Darya Bobyleva

THE VILLAGE AT THE EDGE OF NOON

Translated from Russian by

Ilona Yazhbin Chavasse

ANGRY ROBOT

ANGRY ROBOT
An imprint of Watkins Media Ltd

Unit 11, Shepperton House
89 Shepperton Road
London N1 3DF
UK

angryrobotbooks.com
twitter.com/angryrobotbooks
It's in the woods

An Angry Robot paperback original, 2025
Originally published in Russian as *Вьюрки* by ACT 2019

Copyright © Darya Bobyleva 2019
English translation © Ilona Yazhbin Chavasse 2025

Cover by Kate Cromwell
Edited by Simon Spanton Walker and Andrew Hook
Set in Meridien

ISBN 978 0 85766 990 2
Ebook ISBN 978 0 85766 991 9

Printed and bound in the United Kingdom by CPI Group (UK) Ltd, Croydon CR0 4YY

The manufacturer's authorised representative in the EU for product safety is eucomply OÜ - Pärnu mnt 139b-14, 11317 Tallinn, Estonia, hello@eucompliancepartner.com; www.eucompliancepartner.com

9 8 7 6 5 4 3 2 1

With thanks to Helen Keating, my old friend and evergreen first English reader – who never flinches when I say, yes the whole thing, and can you do it out loud.
– Ilona Chavasse

TRANSLATOR'S NOTE

Literary novels that play with form and language and speak of deep, meaningful things get all the kudos and prizes and clever reviews. But genre is a special test of a translator's mettle and creativity: funny things have to be funny, scary things have to be scary. And a sci-fi, crime or horror novel can tell us just as much about the state of affairs in a particular time or place as its more refined literary cousins. I loved this book - really, Darya's melodic, sardonic, winding narrative voice - from the first lines, and her characters from the first glance. She has a totally original sensibility which manages to be by turns cozy and creepy, gory and funny, familiar and disorienting, as the kaleidoscope of stories shifts and clicks into place. She creates a world where the uncanny is just there, in the corner of your eye, the "others" have main character energy – indeed the whole novel is essentially a side plot, like the Strugatsky brothers' *Roadside Picnic*, or more precisely an *aftermath* – and the inhuman monsters don't hold a candle to the human ones.

Post-Soviet trauma, generational conflict, the hideous wisdom of crowds, the warnings encoded in folklore - it's all there, if you look. But mainly, *The Village at the Edge of Noon* weaves a strange and enticing spell of pleasure and dread in equal part, just like those who call from the river: I hope you enjoy it as much as I did, and that it haunts you too, just a bit.

THE EXODUS OF VALERYCH

Nikita Pavlov trailed Valerych down the street and wouldn't leave him alone until they got to the missing turning. Trying to talk Valerych out of it, waving his skinny arms, his bloated face sweating with a hangover and the gravity of his mission.

"Why don't you fuck right off, lad," Valerych said, not unkindly, and patted him on the back in a fatherly way.

Very few people in the village knew him as anything but Valerych; it might have been a shortening of his real patronymic, Valerievich, but just as easily a corruption of the given name Valery, or even Valerian; there was no way of telling and he never volunteered it. He was middle-aged and pigeon-toed, the steady, reliable sort. He had inherited his plot from his father, who had been something big in the military, but the family had not used the dacha much – only to grow potatoes, and not on anything like a regular basis. The father had preferred sanatorium vacations at Soviet medical resorts, and for Valerych that word still brought up childhood memories of wavering shadows thrown by floppy potted palms, and a grand marble staircase jutting out of a yellow background. Times changed; the faded grandeur of these relics of pre-revolutionary times requisitioned for the health of the common man had to be given up. It was soon thereafter that Valerych found himself in possession of the family plot, comprised at that moment of a fenced-in wasteland, and decided that it would henceforth be a haven of summer rest and relaxation. A family seat, so to say. There wasn't nearly enough ready cash to turn the dream into reality, but Valerych was handy as well as obstinate, and had a genius for repurposing and utilizing old junk in unexpected ways. Up went his architecturally heterogenous but perfectly sound dacha, which he built from odds and sods including, of all things, discarded railway sleepers. Valerych had lined the gravel path from his front gate with shards of old bricks and constructed a pergola out of some random assortment of metal ribs and rods that soon enough were festooned with grape vines and looking perfectly elegant. Valerych marked out and built his raised vegetable beds with military precision and, obedient to his design, his crops always came up in orderly rows: no beetroot would have dared sprout up through the ranks of parsley, nor a pumpkin have the audacity to lounge among the cabbages.

The family seat idea did not work out. Other luxuries became available, and his children preferred gallivanting on foreign beaches. Valerych's only grandchild, for whom he toiled over his best "Queen Elizabeth" strawberries, always seemed to go with her parents. Nevertheless, each spring Valerych decamped to his dacha, building, fixing, sowing, and waiting – above all, waiting – for his children to realize that a dacha was a better proposition than sitting cooped up all day in the "all-inclusive" – which was not much different, by his reckoning, to a prison.

Beyond the missing turning the street ran along one bank of the Sushka, the small local river, and it was this proximity, rather than being sent packing, that caused Nikita to hang back. Valerych carried on walking. His face was crimson from the heat and exertion, but the calm determination written there lent him the air of a handsome old sea dog.

a giant brick villa to be built in their midst and who bought Sveta all manner of amazing consumer goods, they regarded as something of a Bluebeard. His first wife had simply vanished; that is to say, one summer Beroev arrived without her and obviously no one was going to ask him about it. There were confirmed rumors that he had divorced his second wife, the one who had borne him a daughter, and that he had left her with very little by way of a settlement. So on the whole, the villagers felt that Sveta was unwise to go around all stuck-up, so satisfied to have secured a provider. One never knew how things would pan out. And Sveta really did swan about, constantly fingering her delicate gold-rimmed glasses and tripping about ever so lightly on her slim glossy legs.

But Sveta made it up with Narghiz, and even gave the nanny a moderately large banknote to indicate that she was forgiven. Valerych had gotten this update from two old ladies who seemed to be best friends and were always together. The pair walked up and down the path along his fence for some time, discussing the episode in the absence of anything else to discuss. He finished watering and went inside for something to eat, noticing as he finished his repast that his own wind-up clock had also stopped, as if following the Beroev clock's example. He wound it up but it was no use. The inside of the dial sweated with beads of condensation. Valerych put the clock by his wood-burner stove in the hope that it would dry out and revive. And anyway, it was time to start getting ready for bed. It always took a while to set up the outdoor shower, and he liked to read a little before going to sleep...

Afterward, as Valerych sifted through the immediately preceding events and broke them down into fragments, searching for some sign – the broken clock and the trouble at the Beroevs were hardly credible as any kind of warning – he did recall waking in the night to a strange sound outside. It was loud but also weirdly thick, and it clogged Valerych's ears. Or maybe his ears were clogged to start with, and that was why he dreamed that sound before waking. Of course, it was equally possible that Valerych hadn't woken up in the night at all, and all of that was a dream too.

The path finally meandered away from the river, popping Valerych out by the long perimeter fence that once upon a time had existed simply to guard the village from outside disturbance. Valerych scanned the environs, but there was little to see except the long bobbing grass around him and the willows weeping tears of dew on the riverbank behind him. A faint knocking – someone was hoeing diligently – emanated from the dacha at the village's furthest edge, almost entirely concealed behind an overgrown palisade. Valerych cleared his throat and began to undress, folding and stacking his trousers, rough buttonless top, and boxer shorts neatly on the grass. His own private theory, which was not exactly comprehensive and yet necessitated a definite course of action, held that anything that had been part of the cursed village would detract from his endeavor. He himself had spent quite a while in the village, of course, but he was not an inanimate object and therefore had qualities more resistant to being suborned, the chief of these being his will and reason. Valerych considered divesting himself of the earplugs too, then thought better of it. They were small and insignificant; besides he could throw them away at any time.

The unclothed Valerych was a many-hued thing, running the gamut from snow-white to bruised ruddy purple. He no longer looked brave and seafaring but rather tenderly squishy and vulnerable, like a snail prized out of its shell by a nasty young naturalist. Valerych gave in to a strong unexpected urge to make the sign of the cross over himself, then slid the bolt free, pushed through the gate and stepped outside.

Outside was the normal suburban landscape: a field yellow with winter-cress, the riverbank on his right, and the thin wood copses straight ahead. To Valerych's left, quite some way off across the field, was the sprinkling of neat concrete cottages for a new-style outer-burbs development that had roused the solitude-loving dachniks' ire from the moment it was first approved.

Valerych broke himself a walking stick from a little tree and headed left, to the cottages.

That first morning, he had awakened to the sound of a woman's screaming. Valerych's first half-awake thought was that Sveta Beroeva finally got round to murdering her nanny. And indeed, it was Narghiz who screamed, as Valerych quickly ascertained from the reedy, Asiatic shrieking:

"The road has gone away!"

Oh dear, thought Valerych, she's finally lost it. Though he couldn't quite think why it felt like a "finally".

He breakfasted unhurriedly and did his morning calisthenics before venturing out to find most of his neighbors milling outside his gate. The Beroevs were there, and also Nikita Pavlov, the quiet young alcoholic, and the implacable pensioner Kozhebatkin, looking ready as ever to lash out at some unwitting offender. And of course, the dacha cooperative's committee chairwoman, stately and regal Claudia Il'yinichna Petukhova, and with her many of the others.

"Did they bring the milk, then?" Valerych addressed himself to Kozhebatkin, who was nearest to hand.

"You think I know?" Kozhebatkin always found a way to wind himself up. "They're saying the turning for the gate and beltway is blocked!"

"There isn't any turning. At all," Nikita said quietly.

"That's what I said, isn't it?" scowled Kozhebatkin.

Small delegations kept splintering off from the main crowd to essay the village gates. Each returned in a state of extreme confusion, the young people were making an excited racket, and the combined sound of so many raised voices soon escalated into an alarming din. Something had happened – was happening – and it was very strange.

Valerych wavered for a moment between going to open his tomato greenhouse up for the day and having a look at whatever had brought out such a crowd, and chose the latter.

Like any other dacha cooperative, the village was laid out along several pleasantly named lanes: Forest Street, Rowan Street, Cherry Street, and so on. The lanes all joined into one and swerved toward the main village gate – beyond that was a dirt track leading out to the asphalt beltway that in turn led back to the city and civilization. The village itself was situated in a lovely bit of unspoiled nature – there was a small tidy wood, and a river whose middling size and muddy waters were balanced out by a bevy of beautiful weeping willows, with a wooden mooring right out of someone's idyllic rural childhood, and even a little abandoned chapel on a mound above the far bank. Better still, the river teemed with rudd, roach, and bream, and Valerych enjoyed bottom fishing there, rich hauls that gave one a warm manly feeling. He made a mental note to get his rig ready for some bream fishing.

Still thinking about his fishing gear, Valerych went right past the turning. That is to say, past the place where the turning used to be.

It had simply ceased to exist.

Valerych backtracked a dozen or so steps and proceeded up the lane once more, looking around him attentively.

Here was the house of Tamara Yakovlevna, the inveterate old cat lady. Hers was the dacha immediately next to the water-pumping station and so whenever she forgot to open up the valve – which was always – the street ended up without running water. Here was the water pump itself, and then the turning for the exit gate, and then the next street, Forest

No one was going to wait by the fence for his return. Also, just then Antoshka Aksenov shot past on his bike, raising a cloud of dust. He shouted excitedly at them as he rode that some others had decided against trying the back of Tamara Yakovlevna's plot, because the forest was there too, and you couldn't see anything beyond it, but the second village gate, the old one, was still where it should have been and seemed to be perfectly normal.

This was the gate through which Valerych would eventually effect his egress; it had once been the main gate, in the old days before the asphalt road finally caught up with the village.

Never before had the view of the field, river, and irritating new development seemed so cheering. While the gathering crowd chattered with relief and tossed about what scant bits of information there were, the Aksenov family was busy kitting out their bespattered Jeep. They were a shouty, athletic and cheerful bunch, always going off camping and hiking, or else taking the Jeep motor-touring across Russia and even abroad.

"We'll get to the bottom of this!" Natalya Aksenova, heavy-bottomed like a pear, assured them all in her deep, carrying voice. "We'll figure out what's what!"

The villagers hollered various pieces of advice over one another: the Aksenovs should drive straight to the new development and ask around there – no, they ought to go to the village further away, because the new place was only half-built and the migrant laborers wouldn't know a thing. They should drive all the way round the village until they found the turnoff for the beltway, and flag down a car, or find someone with a cell, and phone and ask… No one could verbalize exactly what it was the Aksenovs should ask, and no one attempted to think this through. The very idea of questions like "Where has the turning gone?" and "What exactly is happening here?" was still wild and rather uncomfortable.

Valerych didn't have much use for his cell phone, which was one of those bricks for oldies, with push buttons and large digits. He hadn't even thought to take it when he left the house to join the others. It was only later that he discovered from the young people, who were all staring hungrily at their gadgets with genuine alarm, that no one had any web or internet or anything. The youngsters seemed unable to leave their cell phones even when going to the outhouse – perhaps they couldn't manage in there without internet advice – and now all the phones were blind and deaf. This wasn't the first time, though; internet access did waft in and out of the village, rather. There were no telephone lines of course, which had at one time added to the secluded charm of the place.

Chop-chop and shipshape, the Aksenovs with their Antoshka in tow soon piled into the mud-spattered, brightly stickered Jeep. Aksenov revved the engine loudly – purely for show – and they were off. Everyone watched the large WW2 anniversary sticker proclaiming "All the way to Berlin!" on the Jeep's blacked-out back window judder with every pothole, but soon all that remained was a dissipating swirl of dust. It was barely a minute's drive to the new-builds; someone especially keen-eyed asserted that they could see something moving among the toy cottages in the distance.

The next to leave was a taciturn guy named Sanya, who climbed the fence adjacent to the spot where the missing turning used to be, and into the murky woods. Then the quiet couple from the top of Forest Street, taking with them the current Naida; they felt sure that if they lost their way, the dog would lead them out again. Beroev was the next to drive up to the old gate, but then Sveta raised a ruckus worse than the day before, shrieking and pummeling his large white SUV with her little fists, until Beroev, cursing like a trooper, gave in and agreed to wait for the Aksenovs to come back.

As for who was the first to return... The sun tolled inside Valerych's skull like a crimson tocsin. He sat down in the prickly grass and hoped that dredging up the details would distract him from his terrible thirst and incipient heatstroke. Now who was the first to return? And did they behave suspiciously, oddly? It was probably the dog lovers; they had been proven right on the subject of their animal's abilities. Yes, it was definitely those two, and they came back shaken and frightened, but on the whole, normal.

They appeared on the evening of the day after, just when the villagers' initial bewilderment had turned to apprehension. They reported having tried to leave through the forest, as getting Naida to step foot into the field had proved impossible; something in the field had spooked her badly. The couple was uniformly filthy, scratched, swollen with mosquito bites, and oddly lethargic – probably from exhaustion. They ate and drank ravenously, barely lifting their faces from their plates, and seemed unwilling and slow to answer questions. Only the dog was delighted, wagging her tail across the table leg – *she* had not failed, *she* had led them back out again. Her owners explained, though it had to be prized out of them, that they had gotten lost in the forest, never finding any path at all; they ended up in an impassable wilderness, which after a day of walking was not surprising. So they circled round and round, always coming back to the same spot somehow, then ordered the dog to find home, which she did. They had slept the night under a tree, lucky that it was still summer. They listened out for traffic or the river, and occasionally heard snatches of sound, but never saw anything except forest. This was what the husband, bearded and melancholy, told them. The wife only bobbed her head wordlessly, as she wolfed down bowlfuls of buckwheat and tinned meat. Valerych realized that this silent purposeful eating was what had been quietly bugging him since then, and he was sorry that he hadn't had time to tell anyone before he left.

The return of the dog couple, though fortunate, had a depressing effect on the villagers. Especially when you considered that they had not gone off-piste, but in a straight line for the road, compass in hand. The day before, Nikita Pavlov got on top of the guardhouse roof but couldn't see anything, so climbed as far as he was able up the highest pine and declared from above that everything was the same as it had ever been – river, wood, fields, and plantings on the far side of the river. He shimmied down dejected, saying it was hard to see very far. It was then that they triangulated the rough location of the road and sent the dog lovers off with the compass. The melancholy husband later explained that they'd lost it in their wanderings.

The migrant laborer briefly returned too, although it was hard to say whether this was that first one to go, or one of his countrymen. He eluded any attempt at questioning by blinking at them perplexedly without saying a word. Nikita Pavlov came back – in a state of mounting anxiety, *he* finally decided to simply cross the field, having first tied some twine to the gatepost. Ball of twine in hand, Nikita wandered out to the end of the tether and immediately returned. He was soaked in sweat and completely unshakeable in his conviction that he'd not gotten an inch closer to the cottages. Also that the twine in his hand had quivered weirdly as he spooled it out.

Valerych's mate Vityok came back too, though it would have been better if he hadn't...

The Aksenovs, on the contrary, were gone without a trace, and so were the group of college students who'd come for just the weekend to camp out and barbeque. Their timing was unlucky; they had to get back to their course or be expelled, and so there was no talking to them. Sanya never came back, never mind that he owed Valerych a deal of money. It was after Sanya left, Valerych figured, that people got desperate and started to vanish pretty regularly. People tried the field and the forest, hoping that the true road back to the world, having been hidden by the mysteriously localized anomaly, would reveal itself spontaneously to them. They still had regular village assemblies, and for a time the chairwoman attempted to keep a tally, but it made things all the more confusing – trying to decipher who had actually vanished, and who left before the road winked out of existence, and who hadn't come this year at all – and not a little dreary, shouting surnames out like a prison roll call.

Narghiz disappeared too. But that was different.

None of the strange proceedings had any bearing at all on the Beroev boys' daily routine. Narghiz, looking even more dejected than usual, continued to take them on their morning and evening walks, which consisted of circling once round the perimeter, then to the river and rudimentary playground, then back home.

One evening Narghiz and the children failed to return. Sveta Beroeva hunted through the village, her flip-flops thudding severely down the lanes, and found the boys by the riverbank, swaying contemplatively on a bench swing.

"Where's Narghiz?" asked Sveta, hugging them tightly with relief.

The older boy pointed to the water.

Sveta looked down, puzzled. The murky river wended lazily past clumps of sedge. It was speckled with water skimmers, and there were a couple of ducks. A clumsy garland of yellow water daisies hung down from a nearby bush – the kids must have been playing. There was no sign of Narghiz.

"Has she gone for a swim?"

The boys shook their heads no, vehemently, and pressed up against their mother.

Sveta called Narghiz once, and again. Then she hurried away with the children. No one ever saw Narghiz again after that. Or imagined that it was all just beginning.

* * *

It was lucky perhaps that after the disappearances of the Aksenovs, the college students and Sanya – and oh, all the glum migrant laborers, who stubbornly kept on going in search of one another – no one attempted to leave by river, either swimming or in a boat. The villagers tended to view the river as too much of an obstacle, given the way that other escape routes had turned strange and thorny, even before they realized that the river too had changed. Not outwardly, no – the mosquitoes and the slap of fish against the water was the same, much as the wood and the field appeared, at first glance, the same. But the little river too bloomed strange and otherworldly. After this was discovered, the villagers kept well away and it was only much later that a couple of deaf old anglers and that odd spinster Katya came back to fish at the bank. Valerych couldn't quite put his finger on what the matter was with Katya, from the way she spent all her summer fishing alone, to the way she spent her summers at the village altogether.

The two bosom friends, Tamara Yakovlevna and Zinaida Ivanovna, meanwhile, had tried to put their fingers on what the matter was with Narghiz. This was before the nanny disappeared. They were used to long summer evenings at Tamara Yakovlevna's, bingeing television programs about folk remedies, ghost hunters and cursed bloodlines. So when the turning disappeared and the beloved TV set showed only gray fuzz in place of their favorite channel, the disconsolate old ladies talked it over and decided that it was Narghiz's doing. To revenge herself on bossy Sveta, Narghiz had placed some sort of oriental curse on the village. This theory was no more ludicrous than anything going on at the time, and the pair of them even went to visit Narghiz to see if they could sound her out. After she vanished, protest as they might that they'd been nothing but tactful and friendly, Sveta Beroeva was of the firm and vigorously voiced opinion that they'd sounded – hounded – the nanny straight into the river with fright, and who was going to look after the children now. Maybe she just decided to swim the hell away from Sveta and the Beroev pups, when it started to look like she'd be chained to them forever, reflected Valerych. He looked up, half-hoping for just a single cloud to blot out the blazing sun, and saw something curious.

There was no sun. The whole of the sky, end to end, was veiled in a pearlescent substance, like the insides of the freshwater mussels that bunched in the river. Valerych was overjoyed to see so much cloud until it dawned on him that this was no cloudbank. The vault of the sky itself had gone bleached, and gleaming waves of white-hot aurorae arced liquidly above his head. He felt the blistering breath of a furnace on his face – then molten sand slashed across his eyes – his throat burned. A roiling, churning haze was spreading fast atop the drooping dry grass stalks all around him.

They're not letting me through, Valerych thought. Trying to scare me off.

He gripped his walking stick tightly, eyes closed against the spinning world, waited a little. Then stumbled on, picking at the vague threads of his previous thoughts, anything at all, to keep his mind from the unbearable crackling heat, and from that white-hot sky. Whenever you walked on your own like this, not in the city where every passerby was talking and every shopfront yelled for your attention, but really on your own, didn't your brain always find something to mutter idly to itself? Go on then, brain, mutter away...

...thought that she'd be chained to them forever. Bullshit, no one thought of it as forever back then. What normal person would assume that anything was forever, especially given all the crazy that was going on?

The chairwoman Claudia Il'yinichna, unusually pale but majestic as ever, called a general assembly beside the guardhouse, near the spot where the turning had been. She alerted all present to the need for keeping calm and carrying on, lending a helping hand, and so forth. She also informed them that they were not to leave the village until the situation became clear. This was met with the kind of learned communal inertia that expressed itself in generalized moaning – who was going to make it clear and when would they make it clear – that was normally reserved for rising utility rates and chronic late-payers. Claudia Il'yinichna made the dignified reply that since such a thing, pardon my saying, such a terrible catastrophe, the forced sequestration of so many people, had occurred, the relevant branches were certain to be working on a rescue, matters were surely in hand and they would surely come...

"What, from the outside?" The teenager who insisted on being called Yuki instead of Yulia, her God-given name, called out from a little way off, where she balanced carefully on her bike.

Claudia Il'yinichna gave the inky-haired girl a stern teacherly look and said nothing. The assembly had quietened too, each person privately alarmed by the new set of what-ifs dashing about inside their heads.

"Comrades, we still have electricity, and that means that the outside is..." she shot a warning glance at Yuki, "... absolutely fine. We just have to sit tight. I'm sure a rescue is already underway, and all we have to do is wait." With that, Claudia Il'yinichna seemed to recover her equanimity, like someone navigating at last to a familiar road after a painful spell of being lost.

Overhead, the air crackled with the fury of live electricity and grew more scorching still. Valerych could feel his skin blister. His lips were glued together, while his thick, rough tongue seemed to fill his mouth entirely. Even his eyes were parched, so he only lifted his eyelids now and then, just to get a sense of where he was going. The endless, boundless field and the roasting sky flickered before him and were both subsumed in the ruddy, veined, pulsating gloom.

It was during one of these flickers that Valerych spotted the river. Mysteriously *elsewhere* once again, the rippling river was now behind him – right behind him. Its glistening, sunlit surface burned into his retinas and carried on shining from the inside of his eyelids. The fleeting scent of water was like a promise of sweet coolness in his nose and mouth. As always in the heat, the river smelled of cold watermelon.

Valerych dropped his stick and stumbled to the water, growling hoarsely through clenched teeth. He had his earplugs in, after all.

It was easier to breathe by the river. Valerych got himself clumsily down the mudbank, swearing out loud when a shard of beer-bottle glass bit him in the heel. There were people here not long ago, normal everyday people, drinking and breaking bottles. And there used to be rubbish all along the bank – disposable barbeque trays, scraps of paper, plastic bags, cigarette butts. Where did you take all the rubbish, you fucking monsters? Valerych was furious, and close to tears. You bloody neat freaks, you goddamn tidiers, you want to erase all traces of the old life, is that it? The shard of glass seemed like a small miracle, and Valerych was willing to forbear his own sliced foot, reminder of a time when you could leave the village if you wanted to, when people came to the riverbank to have fun, eat shish kebabs, listen to the smarmy songs that spilled like warm oily vodka from car radios...

Valerych lapped at the river water thirstily. It left an aftertaste of peat and manure in his mouth. He sprinkled some on his blistering skin and didn't even feel the drops; they evaporated like water on a scorching-hot pan. In a last attempt to cool down, Valerych lowered his feet into the water. The top of the river was yucky and warm, full of debris and tightly shut mussels that floated past him, tickling his steaming shins. He had to limp in further, to the knees. His toes gummed up with silt, the throbbing in his foot subsided, and such blessed coolness shivered up from below, that Valerych nearly began to cry again, face crumpling in a grimace of mute bodily joy. He splashed his palms in the water, ducklike, knowing all the while that this was dangerous, forbidden, that he was probably already halfway to perishing. I have every right to cool down in this heat, why should I be forbidden something so innocent, he raged to himself with a rising, vicious desperation. He cast his eyes around, as though summoning a witness to this injustice from the ranks of the weeping willows and the skimmer-bugs, and the blessed bottle shard...

He saw instead a wall of blinding white flame roll silently across the field toward him, engulfing the grass as it went past. In the heart of the flame was not fire but the plasma of the very sun. It had the shape of a gigantic woman.

Momentarily stupefied, Valerych twigged at last in that still moment that the sky had fallen in. That the end of the world had come in a blaze of pale fire, the opium of the masses was at hand, and the archangel had sounded his horn – Valerych just hadn't heard him through his earplugs. The village was no more. The new cottages, the field were no more, and there was nowhere to go now, and he would never leave, because all that was left of the world was this little river, reeking of peat and manure. And there was one more thing that Valerych, a committed materialist, instinctively knew straight away: only merciful water would give refuge against the cleansing, chastening flame.

Mud slippery and silky beneath his feet, further and further in he went.

"Tolya!" The sound of her voice cut right through the earplugs. "Tolya, you idiot, what's all this for, honestly!"

Antonina. His wife. His very own fishwife, born into grinding rural poverty but straining all her married life to make out like a city lady, she had relieved Valerych of her earsplitting presence more than a decade before. Once upon a time he had answered to Tolya – Anatoly Valerievich, Tolya for short – though very few people remembered it now.

"Tolya, where in the world are you going? Don't be so dim, use your nut for once. Get on over here, hurry up. I know what you need, I'll look after you." She was not haranguing now, but caressing, his dead wife.

"You're the last thing I need, you old bag!" Valerych roared, and he struck out for the other riverbank – away from the incinerating flame and the village and his dead goddamned wife – toward the other world, the other shore. It was so close and so normal, muddy and crumbling and wall-to-wall with nettles, not fire.

Something raced underwater and broke upon a piece of driftwood – only the wind. Valerych windmilled his arms as he swam, spluttering and sniveling, but the river, endless and redolent of peat and watermelons, clung to him, plastered his sides and belly with chills, poured into his nostrils. He knew he was waiting for it all to be over, but also felt compelled to keep swimming, eyes fixed on the jagged lacework of nettles that framed the other shore. His arms and legs throbbed; he snatched up air but it could barely get through the viscous saliva filling his mouth before whistling painfully out again. Valerych felt something akin to relief when something finally grabbed him and tugged him sharply down. He couldn't see anymore, but he knew it was her, Antonina – bloated and corpse-blue, with bulging eyes like hardboiled eggs, her face glittering with thin trails of riverweed and a pike-cheek coyly gleaming from one earlobe. He didn't need to see; he knew her by the unmistakable feel of her soft, creased skin, like the peel of a rotting peach. With a flourish of fish breath over the suddenly struggling, kicking Valerych, Antonina took him gently by the shoulders and drew him under, where it was cool and dark.

* * *

A soft breeze riffled through the winter-cress as though nothing was the matter at all, and the woods shivered on their horizon. The little concrete cottages, each with an identical rusty-brown roof, dotted their fenced hillside like field mushrooms after rain. A sudden gust of wind cut across the still surface of the river, spoiling the ripples that still radiated from its center, and gliding down the grass, knocked at the dingy green gate bearing the dacha cooperative's official name, as though checking it was well-barred. The gate squeaked, but only quietly.

2

VITYOK

Vityok, the sinewy, sturdy kind of guy whose age is impossible to guess at, lived in the last house on Rowan Street, just over the fence from Valerych. His dacha was an old-fashioned, timber one, handed down from his granddad, but still robust. Vityok's otherwise inconspicuous wife could usually be seen bustling in and out from the veg patch, and in and out of the house. Everyone called her Auntie Zhenya: she was always sweeping, weeding, scraping, even hammering and painting sometimes, balanced on the top of a rickety stepladder. Vityok spent his time mainly in the lean-to annex, which was the site of the dacha's kitchenette. Everything he needed was right there: the fridge, the radio, a pile of old magazines and a little couch. On occasion, the range was topped triumphantly with the very joy of his heart and apple of his eye: this was a factory-made distilling apparatus, a birthday present from Vityok's enterprising work mates one year. It was the single time they got it exactly right. Vityok tooled around with the thing no less lovingly than classic car enthusiasts kit out and polish their big toys; with his own hands he washed it and dried it, loaded it with unexpectedly imaginative ingredient combinations, observed keenly every stage of the brewing process, and personally sampled the first skim. Something hefty and intense would wake inside Vityok after that first taste, something that moved inside him seeking escape, pushed him out from the lean-to and blew him this way and that up and down his plot: to the outhouse, out of toilet paper as usual, or else to the apple trees, whose heavily laden branches had not been propped up in time, also as usual. And all roads led to Auntie Zhenya, who just then would seem endlessly busy with inessential errands, but never getting round to the things that really needed doing. It was much more urgent, of course, to sort out her plastic bags or make yet another rag floor mat for the veranda, than make sure there was something to wipe your ass with. Flushed and huffy, Vityok would follow her balefully around, while she pretended not to notice his agitation. She'd dash between the various flashpoints of her frenetic activity, but eventually give in:

"Full to the brim again, are you?"

And Vityok could finally rear up at her. His murky sense of ill will toward his scraggy, irritating wife, with her bland smell and the way she always had that moony, concerned expression on her face, ejecting and exploding out of him. He would point at her, with a biblical gesture of rage, and growl:

"You...!"

Auntie Zhenya always tried to scurry away, but Vityok would catch her, shake her, grab her by the hands again: "You... you...!"

Finally, Valerych – who could hear them perfectly well from his plot – would pop up over the fence. Chiding and conciliating in his reverberating low mutter, Valerych would then disappear and pop out again through the gate. Auntie Zhenya would clutch her bosom with her red, roughened hands, apologetic and mortified, as Valerych put his arm about the subsiding Vityok, and drew him inside the lean-to. There they'd do a second sampling, and a third, or however many could be managed. They'd put the radio on and chase the moonshine down with whatever bits of food Auntie Zhenya quickly flung on the table for them, then go promenading round the village, arguing hotly and singing songs, existential suffering writ large on their brows.

This is all to say that Vityok and Valerych were mates, and old ones at that.

In the early days after the way out of the village mysteriously vanished, Vityok took it all on the chin. Naturally he was as astonished as anyone, but for him it was somehow more congenial than for the others. While the dachniks wandered around in baffled clumps, Vityok examined all aspects of the pumping station that still remained immediately before the missing turning, as though looking for a seam in the fabric of reality, slapped his thigh, and said: "That's something else, that is!" Auntie Zhenya confided to her girlfriends, quietly, that her spouse believed it all to be a supernatural event, a miracle even, and expected hordes of scientists and journalists to descend on the village once everything went back to normal. With this many witnesses to hand, and the fact of the disappearing road and gate personally documented by Valerych and his little camera, they would never get away with the usual blah-blah-blah. They would all have to admit that there was an anomaly, right here in the commonplace Soviet-era dacha village. Right here on the banks of their little Sushka, and not down in some cactus-ridden foreign desert, which regular people had only ever seen on TV.

Nor did the disappearance of the Aksenovs, who drove to the next village over, distress him unduly. They weren't fools, he told Valerych stoutly; they'd figure it out. Maybe their car stalled, or something weird was going on in the neighboring village too, so they had to keep going. None of the village phones were working, so they could hardly let anyone know, could they?

Several days after the road out disappeared, Auntie Zhenya heard hissing and stifled moans from the lean-to. It was evening, and the village goings-on had a rather more depressing effect on her than on her spouse, so she felt some alarm; she peeked inside the kitchenette gingerly, holding out a short broom, which was the nearest thing to hand.

Heady gusts of moonshine vapor streamed forth from the open door. She saw Vityok at the table, furiously winding the radio handle. Instead of the usual songs and news bulletins, the radio emitted a steady hiss, enlivened occasionally with eerie, unearthly yelps.

Vityok took another swig, gave Auntie Zhenya a look of pure despair and moaned: "It's not working!"

"Well, of course it's not working. None of the cell phones have got a signal, and the TV over at Tamara Yakovlevna's…"

Vityok plonked his glass onto the table heavily and aimed his index finger at his wife:

"You…"

Auntie Zhenya gasped, shut the door smartly, and beat a prudent retreat to the house. She knew from experience that when Vityok was in a raging mood, the main thing was to steer clear for a while, and he might forget about her entirely.

Vityok did not return to the house to sleep, and Auntie Zhenya, meanwhile, had an uneasy night, waking from sudden tremors to sit up in bed and blink at the inky darkness, and turn on the bedside lamp. She thought she could hear footsteps, or else strange voices. She dreamed that her bedroom door had vanished too, gone the way of the missing turning. When someone rapped sharply on her windowpane at dawn, she nearly vaulted out of her bed in fright.

It was Vityok, bloated and pickled with the mother of all hangovers. He was wearing a dark, overlarge jacket, an old pair of trousers, and a flat cap – his special "forest" gear. He even had with him his particular walking stick, a rowan branch he'd planed down to a smooth finish.

"Where… where are you…" Auntie Zhenya whispered.

"Mushrooming," he answered hoarsely. "Be back before lunch."

Auntie Zhenya ran out in her nightgown, and chased after him, wailing: what did he mean mushrooms, how could he be thinking about going into those woods, people were disappearing, the Aksenovs, the laborers, others, the devil only knew what was going on, the chairwoman had told them to bar their gates and not step foot outside the village, and she was right, they had to wait it out, sit tight until it all resolved itself... Auntie Zhenya's voice gradually took on a remarkable, desperate pitch; even Vityok seemed surprised enough to slow down a little, enough to remind her of the old saying about those who helped themselves. The way out had not reappeared, therefore someone had to go and look for it, and here was Vityok who had to get back to work on Monday, because his boss was an asshole who wouldn't take "couldn't leave the dacha" for an excuse. And besides, maybe something serious did happen out there, but they couldn't get any wind of it, with all communication fried. If everybody just sat tight and waited for things to resolve, they'd never have won the war or gone into space, just sat there waiting for someone to come and do it for them.

Auntie Zhenya gave Vityok a look of pure confusion – she was a simple soul, and had not caught the connection with the war and with space – then carried on:

"But why go now, it's only Saturday... You could hang on, wait a bit..."

But Vityok had had enough. "Wait a bit? Sit around with you, you mean?"

The gate in the perimeter fence that opened straight into the woods was only a few steps away now. Having run out of arguments, Auntie Zhenya simply gripped Vityok's sleeve. He spat irritably, and pushed on, but Auntie Zhenya doggedly hung on, sliding down the path after him, her slippers swishing across the grass. Vityok's jacket twisted around him, the worn cloth close to ripping. Vityok attempted to prize his sleeve out of his wife's grip, but she only tightened it, pinching him painfully through the fabric. They struggled silently for a moment, not even looking at one another. Finally, Auntie Zhenya capitulated and let go, rubbing her blotchy palms together. Vityok righted his clothing with one fierce jerk and swung open the gate.

He loved going for mushrooms almost as passionately as he loved his distilling apparatus. And he inevitably felt better – fresher, you might say – each time he stepped over the boundary between village and wood. No matter that the wood was sparse and rife with human trash; even so, it was a place where Vityok was hunter, provider, tracker.

He rolled his shoulders and flung his arms wide, breathed in a deep lungful of the grassy-piney scent and set off unhurriedly down the forest path.

"Back before lunch," came his wife's tremulous voice behind him.

"Go get cooking," said Vityok without turning, and gathered pace. Auntie Zhenya stared after him until the jacket vanished completely in the dense forest shadows.

He was not back before lunch. Not by evening, nor on the second day. While her neighbors ran through the stages of astonishment, denial, resignation, and then a flaring of hope again, to get back to the world, Auntie Zhenya spent that first week of the village's seclusion simply awaiting her husband's return.

No one noticed her devoted, dogged heroism. Vityok's lunch stayed in the fridge, untouched. Auntie Zhenya did not eat any, just checked from time to time that the sorrel soup had not gone off. Even Valerych had no idea – he spent his days investigating, conferring with the other dachniks, and was generally busy. Auntie Zhenya, meanwhile, stalked up and down the fence, scrutinizing the hostile-seeming, preternaturally quiet forest. She crossed paths with Valerych at some point, when each had the idea of getting down to their respective veg patch for a bit: no point in letting the cucumbers rot, whatever else was going on. Auntie Zhenya said hello and asked for his advice, blandly – did he think she should report Vityok to the police as missing. Valerych gave her a long, baffled look, after which they both fell silent for a long while.

On the seventh day, toward evening, a cloud gray as cast iron belly-flopped over the village and began to pour down. Everyone scurried indoors to shut up the windows, and only Auntie Zhenya remained at her sentry post by the gate. In her raincoat she resembled a squat, shiny mushroom. Her rubber boots left neat, small footprints in the very muddy path.

When it grew dark, Auntie Zhenya was finally forced to retreat to the dacha, but she carried on watching, now peeking out from her porch, now peeping through the window. And then, when she poked her face through the door once more and pointed her flashlight into the gloom, she caught sight of another, bigger set of footprints beside her own. She followed them, stepping into the blurry, slippery footprints first down to the yard gate, then to the shed, and finally down to the lean-to kitchenette.

Auntie Zhenya opened the door a crack. In the unlit room she could clearly hear strange noises, the kind of squelching and rustling you had with a quagmire or bog. Auntie Zhenya shut her eyes and fought hard against the impulse to run back to her safe, warm dacha. She slunk along the wall, felt for the light switch, and…

There was a dark and conical shape in the middle of the kitchen. This was Vityok, extraordinarily dirty, and covered in wet pine needles that stuck to him like bark. Motionless, he stared straight ahead intensely, like someone struggling to process something his mind was barely capable of grasping at all. In his hand was a piece of cloth, knotted like a purse. Squinting hard at Auntie Zhenya, as though identifying her in a lineup, Vityok hesitated, then held out the purse to her. It was the hood of his rain jacket, torn clean off; in it lay some squashed, slimy mushrooms.

Auntie Zhenya spoke quietly.

"Well, you're home at last."

The next morning, Valerych, to his great surprise, saw Vityok stumbling down the path to the outhouse. Once he got over the shock, Valerych rallied and waved his arms in the air, calling out to his pal in a just-woke-up voice not quite his own. Vityok, paying him no mind, wandered up to the peeling wooden hut, and tried to walk into the door. He seemed to have forgotten the idea of the handle, and pushed at the door with his whole body, again and again, unhurriedly but with determination. Valerych stopped hollering and watched him in great puzzlement. Finally, Vityok triumphed over the door, his sleeve catching the handle by accident, and got inside.

Soon the entire village came along to get a look at the returnee. Before Vityok, the only people to come back were that couple from Forest Street whose dog led them out again, but they hadn't related anything useful. A few of the migrant laborers seemed to have come back too but, truth be told, they all looked the same to the dachniks, and so a man who had never left might well have been mistaken for one who returned. Also, none of them spoke Russian properly. Vityok, on the other hand, had spent an entire week in the woods, which would have been extraordinary even in the carefree days when one could drive or walk out of the village at will.

Naturally, they had so many questions for him, the chief of which was, what's it like out there, on the outside? But no matter how they pressed him, Vityok remained silent. He sat at the kitchen table, still in his "forest" jacket, hunched and swaying slightly from side to side. According to the flushed and voluble Auntie Zhenya, he was refusing to get changed – actually pushing her away when she attempted to unzip the jacket – and would neither wash nor sleep, though he looked tired to death. The one thing Vityok did willingly, constantly, intently, was eat. The table before him was stacked with plates, licked clean, and under the table were heaps of empty pickle jars and tin cans: Vityok carried on eating, hoovering up sorrel soup, mushrooms, jam, corned beef, things from the vegetable beds. Auntie Zhenya busied herself by the little range, using both gas rings, and more than once had to prize raw potatoes out of her husband's grip.

By the time Katya looked in on them, the outbuilding was crammed full of people and chairwoman Claudia Il'yinichna had taken over the interrogation, with no great success.

"Listen here, Vitaly..." she said again and again, in a futile bid for his attention. He simply carried on chewing.

"It's Victor, actually..." his wife interjected meekly, but the chairwoman either did not hear, or perhaps was just used to ignoring mousy little Auntie Zhenya, and bent down to him again after a time:

"Listen here, Vitaly..."

The swollen tick attached to Vityok's neck jogged up and down in rhythm with his moving jaws. The room was close and rank with the smells of earth, rotting moss, and unwashed flesh. But by far the worst, most revolting thing was the way that Vityok ate, gurgling and snorting, guzzling food down with frantic little sobs. His face was blank, glum, and terribly focused.

"Well, this is impossible!" With that, Claudia Il'yinichna finally turned back to the large audience.

"It's all right," Valerych faltered. "He'll come to, then he'll talk."

Just then Vityok shoveled in the last spoonful of millet porridge. He bent his face to the empty bowl, then looked stonily at the table and saw the plump, resting arm of the chairwoman upon it. Vityok grabbed her hand and pulled it toward his mouth. Claudia Il'yinichna gasped and tried to free herself, but Vityok would not let go. His gaze was trained on her index finger, which did rather resemble a sausage.

Beroev bounded up the table and punched Vityok in the eye, with enough force to pitch him off his stool. The women squealed. Vityok gathered himself together, jerked his head sideways and, still on his hands and knees, rushed at the door. When strapping and bearded Stepanov went down, headbutted in the knee by the escaping Vityok, everyone else backed out of the way: there was something awful in the way that Vityok scurried so easily on all fours, like a gargantuan bedbug...

Vityok crashed out of the lean-to, sprang to his feet, and ran toward the woods, to the fence. It was almost by the gate that Valerych managed to collar him. Vityok pushed him aside roughly, knocking him off his feet, and made to climb up the rickety old fence. It was as though he had forgotten about the existence of the gate altogether. When Valerych grabbed his feral drinking buddy by the pants leg, the worn material tore, revealing a pale and hairy leg. Valerych leapt up, hooked Vityok, who was still trying to crawl up the fence like an insect, by his belt, and pulled him down to the ground. Vityok resisted, snarling.

"Is that how it is, now," Valerych said reproachfully, as he sat on Vityok and held him firmly to the ground. "Filled your belly and back you go?"

Auntie Zhenya arrived, wheezing, bringing with her a coiled washing line. Valerych spent a good old while making complicated knots, then finally lifted the hobbled Vityok to his feet, dusted him off, and dragged him bodily back to the kitchenette.

They sat Vityok back on the stool again, but no one felt like asking him anything now. Despite their burning curiosity, the villagers perceived in him something alien and frightening; however, this was difficult to put to words without sounding stupid. They began to disperse, carefully keeping their eyes away from Vityok and from Auntie Zhenya too, who could have used some friends and some help, this was obvious, except that how was she to be helped?

Claudia Il'yinichna departed but promised to return as soon as Vityok had come back to his senses. Finally, only Valerych was left.

"Well then... you just, you know..." He gave Vityok a pat on the shoulder. Vityok slowly turned and looked at him sideways. His very ordinary, pale eyes expressed nothing at all. Valerych had seen that look before, but only on a dead fish.

"Here, have some pea soup," Auntie Zhenya said, setting a bowl before Valerych. "It's gone lunchtime already, what with all the fuss."

She slid the second bowl toward herself, dipped the spoon in, and brought it to her mouth, blowing, then passed it to Vityok's lips, already smacking with anticipation. Vityok slurped greedily, leaning forward over the table.

"Easy, easy now, you'll overturn everything. Look at you," crooned Auntie Zhenya. "Hungry, aren't you? Running around in the forest, nothing but pinecones to eat, sure you're hungry. Don't rush, don't rush. Go on, eat as much as you like."

To Valerych, this idyllic feeding tableau seemed horrid and creepy. Disquieted, he spooned a bit of soup, for politeness' sake, then edged out of the tight space sideways, like a crab.

Auntie Zhenya seemed not to notice him at all. Valerych stalled for a moment on the porch, wondering whether it would be rude to leave just like that, without saying a word, then thought to hell with it – spat out a peapod shred that had lodged itself in his back teeth – and made for the gate.

Nikita Pavlov – the youngest "real dachnik" of the village – was perhaps more disturbed than most by the state of the returned Vityok. Tall and lanky, Nikita had a boyish face for someone pushing thirty. His was the generation that almost never graced their large family dachas, the proper old-time ones of mature veg beds and lilacs, with an appearance. This irritated the old-timers immensely. The days of school breaks obligatorily spent watering, harvesting and turning over the rows were at an end, today's young people were rooted in city asphalt. They didn't just go on vacation, they flew to places, risking their lives – to those incomprehensible scorching countries where there were terrorists and sharks and tsunamis – while the dachas stood empty, dried-up orchards choking with labyrinthine thorn, fences collapsing, wood pigeons roosting under the rafters...

No one could complain of Nikita Pavlov, however. He visited his parents' dacha regularly, including in the off-season. His parents never seemed to have the time, and also in their old age they developed a fondness for abroad. But Nikita kept one room habitable – the rest were filled to the brim with perpetual dacha odds and ends, and locked – and did minor repairs, and bits of repainting, and even started up a simple vegetable plot with easy-grow greens. Everything he did was a bit clumsy, and almost shy, but the villagers approved of his adherence to dacha traditions. He wanted to be closer to nature, to his birthright of birches and the little river Sushka – good for him.

But really, Nikita was a drunk. He was ashamed, and suffered from the way his highly educated, well-mannered family treated him, with a reproachful sort of kindliness. The family genuinely pitied him as a poor, sick boy, and let him sponge off them, as he could never hold down a job. Nikita accepted that he was a loser, but he couldn't give up the sole pleasure at his disposal – getting wasted and almost happy. He was a quiet drunk, solitary and somewhat furtive. And you could do that at the dacha, drink yourself into a stupor with a nearly clean conscience. In the fresh air, so to say. You always had a chaser right there too, in your own veg patch.

After the village shut in on itself, Nikita found that he required a bigger hit to achieve a state of relative tranquility. Although his stocks were plentiful, he did panic a little when he imagined his supplies running out before the magic faded and you could walk out of the village again. He wanted out, to be among people and liquor stores.

But of course, it was all just beginning.

The place reeked of stale alcohol fumes. Like that village drunk Uncle Vasya used to smell, long ago, going about knocking on doors, hungover, barging in to ask "if there was anything." Nikita's mom would hand him a little bottle of cheap eau de cologne, or some medicinal spirit distillation, and wrinkle her nose as she watched him down it.

Now it was Nikita who smelled like that. The thing that had calmed him and helped him sleep now flared up inside him, shot a bolt of agony into his skull, and spilled shiveringly into his legs. Nikita could feel his skin blistering and turning blue, turning into Uncle Vasya's jogging bottoms that always had a rip in the groin. Lucky Uncle Vasya, he'd copped it and left the village. Nikita was afraid of death, mostly because of the thoughts that would undoubtedly drill into his skull in those final moments: I was given a life, but I didn't live, I wasted it all. I didn't manage anything, just rushed through it, and now this life is being taken from me, and there's no trying again, even though I've only just started to understand how life should be lived. I've turned into Uncle Vasya. Except he didn't get it, and so he died happy, but I do, I understand everything... It was too hard, when you did understand, the knowledge only scraped away at you, it made you frantic and ran cold beneath your ribs, the horror of seeing everything clearly. So you had to numb yourself, to skate along the shallowest surface of what you knew. Nikita also knew that as soon as his cognac ran out, he would have to face that clarity of understanding once more. He would know absolutely that he was locked in forever among these little houses and apple trees, with the old women and the hoarse roosters, and there would be no more life at all ever, only the allotted time of lucid horror. They would never even find out who had locked the villagers in, or why – nobody, for no reason, just because...

A loud bang knocked Nikita out of his doze, and he gave a startled scream, almost in reply. His blanket had fallen to the floor. A numbing horror – he felt it physically, like a lump lodged in his throat – superseded both his headache and the cold he felt. Alcohol was a depressant, nothing anti about it, said Nikita to himself, feeling hungover and repentant, much as usual. Belatedly he noticed that someone was rapping at the window. Counting the room's corners to get his bearings in the gloom, Nikita leaned heavily on the windowsill and pulled the curtain aside. His first thought was that someone else went nuts the way that Vityok had and was trying to get inside.

But in the predawn twilight he saw that it was his neighbor. Katya, that was her name, wasn't it? Abruptly he realized that he wasn't wearing any trousers, and crouched down a bit, so that his lower parts could not be seen through the open window.

Katya, to be fair, was also not exactly dressed. She wore only a raggedy old nightie, but this didn't seem to bother her in the least. Her eyes were sunken. She stared searchingly at Nikita, then asked:

"Can you hear?"

"I'm not deaf," said Nikita, and promptly winced with self-loathing; here was a woman, who had come to him in the night, distressed and practically naked, and the only thing he could think of was to be rude to her. No, he would never have a real life, it was all useless. He'd been given a little span of time, but it was just to tease him with what might have been possible...

But then he did hear it, the strange sound that came seemingly from nowhere and was almost impossible to describe, except as simultaneously dreary and languishing. It wasn't loud exactly, but it filled the world and drowned out birdsong and the clicking of the grasshoppers, and even the mighty frog chorus down at the river. It soaked the village like cold gloop, seeped into every crack and crevice, oozed into your brain and enveloped your heart, all-pervasive, unbearable... Nikita stood agog, more and more certain with each passing moment that it was that sound that lurched about inside his mind, spinning dreary, self-hating thoughts. The bitter lump in his throat was that sound, too.

"Can you hear it?" Katya said again.

More than anything in the world, they both wanted to either burst their own eardrums, or to find the source of that noise and silence it forever. As they staggered through the dark – Nikita had put on his trousers but forgot about shoes – they discovered that they were not alone in that state of mind. Up and down the village, paths flickered with the figures of awakened dachniks, as they clicked gates open and shut, and rustled the grass.

"Is it wolves?" some shawled woman asked Nikita, pressing her large bosom close. "Do you hear it? Could they get in? My brother was taken by wolves, back in our home village. He was so young... Are they coming now?"

Nikita couldn't think of a thing to say. The woman moved off into the gloom, without a pause in her weepy querying. She continued asking the same questions into the gloom.

They turned into Forest Street, and then the sound abruptly changed. It was now a very distinct, clotted hissing that didn't flood the world but rather emanated, like a beam, from a specific place. This hissing, unlike the cosmic draught that had drawn them out of doors, did not provoke in him the same vast dreariness and cold, and Nikita even perked up a little. Quickening his pace, he was soon at the fence which marked the beginning of Vityok's plot.

"Wait, come on, wait for me," Katya whispered hotly behind him, but he was already swinging open the gate.

The lean-to window shone brightly in the gloom. Peering inside, Nikita saw Vityok, Auntie Zhenya, and Valerych. The latter was sitting at the table, talking, while Vityok rocked slowly on his stool. He was tied up. Auntie Zhenya stood by the window, at the stove. Nikita pressed his face to the glass, the better to see, and Auntie Zhenya, glancing vaguely at the window in passing, shrieked when she saw the ghostly imprint of his face on the other side. Nikita smiled at her ruefully and waved, to demonstrate to the best of his ability that he was not the one to be scared of.

Auntie Zhenya flung open the door, letting out a new wave of the hissing at Nikita and Katya, and chattered at them feverishly:

"Why would you give a person such a fright, you ought to have knocked at least or come straight inside, why the window, give me a heart attack or something, don't just stand there, come, come inside, it's open, we're having some breakfast..."

As he stepped inside, Nikita glanced at the kitchen clock – it seemed that breakfast started at four a.m. And then he saw the source of the ear-scraping, rough hissing. There was a radio on the kitchen table. It was on. Vityok was studying it intently and seemed to be tuning in.

"Oh, that's so he doesn't get lonely," Auntie Zhenya rushed to explain. "As soon as I go out of the room, he's pining for me straight away. You're just messing around, aren't you, to keep me with you the whole time? But look, look how many guests we have. All the neighbors came to visit you, see how jolly. And it's time to have some kasha now, isn't it? You want to have some nice kasha, don't you?"

All this she said in a high, playful voice, like talking to an infant. Vityok was utterly absorbed by the hissing radio, listening with the grave and somber look of someone getting reports from the front line. Nikita felt his left arm break out in goosebumps.

"You know, there's this sound," Katya said, suddenly, sounding unexpectedly businesslike. "This... strange sort of sound, did you hear it?"

"Oh, that's just the radio, playing for him. He was so bored otherwise, he just bashed everything in sight. Bashed his own head at the wall, do you see the bump there?"

Auntie Zhenya turned to her husband.

"Who was hitting their head at the wall, eh, Vitya dear? Who is it won't let me sleep? I'd only just dozed off, too... But maybe you two would like some breakfast?"

Valerych, who hadn't said a word yet, looked at her from the corner, and the look was of disbelief and disapproval.

In the morning there wasn't much talk of the strange nocturnal sound. Only that a few of the women complained to one another that something was humming in the night, making it hard to sleep. The dachniks worked on their plots and helped their more improvident neighbors out with salt and matches; some of the younger people were already running out. Sveta Beroeva promenaded her children round the village as always, strictly according to schedule.

Valerych kept finding reasons to go to his fence, curious to see what Vityok and his spouse were up to, but saw nothing of them apart from a couple of times that Auntie Zhenya accompanied Vityok, walking sedately with his arms tied behind him like a prisoner, to the outhouse. Valerych didn't call out to them though; on the contrary, each time he crouched low in the bushes.

In the night, it was the chairwoman Claudia Il'yinichna Petukhova who awoke with a drear longing and a hitherto unknown stirring in her breast. She thought on how she was an old woman already, and how she'd soon die of causes that were natural but hardly any less unfair for all that. Wondering at this turn of mind, Claudia Il'yinichna laid a palm over her droopy bosom. Time was, when she was young, she had a bosom like ripe apples, and her first – who was not in fact Petukhov – well, he went wild with delight when he liberated them – another first for her – from her stiff and modest brassiere. You could never get it back, your youth and beauty, and that sweet feminine confidence that comes of knowing everyone watches you as you walk down the street. It was all taken from her, taken...

Meanwhile, the fifteen year-old Yulia, nicknamed Yuki, almost choked on her tears in her sleep, and now lay awake and curled up in her bed, crying bitterly over her parents who were beyond the vanished village gates. Where are they, she pleaded with the unseen, and when would she see them again? Who would solve the problems that she was too young for, who would hug her warmly and fiercely like her mother did, and keep her safe from this strange world?

Nikita, who had once again been tossed out of sleep by the piercing idea of his own uselessness, was about to walk out his front door. He was sure of one thing: he had to find out what the hell this was, and get rid of that sound forever, no matter what it took...

The sound ceased. The click of the crickets returned, an unseen fish flipped once and slapped against the river, and sleep overtook him once more. Barely able to keep his eyes open, Nikita stumbled back into bed.

This time, when morning came, there was a lot of complaining, although everyone shied short of saying just what manner of unpleasant thoughts had visited them in the night. No one wished to experience it again. Many, it transpired, couldn't go back to sleep at all, after being awakened by "that whining". A pasty and worn-looking Claudia Il'yinichna was promising a clutch of women who congregated by the closed village shop that she would certainly find the responsible party and end this tomfoolery once and for all. The women hemmed and hawed and put forward theories about the nature of the noise. One of them was certain that the villagers were all victims of some kind of experiment, and it was all connected: the vanishing gates, the way that the woods and river became strange anomalous zones, mysterious and threatening, and now that sound, that very definitely affected the psyche...

Dusk came, and with it the cries of children, who refused to go to bed. They all perceived the sound as part of a recurring nightmare. Nikita Pavlov sat on his porch, swigging an excellent cognac with a chocolatey aftertaste straight from the bottle. This was quite possibly the best bottle in his remaining collection and although this was not at all how he'd planned to drink it, what did it really matter, when the most important thing about drinking was to drink. Still, he was hoping that if his intoxication was of a more pleasant and higher quality, then his sleep would be accordingly deeper. He chased the cognac down with bites from a fresh radish. His stomach gurgled.

The achieved effect was entirely contrary to expectation. Nikita woke up no more than an hour after going to bed, and stranger still, he was sitting up and thinking about the only knife he had in the house. As he sat on his crumpled bed and stared into pitch blackness, in his mind Nikita was already on the porch, and the knife was already out of its case. The blade shone in the strange cold light that came from nowhere. Nikita ran his finger along its serrated edge and his skin parted readily, almost bursting like a ripe watermelon, splitting wide to reveal red flesh.

The sound abated. Nikita stood frozen in the middle of the room. He still wanted to go to the porch, pick up the knife and move from his finger onto the more vital body parts. It was a good opportunity, wasn't it, to shorten the time allotted to this dreary despair... the shards and splinters of the idea rolled around inside him, terribly sharp.

Nikita hurried out through the window and loped away into the night – away from the porch, away from the knife.

The Beroev dacha was the biggest in the village. It wasn't even a dacha really, more of a villa – a two-story brick construction with a plethora of rooms and a remarkably high fence. The wall lanterns also had motion sensors, so that whenever anyone walked past at night, the villa sparked into Christmas-tree brightness, and then winked out just as quickly behind the passerby's back.

This time, the sensor lights spotlit the master of the house himself, out on his wrought-iron balcony. Beroev was affixing a sturdy noose and rope to the arm of the satellite dish. He looked focused and serious, like someone at a business negotiation.

Nikita, who had been the one to set off the motion detectors, stopped dead in his tracks. Beroev glanced down at him fleetingly and carried on with his task. For a moment Nikita actually wondered whether the man was perhaps setting up a laundry line – this must have been the cognac still in his system.

Like most of the villagers, Nikita barely knew Beroev and therefore viewed him with the wariness of the chattering classes – a big "biznesman" was almost sure to be a mafioso, God willing a retired one. But now Nikita could clearly picture Beroev hanging himself before his very eyes and turning from an unpleasant and morose but nevertheless human person, into an inanimate object. That could not happen, must not happen. Nikita didn't even mind Beroev's being a gangster anymore, so long as he didn't have to witness this change of state.

"Hey there!" he called out. He had plugged his ears with his fingers against the sound, so it was hard to gauge whether he was loud enough. "Listen! Hey!" What do you call a person, when you don't know their actual name? It was the perennial problem of both the middle classes and the former comrades, when neither "sir" nor "tovarisch" were in use anymore… "Bero… Excuse me! Hey, don't… you… don't do that!"

Beroev startled; his stern face contorted in an ugly way. Nikita wondered, in astonishment, whether the putative crime boss was about to burst into tears. But Beroev only moved his lips silently – perhaps he was saying something – tugged the rope down and tossed it off the balcony, then went back inside so quickly as to resemble teleportation. Nikita heard the door slam behind him.

Nikita nudged the gate open with his foot, but it proved impossible to barge into someone's house without knocking; kick as he might, the front door resisted. His hands were busy plugging his ears against the sound, and everything hurt. For a long while, there was no response at all to the racket he was making or to the ringing windowpane, which Nikita felt rather than heard vibrate. Finally, a bright spot sailed out from the depths of the dacha – someone was coming with a flashlight. Katya opened the door, looked at him without saying a word, then handed him a little plastic box. There were earplugs inside.

"It's a bit easier like this," came her muffled voice, as he screwed the soft cylinders into his ears. "It quiets the sound a little. But it still… seeps in, right into your brain, and sets you thinking, thinking…"

He saw the way she was absently scratching at her clavicle with her short nails as she spoke and knew that she was in trouble. Frankly, he'd come to her looking for rescue himself. He had wandered about the dread-sickened, dazed village until he found himself on Cherry Street, his own street, again. It was by Katya's gate that he remembered how decisive he'd felt before, trying to impress his comrade-in-arms.

"You get now what we're all thinking about? It's digging out all the nastiest things... Look at me, for example, I'm barren. So that's what it's making me think about," Katya forced it out quickly through gritted teeth, then looked at him searchingly. "What about you?"

"I'm a drunk."

A crooked grin slipped across Katya's face; the left corner of her mouth turned downward, twitching like some sort of nervous tic.

"I don't want to think about it, but that sound is pressing and pressing in on me. It's turning us inside out. Pulling out the worst and most revolting parts of us. I was lying here and thinking... it's crazy, isn't it, so many people... all of them meeting, loving one another, and then it all stops with me, and none of that means anything now..." Katya pressed her fingers into her temples. "I don't want to talk about this, why do I keep saying these things?"

Nikita just took her by the elbow and led her away.

Basically, they knew where they ought to head. The sound faded in and out, and seemed to broadcast from every direction at once, so that finding its source seemed at first a hopeless business.

But there was only one dacha where something incontrovertibly strange was going on.

Vityok sat on his stool, in the center of the brightly lit lean-to. Everything around him was the same as always, familiar and homely: the flowery oilcloth covering the table, the old electric kettle that blocked the view a little, and the vase with the little dried orange lanterns of physalis in its customary corner. Only Vityok's mouth, as he jiggled around on his stool, bloodshot eyes big and wild in his face, was covered with transparent sticky tape. His lips moved as though they had a vivid life of their own, distinct from his face. Spit bubbled under the tape.

"Wow," Katya breathed next to him, and Nikita almost thought she sounded admiring.

Thanks to Vityok's efforts, the tape was beginning to come loose. He wiggled his lower lip free, the tape hanging from his upper like a see-through mustache. His Adam's apple bobbed up and down convulsively, like a cat about cough up a hairball, and something black emerged from his mouth. Nikita didn't just go cold; he was nailed through with it. He was preparing to see the possessed Vityok vomit up a demon, and the black cloud of satanic smoke to rise to the ceiling, incorporating slowly into a human form.

With a red-faced, final exertion, Vityok spat out a black clump which Katya, on looking more closely, identified as a pair of ordinary nylon tights. Vityok, meanwhile, threw back his head and opened his mouth, spewing forth another sonic stream of pure icy despair.

Only now they both saw that the sound was a kind of howling.

Nikita slid downward along the wall, dread balling under his ribcage, stopping his breath. He could never have imagined that a person – no, not a person, himself, Nikita – could, in a mere moment, lose the will to live so completely and finally. All the horror of the insensate, indifferent cosmic chaos, all the impassable pointlessness of the twitching and capering called life performed by a furry pink scrap of flesh called humanity, emanated now from Vityok. Nikita spotted a rusty nail on the wall, hammered in to the hilt; more than anything he wanted to prize the nail halfway out with his fingers, his teeth, anything, so long as it was sticking out enough for him to ram his forehead into it.

A shadow passed across the bright window and they saw it was Auntie Zhenya. They had not heard the door, so she must have been there in the kitchen the whole time. She said something to Vityok in a tone of complaint, then retrieved the tights from the floor, rolled them up tightly and stuffed them again into his open maw. The unbearable sound ceased.

* * *

By the time Nikita barged into the kitchen, Auntie Zhenya was taping up her husband's mouth again, only this time she passed the sticky ribbon round his whole head, laminating the sparse hairs on the back of his neck.

"What else can I do?" she shrugged cheerfully at Nikita, as though there was nothing strange in his sudden arrival. "I leave him for a minute, and he starts that howling again. Auntie Zhenya needs to sleep too, sometimes. She needs to sleep, doesn't she, Vitya dear?"

Nikita took a step forward and tripped against an ancient metal cot bed, by the looks of it a relic of some orphanage or theatre of war. The bedding was crumpled. Auntie Zhenya had indeed been in the kitchen the whole time. She had taken to sleeping there.

Patting Vityok on his taped-up cheeks, Auntie Zhenya cut the last of the loops.

"You have to let him go," Katya said suddenly from behind Nikita's back.

"Let him go where?"

"Back to the forest. He wants to go back..."

Wait, how does she know that, thought Nikita with mounting alarm. He suddenly felt not great about Katya standing so close behind him, breathing into the small of his bare defenseless neck...

Auntie Zhenya's pleasant neighborly smile faltered, her thin brows twitched:

"What are you on about, my girl? What if he doesn't come back, what then? Maybe it's hard for you to fathom, but he's my husband, girlie, and has been for ever so long, thank God. What am I to do without a man, can you tell me that?"

"But he's... he..." Katya mumbled. The undisguised confusion and horror in her voice made Nikita feel better.

"Not to worry, I'll get him well! He's had worse. Or is it that you can't sleep because of him? We're not so fancy here, he and I lived in communal apartments half our life. We survived!"

Auntie Zhenya loomed ever larger somehow, even her brassy curls frizzing upright as she turned on Katya and Nikita, transformed and shining with furious, martyred righteousness.

"Auntie Zhenya, people are going crazy with this noise! Beroev almost hanged himself just now."

"Beroev? That one, hang himself? Who ever heard of people catching crazy from one another. What book did you read that one in, huh?"

They were face to face. Nikita watched the door lantern shimmer in her translucent eyes.

"Have you any shame at all?" Auntie Zhenya hissed at them. "Where's your conscience? Come to stir up trouble for someone else's family, is that it?!"

So lightning-quick was Auntie Zhenya snatching up a ladle from the sink, that it took Nikita a moment to comprehend that this was the cause of a sharp pain in his arm: she had smacked his elbow with it. A moment later, the wall above their heads took a heavy direct hit from a thickly patinated iron skillet.

In their flight from the enraged Auntie Zhenya, the pair shot outside and immediately ran into someone. Katya lost her footing and fell over with a little cry.

Valerych – exceedingly dour and appallingly unshaven – shouldered the panting Nikita aside. Poking his head around the door of the kitchenette, he said but one word:

"Zhenya."

He said it in a way that made clear nothing else needed to be said, and even if the frightened young people didn't quite understand it, they certainly felt it.

Auntie Zhenya instantly lost all her bluster. She looked so miserable that Nikita felt a splintering cold puddle behind his ribcage, almost the same as from Vityok's howling. A second later, however, the bare little light bulb flashed up again and rattled furiously in Auntie Zhenya's eyes.

"Mind your business! You think you're so smart? You think you know it all? You know how he's driven me up the wall all these years? So many years... you know how he's treated me?"

"I know."

Auntie Zhenya shook her head, let off a screechy stream of curse words, then poked herself in the cheek that was dented by an old scar:

"That's his handiwork there, I had to get stitches! You think I've not suffered enough from him? You came to pass judgement on someone else's family, you three saints? I don't deserve to have my husband by my side, is that it? A calm, sober, meatball-eating husband? I don't deserve it, is that the idea?"

"Zhenya."

Valerych stepped inside, shutting the door in Nikita's face when he moved to follow. Katya let out a deep sigh of relief.

They left the kitchen as a trio: Vityok, still ribboned round with sticky tape and held between the other two like a prisoner under convoy, Auntie Zhenya silently and fiercely wiping away tears.

As they approached the forest gate, Vityok began to shuffle wildly, craning at his wife and then at Valerych, who patted him on the shoulder and began to peel away the transparent tape securing his lips. Auntie Zhenya watched him awkwardly attempt to lift it with his grimy fingers for some time; eventually, she simply pushed his hand away and freed Vityok herself, from the tights in his mouth and from the ropes binding his wrists. The keys jangled in her grasp; she dropped them, swore with a sob and finally got the padlock off the gate. The chairwoman had ordered them all to shut every door, she even went round the village checking – so that no one else like Vityok could come back from the woods.

Vityok shot toward freedom with the haste of a puppy on a long-awaited walk. He sucked air in through his nostrils, made a strange noise that sounded like something between growling and giggling, and looked about to lope off to his unknown wildness. But then, as though remembering himself, he stopped to hurriedly divest himself of his clothes.

Katya turned away, and when Nikita continued to watch, spellbound, tugged him by the hand: look away, don't be rude.

"How did you know he wanted to go back to the forest?" Nikita whispered to her.

"I didn't know, I was just guessing..."

Behind them came Valerych's strangled cry:

"Zhenya, wha...?"

Auntie Zhenya was waving Valerych off with one hand; with the other she was tearing at her comfortably stretched out, dank and greasy "dacha" clothes. And then they were standing side by side in the gray twilight of the summer night – Vityok and Auntie Zhenya, naked, reedy-legged, ridiculous. But there was something in that indecent and pitiful sight that was also inexplicably heroic, and even splendid, and made one want to quieten, bow one's head and reflect. Katya, Nikita and Valerych observed the nude pair almost with reverence, as though these commonplace, familiar people were performing some mysterious feat before their very eyes.

Auntie Zhenya grinned at them crookedly and waved, like someone in a departing train compartment. Then the naked dachniks, holding hands, stepped forward and soundlessly dissolved in the forest gloom.

A few minutes crawled by in stunned silence. Valerych was the first to revive. He took a look at the second couple, the younger, fully dressed one, and snapped at them, with a sudden rush of anger:

"What are you two staring at? Get lost!"

* * *

Neither Vityok nor Auntie Zhenya were seen in the village again. The nocturnal sound that put everyone into a state of mortal dread similarly vanished for good. For the dachniks, it was a relief to forget about it, and about their own foolish sufferings over the unresolvable futility of being, that were not worthy of an adult person, one old enough to be inured and resigned to everything.

If Beroev remembered the noose he had worked on the balcony of his villa, he did not acknowledge this to Nikita by a single word or look. And Vityok's distilling apparatus went home with Valerych.

3

THE MOUSE

There was something very much amiss with Sveta Beroeva, but equally hard to say why this took quite so long for her neighbors and the rest of the village to work out; perhaps it was the unnecessarily high fence around her ostentatious dacha that stuck out like a sore thumb, or maybe just because this was only the beginning, and the villagers were not used to suspecting one another. It really did seem as if any day now they ought to hear the chittering of a helicopter overhead, or see a squad of pumped-up, lantern-jawed rescuers emerge from the forest to retrieve or return the villagers to normality – and the comfortable, everyday boredom of normality that now seemed exceedingly out of reach. Unlike the unsalvageable bachelors and the village young fry who were still frothing for an explanation, most of the dachniks had given up on reasons, didn't need them. Certainly the womenfolk, and the old ladies especially, held the view that it was safer not to know too much. They were willing to forgive and forget the whole crazy mess, just as long as it was over already.

No, it was quite a while before any of the villagers noticed that something was amiss with Beroev's wife. After her behavior around the time of the turning's disappearance, they declined to notice it even more conscientiously – after all, they were all neighbors now, and no one knew how long for. Summer had settled for a long spell.

Although they all tried hard not to think about it, the long spell showed no sign of drawing to a close. It was now the end of August, but only according to the calendar. The birches did not run golden-leafed, and nor did the nights noticeably cool. The air did not have that special end-of-summer translucence. On the contrary, the apple trees bloomed – again – the birds continued to trill delightedly from every bush and branch, and there were strawberries – again – ripening above meaty squashes. To the more experienced gardeners, best versed in minute changes of weather, it began to seem like all the summer months had crashed down upon the village at once and hung there without respite.

Kozhebatkin (no one knew his first name) was one of the pensioners who lived in the village year-round, in a dacha that was almost luxurious, though only by the old standards. Of course, it was nothing to the new-build mansions of newcomers like the Beroevs. Shadowed and sheltered by apple trees, blackcurrant bushes and ineradicable ground elder (not an elder at all, but a hideous weed), Kozhebatkin's wooden house with its ornately latticed, glassed-in veranda, all of it painted a dull and now terribly dusty green, was nearly impossible to spot. Once inside, the visitor was struck by a pervading, almost monastic sense of tidiness and order in the profusion of little vases and candy dishes, oilcloths and doilies, jam jars and saucers washed squeaky clean, and walls dotted with framed family photos – men, women, and children, stiff-cheeked with smiling. It pleased Kozhebatkin to decorate his walls, and it helped to conceal the fly marks on the wallpaper. Every little room was festooned with pictures, little icons, calendars, and landscapes cut carefully from magazines with nail scissors. Comrade Stalin's portrait had pride of place. Duchess, Kozhebatkin's neat little cat, confirmed the seemliness of the location by grooming herself on the sofa just beneath, pointing up with one hind foot.

On that terrible night, Kozhebatkin woke up because he was cold. Sucking in his lower lip, as was his habit, to check his lower dentures were still in place, he was not a little surprised to discover his gums newly populated with hard immoveable objects. He ran his tongue around and slowly but surely ascertained that these objects were in fact teeth, though not at all the kind of teeth one might have expected. At this thought, he woke up completely.

A huge fiery moon looked down on him from above, and he shut his eyes, wincing and annoyed. Above was a carefully whitewashed ceiling, and not a moon at all – or should have been. And beneath it, there should have been all the familiar rectangles of icons and photos, and the ornamental room thermometer in the shape of an owl struck through with a glass rod, which Kozhebatkin might have used to find out whether his bedroom really was this cold or whether he was just shuddering with being half-awake.

Kozhebatkin opened his eyes. A swift cloud had veiled the flaming face of the moon. Then, out of the night, a monster emerged and moved toward Kozhebatkin: a round hide-bound head without even the hint of a body beyond, carried aloft by long, spindly, many-jointed legs. The silent monster skittered up slowly, swaying like a sleepy early-morning metro passenger, and halted a hand's breadth away from Kozhebatkin, scanning him with its clumps of eyes. This was a daddy longlegs spider, enlarged somehow to the size of a bull calf. Kozhebatkin tried to scream, but it came out as a rubbery kind of squeak. As he reared back and ran for it, Kozhebatkin perceived that he was moving not just his feet but also his hands, both sets seeming to have migrated, oddly, underneath his soft round belly, and to have been evilly foreshortened to stumps. Slapping his four stumpy feet across something cold and hard, Kozhebatkin hurtled forward, squeaking his terror into the night, and then abruptly lost his footing and fell over, dropping from the windowsill onto the paved path beneath.

His wee pink feet smarted badly from the fall, down to their microscopic little claws. Shivering with terror and pain, the tiny morsel dove into the grass.

Not fast enough for the soft shadow that surged out from among a tangle of sickly-sweet and ant-infested globular peonies. As it fell down upon Kozhebatkin, red-hot pokers pierced his belly and breast. Squeaking frantically, Kozhebatkin squirmed away and ran for it, leaving a trail of blood on the grass. The shadow paused for a moment then leapt again, heading off any escape. Faced with its ancient and pitiless Aztec expression, its luminescent eyes and rotting-meat breath, the maddened pensioner had a final, piercing insight that none of this could really be happening, and that any moment now he would be waking in his bed. That he must have fallen asleep upright while reading an old newspaper, and as a consequence was having a nightmare. Sleeping upright always gave him reflux, he could almost feel the acidic gastric juice sloshing up toward his throat... Kozhebatkin shut his eyes again and tried hard to corkscrew himself back into reality.

Duchess arched elegantly over the plump housey mousey and crunched. Its blood-rimmed head rolled a little when it fell.

The pensioner Kozhebatkin, her master, was at that moment sitting bolt upright in his sweat-soaked bed, though the candle in a jar he frugally used for a nightlight instead of wasting electricity had long guttered out in a squelch of paraffin. He was absently scrunching up yellowing pages of *Your Orchard and Veg Patch*. Nose twitching, his watery, beady eyes gazed into the darkness.

Had anyone known about the lonely death of Kozhebatkin-turned-mouse, the village would have wigged out a lot earlier. But it went wholly unnoticed, while Duchess – being both murderess and material witness – went to live at Tamara Yakovlevna's house, also unnoticed as she slipped in among all the cats in residence there.

Instead, village rumor soon had it that old Kozhebatkin had lost the plot. This made sense given both his age and the nature of recent events. And anyway, absolutely everyone was feeling more and more loopy with the need to go somewhere else, and also with the anomalously hot weather that would not break. It could have happened to anyone. Besides, Kozhebatkin was an irritable and irritating old codger and no one liked him much. He had, for one thing, nabbed a strip of land belonging to parents of that teenage Yuki, and no sooner was the subject of its return broached during a village assembly, he had planted a row of thorny rosehips there. Kozhebatkin had been the bane of the village assemblies; loudest of all with his endless grievances, which he read off a piece of paper, and his demands for immediate expulsions of late-payers and miscreants. On occasion he went as far as to threaten the committee chair herself, who would blanch, then blotch, then attempt for a time to hold clandestine assemblies and committee meetings behind Kozhebatkin's back. Each and every child knew that for a single lifted apple, the old man would show up at your parents' door looking mortally wounded and complaining. Even those old gossips Tamara Yakovlevna and Zinaida Ivanovna suddenly had pressing, hastily invented errands to attend to, whenever they chanced to run into the petty and antagonistic pensioner.

Kozhebatkin's hoarding began to draw notice largely because he collected and stockpiled everything. Not just mushrooms, berries, sorrel, and things like that – everyone was laying food away, with the growing sense that their mysterious and enforced seclusion was not going to run out before the tinned goods did. The old man clawed down inedibly tart false grapes, desiccated old rosehip berries, seed pods from weeds... and also apple cores and potato peelings and bones. Hedgehogs were blamed for the noisy rustling in the village dump, until someone caught him at it. When startled, Kozhebatkin would stuff half his treasure into his mouth and clutching the rest to his bosom with trembling hands, carry it off home. The striped pajamas he wore day and night were caked in crud. It was obvious he was not in his right mind. Nikita Pavlov – who existed at the extremes of nursing a hangover and going cold turkey – being therefore sensitive to the sufferings of others in the hope of empathy returned – deduced intuitively that this was Kozhebatkin's early privations coming to the fore. A child during the war, he could well have experienced the blockade of Leningrad, for instance, and the besieged state of the village might have tipped the old, sickly man into a second childhood. Truth be told, no one had the slightest idea of Kozhebatkin's childhood, nor his youth, nor whether he had children or relations. No one knew what he did before retirement, either, though his zeal to prosecute and "put away" everyone he took against caused people to speculate that this was the nature of his work before he retired; work which, due to changing social mores, he now took pains to conceal. Despite the active part he played in village life, no one knew much about him at all.

Kozhebatkin had also stopped speaking. Valerych was among the first to test this conclusively; the old man's metamorphosis was the final straw that convinced Valerych to try and escape by any possible means. He ran into Kozhebatkin early one morning. The old man was mincing along the dirt path toward him, clutching a gnawed corncob.

"Morning," said Valerych, neighborly-like.

Kozhebatkin tilted his withered little face sharply, twitched his nose, and said nothing. This was awkward – it wasn't as if the man really hadn't noticed him, or was off in his own world, or pretending to be. Kozhebatkin was staring him full in the face, like he was trying to hook something in there. His eyes were focused and vacant. Valerych tried to think of something to break the very odd moment.

"Well then," he finally harrumphed, turning away and pretending to admire some purple-gray plums.

Kozhebatkin inhaled through his nostrils, scritch-scratched at his own cheek – the sound of rusty nails on sandpaper – and hurried off. It was not until the man's shuffling gait faded fully from his hearing that Valerych felt his back and neck unclench, unpleasant tension draining away.

Another time, the teenage Yulia-I-go-by-Yuki awoke with a start in the annex where she'd taken to sleeping at night. Though she dyed her hair a radical black and carried a steel piercing bar in her navel like a pimple, she was only fifteen and not yet accustomed to independent living. She was sleeping in the annex because it was the only room in the dacha with a new door and a strong lock. Her parents were doing up the old place bit by bit, and had gone away for a couple of nights to source discount DIY supplies the day before the village found itself locked in.

Yuki had woken abruptly from some normal nighttime creaking and rustling and lay for a while with a pillow over her face, waiting for sleepiness to overtake alarm. But then something kaboomed just outside the kitchenette, and not in the normal nighttime way. This was the very specific noise of someone crashing into the rainwater butt and then crunching along the wall and up the gravel path. With a cold sort of dread, Yuki eyed the mop propped up by her bedside. She was tempted to grab the mop and run outside, and holler "who's there", so that it would all be over straight away. She really did want to finally get a look at the mysterious visitors whom the village was clearly beginning to believe in, because the village was beginning to talk about them, quietly. There was a kind of balancing on the edge of reality, when a strange silhouette would suddenly de-coalesce into mere shadows and tree branches, a something in your eye. But tonight, with the moon barely on the wane, she would be sure to see them clearly.

Yuki forbade herself to imagine all the potential ways this could play out because she couldn't afford to be frightened. She rolled off her folding cot and scrambled, on all fours, over to the window. She found herself squinting – as though if she found it hard to see outside, the outside would find it hard to see her too. When she felt the dusty end of the curtain touch her forehead, Yuki got her face underneath and on the other side of it, then finally looked.

Something was stirring busily in the pale moonlight, something large, wrinkly and pale. The creature digging up her vegetable patch had on its sides two sharp-looking protrusions reminiscent of plucked wings, and no head. Yuki stifled a shriek and dug her fingernails into the windowsill. Almost at once, she realized that the wings were actually elbows, and that there was a head, only it was hanging down very low. The invader, crawling belly-down on the ground, was the stark naked Kozhebatkin. He was nibbling on the tiny early zucchinis, without bothering to pick them from their stalks.

When he blinked at her guiltily, sticky juice running down his chin, Yuki could almost taste the peculiar and oily substance. Her arms and legs and sides started to crawl, as though the old man was biting her too, her and the delicate, thin-stemmed little zucchinis who had trustingly poked their little faces up from their leaves thinking their mistress had come, only to fall prey to the crazy old devourer.

"Go away!" she shouted hoarsely, rapping her knuckles on the windowpane. "Stop that! You're not well!"

She was a well-brought-up girl and even now couldn't bring herself to use stronger language with a grown-up. But Kozhebatkin took a great and sudden fright at either her shouting or her rapping, leapt up and dove headfirst into a large raspberry patch. The thorny branches closed tight behind him, swayed a little, and went still. All was calm again, and the veg patch, silvery under the moonlight, went back to dozing as though nothing had happened. Except the despoiled little zucchinis were bleeding sticky juice, and Yuki stood at the window, wincing at the unutterably persistent memory of Kozhebatkin's naked rear end.

* * *

Morning brought the news that someone had robbed the village store, although it wasn't a store exactly, more of a wooden kiosk. Situated near the now-disappeared turning out of the village, in the good old days of *before*, the kiosk only stocked this and that, food-wise; but it was a real godsend to all the villagers now. It was tended by Naima Hassanovna, one of the village's longtime residents. She had a wispy upper lip and always wore a shawl. When the village closed in on itself, the kiosk thankfully remained with all its provisions. It was decided at one or another of the early assemblies that it would become a storehouse, and people could apply to Naima Hassanovna in times of need. At first, she charged real money, but more and more often the dachniks asked for credit, and little by little money went out of use. Naima Hassanovna seemed to find this a relief; she felt sad not to be able to spend her earnings, and anyway it was awkward to charge her fellow detainees, when they were all in it together.

The thief had broken a window and pulled out everything he could reach through the metal grate – this included several bags of pasta, sugar, and breakfast kasha. Those who came to commiserate at the scene of the crime discovered, in talking it over, that this was only the latest in a spate of raids. One man was sure he was missing cucumbers and tomatoes from his vegetable plot, another couldn't find a packet of flour. The solitary angler Katya couldn't locate her bait-filled fishing net, though she tended to blame the local cats.

Sveta Beroeva was the loudest and the most outraged: she had lost a bag of buckwheat, stolen right out of her own cellar.

"Why not just ask for some, am I right?"

Katya stumbled back from the force of the woman's vigorous hand gestures, though they were not aimed at her exactly. "Just ask! If you need something badly. But to steal from me? We're all in the same boat! And I've got children, too!"

* * *

Naturally, everyone knew that the thief was not a "somebody" but the lunatic pensioner Kozhebatkin. He had been behaving oddly for some time, and his passion for stockpiling food couldn't go unnoticed forever. Yuki wasn't the only one who had caught him gorging on her vegetables of a night, though the girl stayed silent about this, keen as she was to put the whole revolting experience out of her mind. Valerych had seen Kozhebatkin lollop away to his own dacha with his, Valerych's, sugar bowl, bold as brass and in broad daylight. But there were only a couple of sugar cubes in the bowl, after all, and Valerych felt it would be too much – too weird – somehow, to go and wrangle with the crazy old man for it.

Beroev was not a man for such niceties. He arrived on the scene a bit behind the others, took clocked the broken window, caught a bit of the conversation, and then, plucking Nikita, Valerych, and the tall, lanky Dronov brothers out of the crowd, marched them up to Kozhebatkin's dacha – to "sort it out." It was quite something, the way he formed his squad without saying a word, just using curt but meaningful gestures. The four exchanged uncomfortable glances behind his back but couldn't man up enough to resist his summons.

The old man's dusty-green dacha was locked and barred. His latticed veranda and all the windows had been covered with rags, taped up with cardboard and plywood; not a single airhole one could look or shout into. There was zero response to their loud knocking. Beroev made to break the door down, but Nikita found his voice just in time to try and talk him out of it; Kozhebatkin was an old man, after all, and unwell, and had been through the famine probably. Valerych, who knew everyone in the village and had a modicum of respect even from the taciturn Beroev, rumbled peaceably in Nikita's support. In the end they decided against last resorts and forcing their way into the wooden sarcophagus. They agreed that they would keep a watch on the old man together, grab him when he emerged to go scavenging, and then get him back into his house and his unlawful gains out of it.

Except that just that day Valerych had to get on with mowing the fast-growing grass on his plot, and Gena the former paramedic had invited both Dronov brothers over, to sample his experimental dandelion moonshine. Beroev went home to a massive row with his wife, which reverberated through the village, and momentarily forgot all about Kozhebatkin.

When dusk fell, Kozhebatkin remembered himself to the villagers once more, when the warm belly of summer night was abruptly rent by shrieking and the clang of broken glass. The shrieker turned out to be Claudia Il'yinichna Petukhova, the chairwoman of the village committee – no one had imagined that this stately and royally dignified personage had it in her to emit such piercing noises. The rescuers found her on the Petukhovs' glassed veranda, collapsed in a corner and clutching her lacy nightgown to her voluminous breast, the lace stained horrifically with crimson blood...

She had ventured out to investigate a quiet rustling in the cellar underneath the veranda. Sure that she would find an infestation of mice, Claudia Il'yinichna flung open the cellar door at the side of the house and dipped her candle down into the gloom. In an instant, the crazed Kozhebatkin, sooty and naked, flung himself across her like a scarecrow. There was an apple in his mouth. The chairwoman dropped her candle and beat at the wild creature, screaming. Her blows landed everywhere, and Kozhebatkin, in his attempts to flee, pushed and shoved her, wriggling and snapping his teeth. Locked in battle, they somehow made it up to the veranda, where Kozhebatkin finally bit the chairwoman's hand, leapt through a windowpane, breaking it, and ran off.

In the time it took for Tamara Yakovlevna to disinfect the wound, made difficult by the way the blueish indentations made by Kozhebatkin's teeth bled without cease, the chairwoman's hand swelled up horribly. Tamara Yakovlevna muttered sympathetically as she tended to the chairwoman, while the chairwoman, white as a sheet, closed her eyes and moaned.

Very soon a crowd had swarmed over and began to buzz. Many were keen to know, for example, how that bloody old man had managed to get inside a locked cellar in the first place. Nikita Pavlov, still in the grips of wanting to be useful, climbed down and waved his candle around for some time, peering at the cold damp walls and the wobbly shadows made by the battalion of shelved pickle jars. Then he swore in amazement.

There was a large hole in the half-rotten floorboards in the corner – these had been helped to break. Kozhebatkin had breached Claudia Il'yinichna's shrine to winter stores by tunneling. No one was willing to crawl inside it, dark and dank as it was, and full of worms and centipedes; instead, they searched around the plot itself and eventually discovered that Kozhebatkin had started his tunnel beyond the boundary fence, where they found a mound of earth and a second hole beneath a bushy acacia tree. The barely restrained sniggering that accompanied the search abruptly ceased at the thought of Kozhebatkin, crawling under the earth – everyone imagined their own plot, of course – like a naked white worm. This was truly frightening. Wordlessly, as one, the crowd turned toward Kozhebatkin's dacha, down the lane.

The thing that woke Katya was not the chairwoman's shrieking nor the anxious din of her assembled neighbors, although she would hear plenty of both later on that night. It was a series of strange rustlings which, blinking awake, she identified as footsteps: someone was wandering around her room, pressing lightly on the creaking floorboards. It was not the first time. She sighed, pulled her flashlight from under her pillow and flicked it around the walls and corners. No one there. As soon as the light went off, the same unseen little claws skittered in exactly the same place.

Katya crunched down hurriedly on a bitter pill and buried her face in her pillow. She was more cross than afraid. There were very few of the sedatives left, a testament to how often she was waking from a piercing, terribly familiar sense that someone – something – else was in the room with her. This had started on the very first night of the village lock-in, when an old radio that had belonged to her grandmother turned on all by itself and emitted an earsplitting hiss, or more precisely a susurration, but loud as a roar. Katya couldn't think of anything except to lob it out the window. And the minute it fell silent, she could see in her mind's eye, terribly vividly, her dead Granny Serafima bent over the radio, winding it back up carefully, so as not to break it again...

So when she heard the noises in the street – normal, human noises – she felt a relief not unlike pleasure. By the time the flickering lights reached her vine-covered fence, she was standing out on her porch and peering impatiently into the night.

The villagers, all in their pajamas and nightshirts still, processed past her fence. The Beroevs, man and wife, strode scowling at the head. Sveta Beroeva wore a sexy little silk robe.

Katya went up to her gate. Right now, there was nothing she wanted more than to be with other people, on the inside of a human pack. She waited for the lagging tail of old ladies to shuffle up to her gate then slipped out quietly and joined them.

Droning and pulsating, the little swarm breached Kozhebatkin's overgrown demesne. Someone – it was Tamara Yakovlevna – cried out in pain. She had stumbled into a knee-deep hole in the ground. Nikita and his pal Pashka lifted the old lady out and ascertained her leg was still attached, getting themselves muddy in the process. Pashka waved his flashlight around, then gave a low amazed whistle; the entirety of Kozhebatkin's front yard sagged with long deep trenches, and was pockmarked with clods of freshly turned up earth. It looked like an army of raging moles had rampaged through. Judging by the stifled swearing up ahead, the old lady was not the only one to fall in. Kozhebatkin's plot, some of which had been unlawfully appropriated from his neighbors, as everyone knew, had been terraformed into a warren, one riddled with a labyrinth of underground passageways.

"Not bad at all, for camping out," Pashka quipped nervously.

"What if he's there right now," whispered Katya, looking down at her feet, "beneath us?"

"All the better for him if he is," someone replied.

Already they were rapping on Kozhebatkin's barricaded windows and doors, and the furious noise sounded like shotgun fire. Beroev tried to kick the front door down, but this was met with looks of disapproval. The villagers continued to shine lights into the windows and tap on the veranda glass, but carefully, so as not to break them. They were all mindful of the old man's unquenchable sense of grievance, and even now, paradoxically, preferred not to piss him off. It was easier to pretend this was some sort of unusual, but still essentially neighborly visit and so they cajoled:

"Open the door, please!"

"Dear Alexander... what was his name, again?"

"Alexei! Alexei Alexandrovich."

"Ah. Open the door, Alexei Alexandrovich!"

"Are you sure it wasn't Alexander something?"

"Just break the door down already, for fuck's sake!"

This was Beroev and the Dronov brothers taking the warping wooden veranda door off its hinges, which they did with ease, almost playfully. They parked the door against the side of the house, where it wouldn't be in the way, and shone their flashlights into the opening. Then stopped in their tracks. It was impossible to get inside.

The veranda was stuffed, floor-to-ceiling, with edibles: bruised vegetables, roots and pine cones, bunches of herbs – some part of Kozhebatkin still seemed to remember his love of healthful St. John's Wort and tansy – also tall mounds of unidentifiable kitchen waste, alongside bags, boxes and packets of grain, flour, sugar, pasta, baking powder, and even dog biscuits and fish food. It was a little hard to believe that the villagers, hemming and hawing as they might about the imminent dearth of a "civilized" food supply, had actually quite this much in store.

"Take it all," Beroev told them, making for a large sack.

One of the heaps shuddered, then exploded in a hail of grain, as Kozhebatkin reared up against his uninvited guests. He knocked Beroev off his feet, then leapt back smartly and disappeared behind a wall of his trophies. Beroev snatched up his cudgel and poked it hard into the shadows. The old man leapt out again like a clockwork devil and bit Beroev. The others, coming out of their stupor, fell upon them both, and managed to twist the old man's arm behind his back, but he would not be pummeled into submission. He writhed desperately, throwing his thin knobbly legs akimbo, the tiny pouch of shriveled flesh between them bobbling up and down as he struggled.

"Stop it!" She hadn't meant to say anything, but there she was, trying to interpose herself between the old man and his attackers who had wrestled him outside, and tripping instantly on one of his holes. Katya plopped down, squeezed her eyes shut against the searing pain in her ankle, and tried to glue her worsening double vision into one. In one layer of reality, smudged shadows, silhouetted by flickering lights, were trussing up a plump big Kozhebatkin, while in the second – simultaneously – a velvety-gray mouse struggled uselessly in gigantic human hands, casting a piteous look at her with its bulging beady eye.

She saw the mouse slip out through the men's rough fingers and spring up into midair, scampering frantically before its feet even touched the ground, desperate to hide, go to ground, save the remaining scrap of its pointless and precious life.

This was when the villagers discovered that something was seriously not right with Sveta Beroeva. Leaping at Kozhebatkin, who was once again half-burrowed in the ground, she struck him in the midriff with a garden hoe. Kozhebatkin's thin muffled scream came from beneath the earth. Beroev reached deep into the trench and yanked out the jerking pensioner. Sveta took aim and, with a sporting grunt, whacked the sharp end into the old man's liver-spotted bald pate.

A sudden burst of heavy rain echoed Katya's howl of protest.

Instantly drenched, the villagers stood stony and dumbstruck for the exact few seconds that might have made a difference, just watching Kozhebatkin writhe on the ground with deafening squeaks, while Sveta Beroeva, frowning with concentration, hacked at him haphazardly but with a steady rhythm, tearing into defenseless flesh with metal teeth, hauling out guts and tendons like long dandelion roots...

By the time Nikita, Pashka, Valerych and even her own husband came to their senses and wrestled the hoe from her grip, it was far too late. Kozhebatkin lay unmoving and broken on the disturbed earth that was now saturated with his blood.

"He attacked me, didn't he?" Sveta glared at them, as though arguing with some unseen accuser. "He's a maniac! What, we should let him go scavenging for little kids next?"

Her delicate gold-rimmed glasses were glazed with rain, but righteous fury shone forth from the misted lenses. Katya stared at the flinty, blood-spotted little face and realized, with a start, that poor, unfortunate Kozhebatkin would not be the only one who could never leave the village now. She didn't know Sveta Beroeva well, and didn't like her, but she was sure that the woman would never set foot outside the village, not even if the road reappeared again and helicopters rained down with rescuers. It would be someone – something – else entirely that walked out in her stead. A profound sense of guilt, and fault, rolled over Katya like a cold wave, though she didn't know why...

* * *

While the rain intensified, and the heavens roared, Nikita, careful not to look at Sveta or Kozhebatkin, kept his eyes on Katya's fine-featured face, which was framed by a long and untidy fringe. She had clearly been avoiding him since those two nights they spent searching the village for the source of the hideous whining. Truth be told he'd told her too many personal things, trying to talk over his pervading horror, and it would have been awkward, so he avoided her too.

"Come to mine, afterward," he now told her abruptly, awkwardly. "I have some liquor at home. Better not to be alone just now."

Rather than object to the intimate – under the circumstances – invitation, Katya nodded forcefully, indicating her agreement with both sentiments.

In the meantime, the villagers had shaken off their stupor and chattered loudly and busily among themselves, trying to make sense, verbally at least, of what had transpired. Gena, the former paramedic, confirmed Kozhebatkin's death. The villagers stepped back from the body and from Sveta, who still stood over it, sealing the violated pair into an invisible bubble. Even Beroev stood a little aback, stony-faced, and made no move to approach his wife. The crowd dispersed into diligent little streams and flowed back toward the gate; no one fancied staying behind, and everyone was sure that other people, more qualified people, would sort everything out. Better still, everything might sort itself out all on its own, in time, and the death of crazy old Kozhebatkin could quietly fade from memory. The world was cruel and weird, especially nowadays, but you had to live in it somehow.

Strangest of all was the way that the villagers, as they talked quietly among themselves on their hurried ways home, worked to absolve Sveta even as they dreaded the very sight of her. It was not long before almost everyone who had seen her slaughter of the old man and done nothing, genuinely and sincerely believed that what had happened was this: the dead maniac Kozhebatkin had attacked defenseless Sveta Beroeva, who, in saving herself and her young children from certain death, killed him, but almost inadvertently. No one had seen the Beroevs' young boys for some time, as Sveta had stopped taking them out on their scheduled walks, thinking perhaps that they were safer behind their tall fence, what with all the goings-on. The two boys appeared now, with wonderful synchronicity, in the minds of all present: they cowered in the weedy clumps of ground elder, pursued by the pale and thirsting, wormlike Kozhebatkin. By some strange alchemy everyone on the scene now believed something that had simply not happened, could not have happened: yes, the boys had been right here, with their parents, and the little innocents were in mortal danger. Frantically sifting through the new reality which, together with Beroev's wife, had turned into a horror, the villagers talked it over, nodding and gesticulating emphatically. Who knew what that creature was, really? What it was capable of? It would have killed them, the mother and children all, for sure.

"She didn't mean to," the chairwoman heartily concurred. "I mean, he was a psychopath, completely off his nut."

Katya was the last to leave Kozhebatkin's plot, and so Nikita had to wait for her under a streetlamp a few houses down the street. She limped a little as she followed him, glad of his timely invitation for a nightcap. Both were plagued by the same loudly tolling thoughts of the senseless way a human being's life had ended before their very eyes, and also that Kozhebatkin had not been dangerous, or more precisely, that as it turned out it wasn't Kozhebatkin who was dangerous. What danger was there, really, in his passionate stockpiling, for his numerous and well-fed neighbors? But no one had intervened to save him – a helpless little mouse, torn to shreds over a bag of stolen grain. Not Nikita. Not Katya, either.

Scared of a woman with a bloody garden hoe, Nikita castigated himself gloomily. Katya, for her part, was wondering what kind of creature would now hatch or chew its way out of Sveta Beroeva...

Yuki, puffy-faced from sleep, appeared out of the gray mist and immediately began chattering at them. She'd heard thuds and screaming, something was happening over at Kozhebatkin's and she was off to see what... Katya shook her head no and Nikita bluntly ordered her back home. Despairing of getting anything interesting from her older pals she slipped past them and away.

"Stop, you can't go there, you can't look!" Katya shouted in her wake. Nikita ran after her, but Yuki only chortled in disdain – don't think *you're* a grown-up either, *you* can't tell me what to do – nimbly evaded his grasp, and sprinted through the deserted plot up to the old man's house, right over to the place where...

Nikita caught up with her in two bounds, then halted with a whoomph of relief. Waving to Katya that there was no need to hurry, he began to wonder why he felt relief at all, when things had only gotten all the stranger?

There was nothing. That is to say that the mud, churned up by dozens of feet, was there by the veranda, and the footprints, and the bloodstains too. But there was no sign of Kozhebatkin, not a whiff. Not a scrap.

"Hey, where's..." Katya didn't finish her sentence. It was too wild, too ghastly to ask where the corpse was, here in the dawn drizzle among the apple bloom and the sickly sweet peonies, and unnecessary. Better let things lie.

As though it had never happened. As though Sveta Beroeva was the same as always, still.

"So... what's going on?" Yuki asked.

"I don't know," Katya answered honestly. She turned to Nikita. "Did you say something about a drink?"

4

THE WAR OF CATS AND TOMATOES

The long-standing dacha friendship between Tamara Yakovlevna and Zinaida Ivanovna – never Granny Tamara or Granny Zinaida, always the full respectful address – was the stuff of village legend. This pair of elderly neighbors clung on to life like twin burrs, and no one in the village knew exactly how old either of them might be: many dachniks had been born, raised, and even grown old on their watch. Together they turned over their vegetable plots, together roamed the woods and prized white-fleshed russula and boletus mushrooms from under the deadfall. Together they would drink tea over at Tamara Yakovlevna's (this was back before the televisions went silent), daintily breaking off pieces of bread, sweet dried bread rings, or cheese – for these children of the leanest years, to eat anything in one mouthful felt like ill manners. Together they daydreamed about how their assorted Sasha-Lyosha-Mishas would finally come down to the dacha, and mow down the stinging nettles by the gate, prop up the leaning outhouse, put up a fence. The Sashas and Lyoshas came, wolfed down shish kebabs, guzzled beer until they grew fat-bellied and taut like night mosquitoes, and went back to town, promising to definitely do it next time, the mowing and the sorting out.

There were two passions in Tamara Yakovlevna's life: watching TV and her cats. Just then she had three cats, Mus'ka, Kuz'ka, and Leopard, Leppy for short. Zinaida Ivanovna too was fond of the television, and enjoyed the very same programs, all about the secret sigils of destiny, fatal curses, God's miracles, and the vagaries of the zodiac. But instead of cats, her other great love was her vegetable plot. Unlike Tamara Yakovlevna, who blithely dumped the same things in the ground year on year – greens, potatoes, easy things that could grow pell-mell – Zinaida Ivanovna cultivated tomatoes and eggplants, the weird cabbage kohlrabi, and even little hothouse watermelons. While Tamara Yakovlevna's verdant, but for the most part untended, plot was the preserve of lazily promenading cats, over at Zinaida Ivanovna's no shred of earth was unspoken for: her own realm was a tight parade ground of veg rows and flowerbeds, all of it turned over and weeded out with wonderful diligence. And this was how, though their collective children and grandchildren had never yet found the time to put up a fence between their holdings, the border between the two was perfectly obvious.

It was all because of that fence.

One morning, Tamara Yakovlevna discovered a small heap of grass, covered over by dead flowers, just touching the border, but definitely within her side of it. It was only the day before that Zinaida Ivanovna had mentioned finding a place for a new compost heap. Apparently she had found it. The encroachment was likely to be entirely accidental, and yet it left a bad taste in Tamara Yakovlevna's mouth. They both knew exactly where the dividing line lay, and when they stopped to chat, it was without crossing that line. They even went to visit each other as though the fence really existed, out of one front gate and in the other, not just barging through.

Tamara Yakovlevna went back for a shovel and used it to neatly drop the unsolicited weeds back over her neighbor's side.

Zinaida Ivanovna came over that evening, bearing – as promised – some rhubarb jam. It was sweetened with stevia, a sugar substitute that not everyone knew about, she said. The villagers were making strides at growing their own, but people were also starting to wonder – though not yet out loud – how it would go when supplies of sugar, butter, flour and other currently unavailable foodstuffs ran out.

The jam was sour and strange. The old ladies dunked their bread rings, of which the thrifty Tamara Yakovlevna had five packets still, diligently into the jam and then sucked the preserve through velvety old-lady lips. Despite mutual smiles and compliments to the jam, the small talk kept petering out. There was no mention of the compost heap.

No sooner did the first pallid light fall on the old apple trees, than out from her dacha emerged Tamara Yakovlevna. She was drawn to the imaginary fence, the place that was just yesterday profaned by incursion. It wasn't that she had suddenly and utterly lost faith in her neighbor, more that it was better to check, just in case.

The beginnings of the compost heap, grown larger in diameter and again covered over with earth, were once again on Tamara Yakovlevna's land. What's more, Zinaida Ivanovna had been busy making it permanent. The mound was propped up by sidings of slate and broken brick.

Tamara Yakovlevna stood awhile, breathing heavily and blotching. Then she went to get the shovel. The vegetal garbage was returned to its owner, and for the avoidance of doubt, heaped over with slate. The brick shards, she staked into the earth, conclusively outlining the missing section of fence.

On seeing how her bosom friend had not just destroyed the fresh compost heap (Zinaida Ivanovna had naively assumed it was the cats who flattened it the night before) but had also strewn rotting weeds and slate chips all over a bed of anemones, and moreover had built a ridiculous brick fence to claim a meter of land that did not belong to her, Zinaida Ivanovna's mouth pursed into a thin purplish line. *She* had perfect recall of where the imaginary fence ought rightly to have been.

Trembling with indignation, she set off for Tamara Yakovlevna's. She tripped over one of the cats, on approach, which added insult to injury. Zinaida Ivanovna was allergic to cats, but Tamara Yakovlevna maintained that it was not a real illness, just silly fashion, and consequently never put the animals outside, even when Zinaida Ivanovna set about sneezing daintily and pointedly into her handkerchief.

A bystander might not have known it, but the quarrel sparked with lightning speed:

"Forgive me, dear Tamara Yakovlevna, it's just that the compost…"

"Oh, not at all, I must apologize. I thought I'd clean it up myself, I would have hated to wake you…"

Only yesterday they were discussing, over the sour jam, how in the olden days everyone was up with the dawn to start work, but now all the young people lazed about until noon and expected everything to come to them on a silver platter. Implying, that old hag, that Zinaida Ivanovna slept late and rested, unforgivably, instead of laboring.

"Yes, I was done in yesterday, with so much work to be getting on with," gritted Zinaida Ivanovna. "Not like at yours here, so quiet and peaceful, nothing to do but relax."

"You didn't mind, did you?" Tamara Yakovlevna hissed in the manner of a snake about to launch from the grass.

"Over this foolishness? No, no, I shouldn't have bothered you with it." Zinaida Ivanovna's faded irises twitched restlessly behind her glasses. "Good day to you, Tamara Yakovlevna."

And she coasted back in a stately manner through the still warm air to her own plot. Though not through the gate, but straight across the imaginary fence.

Tamara Yakovlevna gazed at the other woman thoughtfully as she went.

From that day, there occurred a daisy chain of little misfortunes, which in themselves were barely worth a mention, and even in aggregate could hardly be blamed on deliberate provocation. Someone had picked all the cherries from Zinaida Ivanovna's cherry tree – although the tree rooted next to a real fence, not the imaginary one, the imaginary fence was close enough to allow anyone to easily get to the shiny fruit. Then one of Tamara Yakovlevna's cats went lame – maybe it had fallen awkwardly or had a fight with one of its tribe, or maybe someone kicked it. Zinaida Ivanovna's flowerbed, the one with her favorite lilies, developed a distinctly un-lily-like smell, and was discovered to contain a rotting fish. It might have been the cats that buried it but could just as easily have been someone else. One morning, though – early – Tamara Yakovlevna spotted Zinaida Ivanovna creeping along her plot. She was still in her nightgown and carried a rubbish pail. Tamara Yakovlevna flung open her shutters to give her neighbor hearty greeting. Zinaida Ivanovna gave a dazzling smile and said she was just cutting across to her compost heap, making it clear that the territory was no longer contested, but very much her own.

"Would you look at the sun," said Tamara Yakovlevna, "blazing so early." She hadn't taken her eyes off the other woman's face.

"Scorching, isn't it," Zinaida Ivanovna agreed. The tension in her smile was making her cheeks ache.

That was how they left it. The shamed would-be despoiler tottered home, while Tamara Yakovlevna clanged the shutters closed with such triumph, she caught her finger in them.

* * *

Zinaida Ivanovna awoke that night from the upward force of her own thunderous sneeze. The darkness looked back at her as a pair of yellow eyes pinned through with shimmering fish scales. The springy, suffocating sphere that lay on her breast was one of the cats.

"Shoo!" she cried, in a voice preposterously loud for the velvety silence of the night.

Snarling, the cat took a prowl about the room, knocked something over, then batted at the closed window and finally fled, pushing the door open with one paw. Zinaida Ivanovna snatched her housecoat and pursued the cat, to make sure of its ejection. Only half-awake, she was nevertheless sure that the cat had been sent by Tamara Yakovlevna with some nefarious purpose. Its springy steps and the jangling of disturbed objects left a dotted trail to follow. Zinaida Ivanovna burst out onto the veranda and stopped dead in her tracks: where she had expected a pair of yellow coins, a fiery necklace of them stared at her from the dark. Then the cats howled, deeply and in unison. She felt her throat close up, which might have been allergies or terror, and shut the door. The animals carried on dashing about the veranda, making their dreary nasty noise and clattering the glass pickling jars she stored out there. It was her, Tamara, she sent the cats, thought Zinaida Ivanovna as she retreated helplessly into her little bedroom. Of course she had sent them, the traitor…

Tamara Yakovlevna in the meantime, discovered that the paths across her plot had overnight overgrown with stinging nettle and stinky red deadly nightshade that looked like micro-tomatoes, and even henbane which she remembered from her rural childhood but had never before seen in the dacha village. Rosehip and thorny raspberry canes poked through where only yesterday there was lush grass. It took Tamara Yakovlevna a while to see this; at first she just couldn't fathom the sharp, burning pain on her legs. She turned to the shed for gloves and a hoe, to eradicate the invaders.

And froze at the mind-boggling sight of the shed, completely swathed in squirting cucumber vines. There was a lot of it at the river's edge, and the children used to amuse themselves by throwing the spiky little bombs against the asphalt, despite being told a hundred times that the plant was poisonous. But to spring up like this, overnight, and with "fruit" to boot... The green vines wrapped the old shed so thickly and tightly it looked about to start creaking under the pressure.

A thorny, venomous sphere burst with a dry sort of snap. Tamara Yakovlevna shuddered.

She knew of course that this was all Zina's doing. That Zina had always been envious of her: the way her house was a horn of plenty, and her handsome grandchildren, and her TV. It didn't really matter how she'd arranged for this lightning-quick invasion of thorny, spiky, noxious things. The evil eye, maybe. The last program before the TV died was exactly about that, the evil eye, that sort of thing. Zinaida Ivanovna had watched the show with her, crunching dry bread rings all the while, that ingrate.

She went back to her covered veranda, dismayed and scratched up, to be greeted by the cats. They massed around the TV, whose blank screen glowed with a very faint, yellow-gray circle: this sometimes happened, circles or dots appearing haphazardly as the ancient cathode tube was probably breaking down.

Except that there were six cats now, not three. Mus'ka, Kuz'ka and Leppy had brought some friends. The cats gazed at Tamara Yakovlevna thoughtfully and even, she fancied, with sympathy. She stroked the skinny striped backs and the cats purred with a sudden passion, rubbing themselves against her blistered legs like furry waves. The silky touch calmed both the pain and, little by little, Tamara Yakovlevna herself; the cats loved her, they cared for her. She could rely on them, even if her friend was lost forever. She *had* been a true friend, that faithless Zina, a kindred spirit, and they'd been friends for ever so long. How, how had she missed the envy taking root in her heart, like bitter henbane…

Zinaida Ivanovna on the contrary, felt great. Having watched her neighbor wage war on the stinging nettles and squirting cucumber, and blowing gingerly on her stung hands, she was brimming with the certainty that there was indeed justice in the world. Nature herself had given that Tamara – and that Tamara's revenge, petty like her bloody cats' – a lesson. It was a small, petty lesson, but still. Sighing with satisfaction, she put on her favorite green headscarf and went for a stroll. She walked past Tamara Yakovlevna's fence in silence and deliberately slowly.

She returned several hours later, having used the time to complain about her neighbor's difficult disposition to a few acquaintances and to gather fresh news of the village. Two more had disappeared: a pensioner from Flower Street and Tanya, the fractious and unfortunate woman who spent every summer at the village with her mentally deficient son. The resident gardening guru Valerych seemed determined to find a way "back to the world" and everyone was trying to talk him out of it, what with people disappearing left, right, and center: move one step beyond the perimeter fence, and that was the end of you. In other news, some unknown pranksters had erected a strange idol of clay on the plot of the local sculptor, who largely kept to himself, but was known throughout the village for the collection of plaster statues he'd rescued from a derelict pioneer summer camp. This caused quite a commotion. Also, Sveta Beroeva's husband had not been seen in a while. The strange goings-on no longer caused anyone to clutch bosoms or drop jaws; the dachniks were beginning to get used to their inexplicable new life and its odd, obscure rules.

Zinaida Ivanovna twirled a bracingly bitter-scented little sprig of mugwort before her face as she swung open her gate, and then, the bushes by the gate came alive with an unholy screeching and launched themselves at her. She felt her vision dim and her heart take a tumble downward, deep inside her – it took her a moment to understand that they weren't exploding at her, but generally in all directions, and it wasn't the bushes but cats from the bushes. It was also the cats not the bushes that were screeching, or more precisely yowling. She dropped the mugwort sprig as acrid cat smell hit her nose. Then she saw that in her absence her plot had fallen to an enemy raid.

The vegetable patch and the flowerbeds had been turned upside down: uprooted and mangled, the lilies and roses were fading where they lay on the ground; unearthed beets blushed crimson from their rows; torn up tomato plants could be seen through the gaping holes of the hothouse. The reek that cut through the thick scent of drying plants, the paw prints, the shreds of fur, all this pointed at the culprits.

Mercifully, the abrupt onset of allergic swelling deprived Zinaida Ivanovna of her sense of smell. She began to sneeze. This deafening volley roused Tamara Yakovlevna, who peeked out of her window sleepily – she had spent half the day erecting a palisade in place of the imaginary section of fence and had just lain down for a well-earned nap. Not that a row of sticks in the ground were a palisade exactly, more of a dotted demarcation of the boundary. They couldn't actually keep anything from getting through, as Tamara Yakovlevna discovered when she saw Zinaida Ivanovna stride resolutely across it.

Her face was stony with concentration; only her nostrils flared a little. No sooner did Tamara Yakovlevna think it might be a good idea to bolt the door, than the tall branches of a rosehip bush by her porch – goodness knew when it had gotten so tall – swayed violently, as though blown by a strong gust of wind, and smacked into the windowpane with such force as to send glass spraying across the room, narrowly missing Tamara

Yakovlevna herself. A second later, the thorny branches – it was no gust of wind that commanded them – worked themselves inside the breach.

Tamara Yakovlevna crept back in silent stupefaction to the door, while the rosehip unfurled, squidlike, and grew, like sped-up video. Briskly, it crawled along the windowsill and walls, knocking over jars and teacups, knocking off calendars and photos. In the calm, empty "eye" of the thorny tornado, was Zinaida Ivanovna. Like a raging harpy, inexorably she approached the dacha.

Tamara Yakovlevna was suddenly aware that the door behind her was shuddering too. Something beat and scratched at it from the other side. Tamara Yakovlevna recoiled in terror; could the vegetation, wielded by that witch Zina, have flanked her and overrun the house? A familiar demanding yowl came from beyond the door, and Tamara Yakovlevna flung it open with her usual haste. She had to let them in, her poor creatures, who were probably terrified by all the devilry.

A glaring of cats flowed into the room with a deep rumbling holler. It spilled across the floor like a motley rug and attacked the branches crawling up the walls. Roused from her stupor, Tamara Yakovlevna seized a mop and, with a war cry little different to that of the cats, joined the fray. The allies overpowered the bestial rosehip and turned back to the window, ready for fresh battle. There was no sign of the plot, nor of that witch Zina – instead, what they saw was a jungle-like wall of plants: henbane and jimson weed, and stinging nettles, and hemlock, and the most ineradicable of the dachniks' foes, ground elder. A bony tabby cat, the bravest and stupidest of the lot, leapt up to the windowsill and the poisonous stems swayed toward her as one.

"Here kitty, kitty," called Tamara Yakovlevna, panicking. She couldn't bear the thought of the cat poisoned and dying in agony before her eyes. The cat, not turning a hair, carried on hissing at the overpoweringly malodorous jimson weed.

Tamara Yakovlevna swept her down to the floor with a neat flick of the mop and the green wall beyond the window stilled.

Holding a rag to her nose and mouth, Tamara Yakovlevna quickly stuffed a cushion into the hole in the window and retreated back inside. She was knee-deep in cats, hackles raised and ready for war. Tamara Yakovlevna crossed her scratched and bloody arms.

"So that's how it is with you..." she muttered, and the cats echoed with an agitated yowl. "You asked for it now... you asked for it."

And soon enough the village once again began to experience unpleasant changes. These were so insignificant and small at first that even the wariest, the most attuned of the dachniks felt no alarm. What could you read, really, into the way that the hemlock growing on the patches of wasteland seemed to grow ever denser and tiny wild tomatoes proliferated along the streets? Or the sudden activation of the stray cats? Not that anyone had any idea of just how many of the silent, round-faced little beasts actually inhabited the village until now. And who could complain about the way that all vegetation, whether cultivated or wild, grew like gangbusters – anyway, easily explained by the steady heat and regular rain. The dachniks were delighted at this, and readied their pickle and jam jars for a record crop. So far, electricity had been working fine, but no one knew how it was supplied and how long it would last. They might be left without refrigeration at any moment, while a cellar full of pickles and jams would stand the test of time.

Then Lyosha Usov from dacha no. 6 – known to everyone as "Lyosha-don't", his mother's constant refrain – started foaming at the mouth when he ate some micro-tomatoes. Lyosha recovered, but when they looked more closely, the villagers discovered these were not wild tomatoes at all, but deadly nightshade.

Katya startled awake at dawn, her pillow damp and hot: "The meadow is burning!"

Surfacing fully and immediately from sleep, she saw a kestrel hover in midair like a helicopter above the neighboring plot. Dusty brown like all suburban birds, the kestrel beat its wings furiously but stayed in place, as though pinned to the tender dawn sky. Katya couldn't look away; she loved watching living things. Then, something unexpected happened. Like a gray meteor, a cat launched itself from a swaying rowan branch. Reaching an incredible, birdlike height, the cat clawed the kestrel from the air and fell down to earth with its prey. It was all very fast and the morning went on as though nothing had happened, if not for the few feathers still dancing in the air. But Katya decided that she wouldn't stir out of doors that day. Far safer to hide in the bowels of the dear old childhood dacha, to take herself out of the equation, wait it out. She was used to sensing the approaching strange in the smallest shifts within the normal course of things.

Lenka Stepanova from Cherry Street went to take a shower that evening and ended up with burning hives across her whole body, from stinging nettles. She wept the whole time her parents hosed her down from the outside tap; the nettles had, on their own, sprung up around her inside the wooden shower cabin. Stepanov senior, in his capacity as rational adult, went to check and discovered for himself that the nettles were not just there, but growing so thickly up through the shower floor that you couldn't get inside.

The former paramedic Gena, who had of late become irreplaceable to the villagers, had his vegetable patch dug up violently one night by moles or some other beasts, everything down to the garlic and dill destroyed.

Kitties attacked six year-old Anyuta. She raced home covered in tears and scratches, with the kitties in hard, silent pursuit. Just as silently, they threw themselves against the door and windows, driving Anyuta's grandmother nuts.

Pashka, the village lazybones, was a frequent visitor to his granddad's dacha: he was always there, working on his motorbike or messing around with a guitar, until the night he got stuck in the village. Well, a hawthorn bush treated Pashka to an impromptu body piercing. Pashka shook his head helplessly and his eyelid twitched as he told the story: the branches suddenly went for him, and before he could blink, these long-ass thorns were stuck in his face. They pierced his cheek in two places, ragged his ear, and almost put out an eye.

Naima Hassanovna, the proprietress of the village-shop-turned-supply-store had her kid ripped apart. Its mother, the goat – the village's milk-producing treasure – was untouched, but it was a terrible shame about the kid. The mysterious predators had skinned it alive, strewing bits of skin all over the yard as though playing with it, and only nibbled at the carcass – so at least the meat didn't go to waste. Now the dachniks grew concerned: they had a predator on their hands who killed not for food, but just because.

The night that followed the demise of the kid was when the village's everlasting committee chairwoman Claudia Il'yinichna Petukhova awoke from the sound of crackling and a pervasive smell of grass. The smell was actually more of a mist, tiny droplets of plant juice suspended in the air. Claudia Il'yinichna had gone to sleep in the annex, thereby escaping her husband's deafening snores. He'd overdone it sampling some apple cider. But now the walls of the annex were rocking and rolling and there was a heady scent, so acrid it made her eyes water. On top of all this, there was a mournful belly howl outside, as though a host of rounded mouths had opened up directly in the fabric of the night.

The chairwoman flicked her helpful bedside light on and off a few times, but there was no light. She hadn't charged her cellphone in ages, as it didn't work anyway. Somewhere along the hallway there should be a flashlight hanging on the wall, in case of a nighttime foray. Claudia Il'yinichna lowered her feet to the floor and yelped in pain. Her eyes were already used to the darkness, so she could see a quivering rug spread over the floor... The scent, so familiar and hateful to any gardener, gave it away: the annex was overrun by stinging nettles.

A windowpane fell in with a clang. The walls were groaning in earnest, like a watermelon in an expert's grip. A taut wooly ball careened around the room, howling, tearing all in its path, including the curtain, which fell softly on top of Claudia Il'yinichna. The darkness outside seemed thicker than the darkness inside, pressing down on the window. Yes, it really was pressing, there were invisible little cracks icily crunching across the glass already...

The dignified and resolute Claudia Il'yinichna did what little children do when faced with fire, flood, or some other such adult horror. She dove under the covers, cocooned herself head to toe, and screamed as hard as she could.

With the help of the convening neighbors, Petukhov rescued his spouse, but was powerless to save the annex, which was mauled and flattened by the moving vegetation before their very eyes. At the last, it exploded with cats – quite in the manner of a squirting cucumber, of which there was actually rather a lot in there.

It was not Claudia Il'yinichna 's first horrific nocturnal occurrence, so she quickly rallied and recalled that she was in charge.

"What is going on here, then?" she asked the bewildered, half-asleep dachniks in that special chairwoman tone. "Just look around you! What in the world is going on here?"

They were surrounded by stinging, thorny overgrowth, and above it the towering, gigantic heads of cow parsnip, that Martian contagion which during the last decade had descended on the suburbs and seemed to broadcast through its satellite dishes signals back to its toxic home world. Strange animal shadows roamed the undergrowth, all hissing, howling and flashing round eyes.

At some point the village had turned into a jungle.

Claudia Il'yinichna raised her voice. "Something needs to be done about this, comrades!" At this the dachniks produced a baffled collective hum.

"We have to find where it's all coming from," said Valerych.

"What do you mean?"

"What I said. It's thickest where it's coming from. That's where we sort it out."

Such finality there was in how Valerych said "sort it out", it was as though he'd passed a death sentence. The dachniks hummed more confidently.

"Let's go," said Petukhov curtly. He was still brave with last night's drink inside him. "But take something to swing. The cats have all gone loopy."

Armed with gardening implements, the villagers set off, slashing through the henbane and nettle with the grim determination of conquistadors.

Agitated, the jungly foliage swatted them across the face and sprayed them with stinging juice. Cats threw themselves at the flashlights like giant moths. The moist vegetal thicket was congealing around the tired and blistered dachniks; in the end it became impassable. Petukhov made a rough calculation of their direction and speed and guessed that they had reached the disappeared turning, where once there stood a tall streetlamp. What if all this creeping and crawling vegetable mass was creeping and crawling in *from the outside*... Petukhov broke out in a cold sweat. He felt the darkness physically cling to him.

"I need light!" he shouted tremulously. "I can't see a thing! Give me some light, somebody?"

A cat catapulted from out of the jungle and clung on to his stomach. Claudia Il'yinichna prized it off with the handle of a hoe and lobbed it back.

"Gimme a minute!" The lazybones Pashka started hacking sideways. The dachniks broke out in a panicked clamor. One of the young people quietly followed after Pashka.

"We're by the turning!" Pashka's shouting was swiftly receding. "I live right here, across the street! Just gimme a minute!"

They kept losing the weak flashlight beams in the gloom; circles of pale light that slid upward and vanished. Nervously, they shuffled from foot to foot and inched closer to one another. Only now they began to see that the aim of their expedition was not entirely clear, and no one really knew what to do next. Everything around them rustled and shifted to stab or sting. The unseen cats howled without cease; every now and then a furry clump was propelled from inside the jungle to claw at human flesh and, just as abruptly, disappear. They were managing to keep them at bay, but everyone was scratched and bitten.

"Turn them off," counseled Valerych. "They're attracted to the light."

"How are we going to be without light?"

"What if that fool doesn't come back at all?"

"What if he doesn't? It's not as though he's any use…"

But the cats continued to advance, and their mean alien eyes glittered. So the flashlights went off one by one. Petukhov, who longed for light, was the last to power down.

"I don't know what we even came for…" someone sighed after a long silence.

"Even if we find where it's coming from, what are we supposed to do then?"

"We could have waited until morning…"

"Exactly."

"Very convenient, to speak out when no one can see you," said Claudia Il'yinichna tartly. "Anonymity, I think the young people call it."

"Fire!" someone shouted from off on the side, and it sounded like a command to shoot. Valerych, who had done his duty and served, even crouched reflexively. Something glomped and snapped, and a cow parsnip bush that had suddenly appeared from the dark ran with transparent blue lights. Desiccated and hollow, it suddenly looked like a burning humanoid, with its head for a head and its branches for arms.

This was Pashka, lover of barbeques. He had lugged over all his lighter fluid, a backpack-full, and now he was spraying it passionately at the green walls. The dachniks clicked their lighters, someone burned their hand and cried out.

"Not so fast, let it soak through..."

"Hey, hey, that's me you're spraying!"

"Light it up!"

The toxic jungle blazed in several places at once. It quivered wildly, attempting to topple over the arsonists, and dropped flurries of smoldering leaves. Cats, suddenly mindful of the danger, ran amok, shrieking. They clawed at bare arms and legs and faces, the dachniks hit back with whatever was to hand, but the cats boomeranged right back at them. Valerych tore off his shirt, doused it from a plastic bottle, then set it on fire and swung it left and right, an axe in his other hand.

"We'll all burn to fuck like this," he muttered, trancelike, as he slowly made his way forward. "Burn right to fuck..."

Tamara Yakovlevna was first to notice the orange glow. As she raised herself up on one elbow her blanket stirred too – it was covered in warm cats. Carefully, so as not to step on her pets who were currently too numerous to count straight, Tamara Yakovlevna made her way to the window, and saw a pillar of flame beside her fence. Further away there were several more, licking at the darkness. Tamara Yakovlevna drew in her breath – a fire. As though Zina's scheming wasn't enough, now she had a fire on her hands too. She could run to get help, sure, but how do you run anywhere with Zina's nettles and jimson weed running riot. There was no getting away from the green nasties, though the cats tried to help her, the innocent darlings. They chewed and dug relentlessly – yet never seemed to get poisoned. Trust an animal to know what's edible and what's not.

Tamara Yakovlevna pushed at the door which didn't move, of course, she had expected it to grow over again with squirting cucumber or something thorny. Zina was constantly locking her in like this; there were no glass windowpanes left in the dacha, just holes she kept having to plug with rags, and it was coming through the walls so hard it's a wonder the house was still standing. As the glow blazed brighter, Tamara Yakovlevna found herself genuinely frightened. You could burn alive like this, with no one coming to help. The fire was probably Zina's doing too, that old witch.

The fence cracked and splintered – but it was not burning, someone was hacking at it from the other side. Tamara Yakovlevna watched, stupefied, as her rickety ancient fencing came down. Human silhouettes appeared backlit starkly by the blaze beyond. The very people she had contemplated running to for help. Brandishing sticks and hoes and axes and spades they marched on her dacha. Also on her neighbor's; they swarmed right over the line demarcating the imaginary fence. They kicked at the cats and hacked at the wildly roiling branches, vines heavy with tomatoes and grapes – all the lush fruit and vegetable cornucopia that had proliferated on Zinaida Ivanovna's plot. Over the crunching wood, Tamara Yakovlevna could hearnasty, brisk and businesslike shouting as people wreaked destruction: it was fun to do it on someone else's plot. Tamara Yakovlevna was terrified. Torches and axes, just like in the Middle Ages, when they came to burn a witch.

Abruptly she remembered the crumpled, pained face of Kozhebatkin, whom everyone had so assiduously forgotten. It was just the same then, wasn't it – they came for him in the night, a mob… Just ordinary people, they were all dachniks, neighbors, allies in the war against decay and drought. She had thought to go to them to get Zina under control – as a last resort of course, she wouldn't have bothered anyone otherwise.

And suddenly she was anxious for Zina, who was probably asleep and had no idea what was coming. She was all alone up here. They were both always alone, they only ever had each other – the kids never came, the grandchildren never bothered, the neighbors had their own business to mind. You could get knocked on the head like Kozhebatkin and people would forget you were ever there. But when her hoe broke last month, it was Zina who gave her her own. To keep, for nothing. And she was always generous with rhubarb jam, and bread rings, and they had such nice times drinking tea in front of the TV, back in the old days when things were normal. Yes, they'd said a deal of things to one another, and done things to one another too, but you could bet that Zina wouldn't come to her door by night, breaking down her fence, swinging a torch and axe…

And in truth, there was only one person in the world she could be sure of, a decent person: Zinaida Ivanovna, educated, kind, thoughtful. She had always felt lucky to have such a neighbor. Tamara Yakovlevna sank down on her bed, clutched a stupid striped cat to her bosom and wept – because she was frightened, because she was helpless, and because she had, intemperately, done so many stupid things she could not take back.

Zinaida Ivanovna too was sitting atop her bed and watching, through a veil of wild grape vines, the approaching mob trample her defenseless lilies and tender little watermelons. She too wept. What devil had taken hold of her? Didn't they say on TV that sometimes devils got hold of good people, making them do bad things? She was a good person, she never meant anyone ill, and Tamara Yakovlevna was good too, and what had the two of them done…

With a final rustle, the branches stilled – just as they ought on a windless night. The cats fell silent and vanished in the dark. The dachniks, hot and excited, continued to battle for a bit out of sheer inertia, until someone noticed that there was no resistance at all. Just the crackling of fire.

Valerych, covered head to toe in soot, flicked on his flashlight and swept it to and fro. There were no creatures to be seen. The jungle looked faded and dull, turned in a flash from vegetal monsters to boring old weeds. Hell of a lot of weeding, thought Valerych reflexively. Look at the state of it.

"Stamp on it now, stamp on the fire! We need some sand here, or earth!"

This was the chairwoman taking back command.

The blaze seemed extinguished but she could still hear shuffling and muted voices outside, so the knock on the door caused Tamara Yakovlevna to do a little startled jump. Telling herself that a lynch mob would hardly bother to knock, she slid the bolt carefully, but left the chain on.

It was Zinaida Ivanovna, in her nightgown and holding a flashlight. She looked agitated.

"You'll forgive me, won't you, if aught's amiss," she sniffled. "If, you know, anything… some devilry…"

"No, not at all. You must forgive me, Zinaida Ivanovna. If I've offended you in any way…"

Tamara Yakovlevna put her hand out, under the chain. Zinaida Ivanovna shook it ardently. Then the neighbors smiled at one another, politely, with great relief.

The dacha jungle dried up within a few days' time. And while Tamara Yakovlevna's clowder of cats was increased to ten or so – all of them peaceable and lazy – the rest had dissipated somehow.

The villagers, still uncertain as to the cause of the rebellious flora, looked askance at both cats and nettles for a while longer. Their suspicions proved, time after time, unfounded: the cats rubbed themselves against ankles, the nettles meekly died at gardeners' hands. So little by little, the inexplicable events receded from memory – besides, new ones were about to land.

5

SOMETHING TO
REMEMBER ME BY

Yulia-call-me-Yuki had not actually set foot in the village until the ripe old age of fourteen, when she was very nearly grown up, and missing out almost entirely on the archetypal dacha childhood of haring around on bikes at all hours, bosom summer friends and secret forest hideouts. Child Yulia accompanied her parents to the seaside some summers, but as she grew, she mostly stayed in town surfing the web, where she picked up the nickname Yuki, which she worked hard to graft onto her non-internet life. Perhaps it was the lack of an annual socialization course – so perfectly delivered by a dacha summer – that made Yuki such a lone ranger, as her mother ruefully called her. She preferred to spend all her free time buried in her laptop watching movies, or else deep in a book, which for a girl of her generation was tending toward strange. More than anything in the world, Yuki loved munching and being scared, ideally both at once. So naturally she fell hard for anything mystic-esoteric and, by the age of thirteen, operating from firm conviction that she was a hereditary witch, she began to dye her hair a radical black. Her parents were horrified, but what could you do, it was that kind of age.

And all because the dacha used to belong to Yuki's grandmother, who had among her relations the reputation of something between Baba Yaga and the Snow Queen; she lived somewhere far away, on her own, spinning malicious webs against anyone in her path, and it was better not to get too near her at all. Not that she let anyone get near; the grandmother, everyone agreed, was very much a lone ranger herself...

The grandmother's story ended in the most banal, ordinary way, when she suddenly grew old and infirm, surrendered her advantage, lost the icy resolve which Yuki had ardently admired from afar, and willed her dacha to her ne'er-do-well son and his bitch of a wife. Meaning Yuki's mom and dad. She died a couple of months after she made her will. This kind of thing happened in movies all the time, people making a will and then dying soon after. No one ever seemed to warn them of the danger there.

And so the first time Yuki laid eyes on the legendary dacha in the elegiacally-named village – the dacha that everyone in the extended family had drooled over – was only after her grandmother was no more. It was then she discovered that there was really nothing special about it, beyond the combination of woods, river, and relative proximity to town, that the adults valued so highly. What else? Mushrooms, swimming, gloom, and decay. A neglected, overgrown plot, a sagging wooden house infested with busily active mice, endless little pots and pans and old glass jars, and crusty dishcloths and stunted stools and tables, the kind of cozy, comfortable detritus that old people loved so much. And everywhere, rampaging ivy – though it looked like this was left deliberately to grow wild and cover up everything especially unsightly. Yuki liked the ivy; it engulfed the dacha wall and the outbuildings and fences so densely and profusely that it was possible to pretend you were looking not at your departed granny's old wooden dacha, but rather an ancient keep inhabited, obviously, by specters wrought of cold mist. And anyway, what would be the point of leaving a house to your descendants if it didn't have even a single little old poltergeist?

Arriving for the first time in early spring, Yuki gazed at the ivy – the ancient branches still dormant but already so heavy they were over-toppling the fence – appraisingly. Then she plucked one of her earbuds from an ear and proclaimed, at a volume her parents would be sure to hear, that it was all right, actually, nice and gothicky.

That first summer, they only managed to visit sporadically, tackling the worst of the old rubbish on the plot and clearing out the sturdiest outbuilding so it could be used as a base. The grandmother hadn't come to the dacha for the last few years of her life and the "main house", as they called the dacha itself, was in a continuous state of rot and sag, not fit for human habitation. Yuki snuck inside a couple of times, with a candle in the dead of night, and it was better than any horror movie. The house flooded with racing shadows, it rustled and creaked, and if the weather was blowy, it even moaned, like a wounded giant. Yuki tried earnestly to summon the spirit of the dead grandmother, but it never seemed to work.

A regular lurker of esoteric forums and chatrooms, Yuki had plenty of research material on which to reproduce well-known spells and develop her own, more potent, rites and incantations; these she wrote out laboriously in a notebook, because they only worked if you copied them by hand, none of that amateur copy-pasting. She had a special box for amulets and magic stones. There were not many teenagers around that summer, so she had but a sparse audience to regale with tales of her strong bio-field and unusual aura, which came from her late grandmother, a tremendously powerful sorceress. Yuki had hoped that her witchy bloodline and magical talents would impress the old-timer kids so much they'd let her into their pack, but they let her in anyway, just because. She was soon disappointed in them, however – the summer crowd of village teens seemed to her, on the whole, a loutish and provincial lot.

Her parents continued steady improvement works over the course of the following summer. Really, they were rebuilding the old house; shoring up walls, knocking out and rebuilding partitions and floors. The empty, echoing interior smelled of fresh wood and paint and even in the dead of night held no thrill at all. Yuki's mother was happy though, planning out which room should go where, and looking forward to setting up a studio – she was an illustrator – in the spacious attic.

Her parents got wind of a job lot of the boards and planks they needed an endless stream of, at a knockdown price, but only if picked up immediately at some remote industrial park. So they hared off, leaving Yuki to "hold the fort". They would be back the following day, or at worst the day after. Her mother left a pot of chicken soup in the fridge (the chicken veiled by a thin coating of fat) and some stuffed peppers for her dinner. Yuki was a little put out: everyone knew she hated stuffed peppers.

The village had shut in on itself on the first night of her parents' absence.

Unlike the majority of the adults and the more rational members of everyone else, Yuki had no trouble accepting that there was no leaving the village. If you can't, you can't, Yuki reasoned, and there was clearly some sorcery at work. Ordinary magic, just like in her favorite books and movies – except that in those, the magic was foreign and glamorous, but here in the village it was homegrown and a bit wild.

And to be fair, this was only to be expected when you were a hereditary witch. As she rifled through her film collection, Yuki dipped dry sweet bread rings into her tea and mused that perhaps it was her destiny to solve the mysterious disappearance of the turning and release the village from an evil spell. Quite possibly, her own dormant but formidable magical gifts had been the thing to spring some enchanted trap, or it was just malevolent forces ranging against her in the traditional way. It followed that her own magical talents – hitherto only expressed rather vaguely in nebulous premonitions and prophetic dreams about pop quizzes at school – would soon emerge for real.

In the meanwhile, you had to just get on with it. Yuki quickly twigged that no one had the slightest intention of looking after her: in fact, the adults barely noticed her existence. She suffered in solitude for a bit, even learning in that time how to cook buckwheat kasha, then finally attached herself to a cluster of elders, who happened to be the village's "young people". This group consisted of her own next-door neighbor Katya, the morose Nikita Pavlov, who lived opposite them on Cherry Street, and his buddies Pashka and Andrei. Hanging around them was much more interesting: quietly but steadily they were investigating the weird goings-on, and they treated Yuki almost as an equal. Katya, the quiet angler, took charge of Yuki. It was impossible to say how old she was; it might be thirty as easily as twenty, and Yuki was too shy to enquire. Katya was not scared of worms or the river, meaning that to Yuki she was almost heroic. But there was something disquieting in her strange, crooked smile, and while Yuki admired Katya greatly, it was the jolly lazybones Pashka, next youngest of the bunch, with whom she made fast friends.

It was actually kind of idyllic. Katya taught her to cook, even bringing fish from the river and showing Yuki how to descale and bone them, though Yuki did feel a little sorry for the silvery sticklebacks and perch, with their meekly gulping mouths. Yuki learned to manage the kitchen garden too, and enjoyed playing the part of a veteran dachnik, mistress of beets and zucchinis, expert hoe-wielder. Basically, despite the fact that summer had already lasted a full four months, life went on in one way or another. It was now the second half of September, but the village carried on enjoying a verdant, generously warm July. Yuki was not displeased at this particular anomaly, however, since there was really nothing drearier than a soggy back-to-school September.

* * *

Then came the day Yuki decided to expand her blooming vegetable patch into the late Kozhebatkin's plot. After all, when he was still alive, the pensioner had done exactly the same, pinching off a strip of land from her grandmother's plot, and nastily planting it over with spiky rosehips. This was how Yuki's parents came to have the smallest plot in the village, where every inch had to count. Meanwhile, all the older dachniks were now saying that the food stores, even the ones inside the former shop that were being rationed, had to come to an end eventually, and then... Also, the day before, Pashka had brought her a dozen little sprouted potatoes, but Yuki had nowhere to plant them.

The fencing between the plots was old and rotten through. It didn't take Yuki long to loosen and break out a section. She dragged the surprisingly heavy planks of wood to the side, grunting with effort, then set to digging. This was easier said than done, despite it having rained the night before, and the thoroughness with which the crazed Kozhebatkin had furrowed up his own plot. It seemed he hadn't quite had enough time to tunnel over to this side of the boundary fence.

As she turned up another dense clod of earth, Yuki felt her shovel clang against something metallic. She broke up the clod carefully, avoiding the profusion of earthworms, and unearthed a small object that glimmered red in the sunlight. Intrigued, Yuki thumbed off the deafening "Beats for Fitness" track in her ears and kneeled down for a closer look.

It was a single, mud-encrusted earring. Yuki had found things in the veg patch before, once even a fishing hook that she lifted out of the ground together with a couch-grass root, and later gave to Katya, but never anything valuable. Certainly she never imagined finding an ancient – it had to be ancient to have been buried so deep – artefact. Yuki excavated the area with great care but there was no more treasure to discover, only a couple of beer bottle tops and an underground anthill. The red ants immediately dispersed along her unfinished row and up her bare legs, nipping formic acid into her skin. Yuki dropped her shovel and retreated, whimpering.

She washed the earth from the single earring, then polished it using an old toothbrush and wood ash, which she'd once read on the web was a good way of shining up old precious metals. Cleaned and burnished, the cheap trinket looked beautiful in the palm of her hand – and was revealed to be a work of finely wrought sterling silver, with a delicate latticed tracery and a translucent red gemstone.

Forgetting all about her potato bed, Yuki toyed with her unexpected treasure – trying it in her ear first, then as a head necklace on a length of string. It was definitely better on a string. Yuki curled the earring's hook closed with a pair of pliers, turning it into a pendant which could be worn around her neck, which she did. Next, she put on some make up and her favorite linen sundress, and spent a long while looking at herself in the mirror. The only problem was, the mirror was rather small and so she had to admire herself piece by piece.

In the dead of night, while the village was sound asleep and only the silken night birds lingered, whistling quietly to one another over the double-pitched roofs, Yuki sat up in her bed with a strange but familiar feeling that uncoiled in her suddenly, like a cold spring. Like someone had cried out loudly just above her sleeping face. She trained her ears, still echoing with that cry, on the darkness. Her eyes went wide into the darkness too. She knew instantly that the velvety night all around her was silent and still. No one had cried out. It must have been a dream. She plumped up her pillow and curled herself up under the blankets once more, but a moment later realized with a pang that there was definitely some kind of sound, and it was coming from a little porch between the inner and outer doors of the annex, where they normally stashed things like muddy boots, raincoats and assorted rubbish without a place of its own. Something was flopping around on the wooden floor there, softly but distinctly. It went quiet again, then made a glassy ding – knocked into an empty pickle jar most likely – then set to flopping again. It went wall to wall, one way and then back again.

It's a frog, Yuki told herself, just a frog that came to visit but doesn't know how to get out again. They came along often, frogs, all puffed up and dignified. Yuki would find them in the little porch, and they always croaked irritably, demanding due respect, as she bundled them back outside. Frogs were charmed creatures, to be sure, and magical. They stored up night energies, same as owls or cats. That was why witches in the Middle Ages used to dip frogs in their potions. Yuki had learned this on the internet: and yes, it was dipping, not boiling frogs alive as everyone believed, and only to power up the potion a bit more with night magic. The boiling part was invented purely to blacken the characters of those wise medieval guardians of the secret lore...

She knew she should get up and go set the frog free, to carry on its magical recharging. But Yuki suddenly couldn't keep her eyes open. Sleep overcame her like a warm wave, and there was no leaving her cozy nest of blankets. "It's ok, she'll find her way out," thought Yuki, as she surrendered to sleep.

As predicted, the frog was gone from the porch by morning, if it had ever been there in the first place. The kind of girl who always let out butterflies stuck bumping against the window and carried dopey lost grass snakes to safety from the road, Yuki made a careful examination of every nook and cranny but found no sign of anyone at all.

She spent most of that morning pottering around in the kitchen garden – turning over earth, weeding, giving the carrots and cucumbers positive verbal feedback about their rapid growth and healthy color – all while plugged into some random yoga mix on her music player. Yuki felt sure that mother nature communicated with people via its gifts and its creatures: like frogs, perhaps, or the birds. And you were obliged to make reply, if you wished to be on good terms. Hadn't they proved, scientifically, that plants who were spoken to or played music to, grew taller and hardier?

After lunch, Pashka came by to see if she wanted to go for a bike ride, but no sooner did they get to the nearest turn, her chain fell off and broke into pieces, so they had to drag the bicycle to Pashka's garage to fix it. It then turned out that it was the day of the weekly all-village meeting, recently ordained to be mandatory. Yuki loitered by the crowd's edge for a bit, hanging tight to the antlered handlebars of her repaired bike, listening. It was just the same speeches as before. No need to panic, but be vigilant, stay together, help is probably on the way, don't go near the water or into the forest, lock your gates. And keep an eye on your neighbors' lots, people are still disappearing. The Rose family from Flower Street vanished without a trace this week, and no need to snigger, nothing funny in that at all. The chastened young people quietened down and the committee chair carried on, fiercely. Yes, that's right, the Roses vanished from Flower Street and so has Tatyana from Cherry Street, the one with a mentally-impaired son, she was so keen to get to town to refill his medications. And what did she do, she went into the forest and there's no hide nor hair of her for days now, her son helpless and all alone in the world. So don't move an inch beyond your gates, if you don't want to end up the same way.

* * *

Yuki pictured the hulking young man with a bland, moony face. In view of his arrested development everyone still called him Romochka instead of Roman, like a little boy. She was always a bit wary of him, because who knew what he was thinking in that empty head of his, he might well turn on you without warning; but now she felt awful for him, imagining him being all alone at home. She was all on fire to go and visit Romochka, and help him out, cook something for him or tidy, but Katya, who usually kept out of things, unexpectedly took it upon herself to talk Yuki out of it. He's got people to help out, you'll only be in the way, and anyway, if you want to tidy, start with your own place, said Katya, and Yuki felt insulted until she realized that Katya was wary of him too.

She went home to sweep the floor and wash the dishes, so Katya couldn't rag her about her mess again. Then she and Pashka went over to the Roses' dacha to see if they could gather any clues but found nothing at all out of the ordinary. Yuki was about to suggest they held a séance to inquire of the genius loci of the place where the Roses might have gotten to, but remembered in time that Pashka was an unrepentant sceptic, and anyway, it was time to water the veg again.

As usual, that night Yuki went to bed with her laptop and headphones, ready for a bedtime movie, which was of course a horror film. She had a special folder for these, that she'd downloaded before the summer, just for such a purpose, and now the stash proved even handier than she'd expected. The cozily creepy plots – always with a mystical mystery as the engine – opened a window through which she could contemplate nostalgically the old, quotidian world where people travelled from place to place, used the internet and cell phones, watched TV. Yuki felt a little resentful of their humdrum, predictable, and comfortable lives, and got cross when they panicked. A curse? A ghost? Please, don't make me laugh. Try living right here, why don't you.

Eventually she put aside the laptop and rolled herself up in her blankets, wiggling her left heel outside the cocoon for temperature control. She was almost asleep when from the porch came the familiar slapping sound, like wet little footsteps. Come to think of it, they were too fast and too ringing for a frog, unless the poor creature was hopping uncontrollably over tiny patches of floor and smacking hard down onto its belly. It sounded even less like a cat or a hedgehog, Yuki thought, cocking her head toward the sound. The unseen visitor flip-flopped over to one corner of the porch, then crossed to the other, and finally seemed to come to a stop and quieten. Only a thin single-ply wall separated the living space from the porch, with a flimsy metal latch hook holding the door shut. The door beyond which there was clearly a something.

In the long silent pause, Yuki had time to feel a little bit disappointed, since it looked like she'd never get to the bottom of the mysterious sounds, and they would remain as unsolved as the spheres that – as urban legends had it – rolled noisily around the floor of a vacant apartment, frightening the neighbors below. Then came a new sound. This was louder and more scrapy. As though someone was cautiously scratching at the door from the other side.

Yuki was by now dying of curiosity. She tiptoed to the door, lifted the hook, then flung the door wide open. Of course, she was not only curious, but also somewhat frightened. That was why she moved fast, without thinking, or giving herself a chance to retreat.

The porch was swathed in an impenetrable stale gloom. Yuki moved toward the solitary small window to twitch back the tightly drawn curtain and caught herself on something. An obstacle that didn't seem to be one of the things that she usually stubbed her toes on in here, like a pickle jar or her mother's rubber galoshes. The unfamiliar object that touched her right leg felt dense and cool, and as tall as her kneecap or so. The thing was, it was moving... Again came the sound of the rapid, hurried flops, and when Yuki thrust her hand down to the strange obstacle, she found nothing there.

She raced back into the room, slammed on the lights and, snatching up a flashlight, hurried back to the porch to sweep every inch of the walls and floor with its beam. Nothing. For sure, there was assorted rubbish everywhere, but a knee-high creature would surely have found it impossible to hide in it. Yuki shone the flashlight at the ceiling, and then, just to be sure, inside the defunct "Fairy"-brand washing machine that had belonged to her grandmother. The ancient appliance smelled of warm mold. There was no one in there. Naturally the porch door was also still locked from the inside.

Yuki felt extremely agitated, and not just because she was frightened. On the contrary, she could feel in her gut that she had stumbled onto something supernatural. Until the assortment of weird events that descended on the village, the world had not played fair with her. For a girl who so earnestly believed in anything esoteric, from astral projection to angels and aliens, Yuki had never come across even a hint of the wondrous in real life. It was unfair, that for someone who had read so many books and internet threads on unexplained phenomena, she didn't have a single personal experience that even came close to being unexplained. Yuki's present life was a daytime soap, gray and bland as a bowl of porridge, and not the mystical thriller she longed to inhabit. Even the village anomalies, that had seemed so promising, seemed to pass her by, almost as though ignoring her altogether; mysterious goings-on went on with everyone but her. And while the dour and sensible adults hid from the supernatural behind their seven seals, Yuki was waiting with a lantern, metaphorically, the door flung open. But she waited, hoping, and thrilling to the idea of such an encounter, in vain. Absolutely nothing happened to her, except perhaps the visitation by naked Kozhebatkin in her vegetable patch, and you could hardly call that supernatural.

At all costs, Yuki was determined to catch sight of her nocturnal visitor. She felt that she was morally prepared for it turning out to be a feral cat or some such small livestock.

Yuki now retrieved a heavy metal box from the top of a wardrobe. She had inveigled her mother to hand over the small ornate casket by pretending it was for girly jewelry, but really it held her trove of amulets and assorted magical objects. Yuki had quite a collection, ranging from a yin-yang charm to a real bird's foot. There was also an assortment of gemstones, which had at one time cost the bulk of her saved-up pocket money: agate, which protected against evil spirits, and jasper, known to supercharge a person's extrasensory perception, and also wine-red garnet, Yuki's birthstone. The casket's dusty velvet interior also cradled a dried four-leaf clover, a five-petal lilac flower and an aura-cleansing conker.

Yuki spread her magical kit out on the table by the door and lit a beeswax candle in the center of the table. She poured a little heap of salt by the threshold, so that no creature could enter without invitation. She attempted, for good measure, to draw a rune for calling on spirits onto the door, but her piece of coal was dried out and crumbly, and you could hardly see it on the old dark wood – so she had to use a piece of cockroach-poison chalk instead.

Preparations complete, Yuki placed a silver spoon inside a mug of water, thrice washed her face with the water, and waited eagerly for night to fall. She forgot to praise her zucchinis and didn't go for a bike ride, preferring instead to bring her folding cot outside for some sunbathing in the yard. She thought she had better stay close to home, in case her mysterious guest decided to come by daylight.

Under the warming sun, Yuki soon drowsed. When she awoke, the sun had gone down, only the last of its setting rays still glowing orange on the tops of the pines. Her sunburned skin felt unpleasantly clammy, and there was a mosquito buzzing in her ear. Yuki yawned and stretched out, setting off an arpeggio of unpleasant sensations – on top of the sunburn, her leg had fallen asleep. Besides, it was all a bit strange: she never slept all that much and was definitely not one to conk out like this for the whole afternoon.

Recalling her appointment with the unseen, Yuki was suddenly anxious that if she went on like this, she'd miss the whole thing. Hurriedly, she folded the cot and propped it up by the porch steps, then opened the door.

The evening light gave her a clear view, without any mystical shimmerings or shadow play, of the thing that flopped sprightly toward her across the floor.

It was a child, and judging by the dirty white dress with ruffles, a girl. Locks of brown hair hung like icicles over her furrowed little brow, covering her eyes. The girl was very small, and not just age-wise – Yuki always had trouble gauging the ages of little children – but in size. In fact, she had a deal less size than what could be expected for a child of any age. This was because she didn't have any legs. Her torso ended beneath the dragging hem of the short dress. The abruptly severed creature hitched herself across using her arms, little palms slapping down neatly on the floor as she moved.

Yuki had one endless second in which to ascertain all this, while each girl, momentarily frozen in place, studied the other. Yuki could feel a rapt, searching look emanating from underneath the long fringe, and she would have sworn that there was ravenous sort of curiosity in that look.

Then the girl opened wide an unexpectedly huge, toadlike mouth that seemed to cleave her little face in two, right to the ears, and emitted a high-pitched, piercing shriek. The glass windowpane juddered in reply, and the pickle jars in the corner shivered and rang out. Still shrieking, the girl made straight for Yuki, palms slapping rapidly across the wooden floor.

Although Yuki had always intended to comport herself, when faced with the supernatural, as brave investigator rather than terror-struck civilian, it was not to be. With a scream of horror, she slammed the door in front of the nightmarish creature's face and worked the key with shaking hands. From beyond the door there came knocking and crashing, and then, the unmistakable sound of wood being clawed. Yuki vividly recalled the child's unnaturally long, yellowing fingernails.

Stumbling in her unlaced sandals, barely knowing whither she went, Yuki retreated shamefully, no better than any terror-struck civilian.

When she finally stopped to catch her breath, she saw that she'd made it, quite without thinking, over to Pashka's place. She could see him through the chain-link fence, gloomily chopping wood, the dope. In desperation, Yuki called to him hoarsely, but he didn't hear her. Yuki went cold all over. Maybe this too was part of the visitation, that humans couldn't see or hear her anymore, or maybe the hideous legless girl had already killed her, and now Yuki herself was a phantom... At last, Pashka spotted her gesticulating out of the corner of his eye and took out his earbuds.

Yuki's recap was lengthy and confused, but eventually Pashka puzzled out that there was a strange child inside her dacha, who had come from nowhere, and was very, very frightening. Pashka felt mild surprise at this; he wasn't a great fan of small children, but he didn't see what was so frightening, provided the kid wasn't your own. Meanwhile Yuki ranted hysterically, something nonsensical about missing legs – this was definitely her imagination, there were definitely no legless kids in the village – and a vast, horrible maw, salt by the threshold, stuff about magic stones that were supposed to protect her from the monster infant, except she was on the other side of the door, and this was no coincidence, no, because she never, never slept in daytime, not even when she was little...

Pashka handed her a bottle of water in the hope that it would shut her up, wrapped his jacket around her shivering, short-shorts-and-bikini-top-clad frame, and set off to see who or what had barged into her house. Yuki trotted along behind him, chattering and whimpering without stop, despite the bottle.

Pashka knew that that the tales of schoolkids – girls especially – should be taken with a bag of salt; but bearing in mind the weird village goings-on, judged it prudent to approach the porch with caution. He cocked his head, then put his ear to the door gingerly, fully prepared for a hard kick from the other side. All seemed quiet, until Pashka's keen ear caught a faint, barely discernible rustling and rapping. It being sundown, Pashka had not neglected to bring his flashlight. Yuki, on tenterhooks, let out a quiet gasp and shied from the cold, bluish beam that suddenly sprang to life. Pashka turned the key slowly in the keyhole, and grimaced as the metallic clicking of the lock ruined their silent ingress for sure. He flung open the door.

The porch was empty. Household detritus lay scattered over the floor: a ball of twine, a roll of duct tape, some spilled nails. The remains of a broken jar crunched under his shoe. There was no one inside, if you didn't count a lone, silvery moth that rustled overhead, bumping into the ceiling slats and shedding fine wing dust that shimmered in the flashlight's beam.

"She was here, it was her crashed around in everything!" Yuki hissed mulishly. "I double-locked it, she couldn't have gotten away!"

Pashka shrugged. "Maybe she crawled into the main room?" Yuki imagined the bloodcurdling little girl crawling around underneath her bed and shuddered.

They didn't find anyone in the main room either, though they checked everywhere, getting covered in dust and cobwebs, including under the bed. Yuki caught Pashka looking askance at the magical amulets laid out by the door and hastened to put them back in their casket, the jasper, the beeswax candles, and the bird's foot.

By the time she got to wiping down the roach-poison-chalk rune off the door, Pashka was feeling sorry for the hysterical kid, and suggested she might want to sleep over at his that night, if she was that scared.

"Seriously?" Yuki's eyes went big and round.

"No, I mean... there's two couches, and anyway, I can sleep on the veranda... there's enough sheets, and pillows, three pillows actually..." Pashka was momentarily flummoxed. "Or you could go sleep at Katya's, what about that?"

Yuki pictured changing her clothes and sleeping at a stranger's house. It would mean hiding her, frankly, worn out undergarments under a heap of other clothes, sleeping with one eye open so as not to throw her blanket off and accidentally expose her exquisite un-depilated self to public view. She would have to be constantly on the alert when dashing to the toilet in her short nightie, and she still went at least three times a night, her mother even took her to the doctor about it, saying it's not normal for a girl to go so often, maybe she caught cold down there, but after fifteen mortifying minutes the doctor said that everything was fine, it was just one of those embarrassing things. It wasn't like she could ask Katya for a bucket, like the one she kept in the porch, never mind explaining the intricacies to Pashka. No, not a good look for a young woman of mystery, and a hereditary witch at that...

"I'm not going anywhere," Yuki carped. "You said it yourself, I just imagined it. I'm better off here. I can lock the door."

But Pashka was starting to feel vaguely anxious himself. "But what if... I mean – people are disappearing... You never know."

Yuki almost swooned with pleasure. Pashka was worried, actually worried – about her!

"So why don't you stay and guard me?" she giggled. "I'll bring a cot down to the porch for you. And we'll find out if it was my imagination or not."

Her coy and flirty tone barely masked a childlike and earnest hopefulness. She really did want Pashka to stay and defend her, like a gallant knight of old... Not that she was a princess, that would be too cringey, and anyway that was for blondes, but she could easily be a beautiful enchantress. Alas, Pashka was not one for subtleties.

"What am I, a mutt, to sleep in the porch?" he said, sounding a little offended. "Up to you, sleep where you like. But if something happens, you holler."

"I will." Yuki was a little offended too. "See if I don't."

Pashka stayed until late into the night, entertaining Yuki with tales of his dopey mates' haphazard adventures and telling jokes. But eventually he left, after poking the mop into every corner of the room, to show her that there was no one there, nor could be. He left the door between the room and the porch wide open.

Yuki stared awhile at the tiny, harmless square of space between the peeling walls, and decided at last that she would not be sleeping down here. She had the whole big house at her disposal, with new floorboards already laid, so she could set up her cot anywhere she wished, without worrying about falling through to the cellar among the mice and centipedes.

So she set to, moving her bed things into one of the almost-done-up rooms inside the house proper. Another person might have questioned the wisdom of retiring for the night to an old empty house as a place of safety. But there was no one around to give her advice, and also not forgetting that Yulia-call-me-Yuki was only fifteen, as well as hampered in her critical thinking by a sense of fright-flavored euphoria: it was her, Yuki, that the supernatural being had chosen as an object of interest. And now it was up to her to figure out who it was and what it wanted. The main thing was not to panic.

Or at least not to panic straight away.

Yuki spread the amulets that Pashka, that meanie, had sneered at, around her bed. Then she made an economical circle of salt – no need to use the whole packet on spirits, she would still need some for soup – and went to bed. She stashed a flashlight and a penknife under her pillow, thinking that although these items were not directly magical, they might well come in handy.

Her grandmother's old house was far removed from that peaceful cotton-wool silence so treasured by the proponents of dacha vacations. No, it was full of cracklings and creakings and clickings, mice audibly busy beneath the floor and something else making noises under the roof above. It smelled of fresh untreated wood and renovation fluids. A fuzzy night moth thumped into a newly installed, still-stickered windowpane, and dropped down with a dry rustle.

Yuki listened hard and peered into the gloom. Twisting this way and that, eventually she made a clump of her bedclothes and lay there, certain she would never get to sleep. Her heart beat so violently that her ribcage seemed to shudder beneath the covers, and her mind was apprehensive and clear...

And then, the bare bones of the room, which she could still clearly distinguish, twitched, fogged up, and began to flesh out. An ornamental squiggle snaked up one wall and spread, flowering and blooming into Soviet-era wallpaper. Something pushed at it from the inside, and the wallpaper ran with ugly protuberances resembling knots of birch tree fungus. The protuberances spread out, fleshed out and coagulated, then broke out of the walls entirely and resolved into wardrobes, chairs and mirrors. A large quantity of old photographs in square and oval frames evanesced and scattered out of the wallpaper. It was impossible to guess who the photographs were of, you could just about make out pale, featureless faces. The window rippled with a net curtain and there was that sudden musty smell of someone's old house – the smell of dust, old paper, laundry powder, the sweetish scent of something rotting... And then her grandmother – tall, straight and spare, as though kiln-dried – glided soundlessly into the room. The Snow Queen, whom old age had transformed into Baba Yaga. Her face, which Yuki didn't remember any more, was softly blurred, as though veiled with darkness. Her grandmother was holding a large dish covered with a napkin.

"Here, I've made a pie with jam for you," she said. "So your life runs sweetly."

Yuki was about to say thank you, but found that she couldn't make a sound, or even move her lips.

"We need someone to live here. To keep an eye out. A baby always needs looking out for."

Her grandmother whipped the towel off, but instead of the promised pie with jam, the dish held an oblong parcel, wrapped in lace and tied with a ribbon. With a scream, her grandmother dropped the dish, and the parcel, having fallen to the floor, began to crawl over to Yuki's bed like a diligent caterpillar.

Yuki thrashed about, trying to leap out of bed, and woke up. Her grandmother's piercing scream still rang in her ears – just like the night she first heard the strange sounds from the porch. Yuki's hands were shaking when she plucked the flashlight from under her pillow. The beam of light skittered over the unvarnished wooden planks and found the doorway, darted over the ceiling, then down below. Yuki breathed out and changed her grip on the hard flashlight case which was biting into her palm. The beam shuddered briefly onto the floor... and the unnaturally foreshortened white figure leapt right inside the circle of light out from God knows where. Yuki had a clear view of the rotten baby-teeth stumps inside its gaping toadlike mouth.

She wasn't sure how she ended up in the adjoining room. She was shuddering with terror and the night's chill, the flashlight's beam rattling along the wall in her unsteady hand. She was sure however, absolutely, convulsively sure of what she had seen: the way that the lace-swathed creature leaped effortlessly up onto her bed, demonstrating the complete inadequacy of all those amulets and wards. It had landed on Yuki's legs; she had felt its unmistakably real, cold weight through the thin blanket. Shit, she could feel it now.

Yuki swept the room with her beam, found the dark empty opening of the doorway – they hadn't gotten round to hanging a door here yet – and ran for it. She didn't clear five feet before stumbling painfully on something that rolled away from her with a sonorous clang, as she skidded, skinning her knees, in the opposite direction. This was an enamel washtub, yellow in color, that had seemed to materialize out of thin air. It was probably her parents who had brought it in, for thinning out wallpaper glue or some such thing.

Behind her came a hurried flop-floppety-flop. Yuki flipped the flashlight off again, hoping to dash away unseen; she dove for the doorway and crashed into the locked door. The locked door that could not have been there. She ran her palms frantically across the old, desiccated wood, but couldn't locate a latch, or a hook or anything, but did find a wall with shreds of old wallpaper to the right of the door frame. This too, could not be: all the wallpaper had been stripped off before the renovation proper began. Yuki gasped violently and turned the flashlight on again...

...onto a different room. The walls were papered with the teeny Soviet-era flowers she had already seen in her dream, the slatted wooden floor was painted, and the room was full of furniture. There was a table, a sagging metal bed, a nightstand topped with a crocheted doily, and a wardrobe – a monumental, incongruous wardrobe with an empty eye socket where there was once a mirror. The wardrobe that the three of them had barely managed to disassemble enough to drag out to the yard, where her father chopped it into firewood.

Next to the inexplicably resurrected wardrobe there was another door, narrow and invitingly ajar. Yuki had no time to deliberate on this course of action, the quick, efficient flops were very near now, and the door she had been trying to crash through seemed locked. Yuki threw herself at the second, new door, tugged at the cold metal handle, and scurried inside.

The flashlight's beam revealed neat, tidy rows of shelves, all filled with pots, crocks, and boxes. Pale pickles floating inside glass jars like fetuses in formaldehyde. It was a storeroom. A tiny, windowless, claustrophobic storeroom, a cupboard really, which her parents had pulled apart long ago, and incorporated into the room, because they already had a shed and a cellar, and it could make a useful addition to the small room, like a niche for a guest futon, or something...

Flip-flip-flop. It came distinctly from beyond the door. Yuki pushed a large carton full of some kind of rubbish against the door and retreated into the furthest corner she could manage, among the rot and cobwebs. Cans and jars rained down from the lurching shelves, with an unholy racket. The door creaked and shook, and Yuki remembered, through a new wave of icy terror, that this door opened out, and no boxful of crap was going to prevent it.

The door creaked again; it appeared that the vaulting creature had somehow managed to reach the handle. Yuki pictured, with revolting clarity, how the girl must be hanging there, swinging her stumpy body from side to side, in an attempt to turn the handle. The door is heavy, Yuki told herself, she won't manage, it really is very heavy... And saw, in the dancing beam from her flashlight, a child's fingers slither around the widening crack between door and frame. Leaping forward, Yuki grabbed the handle and pulled hard. The fingers retreated, there was a squeal from the other side, and the door shut firmly once more.

"Go awayyyy!" Yuki roared. "Go! Away!"

She was abruptly aware that the hands pulling the door to were not her own. They were a stranger's hands, a grown-up's – rough, with bruised fingernail beds – yet they responded to her. Not only did she feel the coolness of the door handle, but the stinging from a hangnail, someone else's infected hangnail on someone else's index finger. Yuki peered down in utter dread, to find someone else's body there, too: thickset and bosomy, the body wore a blue flannel housecoat that smelled strongly of old sweat and onions.

"Go awayyyyyy!" Yuki howled, but her cracking voice was that of a middle-aged hysteric. Everything seesawed and went blurry, and then around her unfolded a greenish murk the color of pondweed.

That dopey Pashka, and Yuki's neighbor Katya, found her the next morning, sat in the corner of an empty room, arms wrapped around her knees. She appeared to be dozing, so Pashka, who had already got it in the neck from Katya for his recklessly casual handling of the night before, immediately assumed the worst. But no sooner did a floorboard creak than Yuki startled and stared at them, wild-eyed.

"Well?" Katya crouched down beside her. "Who did you see?"

Stuttering and stumbling from one thing to the next, Yuki apprised them of the night's events. Just as before, her story came out jumbled and unconvincing, but Katya listened with the look of someone who completely understood what she was talking about. She proceeded to give Yuki a lecture about using the stones, and the wormwood, and the circle of salt. Pashka had also snitched about the rune chalked on the door, so she had to hear about that from Katya as well. Yuki sat and blinked wetly, her terror from what she'd experienced morphing into confusion and grievance, while Katya went on and on: we don't know what's going on all around us, do you really think it's a good time to mess around with magic, even if it's all pretend. Didn't Yuki consider, under that dyed mop of hers, that her cockroach runes might annoy someone she'd rather not meet, or even be a lure for some kind of...

"Devils?" Yuki interrupted.

"Devils, why not!" snapped Katya, whom Yuki had never before pegged for someone so old-fashioned or weird and orthodox.

Yuki didn't argue, since she couldn't just then be bothered about defending her magical arts. Katya ordered her to gather up all her things – though not the casket with the amulets – and marched her to her own dacha, where after a cup of herbal tea and some sort of pill that Katya pressed on her, Yuki began to feel better. Katya, who now more than anything resembled a stern teacher, insisted on hearing the whole story again from the beginning, slowly. She listened attentively, even jotting things down in a notepad, and Yuki felt vaguely surprised that her odd, self-contained neighbor could be that interested in devils. Could it be that she knew something, or had some kind of abilities, and maybe even had sensed a youthful competitor? She lived alone, after all, and kept to herself; she was always messing around with creatures of water and earth, and her brown hair definitely had a red tinge, if you looked closely... things rather pointed to Katya being a witch herself, didn't they?

Toward the end of her tale Yuki could barely keep awake, and Katya packed her off upstairs, where a bed had already been made for her.

"Is there any salt," Yuki enquired, stifling a huge yawn.

"I'll show you salt! Go on, go to bed. She won't get to you, not with a staircase this steep..."

Yuki's last conscious thought as she burrowed into her pillow was that for sure, Katya knew something, and it was something she didn't want to say...

...The downpour had made the dirt path into a squelching mud pit. She had to yank the over-large galoshes out of the mud with every step, and they slapped against her heels. The orchard, wet and waterlogged, was barely recognizable, and it wasn't just the rain. For one thing, the gooseberry bushes by the front gate had for some reason been replaced by an old apple tree, and where her mother had planted lilies, her favorite flowers, a row of potato plants twitched under the heavy raindrops.

She turned back to the house, solidly manifested now and painted a deep green, with latticed fretwork and frothy lace curtains at every window. So that's what it was like, before. She would bet that inside the house she would find the flowery wallpaper, and the store cupboard, and the yellow enamel tub that everyone tripped over.

But she had to keep going the other way, to the fence. The best place was over there, where purple irises bloomed in summer, and bright asters in fall, where no one would disturb...

In her arms was the lacy oblong parcel, while a heavy spade dragged through the mud behind her, the handle pinned awkwardly to her side. The very idea of lifting the lace to see inside was awful, agonizing. She just had to bury it, deep enough that no one would find it, no one could wake it up. It was a good thing the earth was sodden and easy to dig.

She dug for some time, effortlessly turning up large clods of earth. In the deepening gloom, the parcel, lying in a cozy bed of burdock leaves, gleamed white. She picked up the parcel and carefully lowered it into the sludge.

A thought – piercing, and not her own at all – struck her just then: she didn't kill it, she didn't, no-no-no, she could never, she just fell asleep, was all... The thought was a stranger's and so was the body, that familiar thickset, bosomy woman's body in the sodden housecoat.

She wiped the salty water from her face, and in doing so accidentally caught her dangling earing with her pinkie. The memory flashed so vividly that she longed to shut her eyes and die on the spot: how the little one had loved those earrings, always reaching with her tiny fingers for the translucent crimson stones, snatching at them, playing with them. Now she couldn't get the latch loose, almost ripping the earring from her earlobe, drops of blood falling on her neck. She kissed the warm metal and tossed it down to the parcel: "Take it for a toy, to remember me by..."

"To remember me by," Yuki said, still half-asleep, and opened her eyes wide. "To remember me by!"

So loudly was she screaming that Katya woke instantly and hurtled up the stairs. Sniffling, Yuki handed her the charm she had made from the unearthed earring. That whole time, it had been with her, and she had forgotten about it completely. It hung from a string around her neck together with her beloved cat's eye beads and a little icon from her mother. Yuki had a habit of wearing her favorite trinkets without taking them off to sleep, and she'd simply stopped noticing the extra lace around her neck. Katya peered at the earring thoughtfully, while Yuki wept and wailed what an idiot she had been, how she had never thought of that, she, who had seen so many horror movies...

"You remember where you found it?" asked Katya.

"More or less..."

Katya nodded, looking thoughtful.

* * *

It took them most of the day to dig. Yuki dreaded that sooner or later her spade would catch on slim, time-worn bones, so every clink and creak made her start. Fortunately, it always turned out to be just a stone or a root. Yuki related her dream to Katya in every detail, though she couldn't remember exactly how deep the dream hole had been. Finally, their palms blistering, they agreed that it was deep enough. Katya threw the earring down the hole and said, earnestly:

"Take back your earring, and take your remembrance too."

Yuki looked at her sideways. But Katya only handed her the shovel and told her to cover it all up again.

Afterward, having tamped the earth down and laid some wooden fence posts on top for good measure, Katya and Yuki went to visit Tamara Yakovlevna, over in her cat kingdom. After the quarrel that had nearly suffocated the village, the two pensioners were once again coexisting in peace and harmony, but Zinaida Ivanovna's plot was still overrun by wildly proliferating vegetation, while Tamara Yakovlevna's continued to be guarded by feline legions. Katya had a string of dried anchovies ready for them – occasionally, the cats would not allow a visitor past the gate, ringing round anyone they took against, hissing nastily and preventing entry.

They had a good excuse for visiting – Katya had recently borrowed a cup of flour. Yuki filled a cup from her own stores, and they also took along a bottle of excruciatingly cloying raspberry cordial which had lain in Katya's cellar for several years awaiting a special occasion.

Tamara Yakovlevna was not entirely well – she maintained it was on account of the strange weather – and they found her recumbent on her sofa, propped up by cushions and cats. As the cats turned their unthinking, focused gaze at the new arrivals, Yuki was unpleasantly reminded of the nightmarish little girl, and her normal shyness escalated into real disquiet.

But then the raspberry cordial worked its magic on Tamara Yakovlevna who, ruddy with pleasure, kindly complimented Yuki on her hair and said she ought to grow that lovely hair of hers into a proper braid, just wash out that horrid black dye first...

They chatted about the weather, seemingly stuck in a high barometric pressure system, and came on to the tomato crop, current conditions making it entirely unclear whether to harvest or leave them on the vine. And then Katya, with the gentle insistence of an experienced TV detective, turned the talk to the olden days, back when the weather was predictable and the summer only lasted as long as it was supposed to, when one could leave the village at any time and the plots all belonged to deserving, decent people. Like Yuki's grandmother and her family, for example – they had been a big family, hadn't they, worked hard and stuck together...

"Sticking together, for sure," Tamara Yakovlevna readily concurred. "The size of that old house, that big orchard, they put it all up themselves. You ought to keep it all going, look after it, with so much work gone in already."

"Absolutely," said Katya. "Why did they stop coming, actually, did they just get tired of it or maybe something happened?"

"The wonderful gazebo they had out there, and the Dutch apple trees, and that big swing behind the main house..." Tamara Yakovlevna was away in her pleasant memories, clutching a large ginger cat to her breast like a lifesaving buoy. "They always had guests to stay, lots of young people and dancing, I went over myself sometimes... Mind you, they worked hard too, none of them work-shy. They used to get ten-kilo cucumber harvests in, and everything always neat and tidy, too..."

"But then they just gave up, on such a wonderful dacha?"

Yuki was privately admiring Katya's unexpected persistence, and even guile.

"I told them, didn't I, no sense to abandon it, when you've put so much into it. But they lost all their pleasure in it. This was after Zoechka's mishap, you understand. I'm sure you've heard about that. A terrible, awful mishap..."

"The mother killed her baby, is that right?"

Tamara Yakovlevna reared up sharply, to the cats' displeasure, and sliced down with the side of her palm.

"She did no such thing, never you mind what those gossips say! None of you know a thing about it, but you're all so quick to judge, shame on you..."

"No, no, I just meant..."

"She didn't kill the baby! It was an accident. Zoechka slept so heavily, she just smothered the baby in her sleep. Lost her mind with grief, afterward. She buried the baby in the orchard, and then took herself to the police station, to confess..."

"Wait, how do you know it was an accident?"

Katya dug her elbow sharply in Yuki's side at the inopportune interruption.

Tamara Yakovlevna's eyes went narrow and glimmered like a cat's.

"Ah, my lovely, I know everything that goes on round here... They declared Zoechka mentally incompetent, put her in a mental hospital and that was that, God rest her soul. But no one ever found the baby girl. Mind you the cops came down, they dug over the whole plot but didn't find any trace of a little corpse. Maybe they didn't look too hard, they're lazy buggers, aren't they, always have been... Except that your granny, used to tell me that her niece came to see her of a night. Growing up a little each time, she said, as she'd been such a wee mite when she died."

"Came to see her... like, on legs?"

Tamara Yakovlevna raised her eyebrows quizzically at this, and Katya elbowed Yuki again.

"The little girl... she was... she was disabled, right?"

"Wherever did you get this stupid idea? She was a delightful baby, perfectly fine."

* * *

It was late by the time Katya walked Yuki back to her plot.
Yuki was quiet, digesting the story of her grandmother's
unfortunate sister Zoechka, the one she had never known
anything about. When Katya pushed the gate open, Yuki
looked over her demesne and saw it all again in her mind's
eye, with extraordinary clarity: the child's palms slapping
across the floor, the close, cramped storeroom in the strange,
frightening house, the lacy parcel, the blue flannel housecoat...
She clutched Katya's hand and then lost it completely. You
couldn't spend the night here, she wailed, you just couldn't,
who knew whether that thing was done wandering around,
what if it came again, what if they'd buried the earring in the
wrong place, or done something else the thing didn't like...

"Quiet down," Katya said, and drew Yuki up into the porch.

She set up the folding cot by the door and inquired
whether Yuki had any extra bedding, a blanket and pillow
in particular. And Yuki knew by this that she was protected,
"safe at base". Just like when her mother would come in,
after another one of Yuki's terrible nightmares, with a folded
blanket under her arm, and set up camp on the little sofa
next to her. Yuki would fall gratefully asleep, even though
she knew that in the morning her mother would grumble
about not getting any sleep at all because of her, everyone has
bad dreams, don't they, there's really no need to holler fit to
wake the whole house...

"But what if it does come?" Yuki whispered, as the light
went off.

"We're going to see if it does," said Katya from her cot. She
was silent for a moment, then asked: "Are you sure she didn't
have legs? Maybe she was just crawling?"

"She really didn't. Not at all. Although Tamara Yakovlevna
said..."

"An igosha, then."

"Wha...?" Yuki strained to hear.

"Nothing. Go to sleep."

Yuki could tell from her voice that Katya was smiling in the dark, that odd, crooked smile she had.

The night passed quietly, without anyone coming to visit, or flopping up and down the floor or scratching at the door. In the morning they got Pashka and Nikita to come put the fence back between Yuki's plot and the deceased Kozhebatkin's.

Yuki knew that Katya had classified the terrifying little girl with some strange word, but could not recall, try as she might, the word itself. It seeped through her memory and splintered into mere sounds. There was something zoological in it, she was sure. Something to do with an iguana? Yuki thought that Katya might laugh at her, and there being nothing more dreadful to a fifteen year-old, decided against asking her any more questions.

The main thing was that the dead little girl in her lacy dress never came again.

6

MOTHS TO A FLAME

Vitaly Petrovich lived a sedate and solitary life and took a quiet pleasure in it that none of the busy, bustling dachniks could understand. The rotund pensioner never seemed to organize deliveries of well-rotted manure from the usual shady operators and didn't spend the beginning of the season frantically digging, later to pile the decaying, fly-blown excess fruit and veg that you couldn't eat or pickle or feed to the grandchildren anymore into a compost pit, like everyone else. Indeed, to the villagers he seemed not to be living so much as vegetating over on his unfurrowed plot, alongside his modest, unpainted wooden dacha, chain-link fence, raspberry cane, and cozy-looking hazel coppice.

He took little interest in the dacha cooperative's goings-on and was suspected of not knowing the chairwoman by name. It was quite possible that he had no idea at all, until the last possible moment, that something hitherto unknown and undesirable was happening to his sheltered domain and to the village at large.

Vitaly Petrovich was a humble and fervent devotee of art. His small dacha was festooned with pictures of masterpieces, the faces of Renaissance Madonnas slowly eaten away by patches of mold. His homemade shelves held gilt-spined, multi-volume series with names like *ART*, *Masters of Landscape*, and *Art Masterpieces*. When it was especially cold, Vitaly Petrovich shamefacedly used lesser works like *Foundations of Architectural Harmony* to light the stove – though of course these would already have been read and reread until the pages went greasy and translucent with handling.

His regrets, if indeed he had any, would have been that he had lived a quiet and mediocre life, toiling at some insignificant job, while somewhere far from him, the chosen ones fluttered their brocade dragonfly wings: the artists, the sculptors, those who created works for eternity, and writ their names on posterity, outstripping time with their genius and bringing Beauty and Harmony – obviously capitalized – into the world. He couldn't do without those capitals, when he considered on Art. Feverishly, Vitaly Petrovich traced the capitals in the air with his little hands: his musings seemed too ordinary and even inappropriate without them. Not that he found much opportunity to talk about the subjects dear to his heart, kindred spirits being hard to find.

To Vitaly Petrovich's mind, qualification as a genuine work of art required that the art be old, beautiful, and based on real life, because, as everyone knew, life was reflected – artistically enriched and ennobled – in art. Naturally, Vitaly Petrovich was not the slightest bit interested in the avant-garde or any of the new-fangled nonsense. You didn't need much talent to paint a black square and sell it at a premium as "contemporary art." Even so, he didn't approve of the way they had been castigated in the more severe old times, those painters – they were yearning for beauty too, were they not, even as they slapped down their black squares. That yearning ought to have been nudged in the right direction; take them to an art gallery and make them copy somebody's well-made still life, that's what the powers that be should have done.

Yes, the severe old Soviet times had been rife with real artists. It was ten years before that Vitaly Petrovich had experienced genuine, powerful catharsis, when out mushrooming with a friend: they had lost track of time and were almost out by the beltway, when they happened to wander into an abandoned old pioneers camp. There were many forgotten places like that now, birds nesting in crumbling huts and teenagers hiding out to drink and smoke, while a difficult but great epoch crumbled and melted away around them. They stopped Vitaly Petrovich, with his raincoat and mushroom basket in hand, in his tracks; the fine, exquisite faces of the plaster pioneers, their arms raised for an unwavering final salute from out of bushy nettles. Something of the great Italian masters' seductive Madonnas and martyrs, so beloved of Vitaly Petrovich, was there too in the fragile figures and delicate features of the plaster children.

He couldn't have left the statues there, left them to a certain doom. He had to liberate these unknown master's creations from the stinging nettles, rife with stinkbugs. Some of the troop were already missing limbs, and several had lost their musical instruments. He returned to the sacred spot with an axe and cart, lifted the austere youths from their pedestals, and quietly took them away.

And that was how the gleaming-white pioneers came to live with Vitaly Petrovich and became the secret local attraction. People took their visiting friends to see them, once the barbeque was all eaten but there was still some wine left. The bike-crazy dacha kids showed off the statues that looked out from Vitaly Petrovich's bushes to their visitors, but furtively.

Furtively because no one really knew what the eccentric dachnik wanted with them, having brought the plaster Soviet children to his plot and patched up their cracks and stains, though he hadn't gone as far as to give them new limbs. He had only cut off the inner armature rods that stuck from the broken arms like rusty bones, and the pioneers carried on looking like handsome, disabled Greek antiquities. Indifferent to the furtive viewing forays along his fence, he dreamed that future archaeologists would be glad of the missing parts, when they unearthed the statues he had saved, just the way that Vitaly Petrovich himself – when he gazed at the Venus de

Milo or Winged Victory – was glad that they did not survive unblemished. How awful would it be, otherwise, to be taunted by all that blinding, unattainable beauty? The artists grew ever smaller with each passing age, and it must have been painful for each new generation of creators to look upon the geniuses of time gone by...

A good thing that Vitaly Petrovich only let himself go off and daydream like this infrequently, really only when he drank – also, as a rule, in solitude. He would sit on his porch and breathe in the milky-warm summer air, and look lovingly over his domain. There was the hazel growing from the earth and there the pines, and here were the pioneers growing, and Vitaly Petrovich growing with them, and all was well.

It was a few years after the pale plaster children appeared that Vitaly Petrovich presumed to add a new exhibit to his dacha collection; a tree stump that marvelously resembled a horse's head. Vitaly Petrovich felt able to display it amid the real sculptures because he hadn't made it himself, only found it in the forest, polished it and painted it with a special solution. Later on, he added a piece of driftwood that looked like a crocodile, and a nameless three-horned beast he'd carved from the remains of a wind-toppled apple tree that hadn't belonged to anyone. Then he grew bolder and got carried away: the pioneers had nothing to do with it. And after all, he had always wanted to create, and sooner or later he would have started anyway.

Though he despaired of modern art (in his mind this was represented by the Black Square though it had been painted before he was born, as he thus repeated the error of many an art-loving pensioner), his own works were closer to the contemporary than to the classical school. Then again, Vitaly Petrovich didn't set himself up for a great artist and he liked his own works, which seemed to him to complement his dacha holdings, the impassive pioneers, and his collection, stowed

behind lush greenery. He sculpted in any and all materials;
sticks and stones, old hubcaps and bicycle wheels, wire and
pots and ladles, leaky buckets and boots. There was lots of
material around owing to the fact that a dacha was a natural
repository for rubbish: a place where one would always find
the physical detritus of the past, battered and broken but kept
back nonetheless. Perhaps to the villagers, and all dachniks
everywhere really, their granddads' transistor radios and their
grandmothers' old pots meant as much as his pioneers meant
to Vitaly Petrovich. The others couldn't abandon their old,
dead things to their fate any more than he could.

His own works he considered sheer tomfoolery, and never
explicitly showed them to anyone, yet the villagers enjoyed
them and were more fond of them even than the stern-faced
Soviet angels that came before.

It would forever remain a mystery whether Vitaly Petrovich
even noticed the date of the village closing in on itself so
strangely, because just around this time he was busy settling
a new tenant in his cool green bower-cum-gallery. A metal
lumberjack with a funnel atop his head, just like the tin-man
illustrations in children's books, it had a dented dog bowl for a
face. Vitaly Petrovich's creations were always blank-faced, and
often did not suggest a face at all: he much preferred making
animals and abstract constructions that chimed melodiously in
the wind. Faces and hands, they were too intimate and detailed,
too easy to get wrong. He didn't want to spoil everything by
making, in his untrained way, something ugly and ridiculous
where he had sought to create beauty. Within his bower of the
beautiful, only the plaster pioneers were allowed to have faces.

Having erected the tin man beside his gate, Vitaly Petrovich
stretched and sighed, reveling in that feeling one gets at the
end of a job well done. Then he noticed a bright little cap just
beyond the fence: some phlox. The flat blade-like petals on
the ends of furled tubes radiating out from the center of each
flower were fuchsia, that color beloved of old ladies who liked

to dress young. Vitaly Petrovich shrugged as the word came to him; who'd ever seen an actual fuchsia colored like that. They should have just called it phlox, that color. The flowers appeared beside every dacha, last of all the blooms, old-maid flowers, like the first needling stab of autumn in the heart. Seeing them meant that Vitaly Petrovich's shady summer haven was on the wane. It didn't matter that he could stick around until the first frosts, even the winter long: he had done that several times, pulling logs from the shed on his sledge, and knocking the snow from his pioneers, standing frozen in place like the heartless little boy in the story of the snow queen... His slice of joyful summer, elusive and dreamed of since he was a boy at school and a man at work, was melting away... School, work, these had been invented to steal time away, and to make for undeserved, pointless nostalgia years later.

All this swept through Vitaly Petrovich's mind in a moment, without resolving into coherent thoughts. He opened his gate, reached out to pull up the autumnal phlox, and tossing it into the gutter, went back home with a whistle.

Later on there was some sort of tumult – clumps of dachniks wandering past his fence and making noise, the chairwoman came to order him to go to some mandatory meeting, talking all sorts of nonsense. Vitaly Petrovich asked her if this was about the water supply being turned off for the winter, but she just flapped her hands, that wasn't it at all, and didn't he realize, hadn't he seen... From this he gathered that the water wasn't about to be turned off; it really was too early for that. So he didn't go to the meeting. The others mooched about some more, making noise, somebody climbed the perimeter fence straight into the forest, then everything seemed to settle down again.

It would only be much later, when the others were already making adjustments and learning to live in their new and sometimes inexplicable reality, that Vitaly Petrovich first noticed anything strange. For a long while, he simply enjoyed the way the summer came to a standstill at its height, wafting gently along with the undimmed green leaves, and the way that there were no more phloxes, and his serene happiness just went on without end.

It began abruptly and unexpectedly. Vitaly Petrovich walked outside one morning, mooting whether to do some raspberry picking, head out in search of new material for his sculptures (it had been a while), or just go back inside to brew up some tea and leaf through his art books. Suddenly he had a sense of being watched. Vitaly Petrovich had always had an instinctive awareness of being looked at: his long-ago wife used to have fun waking him up just by "telepathically" staring at his face, or even the back of his head.

He looked around. From under the hazel branches, the deathless pioneers watched him through the convex, fingertip depressions that served as the pupils of their white plaster eyes. How strange that he felt that gaze so sharply and forcefully, he really ought to have been used to their exacting stares by now. But perhaps it was the work of a falling shadow, or on the contrary, a sunbeam that lit up the pioneers' eyes and made them look at him, from the depths of their happy childhood, in a different light.

In the middle of the night, Vitaly Petrovich, on his way to the little green outhouse, was once again struck by the same feeling of being watched. A wave of atavistic shivers rolled down his back and arms; had he hackles, they would have stiffened. Reflexively, he hunched and drew himself into a wary, animal-like posture. It wasn't that the watchful eyes seemed malicious or bloodthirsty exactly; more that there was something strange and alien in that stare. It could not have been his beloved pioneers, whom he had come to know down to the last scratch and bump.

Vitaly Petrovich scurried warily to the little green outhouse, flung open the door and tugged the lightbulb cord. A frog hopped out, smacking on top of the grass and making the nearest bush quiver. Beyond it was a dense blackness, out of which something was staring at the pensioner, illuminated by the outhouse light and defenseless.

He shot inside, slamming the door behind him. Only now he realized how cold and clammy he was, like wet clay. His heart jogged painfully in his throat, his chest heaved. I really ought to check my blood pressure, thought the frightened Vitaly Petrovich.

In the morning, when the night's scare was assuaged by sleep and seemed not so alarming, Vitaly Petrovich went looking. Without a doubt, there was something on his plot, and that something had, without a doubt, been staring at him. He just had to find out what the something was.

First he checked the pioneers, but as usual, their eyes caused him to feel nothing beyond a soft and wistful yearning. Then he checked, methodically, every nook and cranny. Eventually he climbed up to the dacha's attic and there, through a little glass ventilation pane, saw a new path snaking through his hitherto untouched raspberry patch.

That was where Vitaly Petrovich found it, after forcing his way painfully through the scratchy, unyielding raspberry cane. A thing of astonishing ugliness, like some sort of dreadful idol or freak, made from gray clay mixed up with grass and sand, it sat crookedly atop a large log. The freak had no neck, and a misshapen torso, and broken river shells for ears. It looked like an ape, terrifying in its sheer hideousness. The widely stretched mouth had been stuffed full of white pebbles for teeth, and it also had eyes – so piercing and awful these were that it took Vitaly Petrovich a moment to comprehend they were made of night moths, nailed onto the wooden head. The freak watched

Vitaly Petrovich unblinkingly with ferrous-brown eyes that even had pupils: these were the tops of the tiny nails piercing the furry little bodies of the moths.

Stunned, Vitaly Petrovich plopped down on the mossy ground. Who could have done such a thing? Trespass on his plot, plant this dirty-mud-thing, so carefully stuck together, just to mock him and his modest and private art collection? Sure, they used to come to look through the fence, and have a giggle – he'd heard them – but he always felt that it was on the whole benign, and that his neighbors were glad to be living next to someone who valued beauty. What has happened to this village, he wondered, that they could treat him this way, crossing all the lines, dumping that horrible mocking thing in the middle of his tiny harmonious kingdom. And it was no accident, it took time to make that thing, they had planned it, had prepared it...

So for the first time in a long while, Vitaly Petrovich left his plot. All the way down Rowan Street, he accosted everyone he met – though there were not many dachniks about – asking what they knew about the new sculpture dropped over on his plot, a sort of ape with moths for eyes, you see, maybe it was the teenagers fooling around? They all gave him incredulous looks, but eventually he came across a tender-hearted old lady who listened attentively, then told him, with a gesture of resignation:

"Well, these days, what do you expect?"

Finally, he came upon a clutch of young people and recalled, with a start, that one of them, a gangly young man who always seemed half-cut, had banged on his gate not long since, asking for permission to try the forest from his plot, but all in a very garbled way, as though there were no more places to get to the forest by.

Vitaly Petrovich bounced up to him and grabbed him by the t-shirt.

"Was it you put that freak thing on my plot?"

The youths all started speaking at once, while the young man – this was Nikita Pavlov – immediately looked alarmed. Vitaly Petrovich had no use for anything the young people might say. Clutching a fistful of t-shirt, he dragged the probable culprit behind him, toward the scene of the crime. Vitaly Petrovich was lame in his right foot and puffed heavily as he went, and he barely reached to Nikita's shoulder, but the younger man followed meekly along without protest. He just kept asking, and looking spooked, what do you mean a freak, and where was it, and how did it...

Once in the raspberry patch, the young people took their time looking over the hunched monster, touching its wooden face and professing astonishment. They all swore, of course, that it wasn't them, they didn't know a thing about pottery or wood carving, except for making those wooden stools in shop class at school. And anyway, why would they even come here, where would you even get the idea, except that they only looked over the fence sometimes, at Vitaly Petrovich's wonderful open-air art collection, with all his wonderful statues, they all remembered the pioneers that were here before all the other artworks came...

Looking at their clumsy, clean hands, only good for fiddling on gadgets, Vitaly Petrovich calmed down. They were probably telling the truth after all.

"Why don't we carry it away," Nikita finally offered. "It really is a freak, you don't want it here, do you?"

Vitaly Petrovich was about to agree wholeheartedly, but then he looked from those moth eyes to the austere profile of a plaster pioneer just beyond the raspberry patch and thought again. He too, had placed his silly handicrafts alongside classical beauty. The idol had been made with a certain diligence, you could see that, there was imagination in it, and even some talent, even if the talent was going down a wrong, perverse path, creating the devil knew what instead of something beautiful and edifying. It was called degenerate art, wasn't it, and it had been destroyed, which was probably fair. But then Vitaly Petrovich recalled that it was the Fascists who did the destroying, and was horrified at the thought, so he quickly said:

"No, don't throw it away. It can stay. I mean it's a kind of… sculpture, too."

And so the idol came to live in Vitaly Petrovich's raspberry patch. It wasn't at all in the way, you couldn't even see it in the bushes, and very soon Vitaly Petrovich stopped being aware of those moth eyes. It was only that he couldn't quite finish his new work, based on a lovely piece of driftwood in the shape of a wave, though he had already prepped and sanded it smooth. No sooner did some creative idea enter his mind than he thought of the idol in the raspberry cane and was spooked, and the idea itself suddenly seemed silly.

More washed-out midsummer days crawled by. After a long run of rains there came a bright clear morning promising a day of cloudless sun. The dewy grass was still that opaque green of an ice-cold beer bottle and shadows still lay unpleasantly cold and thick, but already the melted butter of the sun was spilling smoothly across the village.

Vitaly Petrovich trundled out onto his porch, took a look around his plot, then gave a scream of fright and rage, stamping his feet and gasping for air. It was right in front of the house, on the cobbled path he had laid with his own two hands, each cobble his own find.

A new idol.

This one was taller and broader than the one in the raspberry patch, and it had a long snout. The style, the mixed media, these were the same. It was made from unwashed clay shot through with grass and twigs and had a beaky mask, like a plague doctor's, carved – Vitaly Petrovich now saw with a suffocating horror – from a piece of driftwood, the very one that he couldn't quite transform into a new work. He had put it aside, thinking to let it lie, and hadn't set foot in the shed where he kept his supplies. So then – they'd broken in, stolen it, sawed it in half and made this awful crocodilian... no, it wasn't a face, it was a horrid mug...

The horrid mug ogled him through its moth eyes, nailed to the wood. The shape of those fragile, narrow little bodies gave the mug a kind of coy, flirtatious look, like it was winking slyly. It was hard to say whether it was this sly look or the array of feelings, including among others indignation, fury, and superstition, that roiled in Vitaly Petrovich's hairless chest, but the pensioner lost it completely. He snatched up a stick and struck at the idol. It turned out to be surprisingly fragile: the torso broke in half and toppled, the driftwood snout fell away, and Vitaly Petrovich was showered with clay dust. He looked triumphantly at his fallen foe, then stumbled back at the sight of the bones inside.

The thought of killing someone, that the thing had been alive, sliced through Vitaly Petrovich's mind but was immediately dismissed as too insane. He looked closer and discovered that the bones were chicken bones, from a cooked chicken, sucked clean. Poking around the remains with revulsion, he found other bones, and also some sticks and one bicycle spoke. The unknown, obviously inexperienced sculptor had used whatever was to hand to build a frame.

The head lay a little way off like a dark clump. When Vitaly Petrovich pushed it gingerly with his foot, it rolled over to glower back at him from a cat's skull, its teeth bared.

Vitaly Petrovich carted every last bit of it out of his gate and threw it all into the gutter. Then he executed the second idol, who also turned out to be stuffed full of crap, chicken bones and twigs, with a big marrow bone for a skull. Vitaly Petrovich even wondered if this was some kind of magic, someone trying to get rid of him in a particularly clever and repulsive way. Vaguely, he turned over in his mind the little he knew about the evil eye and hexes, and Maundy Thursday salt – whatever that was – but he'd never heard of clay sculptures appearing out of nowhere with such contemptuous perseverance.

* * *

Having rid himself of the freaks, Vitaly Petrovich had another close look at his plot and located track marks and bits of dried mud leading to his gate and thence down Rowan Street. Eyes down on the patchy asphalt, he followed the trail all the way to the riverbank. That was where they got the clay from of course, from the slippery bank. All the evidence was here, from the actual holes in the ground to the footprints of someone stomping about, who didn't look to be alone. A whole gang of them. Digging, those fuckers, carrying off the clay, working so diligently... Too bad he had no sniffer hound to send after them...

"Hey, whatcha doing down there?" came a shout from the top of the bank.

Vitaly Petrovich looked up at a tanned boy in blue shorts.

"Whatsa matter with you?" shouted the boy again. "You can't be here! You better scram!"

"Oh, is that right?" snarled Vitaly Petrovich. He scrambled up the slippery slope. The sight of his face, purple with rage, sent the boy running for his bike and jangling speedily away.

"You creeps!" Vitaly Petrovich made it up the slope. He was close to crying, but all he could do was pump his white-knuckled fists. "You creeps, you creeps, you creeps!"

That very day, or more precisely that very night, Vitaly Petrovich began to guard his plot. The freaks had appeared in the night: therefore, the delinquents who left them would be caught in the night also. He would either catch them at it red-handed and give them the what-for, or better still, they wouldn't dare trespass on a carefully guarded plot. Vitaly Petrovich spent every night thereafter sitting on his porch or making rounds with his flashlight, carefully lighting up and examining the site of the smallest suspicious rustle.

* * *

All was quiet at first. The modest and overgrown plot transformed by night into a vast space filled with crackling and whispers, but these were familiar, everyday noises, the sleepy murmurings of nature itself. Vitaly Petrovich grew sleepy too, sitting by his house with cudgel at the ready. Although he sensibly got his forty winks during the daytime, the night would rock him gently toward sleep, gum up his eyes. A drawn-out cry of some soft night bird, a butterfly thumping into the window... then all again would be sleepy and still, and silent.

Then bang in the middle of one of Vitaly Petrovich's guarding shifts, as he drowsed by the cool light of the moon, came a loud, unmistakable crunching. It came from the hazel copse, where Vitaly Petrovich's favorite pioneer, the child bugler long without his bugle, stood. The sound was not being made by a hedgehog working its way through the bush, but by something large and impressive.

With a sudden gusto, Vitaly Petrovich hared after the noise, his flashlight's beam skittering wildly across the inky branches. And a new burst of crunching came from the opposite end of the plot. Vitaly Petrovich reversed direction, screaming that they wouldn't dare, that he'd show them, but once again his cudgel only cleft the darkness itself. By this time, the crashing and crunching came from somewhere else entirely, behind the raspberry patch, and there was a noise coming from the house, and the gate latch squealed, and Vitaly Petrovich seemed to be surrounded by a legion of nameless foes.

Rushing valiantly at every new sound, he found himself in the hazel copse again, and then something thumped him in the back. He turned with a cry, to discover that he'd backed into the cement block that served as the child bugler's makeshift pedestal. Vitaly Petrovich raised his flashlight high and screamed again, madly flailing the flashlight.

The bugler was gone from his pedestal. The unseen foes had changed their tactics, it seemed: instead of dumping their own disdainful statues, they'd taken to stealing his...

"Creeps…" he moaned.

The bushes crackled very near now, the grass rustled as it bowed beneath a sure and steady tread. The ring was tightening around Vitaly Petrovich. At last, the shaking beam prized a face from the darkness. It was the serene, pale face of a plaster pioneer, the stern Soviet angel. His concave pupils seemed exacting and sad as they gazed at the world's irksome imperfections. Vitaly Petrovich veered aside but fell straight into a hard and cold grip. His flashlight dropped to the grass and lay there, making a dim greenish stain. The light of the moon was plenty, in fairness, as the pioneers worked openly and without guile. They surrounded the struggling Vitaly Petrovich, stuffed a clump of grass into his mouth, caught up his hands and feet smartly and carried him off. The whole troop was here, and they all helped one another, even those with missing limbs.

He howled and fought at first, hurting himself on their stiff white bodies, looking pleadingly into his beloved children's handsome faces, trying to catch their aloof and distant eyes. When he felt the cold clay pressing close, he understood and he was still. The diligent young sculptors had finally found appropriate material and were applying themselves.

With careful intent, stony fingers clad him in a damp clay armor, molded him and cast him anew. Slowly and painfully, Vitaly Petrovich was being transformed into a work of art, and no one including him could possibly object, no matter the final piece, because the work was based on real life and genuine suffering. He had never even dreamed of sacrificing himself on the altar of Art. The unremarkable life of Vitaly Petrovich took on, in his extinguishing mind, a meaning as pure as the perfect lines of antique statuary. He just wanted it to be over already, because his corporeal, bodily terror and despair were suffocating him, distracting him from the wonder of what was happening to him, a thing given to the chosen few, but only the once, the last time…

Underneath a layer of clay, his lips moved gently as Vitaly Petrovich breathed his pacified last, with the silky wings of a moth upon his eyelids.

7

THOSE WHO CALL FROM THE RIVER

The first time Romochka saw the one who wandered up from the forest and prowled along the perimeter fence, sinking into the earth without a trace and then coming up again, he told his mom straight away, but she didn't listen. Mom often didn't listen to Romochka. As though his talking was like some noise in the air, or bird calls. He didn't mind, it was just how mom was made. It was always warm with her, and with nice things to eat, and at night she always-always tucked him in so Romochka could sleep safely in a soft cocoon. He was very scared of the one who sat under his bed at night and would snatch at a hand or foot, if it happened to hang down. Romochka had never seen that one properly, only the snatching paws – they were gray and hairless, and many. One time, when his aunt came to visit with his cousin, they all went to a special place all about the sea, where they had many aquariums with water animals. Romochka had been very scared of the prawn-animal, because if you took it out of the water and made it many times bigger, the paws would be the same as the paws belonging to the one under the bed. Romochka tried to tell his mom about the giant under-bed prawn but she wouldn't listen, not really. She always tucked Romochka up, though, to help him feel less scared. Even when they went to the dacha, though it wasn't as important there – the many-pawed animal always stayed behind, in town. He probably could only live there.

In the before, Romochka was happy in the summer dacha world. Sometimes kids in the street called him mean names, or threw yucky things at him, but it was only because they were silly. It wasn't them he followed out the gate. He went to see the woods and the river, the dragonflies and shiny beetles that dug themselves into the earth, quick-quick. Before, everything was good here, and Romochka liked it, until he woke up one day in a different world, very different and very puzzling. Strange creatures with changing shapes had come from somewhere else and started to live in the village. Romochka couldn't even describe them exactly, so he had a vague, tongue-twisty name for them: "othery-strangery". He saw the first one on the day the world changed, at dawn: something tall and dark standing in the forest just beyond the fence, and swaying. The trees swayed one way, and the something swayed the other way, and it was looking straight at Romochka, except not with eyes, because it didn't have any eyes.

All the dacha people, they also saw that the world had changed. They wandered around the village in frightened flocks, they were noisy, trying to explain the changes. But they never seemed to notice the othery-strangeries, people would walk straight past them, or even straight through them. That was because they hid: they skulked in shadowed corners or else pretended to be shadows and sunspots. Even Romochka couldn't see them all at first. He had to learn to recognize them; like a hunter in the forest, he looked for their tracks and listened out for their sounds. He would have liked to hunt them with a big gun, and hang their empty skins on the wall, because they were strangers, these others, horrible and unexplainable, and just the sight of them made him go cold under the ribs. Why did they have to come, thought Romochka. It should have stayed the way it was before.

* * *

Though she was a woman in her middle age, Tatyana's neighbors continued to call her, as when she was young, Tanya. She lived in a decrepit little blue dacha on the corner of Cherry Street, just by the river. Tanya had no friends, and no truck with the villagers unless in dire need. She spent all her time on keeping up her dacha and plot, and her son Romochka, who was indeed the reason for her gloomy reserve. She did not see herself as one of those mothers of "special" children, who form a pack and campaign for rights and vaguely defined ideas of specialness. She wanted no knee-jerk pity from those with better luck, either. So the life she led was a lonely one: having removed herself from the sphere of the one kind and the other, she dedicated herself to her son. And anyway, she had no one else to live for, besides Romochka. Big, gangly, nearing the legal age of adulthood but stuck for some reason none of the villagers understood in a scatterbrained semblance of childhood. He bicycled around the village, looking out from underneath his grown man's eyebrows with bright, unclouded eyes; he paddled in the Sushka, diving in from the jetty and returning immediately to the shallows, as he couldn't swim; he wandered about the woods, keeping per his mother's instructions close to the fence, appearing silently from out of the bushes to startle mushroom hunters.

Tanya had been the first to openly panic in one of the communal gatherings they held after the village mysteriously closed in on itself. She was outraged, and she shouted. They had to do something, sort it out, this inexplicable situation, because she needed to get to town, she was running out of her sick child's medication. No one had even known until then that Romochka daily consumed a fistful of pills. They tried to calm her down, explain that those who went in the forest were lost, and those who tried to leave by the field didn't return. It was better to wait and see, it still could all resolve somehow,

change, work itself out. At that time, the villagers still had a
strong idea of help from the outside – surely they couldn't
have simply been forgotten. The extraordinary disappearance
of so many people could not have gone unnoticed. But even
Claudia Il'yinichna's forceful arguments to this effect quickly
lost any hold over Tanya. The chairwoman began to worry
in earnest and even consulted her spouse on how they could
get the gloomy disheveled woman to stop making scenes and
freaking out the other dachniks, who were already scared
to death. The situation resolved itself, though, without any
further exertion from Claudia Il'yinichna: after one of her
scenes, Tanya stopped going to the meetings altogether.

Romochka knew Mom was upset about something. And he
tried to explain to her, that there was no need to be so scared
of the new world and the strangeys that wandered around just
out of the corner of your eye. Romochka himself had suspected
every shadow of some bad thing, at first, and couldn't sleep
at night. But then he got used to them and realized that the
strangeys were scared too. They even looked confused, just like
the regular, normal dachniks. Like the changes were sudden and
strange for them too. Like they had dropped out of nowhere
and were trying to get used to it, get comfortable. Mostly they
were like refugees – like displaced people, meekly carrying their
belongings on their backs, like in old movies. Realizing this,
Romochka felt sad for the strangeys. It was only some of them
that noticed people, trying to get a closer look or to touch them
even, like the one from the forest, the one Romochka saw first.
You could definitely start to be scared of that one though; he
studied the dachniks, rising up noiselessly out of the ground
in the shape of an earthen pillar. He was right on the other
side of the fence, he tried to touch people and didn't seem to
mean well. But the others were interesting to watch, and he
wondered at their many guises; neither human nor beast, they

only *looked* like bears or driftwood or ladies, their outlines were hazy and changeable. Romochka asked the grown-ups what kind of visitors they were and what he should call them, but the grown-ups seemed as confounded as the strangeys did when he tried to ask *them*. It was hard to know what they were looking at him with, but he did feel them looking.

Mom got more and more upset, and then cross, and then Romochka's favorite potato pancakes kept coming out all burned. He carefully spat out the burned crusts and piled them on the oilcloth, in the heart of a large flower picture. But mom shouted at him, saying that he was making a mess, and even smacked him a few times with a tea towel. For the first time ever, she didn't tuck him in at night anymore, and Romochka sensed that some catastrophe was creeping close. Mom was starting to be as alien and strange as the new arrivals.

Then, one morning she woke Romochka so early even the frogs hadn't started to chorus on the river. She was standing by his bed, wearing a striped top, hair neatly pulled back beneath a headscarf. How she usually was dressed before she made a trip into town. Romochka told her that you couldn't go to town just now, because there was no road, and in the meadow was the strangey – you couldn't see him very well because he was spread across the ground, stretching out the meadow, not letting anyone leave. Mom started to cry. She told Romochka to behave himself and to remember to eat – she was leaving him a big plate of pancakes – and to obey Auntie Lida, who would look after him until she came back. Romochka readily scrunched up his face, gave a deep moan and cried too. Mom tugged sharply at her handbag and shut the front door behind her.

Romochka ran after her all through the village, still in his briefs with the funny carrot pictures, crying and begging her to come home. She kept turning away from him, so he could only see her bowed back. Then she suddenly grabbed a stick from the ground and turned on Romochka, waving the stick clumsily:

"Go away! Go on, go! How are you going to manage without your pills? What if you have an episode? Go on!"

Mom's voice, her flushed face and pulsing veins – they were so frightening that Romochka fled, obediently, back to his own gate. He didn't have time to tell her that he hadn't been taking his pills for many days, just putting them under his mattress, and there was no need to worry about running out, look how many they still had left. And that he was fine, much better than usual, and he didn't have any episodes now, and he probably wasn't sick at all anymore...

Auntie Lida, who lived in the dacha opposite and looked like a little gray nun, did come from time to time, to feed Romochka and wash his face, and talk to him a bit. But Romochka could sense that this was out of obligation, despite her play-acted meekness, and that she found it burdensome, and that she disliked him. She always tried to get away quickly, though Romochka could not see what was so unpleasant about him. He studied himself in the mirror, and sniffed himself, and even blew his nose thoroughly, the minute he saw Auntie Lida's kerchief bob along the fence. No one else ever came. It was as though no one noticed his mom disappear, or his being left all alone, the kind of loneliness that made a rasping pain in your chest.

Mom wasn't back, but the dacha still smelled of her. To escape the suffocating sadness, Romochka spent as little time as possible indoors. He roamed the streets, gathered raspberries by the perimeter fence, caught minnows by the river. The grown-ups said there was no more swimming there, and Romochka obeyed without complaint. And it was true, the sloping banks that once served as the village beach were bare: no more swimmers, no more boys screaming as they launched themselves from the jetty, no more grannies and grandkids in matching sunhats taking their strolls. No one went to the river anymore, except that quiet fisher-lady Katya. She still cast her lines and sat motionless, waiting for the first shiver of the float.

It was said that the river had terrible creatures, and they drowned people. Romochka had seen those who lived in the river now, and they didn't seem to him so terrible. He thought they were shy and fearful. They hid underneath the driftwood at the bottom, so all you could see was flickers of murky shadows and quiet splashing. Romochka still hoped to track them down and get a good look, or maybe even catch one in his butterfly net, but they spooked at the slightest rustle, like minnows in the shallows.

In the meantime, other creatures got comfortable living in the village, getting bolder and more visible as they fleshed out their forms or even changed them for more familiar ones. Their shifting, shapeless tissue, made of who knows what, coagulated into faces and eyes, as though they were carving themselves out in the humans' image. Like an octopus changing color when placed onto dyed sand. Romochka remembered a TV program he'd seen, where they threw an ugly little octopus into different-colored aquariums; that very evening he saw something octopus-like, with many tentacles and a round mouth in the middle of its pulsating bag of a head, crawling around the raspberry bushes. It really scared him. He decided that since they could get inside his thoughts and were pulling pictures out of them to use, he would only imagine nice things from now on – birds, kitties, pretty girls.

Later on, Romochka did see his mom again. He was walking up and down the perimeter as always, and then, under a pine on the other side of the fence he saw the familiar shape in the striped top. Romochka's heart gave a hot, fervent thump. He hadn't even seen her properly, but knew it by the shape of her, knew her shape by heart. He ran to the fence. Froze, before he could take the final few steps.

It wasn't Mom. It was a scary not-alive thing, a copy of Mom that was rough and ill-made. It was standing still, staring at Romochka, a yawning emptiness in its stopped eyes. Romochka was horrified, because he finally understood. First, they had learned to resemble people, and now they were learning to impersonate them. It was him, the one in the forest, he had taken Mom and sent this hastily assembled fake out to the fence. Dead-eyed, and hollow inside like a rotting tree stump. Romochka could see that there was nothing there, behind the face that looked like Mom's, except for white threads of mold and burrowing woodlice.

The fake Mom thrust out its hand and felt blindly in front of her.

"Go away!" Romochka roared. "Get thee gone!"

The fake Mom grinned a hideous wide grin and withdrew into the forest rapidly, as though she had eyes at the back of her head. Romochka would never forget the way the blood-curdling copy-thing loped backward, still grinning at him and bending its knees all wrong. But he wouldn't remember how he ever made it to the dacha, where he lay a long time sobbing on Mom's bed, beating at her pillow with his big, grown-up fists.

He didn't leave the house for a long while after. He locked the door and wouldn't open it even to Auntie Lida, feeding himself with dry oatmeal and tins from the cupboard, doing toilet on his childhood potty and tossing the contents out the window. If Mom were there she would have worried about him, but she wouldn't have been surprised; this was how he always reacted to stressful experiences. He would shut himself away in his bedroom and wait gloomily for the wrong reality to go away, so he could come out into a new, good one.

He couldn't sleep very well at all, because of a strangey that had taken over Mom's vacant bedroom. This one was very small, with a body like a person and the face of an owl. He clattered along the floor with his claws, moved stuff around, clanged the dishes and even pulled the curtains down to the floor for some reason. Romochka shooed him away with stomping and shouting, but in the morning, he would wake with his hair in matted clumps – that was how the little person took his revenge.

A week passed, or more, before Romochka could bring himself to turn the key. He came out and breathed in deeply. The evening air was especially sweet after stewing inside the dacha. He went to the river, to wash. He forgot all about how it was forbidden now to swim there, and it didn't matter anyway: enough time had passed, he thought, for the world to have changed again and finally got right.

He left his clothes in a little pile on the bank and went into the water to splash about awkwardly. Someone called out to him, quite clearly:

"Romochka."

The voice was not outside, but inside his head. It was pure and joyful, like Mom's voice when she came back from a successful shop, with a haul of reduced-price chicken and candies in a paper bag, and a pair of quality men's socks.

"Romochka, look what I have for you."

They were looking inside his head again. But the voice that repeated Mom's words to him was so kind and tender that his heart leapt gratefully. From murky water something splashed in reply.

"Look at this, Romochka..."

"What's the matter with you? Get out of there now!" Someone was yelling at him from the bank.

A stranger, wearing glasses, skidded down to the shore and hopped about by the waterline, unwilling to go further.

"Get out! You can't be in the river! People vanish out here!"

"It's probably they get called," Romochka explained, after a moment's reflection.

The man was taken aback: "Called by whom?"

"I don't know. Called from the river."

That was how Romochka accidentally gave the village the appellation for "those who call from the river". But he never knew that. Obediently he returned to the riverbank, gathered up his clothes under his arm and followed the nervous stranger man back up the steep incline. The bespectacled stranger was actually the former paramedic Gena, from Flower Street, but Romochka didn't think to make his acquaintance.

From then on, he never missed an opportunity to sneak away to the riverbank to watch those who called from the river. He tucked himself behind the bushes on the high ground above, so they didn't spook at seeing him, and also to keep from forgetting and going in the water. Their dreamy, inviting call turned out to be more of an all-purpose birdsong, one that they tuned in different ways, paging through the images and memories in Romochka's head. They probably did this to everyone who came by the river.

Eventually they grew bored with Romochka's few simple thoughts, and they also stopped being so shy. They swam up to the waterline, tugged brusquely at the rubbery reeds and plaited garlands of fat-bellied yellow blooms. Romochka watched, wide-eyed, amazed how he had ever been so silly. Before, he had thought of them as indescribable beasts, that looked like living driftwood or cyclopean water bugs with repulsive, tenacious tentacles. But now, watching them at play, he could see that they were just girls, lovely gentle girls in white clothes that stuck wetly to their bodies. They chased each other, making the water foam, and climbed out to sun themselves on the trunks of trees felled by beavers. Spooking at any sharp sound, they would flee, leaving only ripples on the river's surface. They were so beautiful, so fragile, that Romochka's heart melted in silent worship. His longing to tumble down the grassy bank and dive in after them was unbearable. But the man in glasses had absolutely forbidden him to go near the water, and Romochka trusted grown-ups. For him, their prohibitions were akin to a scared taboo. Even his returning to the river again and again was bordering on sacrilege; still, his forever childlike consciousness could not master his overwhelming love for the wondrous girls.

One morning, when he came to his favorite spot, he was almost forced to turn back when he saw the lady fisherman Katya. She never seemed to cast her lines just there, as it was shallow and clogged with waterweed – and yet there she was. Romochka was about to retreat before she spotted him, when he saw one of the white girls very close, just under the weeping willow. He had gradually learned to tell them apart, and this one was one of his favorites: she was slim, with a neat smooth head, and looked just like a little porcelain ballerina ornament from Mom's bedroom.

Somehow, he ended up at his usual spot, because he couldn't bear to leave the porcelain ballerina all alone.

"Romochka," said the pure, joyful voice inside his head. "Romochka has come."

The ballerina wasn't playing or sunning herself. She was carefully and quite slowly moving toward Katya under the cover of the drooping willow branches. Something about Katya had caught her attention – probably that she was a lady, but a fisherman too. Romochka had also thought this surprising, that was why he remembered her name, the lady with the fishing lines. When Romochka was little, she showed him a couple of times how to bait the hook with a worm, and how to cast the float not into the japonica bushes or the trees, but exactly where you wanted it to go. Romochka liked Katya, he liked her fluffy dark fringe and the ginger freckles by her nose. Except she always seemed sad, somehow. Was she sad now too? Romochka crawled down the bank, puffing with the effort, eager to catch a glimpse of Katya's face, to discover that she was not even thinking about fishing. Her net and float lay idle in the grass, while Katya herself, tense with concentration, was staring exactly at the spot where the ballerina's glossy head rocked gently just above the water. Katya had noticed her! She could also see the strangeys! Romochka crawled forward, twisting away from the fiery kisses of the nettle, closer and closer. He was nearly at the water's edge when he realized that Katya was not merely watching the girl who hid beneath the willow, she was talking to her, very quietly. He couldn't hear a word, but Romochka's favorite girl came closer and closer, as though enchanted, as though Katya was calling to her...

He lurched as his foot suddenly found no purchase, lost his balance, and slid down into the water with a clatter and a scream. Katya startled and turned. The porcelain ballerina vanished into the river depths.

A minute later Katya was hauling Romochka out of the river and to his feet, and scolding him under her breath:

"Why are you even here?"

"To visit the girls," he said shyly, in that low, grown man's voice of his, and wiped river mud on his trousers.

Katya knitted her brows. "What girls?"

"The ones in the river... you saw them yourself... I come to watch them, same as you..."

As he mumbled his explanations, vaguely flattered by the attention, Romochka studied Katya's face. No, it wasn't sad anymore; every line of her face now held a deep, long-carried horror. Mom got that face when she saw a spider. She had been terrified of spiders all her life, and not the usual shrieking like all grown-up ladies do, but in a deadly way, for real. Romochka's intuition, and not his mind, told him: Katya had seen her own spider.

"Girls…" Katya echoed, then began to whisper hurriedly. "You can't come here. They'll take you away. Draw you down in the water, and that's it. Or swap you for a changeling, send a big frog back instead, and everyone will think it's you."

Romochka imagined a frog strolling importantly through the village, and everyone saying hello. It made him giggle.

"I'm telling you the truth." Katya peered into Romochka's clear, untroubled eyes, and something in his look made her shiver. "Don't even think about coming back here. Where is it you live? Go on, show me."

Romochka shouldn't have trusted her, because she turned out to be a mean tattletale. She told on him to Auntie Lida, that he loitered by the river, and even fibbed that he'd almost drowned. Auntie Lida oohed and aahed, and flapped her hands, and then, not knowing how to punish someone else's great big child – punish him to teach him, otherwise it wouldn't stick – shut him up inside the dacha and forbade him to come out. Being locked in against your will was horrible and hurtful.

Like a beaten Saint Bernard, Romochka wandered about the dacha, weeping, even calling both Auntie Lida and Katya idiots, both of them. The two of them had taken away his lovely girls and now they would play without him, and he didn't deserve that at all, it was so unfair…

Romochka spent two days in dejected captivity. Auntie Lida came by to deliver a jug of soup and yucky fish patties, then locked the door again. She was a little surprised that Romochka hadn't tried to escape – through the window, for instance. But what was the point, and where could he have escaped to anyway, when the river was forbidden. Katya had warned him that she would be watching for him. Romochka could imagine her guarding the riverbank, like a border guard, with the Alsatian, Naida, on a leash. Auntie Lida would probably be keeping a watch on him too, that's how cross she was. They would both be patrolling the river day and night, guarding it from Romochka. His secret friendship with the girls had been found out, and shamed. He would spend the rest of his life here, divided from them forever.

The noise woke him that night. It was the tiny person with the owl's face, fussing around on the shelf where books and assorted dacha bits and bobs were kept. Lately, the tiny person had acquired more definite contours, a neat and tidy little gray gnome emerging from something knotty and indistinctly shaped.

There were books, and boxes, and vials bouncing down onto the folding chairbed below. Romochka was cross, shouting and clapping his hands, but the tiny person would not go. Romochka had to get up and turn the light on. Immediately, the strangey fell from the shelf and darted under the wardrobe. He always vanished without a trace, unwilling to be looked at in the light.

There was a strange yellow brick lying on the armchair, atop all the fallen things. Romochka turned it over a few times until he recognized the little radio Mom sometimes used to listen to the news. When he twisted the dial, the tiny sound bar began to hiss, the sound waxing and waning like the murmur of a forest at night. The dial turned smoothly this way and that but the sound, although it changed, never changed for the usual voices and music.

"Ro..."

He stilled, hurriedly twisted the dial back and pressed the radio to his ear.

"Romochka," came an airy, tender voice. "We're coming. Coming to see you..."

* * *

They came the next night. Romochka spent the day in an agony of waiting, scared to leave the window for even a minute, and only managed to eat a single apple. And just after sundown, orange streaks still flaming in the sky, the orchard was filled with rustling and laughter, and the wonderful girls appeared out of nowhere: they lounged in the grass, swung happily in the branches. The girls played idly with the cups and dishes left behind on the veranda, tossed apples at one another, and poked at the bicycle leaning on the porch – until the sudden clang of the bicycle bell made them scatter fearfully like drops of water.

Romochka was rooted in place by the window, in silent adoration. He did nothing to betray himself, but the girls quickly found him anyway and came close, to tap at the window with their long white fingers. In the gloom, they seemed to emanate barely visible, soft milky light. Romochka came to, struggled for a moment to unlatch the window, sticky with spongy old paint, and opened it wide. A myriad of tender and very cold hands reached out to him, and he seemed to flow across to them, and come to rest outside the dacha, in the center of a white daisy chain. The girls surrounded him, and each girl was trying to touch him, stroke him, tickle him. They smelled of the river, and waterweeds, and clean river fishes. Romochka's heart slowly steeped in icy, glasslike joy...

There was a sudden burst of shouting and noise. The girls scattered again, like a shoal of minnows, and Romochka was looking at Katya. Disheveled, stern-faced and pale, she was coming up the orchard path, swatting at the girls with a large sheaf of something green, and chanting:

"Wormwood and rue! Away with you! Wormwood and rue!"

This looked silly, and the chant was silly too. Romochka couldn't help giggling. The poor girls weren't laughing though, they cowered in fear from Katya's broom of bitter wormwood, crying out helplessly like birds and dissolving, as they softly wept, into the twilight. Romochka tried to hold them back, catching pleadingly at their fragile hands and white garments, but they slipped from his grasp and melted away, melted...

"Stop it!" he roared and balled his fists, close to throwing himself at Katya. But he halted before he got to her. Probably because you shouldn't hit grown-up ladies. And also because he saw, in that instant, that Katya was lit up from the inside with something inhuman, something belonging to the strangeys – except she didn't seem to feel it that way, didn't know she was different now. Romochka had no words to describe what he was seeing, nor did he think to describe it: if he'd been asked, he would have been at a loss to explain that Katya had come alight from the inside, and it wasn't with the soft glow of the river girls, but a true blaze, pulsing with hot, hazy waves. Flame flickered faintly in her contours and smoldered in her eyes, and Romochka knew instinctively that it was not just beautiful but dangerous, to touch Katya now would mean getting burned.

The wonderful girls had vanished and all was quiet. Katya drew a labored breath and the fire went out. Then she smacked Romochka with her bitter broom, on the head and shoulders, as though dubbing him a wormwood knight.

"Why do you have to be such a dummy," she said hoarsely. "I told you, they'll take you away. Take you with them to the river, to live with them, and never let you come back..."

Romochka snapped out of his white-blaze trance and comprehended the terrible thing she had done to him.

"I want to go! I want to never come back!"

He cried and cried, with all the force of his long suffering, and tried to explain to her, in his muddled way, that the girls were kind, and he wanted to go with them, if only they called him. Mom was gone and he was alone, sad and cold – cold on the inside, because everyone had forgotten him. No one cared about sick, ugly Romochka who was a burden to everybody; even to Mom, and so she left him and went to the forest. The girls were nice, and kind, and they told him that they liked him, when no one in his life had ever liked him. He loved the girls and would have followed them into the river gladly, if mean Katya hadn't chased them away. Now they would never come back, they were so easy to scare, and you had to be gentle with them, not like that, with a broom. The girls promised to make Romochka just like them, light and pretty, promised that he would live with them, and rock on the waves, and play with the fish and make daisy chains, but now it was all gone...

Katya led him to the gazebo and sat him down on a bench. Romochka was hoarse and puffy from crying, his eyes stung. Katya was frowning, twisting leaves off her wormwood broom.

"Can I sit in your lap?" Romochka asked. He was done crying but not quite recovered himself.

"What?"

"In your lap," he repeated gloomily and, climbing onto the bench, did his best to fold his large body into Katya's embrace, with his shaggy head on her shoulder. That was how Mom usually made him feel better, rocking with him as though he was a little boy on the outside too.

Katya started and harrumphed from the sheer weight of him, but when she saw that he had no intention of going anywhere she arranged herself more comfortably – as far as that was possible – freed her hand from his grip and gingerly stroked his head.

"They're mermaids, right?" Romochka asked her. His eyes were closed.

Katya was silent, remembering the dark, hideous shapes with their sensitive articulated tentacles.

"Maybe..."

"So why are you scared of them?"

"Because they're scary, Romochka."

"So are you, but I'm not scared of you."

Katya smiled at this, and Romochka felt better.

"Can you rock me, like Mom," he said.

Katya swayed with him awkwardly from side to side, then sighed, apologetic:

"I don't know how."

"Why not? All moms know how."

"I don't have any children, Romochka."

Romochka was silent for a moment, while he considered whether to tell her or not, then decided he should:

"It's because she won't let you..."

"Who?"

Katya's fingers were suddenly digging into his shoulder, filling with heat. That was when a sudden, almost sly idea glittered in Romochka's simple mind.

"Let me go to the girls, then I'll tell you!" And he shut his eyes in terror at his own desperate nerve.

Katya gave him a shake – roughly, not like Mom at all – and repeated in a low, stranger's voice:

"Who?"

"Let me go to the girls..."

Katya bit her lip, looked him full in the face, like he was a grown-up, and nodded:

"All right."

"The lady made from fire. She's super tall, and on fire, like you."

"I'm on fire?" said Katya, and felt her own forehead for some reason.

"Not there, here." Romochka tapped a finger at his chest. "I saw."

Katya was silent for a time, then asked, quietly:

"Did she say anything to you, the lady?"

"Nope." He gave a wide yawn. "She just watches."

"Is she watching now?"

"Yep." Romochka waved vaguely upward. "She's right there... Are you really going to let me go?"

"Romochka…"

"You promised."

"I did."

"Well, then." Romochka smiled blissfully, sniffled for the last time, and fell asleep.

Katya sat in the gazebo until dawn, cradling the unexpected baby in her numb arms. Romochka did little snores and mutters as he slept, but Katya seemed turned to stone, gazing without moving into the gray murk.

It was still early when Katya roused him, ordered him to wash his face and hands, so no trace of wormwood remained, and dress himself in clean clothes. Romochka knew immediately where they were getting ready to go; he went silent, nervous of jinxing his great good fortune. Brimming with joyous excitement, he pitied Katya – who was sad again – with all the earnestness of a truly happy person.

Quietly, they walked through the sleeping village and down to the riverbank. The river was sleeping too, only some pond skaters slipping along the brownish, still surface.

Katya broke the river-mirror by tossing a stone and setting the trunks of the weeping willows alight with the skittering reflection of the ripples.

"You've got company."

In answer, something splashed by the jetty. Romochka was overjoyed to see the dear little glossy head with its threadlike parting. Katya saw it too, and he could tell from her instantly stony expression that she didn't like the river girls, didn't trust them. More than that, she looked like she hated them. Panicking that she would change her mind, Romochka kicked off his sandals and would have made for the water if not for Katya's restraining hand on his arm.

"You promised." His gorge rose up like cast iron. "You promised!"

Katya didn't say a word, just gripped his wrist more tightly. Romochka burst into tears. He was a good deal taller than Katya, and could simply have pushed her aside, but you couldn't do that. She was a grown-up, she was in charge, and she couldn't, just couldn't have been lying to him...

"Give me a sign," Katya finally said in a strangled voice. "When you get there, give me a sign."

Romochka wasn't completely sure what she meant, but he nodded so furiously it made him dizzy.

And then she let him go.

With a beatific smile Romochka paddled through the shallows. It was harder going once the water reached his knees, he huffed and puffed, steadying himself with his outflung arms. Katya watched him from the waterline. Her face was serious, like he was a grown-up. Finally, he felt cold, tender arms wrap themselves around him, pulling him softly down to the bottom, or else to their own promised world.

Even when circular ripples on the water were all that remained of Romochka, still Katya stood on the bank for a long time, waiting for a sign. The dragonflies were crackling, a silver fish skin flickered above the water. A frog surfaced momentarily and gave a ribbit, thinking of its own affairs.

But there was never any sign at all.

8

DOLLY-KNOCKEY

The reason that Lenka Stepanova, the one who had been nettled to ruddy hives in her own shower, was one of the first victims of the mysterious vegetational rebellion that almost destroyed the village, was simple – her parents' plot bordered that of Zinaida Ivanovna. No one knew, of course, that this was the reason. Zinaida Ivanovna always felt that she'd lucked out with the neighbors; the cat-loving Tamara Yakovlevna, her friend of long standing, on the one side, and the Stepanovs – decent family, no drinkers – on the other. They did have the occasional argument, or the odd neighborly spat, but that was to be expected.

They really did have a decent, stable look to them, the Stepanovs, and they were all sort of, just correct. Tall and strapping they were, and golden-haired, as though they'd stepped out of one of those ubiquitous paintings depicting the serene lives of Soviet collective farm workers, or wise ancient Slavs, which was the same idea really. They didn't have the paintings' saccharine, pretty faces though, just regular faces, open and large-featured, maybe a bit rough-hewn. The paterfamilias had even once got caught up in some neo-pagan sect, in his youth, whose interest in him was probably explained by his inarguably Slavic looks. He succeeded in beating a hasty retreat from the sect, but kept his wide, wheaten beard. Though streaked with gray these days, it was too nice not to keep. His plump, pleasant-looking spouse, Irina, resembled a kindly merchant's wife. Tow-headed Lenka, their daughter, did not exactly have the looks of a future Russian beauty, but then no one expected it of her.

The Stepanov dacha was similarly large, light-filled and altogether correct. Two stories, with neat, sectioned window frames that threw lacy shadows over the unpainted floorboards on sunny afternoons. Irina was a dab hand at making rag mats – multicolored and shaggy, they reminded her of marigolds, her favorites – which she spread around the house. She liked everything that was cozy and soft, things you could snuggle into for an afternoon nap, and so she surrounded herself with little settees and armchairs, and scattered cushions, featuring lilacs, cherubs, kittens also embroidered by her. Much of the indoor furniture and the comfortable benches outside were the work of Stepanov himself, whose hands were not just made for work, but hungry for it too.

This is all to say that everything was so correct and comfortable over at the Stepanovs' that even the village's mysterious isolation and the strange occurrences that were gathering pace, did not intrude on their tranquility. At least that was how it seemed. Even when they had to hose down the blistering Lenka, and the whole plot got overrun by jimson weed and ground elder, and then the toxic jungle died back in a single night, Stepanov only shrugged:

"Nature."

Then he pulled on his tarpaulin gloves and went to clean up.

It all began on one orange-lit evening. Lenka was already in bed, reading a book from the house assortment, the kind you find in every dacha: a mix of school-day classics read cover-to-cover, and thick tomes with uninviting author names on the spines that no one ever wants to read. The sort of books with a double purpose – you could pick one up out of boredom or use it to kindle the fire.

For the second week running, Lenka was reading a novel about a dynasty of tyrannical landowners and their sensitive serfs. The cover and first twenty pages had previously gone into the stove, which made it all the more intriguing. Still, it was making her yawn, but she was more bored with the alternative, another walk around the village. The internet was gone, and the games she had on her tablet, charging it in secret since her dad was suddenly economizing on electricity for some reason, bored her to tears as well.

In places, the book was interesting. Just as the slatternly lady of the manor had ordered that the handsome blacksmith, ever-faithful to his beloved Marfa, be whipped in the stables again, there came a knock, hard and loud. Her mother was doing her embroidery on the terrace and so Lenka, assuming she would just open the door and come inside, was about to lose herself once more in the maelstrom of serf passions, when the knock came again, louder than before. Lenka shouted to her mother, who was probably asleep over her embroidery hoop, that the front door was open. A second later, Irina peeped into her daughter's bedroom to ask what in the world she was doing, hammering a nail in or something?

"It's not..." Lenka began, setting aside the book, but whatever she said next was drowned out completely by the subsequent dose of knocking.

Together, they made a tour of the house and established that there was no one else there, and that the knocking was not coming from a door, not the front door nor any other door. And not from a window, either.

It was coming from a little spare room, where they sometimes had guests staying overnight. And it was coming from below... Lenka was sure of this, having carefully laid a palm along the smooth floorboards and immediately feeling them shiver from the insistent, even sort of pissed-off, knocking underneath.

They got Stepanov, who was outside building a gazebo, which he had been at for some days now. He listened to his wife and daughter, then shrugged: big deal, some cat or a mink or something, lots of them down by the river, had gotten into the cellar. At first Lenka and Irina were embarrassed to be so female and easily scared, but then began to argue that animals scratched and rustled, but definitely didn't knock with what sounded like a fist.

Stepanov shook off the wood chips and went to the spare room, stopping firmly with hands on his sides. It was so quiet he couldn't hear even the usual swish of mice, never mind any knocking. He gave it a moment, then, with a meaningful look at his family, knocked on the floor with his heel. No one answered from below.

"That's it, she's gone, your pussycat," he harrumphed, then went back outside.

That night, with everyone asleep, the knocking returned with such force that Lenka, in her fright, shrieked the house down. Stepanov, extremely cranky at being woken up, returned to the spare room, but this time with a mop, which he thumped furiously on the floorboards, as he used to do in town, when the downstairs neighbors partied too loudly, too late. It usually helped – the music would go off and the laughter die down.

The reaction was immediate and counter to expectation: a deafening bang that shook the floor, rattled the windows, and knocked a cushion from the guest cot. Irina and Lenka, who had been watching Stepanov's exertions from the doorway, hastily retreated.

The head of the family, however, did not seem frightened at all. Rumbling irately like a disturbed bear, he went and got his toolbox, an axe, and a head-torch that made him look like a miner. To his family's astonishment, he proceeded to pull up the floor in the middle of the room.

Beneath the floor, it was murky and shallow, and smelled of rotting fungus. Stepanov adjusted his head-torch, lay down, and hung over the hole, trying to see what was going on underneath the house.

"Sasha, maybe don't…" his wife said nervously.

Just as the words left her mouth, Stepanov slid into the hole, as though jerked hard from the other side. His pajama-clad legs momentarily took on a vertical position, a slipper fell sideways, and there was a muffled crash under the floor. Irina and Lenka froze, clutching at one another.

From under the house came more crashing and then furious swearing. Then Stepanov recalled himself.

"Don't fret, there's no one down here," he said thickly. "I fell in all by myself. Banged my nose up good, damn it… Irina, stay away, you'll topple in too."

Stepanov climbed up from the hole, dirty and covered in thick spiderwebs. Once again, he reassured his wife and daughter that there was nobody – not even mice – down there. His epic descent had driven them all away. His nose was swollen and bleeding lightly. Irina rushed off to find cotton wool and antiseptic.

"Really nobody?" Lenka whispered to her father, looking unconvinced.

"Have a look for yourself, if you like." Stepanov drew her by the hand, but she wouldn't go near the hole, even clutching at the door frame in her distress. "Don't you believe me? There's nothing there, really nothing, stop shaking like that."

They stayed a little longer, listening. There was no knocking underneath. Her father, sniffling his banged-up nose, looked pathetic and very dear. Lenka breathed a sigh of relief and finally accepted that no one had pulled him into the hole or done anything to him. And then her mother arrived with the first aid kit.

In the morning, Stepanov returned all but one of the floorboards back to their places. He left the room, stamping purposefully, and then crept in again on tiptoes, stationed himself by the gap and listened. His wife and daughter, sleeping peacefully after the night's adventures, would have been puzzled to see his maneuvers. Stepanov stayed and listened for a while, but the malicious knockey, or whatever it was, eschewed any further activity. Stepanov harrumphed again and went to finish his gazebo.

The day passed as usual, if you didn't count Lenka being spooked by her mother's chopping cabbage, when she ran into the house for a drink. To be fair, Irina really was wielding that cleaver furiously, making a racket. Lenka guessed at once that Zinaida Ivanovna had been over to complain again. She was always very polite with her complaining, very retiring, but she did complain rather a lot, she barely needed a reason. First their lilacs were overshadowing her vegetable rows, then it was the moles they must be keeping – did they have a farm of them out here, for making coats, she shouldn't wonder – that dug up all her flower beds. Now the capricious old lady was convinced that the Stepanovs were draining water "with some kind of chemicals" under their dividing fence, causing her lilies on the other side of the fence to die off. She even got Irina to go over to her side and showed her the balding and fading lilies. It was then that the other woman, who was, equally, a soft-spoken and educated person, finally lost her patience and told Zinaida Ivanovna in no uncertain terms that everyone always poured the wastewater away by the fence, since they couldn't very well be expected to do it by the house, but that there were no chemicals in it, and no one was poisoning her flowers, she just ought to look after her lilies better. Afterward, of course, she apologized, and Zinaida Ivanovna apologized, and they agreed that the Stepanovs would empty their buckets by their other fence, the one bordering the woods. But here she was again, this batty old flower-botherer, again with her lilies...

Stepanov put the final touches on his gazebo and showed it off to his family. Everyone was very pleased with it. The gazebo had come out handsomely, lacy with carvings and a weathervane on top: Stepanov really was a master at unexpected ornaments. They had their dinner of stewed cabbage right there in the gazebo, and eventually began their unhurried preparations to turn in. Since the radio, TV, and internet disappeared, there was not actually much to do in the evenings. Better to have an early night. There was no going to the river for a stroll anymore, never mind that Katya from Cherry Street, who fearlessly continued to fish there, maintained that you could sit on the bank, if you took some odd-sounding precautions. The woods too, had become a terrifying and forbidden place, especially after the vanishing, return, and final re-vanishing of Vityok. The field had swallowed up the Aksenovs and then Valerych, whose folded clothes were recently found by a gate. People disappeared within the bounds of the village too, didn't they, and the chairwoman made house-to-house rounds, making sure everything was well. They all said they were going to look for a way out, but how could you be sure? So it seemed that even a stroll out of doors was risky, you could just about walk up to your own gate before bedtime, and even that carefully, keeping an eye out. Yes, that was the shape of things now, sighed the villagers. No one had figured out why yet, but you had to carry on living, didn't you, somehow.

The husband and wife slept in a giant bed, beneath a big communal eiderdown, light and frothy as whipped cream. As he lay facing the wall, mooting whether to plant Boston ivy around the gazebo or leave it bare of greenery, Stepanov was aware of a sudden, playful sort of rustling under the covers. Irina always began her caresses silently, modestly – as though still shy of her own husband. A playful stroking between his shoulder blades, then a tickle at his neck. Then, an unexpectedly passionate bite on the shoulder.

"What's with the biting, hmm?" Stepanov said, feeling amorous.

"Mmm?" Irina mumbled sleepily, but not by his ear, which he had expected from the way her cool fingers were still on his neck. From the other side of the bed.

Something clawed at his belly, not in the least playfully. Stepanov cried out and jerked upright, flicking on his bedside lamp.

Irina was there, in her usual spot on the far side of the bed. But the deep bite marks were there too, already bruising ruddy and blue. Two incomplete ovals, puffy and almost pleated in the gaps between the biting teeth... As though it was a human bite, but fanged, too – fangs that had punctured the skin as smartly as a dog's would.

Turning over, Irina saw the livid marks. She gasped and covered her mouth. Stepanov now faced her with the leaden look of a calm and reasonable man who had finally lost it:

"Show me."

Irina shook her head, bewildered.

"Teeth. Show me your teeth."

Irina goggled at him, but kept her hand pressed tightly to her mouth. Then Stepanov, wincing at the hot, dull pain in his stomach, reached out for her. Irina let out a smothered squeak and hid under the eiderdown. She did have a stubbornness inside her, that sometimes overtook, even when it did her more harm than good. Stepanov had encountered it for the first time eleven years ago, when she was breastfeeding Lenka and came down with mastitis. For some reason, she kept refusing to go to the doctor. When Stepanov decided to take her to the surgery himself, the silly fool, she went demented, hysterical, with seizures and everything. Hormones on the brain, the usual woman thing... But now Stepanov was thinking how she bared her teeth at him back then, squealing – and those long incisors of hers, he'd been surprised at the time how he'd never noticed those long, predatory fangs...

Stepanov clamped down on her under the covers and started to haul her out.

Over in a shadowy corner, something knocked a sharp tattoo, and even seemed to giggle. The reading lamp wasn't much use and most of the room lay drowned in darkness. Stepanov let go of the half-heartedly struggling Irina and got down from the bed. He was going to find out once and for all who was messing around. It wasn't going to be Lenka, was it. A broom shot out from the corner and poked him right in his savaged belly. Stepanov groaned and bent double – which was lucky, as a mug still half-full of herbal tea sailed over his head and smashed into the wall, spraying everything with dank herbs.

Stepanov swore, using language he hadn't used even when he fell through the floor. He yanked the string of an ancient ceiling light, momentarily blinding Irina, who had barricaded herself with pillows and was silently weeping... There was no one in the corner. There was no one in the bedroom, aside from the two of them.

A banging at the wall, then a thunderous crash, and the house filled with Lenka's terrified screams.

"The hell!" Stepanov barked and, snatching up the first thing to hand – a wooden stool – dashed out in pursuit of the elusive enemy. The next room rang with a quick patter of little feet, the insistent knocking came again, this time from the other wall. Five knocks, six, seven... thirteen.

Irina felt her legs go out from under her, as though she was melting into the thick mattress. She hadn't the strength or the will to stand, she only wanted to stay in bed, burrow into the soft covers, wait it out...

She saw the lamp from her bedside table climb into the air as vertical and solemn as a rocket taking off from the cosmodrome at Baikonur. The lamp hovered for a moment, about five feet from the floor, made a slow turn about its axis as though wishing to show itself off to Irina, then bashed against the wall forcefully, sparks flying. Irina screamed and, cutting her feet on the shards she couldn't see, fled her bedroom.

All night long the Stepanovs' dacha rattled and shook in a devil's dance. Literally. The elusive knockey deployed in one room and then another, broke dishes, tossed chairs about, and shattered lightbulbs. Stepanov chased it round the house with the stool at first, and then with the axe, tirelessly, but in vain.

Worst of all, it didn't cease when morning came. Dawn found Irina and Lenka still sheltering in the gazebo and listening in horror to the racket coming from inside their house. There was no sign of Stepanov, who seemed to be actually enjoying his small, hopeless war.

Finally, Irina couldn't take any more. She winkled a thick quilted jacket and high forest boots out from the shed and donned them like it was riot gear, rather than done-in old stuff. Lenka, when she twigged where her mother was going, started to cry again, but Irina smacked her upside the head. She told her to hide under the blankets they'd hauled out to the gazebo in the night, and not to stick so much as her nose out until her mother came back.

Irina actually found it a little strange that the house was the same as always – filled with light, bright with multicolored mats and settees, still their house. Of course there was a mess, but not as bad as she had anticipated. Doors flung open, mats heaped up, all manner of stuff strewn about the floor. Some kind of tumult was still going on in the bowels of the house, accompanied by a muffled monotonous knocking.

She peeked into the first doorway and recoiled with a shudder. A crooked figure, wrapped up in rags, had moved on her from the far end of the room. A few unbearable seconds passed until Irina noticed the long nightshirt sticking out from beneath the rags, and realized she was looking at herself – or to be more precise, her reflection in a cracked mirror. Looking in a broken mirror was bad luck, so she made a quick sign of the cross over herself.

All of a sudden, the bent figure sprang from the wall and rushed her. Irina didn't have time to think anything, she was eye to eye with her own madly grinning face, a glass crack running right through it. She was knocked off her feet and peppered with stinging pain...

Irina got up laboriously from under the mirror – her grandmother's, heavily framed in wood – that had fallen on her. She tried not to think about how strong it must be, the thing that had flung it from the wall at her. The glass shards glittered across the room like water droplets. One was lodged in the fleshy part of her palm between the thumb and index finger, and she could feel tiny, cold splinters in her forehead and cheeks. Lucky she'd had the foresight to put on the old jacket and boots, or she would have been properly shredded, and if some major artery was nicked it was goodbye and goodnight. Irina cautiously put a hand to her neck – thank goodness the high collar was still tightly buttoned. Before, it used to save her from mosquitoes and ticks, and now from certain death, you could say. Would be good to take out these glass splinters, but she felt ill just looking at them. She wasn't scared of blood – what woman could be, you couldn't exactly go fainting every bloody month – but wounds, torn skin, turned out flesh, a healthy intact person was not supposed to have those... She had always been frightened by that kind of thing, even when she cut herself with the kitchen knife, it was her husband who washed and dressed the wound. She would look aside until he covered the scary thing up with a Band-Aid.

"Sasha...." she called out softly. "Sa-aash!"

No answer from her husband, though still that monotonous knocking. Hands over her head for protection, startling at every noise, Irina went toward the sound.

Something fell right next to her, several times, and once hit her on the back of the head, but she forged on, clutching at the single, both stupidly helpful and helpless idea that she needed to find Sasha, he would take out the splinters and apply iodine solution, she was too scared to do it herself...

And then she did find him, finally.

In Lenka's bedroom, Stepanov hung in midair – arms akimbo and feet well off the ground – unsupported by anything that could be seen. He was facing the wall, with the window to his left, and to his right a miraculously unharmed, out-of-date wall calendar featuring a horse's wise face. Stepanov was being smacked into the wall, face first, repeatedly, with force. The floorboards beneath his helplessly drooping legs puddled with crimson blood. His face, meanwhile, was swollen blue, and you could tell from his bared teeth and the way the veins were popping in his neck, that he didn't want to be ramming the wall with his head at all, that something invisible was making him, pushing him, while he resisted with all his might.

"Get... hel... ppp," Stepanov managed hoarsely, with a wild, equine sort of side-eye at Irina. "Call... people."

The villagers arrived on the scene quickly and in numbers. They were getting used to rushing over without delay if something was happening somewhere. Like going to an impromptu village meeting. Claudia Il'yinichna and spouse were among the first to get there, and everyone clumped around the chairwoman. Tamara Yakovlevna took this opportunity to express her concern that the municipal water supply would be cut off, but they waved it aside: water wasn't the main thing, they had a well, didn't they. Better hope the electricity stayed on...

It was Pashka, Nikita, and the dog breeder from Forest Street – the one who spent twenty-four hours beyond the fence – who volunteered to go and liberate Stepanov. For a moment, they stood inside the room, looking at one another, baffled. Each of them needed to be sure they were all of them seeing the same thing.

The unfortunate Stepanov was still banging his head at the wall, still pinned in the air by an invisible force. You could see him desperately trying to stiffen his neck, to lessen some of the impact of each bang. The wallpaper ran red.

Nikita was the first to get up the nerve to approach him. As he grabbed Stepanov by the belt, the air around him went solid and thumped him in the chest, so hard that Nikita almost toppled. Pashka also tried to get near Stepanov, and did fall over, lamped in the jaw by something unseen.

"I suggest we all three of us hold on to him and pull. It will be harder to deal with all of us at once..."

Although he'd run out of being surprised by this point, so to say, Nikita nevertheless *was* surprised to hear the Forest Street dog breeder speak, thoughtfully stroking his little beard. Nikita figured he'd never even heard the man's voice before. But more important, the dog breeder was speaking sense.

On the count of three, they lunged at Stepanov from three sides, as agreed, and hung on, pulling him downward. Something brisk and invisible showered them with pinches and slaps, fighting hard but with a kind of petty, almost pathetic, malice – pulling them by the ears and hair, gouging Nikita's hand. Sharp teeth perforated Nikita's shoulder like a trolley conductor's ticket puncher, leaving a bloody oval. He felt the bite perfectly well but didn't see a thing.

The dog breeder bent double, moaning, and his curly hair suddenly not just stood on end, but in two hornlike clumps, as though the gloomy-looking man had been harboring a devil or satyr.

"On my back, it's on my back!" He was shaking his head frantically. "Chewing my neck!"

Nikita realized that the dog breeder was being pulled by the hair, by whatever it was that just stopped biting and smacking them so it could cling to the poor man's back. The dog breeder groaned and grimaced but held on to Stepanov's foot.

"Don't let go!" Pashka hollered at them. "One! Two!"

Stepanov went limp and dropped to the floor. It seemed that the malicious thing had had to loosen its grip when it switched to the dog breeder, who was spinning around the room like a top, pleading for them to get it off, get it off, get it off... Supporting the whimpering Stepanov with one arm, Nikita grabbed some stick that was propped up against the wall and clobbered the dog breeder right between the shoulder blades. The stick turned out to be an iron fire poker; Nikita had just enough time to be horrified – before it came down – that he was about to break an innocent person's, really a stranger's, back. But the poker smacked into something dense five inches above the dog breeder's faded denim jacket. There was an unholy squeal, and the dog breeder, clutching at his withers, ran for the door. He didn't scarper, as might have been expected, but held the door open for Nikita and Pashka to drag out Stepanov.

"Thank you so much," the dog breeder puffed hoarsely once they were in the hallway. "I don't believe we've been..."

"Nikita." He was a little worried that the courtesies might slow down their escape.

"I'm Yakov Semyonovich."

They shot out onto the covered veranda. The door was open, and dachniks massed outside. The first to approach was the weeping Irina, and Katya. "Of course Katya," Nikita said to himself as they made the final lurch down the porch steps. "Nothing happens without Katya."

All the villagers were staring at the four men, but Katya wasn't. She was staring at something behind them, deep inside the dacha still. Her eyes were very round.

The men clumped down the porch steps and collapsed, panting, into the grass. The villagers ringed them round thickly, so no one noticed Katya's dashing up to the front door to slam it shut. She tugged at the handle, making sure the lock had snicked, then peered inside through the terrace window. Backed away. Looked in again and, after a moment, returned to the others.

Gena from Flower Street, who had worked as a paramedic before going into business, treated and bandaged the wounds on Yakov Semyonovich's neck, saying that it wasn't too bad, as long as the animal that bit him didn't have rabies. Yakov gave him a miserable look but said nothing. The unconscious Stepanov, however, was diagnosed with "concussion – and that's the best-case scenario." Irina too, needed mirror splinters tweezering out.

"I'd lay stitches on, if it were me, but it's up to you," Gena said phlegmatically, as he stuck the last bit of Band-Aid to her face.

The bravest of the lot, meanwhile, headed by Nikita, made a survey of the house. From the outside, as no one wanted to go in there again. Gradually, it was established that outside the dacha there was nothing unusual happening. Nothing happening at all, in fact. Inside, it continued to clang and knock. Somebody plucky peeped into a broken window and got smacked in the head by a flying frying pan. Fortunately, it was the kind with the Teflon coating, and not an old-fashioned cast-iron one. Nikita picked up a fallen apple and lobbed it inside. Instead of clodding against the wall, the apple sailed back out in silence, so fast that Nikita barely managed to dodge a black eye.

Whatever was raising the roof at the Stepanovs' dacha, it either couldn't get out or just didn't want to.

They held an emergency meeting after all, right there on the Stepanovs' plot, primarily to douse their own agitation. This was the first time, after all, that something supernatural was happening in broad daylight, was incontrovertibly dangerous to humans, and utterly resisted any logical explanation.

"It's a poltergeist," Claudia Il'yinichna declared. "That means 'noisy spirit', in the original."

"Yes, that's right, there have been cases…"

"A bogeyman!"

"A ghost! Maybe there's someone buried under the house…" Yuki began, but then caught Katya's quick and displeased glare.

"The devils' dance," pious Auntie Lida from Cherry Street mumbled meekly.

"Alien life forms," said Pashka abruptly. "They're hovering up there, doing experiments on us. What you call it… remotely."

Everyone looked to the bright summer sky. Only sparse white clouds hovered over the village, and there were swifts, high up, which meant clear weather.

"You're an alien life form," Nikita groused.

"Maybe it's a domovoy, a house spirit?" conjectured the Stepanovs' elderly neighbor Zinaida Ivanovna, who was standing a little apart, by the fence. "If you offend him, he can make trouble. Once, in my father's village…"

"We didn't offend anyone," Irina said loudly, though her voice was tremulous. She'd just come back from the gazebo where Gena was tending Stepanov.

"No, of course you didn't," acceded Zinaida Ivanovna, but with a pursing of her lips.

"And no one poisoned your flowers, either!" Irina yelped. "When are you going to let it go already?"

"It was a kikimora."

A titter travelled the breadth of the assembled group. Even Irina couldn't help sniggering anxiously.

"Ki-ki-mo-ra." Tamara Yakovlevna said it again, in a tone that brooked no argument.

"What, like from the bogs?" Petukhov raised an eyebrow and looked over at his wife.

"Why does it have to be from the bogs? It can be a land one. I saw it once on TV…"

But everyone knew all about Tamara Yakovlevna's viewing interests, and so no one was listening anymore.

"Enough." Claudia Il'yinichna raised her voice. "This is the question: do we leave the house as it is, preferably battening the windows and doors, or do we… resolve the poltergeist issue somehow."

She made it sound like sorting out some problem with garbage collection or water supply. And "the master's voice" did its usual magic, bringing them all back into the realm of the routine, quotidian, slightly quarrelsome village assemblies of the past, and stiffening spines nicely.

Seeing that no one cared what she thought, Tamara Yakovlevna shrugged and walked back up the path. Halfway, though, and with a furtive look around, she turned at the shed and made her way, behind the bushes along the fence this time, back to the Stepanovs' dacha.

None of the dachniks, deep in discussion of how the poltergeist issue might be solved, nor the former paramedic Gena and Lenka, who were still in the gazebo with Stepanov, noticed this maneuver. Katya, who was taking no part in the discussion, did. She watched Tamara Yakovlevna creep along the fence under cover of blackcurrant bushes, then with a furtive look around scurried after her.

The queen of the cats was taking her time crawling on hands and knees around the Stepanovs' house. Katya watched her from hiding places in the blackcurrants and raspberries. Finally, Tamara Yakovlevna paused beneath one of the windows, the one in the little guest room where Lenka Stepanova first heard the knocking.

Tutting to herself, Tamara Yakovlevna dropped creakingly down to her knees again and dug in the earth with a little stick. Her fingers were stiff, and her back was aching. Katya watched her work and dab at her forehead for a while, then emerged from her hiding place.

"Why don't I help you."

"Do, Katya dear, do," Tamara Yakovlevna nodded gratefully without turning around. "Can't spend the rest of my life down here in the blackcurrants..."

The ground was soft, as though recently turned over. Together they quickly unearthed a crack in the foundations, stuffed with a small rag of some kind, like a handkerchief. Katya was about to take it, when Tamara Yakovlevna smacked her hand away. Spitting over her left shoulder, she pinched the very edge of the object, pulled it out of the crack and tossed it, without looking at it, behind her.

It really was a muddy handkerchief, fine thin cloth dotted with blue flowers. It had been knotted in several places to resemble a person.

"And there's your dolly-knockey." Tamara Yakovlevna rose to her feet effortfully, holding on to the wall for support. "For our sins... Casting a kikimora at somebody, that's how it is these days, no shame at all, no conscience..."

"But how do you..." Katya was arrested by the familiar sly flame dancing in Tamara Yakovlevna's eyes.

"Oh, I've started to make sense of the new ways, don't you fear. I know all about how to do that. I've lived under the communists, and under the capitalists, and I'll manage now too, dear, with whoever's in charge these days. Who did *you* see, by the way?"

Katya blinked at her, puzzled.

"Save your pretty eyes for someone else, you don't fool me. When those lads were hightailing it out of the house, who did you see back there?"

"A pig. On two legs. Chasing them."

Tamara Yakovlevna did not laugh at this. She only narrowed her eyes at Katya, and for a time they looked at one another, both of them suspicious and curious in equal measure. Tamara Yakovlevna was the first to speak.

"A kikimora for sure, then. It rolls round the house like a pig or a hare, or else a dog. But how come you can see them, Katya dear? And you're always just there, to hand..."

Katya said nothing.

"All right, don't tell me, I've enough to deal with. Hand me that dolly, it's hard for me to bend."

Obediently Katya bent down and reached for it – but then she stopped herself abruptly, without touching the little cloth person.

"You think I'll set it on you?" Tamara Yakovlevna was shaking with silent laughter. "Take it, take it, it's safe now."

Katya stalled for a bit then picked up the dolly and handed it to Tamara Yakovlevna who, flattening and smoothing out the cloth in the palm of her hand, shook her head: "A fancy lawn handkerchief too, don't you know. God forgive me, but what a fool..."

Forgetting about Katya completely, she went back to the others.

It was decided that for the time being the Stepanovs would take over Naima Hassanovna's guest cottage, and Nikita, with some of the other guys, could check on the abandoned house periodically. The optimists of the group hoped that the poltergeist was a temporary occurrence and would soon clear up.

"How can you say that!" raged ancient little Volopas, a long-retired history teacher. "A geomagnetic anomaly is forever – you get a breakage and that's it! For–ev–er, you understand?"

A litter was being made for Stepanov. Irina stood apart, looking at her cozy dacha, full to the brim with cushions and rugs, and sniffling.

Tamara Yakovlevna and Zinaida Ivanovna were engaged in tense, whispered discussion by the fence. Katya did her best to eavesdrop but could only catch fragments:

"I only wanted to..."

"How about I take it over to yours?"

"I beg you, Tamara..."

"...could have been killed!"

"... it was all so sudden, I had no idea..."

"... were you thinking, setting a hex?"

"They ruined my lilies..."

"...to human beings, over some lilies..."

The old ladies' serpentine hissing at one another grew indistinct but Zinaida Ivanovna looked sheepish and upset, while Tamara Yakovlevna puffed up and loomed over the other woman, still clutching the white cloth in her accusatory shaking fist. Then Zinaida Ivanovna, hanging her head, tottered back to her dacha, and Tamara Yakovlevna went over to Irina.

"Irina dear, don't take it so much to heart. Just wait a week, then you can move back in."

The glower Irina turned on her was both mournful and suspicious.

"You get your husband well, that's the main thing. And don't fret, you'll have the house back again soon."

Late that night, his front door shook from such a knocking that Nikita choked on his cognac. Stashing the bottle behind his armchair, he went to open the door. It was Katya, with a bunch of orange flowers wrapped in a wet rag. Nikita – relaxed because he was already a little drunk – nevertheless felt suddenly wary. The last occasion for a neighborly visit from Katya was Vityok's soul-destroying nocturnal howling. Katya did not come in, just stood in the doorway, crumpling the flowers, looking at Nikita. She also seemed wary.

"God, she's strange," thought Nikita. But he wanted to break the mood, and so he quipped:

"Those for me?"

"Oh." Katya had clearly forgotten all about the flowers until now. "No. I got these from Zinaida Ivanovna.... They're marigolds. Flowers of the dead."

Nikita, to his shame, was spooked at this. Katya noticed, and explained:

"In folklore, I mean. In Mexican folklore, marigolds are the flowers of the dead. But that's not why I... Listen, Pavlov, I know what's going on. I've known for a while."

The drizzling sky behind her flashed once with a silent lightning bolt. Or perhaps it really was that Katya's eyes blazed fleetingly with bright white flames. Nikita's pleasant sense of being half-cut vanished; he was terrified for real. To make it worse, Katya actually grabbed him by the hand, raking his wrist with her fingernails.

"Come on, I'll show you. I need a witness..."

"Like a Jehovah's Witness?"

"What?" Katya let go of him and took a step back. "You think it's funny? Is that what you think?"

Sensing that his saving grace was to keep snarking, Nikita carried on:

"You've got a theory now too? Get in the queue. Geomagnetic anomaly? Psychotronic weaponry? Apocalypse? Aliens?"

"You drunkard," Katya whispered at him with real hatred. She turned on her heel and vanished in the wet dark.

"You nutcase," Nikita volleyed in her wake. Shutting the door, he let out a sigh of relief. Didn't Pashka say that there were all these rumors of her not being right in the head, and that was why no one ever married her?

But already he felt ashamed, about his girly moment of terror and about how he'd treated Katya. He picked up the cognac bottle again and swigged.

Nikita was very sure, though, that he hadn't just imagined it – he really did see a pale fire flicker for a moment in her eyes.

9

THE HUNT

Lydia, though she went by Lida or Auntie Lida, was a bookkeeper by trade; her dacha was small, unprepossessing, and modest, just like its owner. At a little past forty, Lida had every reason to consider herself an old maid, even though she didn't look old, just old-fashioned: she wore long skirts and always had a headscarf over her thin graying braid. Lida always arrived at the very start of the dacha season and set straight to work. Each weekend she labored scrupulously on her own, digging, planting, fertilizing, and pruning. She swept away last year's dried up old leaves and twigs, scrubbed her tiny dacha until it shone, and helped the first flowers break through by fencing them in with wood chips, so that they wouldn't get stepped on. Then, when the blessed long breaks came she would move into her small, well-cared-for kingdom for the summer. Not that she sat around sunning herself. She carried on working tirelessly, so that her orchard and kitchen garden were exemplary, so that she could look around and feel a quiet joy, and that certainty of knowing you weren't living in vain. "She's a toiler, that Lida," – her neighbors all said it with respect, and this too brought her a quiet pleasure. Not pride, though, pride was a sin.

That morning, Lida was weeding the strawberries. Perching comfortably on a kneeling bench, she pulled up tiny dandelion and thistle rosettes: you could never be rid of those foes, no matter how hard you tried, even digging them right out to the long fleshy roots. Her little strawberry bushes groaned under the weight of fruit, the third crop already. Lida had made jam with stevia, the sugar-grass, and gave some away to the neighborhood children, and ate more of it herself than she'd ever eaten in her life. The strawberries were sweet and tasty but Lida did worry that this endless fruiting would deplete the soil. Adding fertilizer wasn't always a good thing either. Lida popped a shiny berry in her mouth – sweet beyond description. How nice it was at the dacha, and even being unable to leave was nice too, all in all. There was nobody there, in town, waiting for her, except perhaps her bosses. An endless summer – five months already – what a wonderful thing, mysterious are thy ways...

The gooseberry bushes by the fence swayed violently, though there was not even the hint of a breeze. Lida tidied her fringe where it peeked out from under the kerchief, and looked more closely in that direction. Nothing unusual in the bushes, and besides, her gooseberry was always neatly pruned, so there wasn't much room to hide under there. That was cats for you, coming and going as they pleased...

The unseen visitor had meantime moved from the gooseberry bush to the dense profusion of girasol. Lida cultivated this earth pear – nothing to do with real pears in terms of taste – for ornament mostly. Its tall stems made a nice living fence, and now the stems were swaying from side to side restlessly, and Lida could hear creaking and rustling in there. A hedgehog, of course it was – unseen, it was making an elephantine racket. It would be good to get a photo, just for herself. Lida was a keen documenter of the fauna visiting her plot. She loved animals, had even wanted to be a zoologist – though she ended up a bookkeeper without quite knowing how it happened.

She kept her little red camera on a shelf in the inner porch, just for moments like these. Lida dashed noiselessly to the house, grabbed the camera without even looking, and tiptoed back to the girasol bush. Something was still fussing beneath. Hedgehogs could be very fast when spooked: one sudden move and the spiky little droplet would be gone.

Lida was looking at the camera display window as she moved apart the shivering stems with one hand. What she saw was so unexpected that she pressed the button at once.

Something large and dark lurked in the bushes, and it was not in any way like a hedgehog or a cat. In her amazement, she struggled to distinguish the creature's head, or feet, or anything at all. Barely a moment passed, then a huge maw gaped wide amid the shapeless shifting mass. There was no tongue inside or jaw, only rows of countless sharp teeth receding into a ruddy hole. Lida shrieked and recoiled, the camera fell from her hand, and the fiend launched itself at her. The last thing Lida knew was the warm surge of rotten-meat stench from the maw that suddenly blotted out the world around her.

A neighbor stopped by toward evening to pick up the strawberries for jam, as they'd earlier agreed. She hung for a while by the gate, calling out to Lida, then walked up and down the plot. Everything was as usual, clean and tidy. No sign of the owner. The neighbor called out once more, then left, figuring that Lida was away on an errand somewhere, or else napping after her labors.

So lonely and modest was her existence that it was only a few days after a different to-do that the villagers discovered that Lida was gone. The different to-do happened on the other side of the village, on Forest Street, dacha number six.

This was the residence of the Usov family: Maksim, Anna, and their son Lyosha, known more generally as "Lyosha-don't" because that was usually how his parents addressed him. He was the one to get poisoned by the deadly nightshade, when it overran the village the month before.

The Usovs were politely and silently disliked – just like the Beroevs and to the same degree. They also did not fit into the serene, old-fashioned dacha ambience. They hadn't owned their dacha for generations and didn't have it passed down to them as was right and proper, but just went and bought themselves a plot, put up a big bland house without any lattices or lacy verandas. On the side of the house, they stuck a garage, equally enormous, to store their coffinlike four-by-four, the one that barely managed the little village lanes. Everything belonging to the Usovs was massive and heavyweight, including themselves. Even Lyosha-don't; he'd scarfed all those nightshade berries because he was used to stuffing himself, to feed his uncontrollably growing body. On the whole, the older generation of dachniks approved of bodily heft as proof of health and plenty, and besides, you never saw the gym bunnies vacationing at a dacha. It was more that on top of everything else, Maksim Usov and his wife Anna lived their lives in an incredible attitude of force and noise. They spoke to one another so loudly that at first their neighbors would assume a quarrel where the couple was only discussing the lunch menu, or a walk down to the river. Obviously they quarreled too, and Lyosha-don't regularly got it in the neck and various other body parts, howling as he escaped. Sometimes the Usovs had visitors, just as large, in enormous vehicles – their extended family, you shouldn't wonder – who all hooted with earsplitting laughter as they inhaled shish kebabs and vodka.

The only quiet, fragile one among them was Lyosha's grandmother Lizaveta Grigorievna. So ghostlike was her existence, that even the Usovs themselves regularly seemed to forget she was there. Faded and pale-eyed, she sometimes went outside their gate to wait for the first random passerby, so she could accost him with the long, muddled tale of her interminable and unexciting life.

* * *

It happened in broad daylight. The outhouse pipe that led into a trench emptying in the woods on the other side of the fence was blocked, so Anna shouted to Maksim to get it fixed right now. Maksim shouted back at her from the house that he'd tried it already and got nowhere, and since he wasn't about to go into the woods, they'd just have to use a latrine bucket like everyone else. Anna replied that she didn't want to live like everyone else, she wanted convenience, so Maksim had better try again. Maksim refused but wished her every success in her sanitation endeavors, since this was clearly so important to her. Lyosha chose this moment to inform them he wouldn't be picking any more raspberries because someone was walking around in the raspberry cane, and he was scared. His furious mother, who was just then busy with the outflow pipe and some buckets, gave him a smack upside the head with a soiled palm and warned him he'd better do what he was told. Maksim was about to emerge to have a straight talk with his son, but Lyosha, hollering and crying, escaped out to the street. He didn't want to pick the buggy raspberries at all, he wanted go ride his bike.

Maksim was putting on his outside shoes – Anna was strict about keeping the house tidy, with different footwear for indoors and out – when a visceral squeal that pierced even his veteran ears brought him running outside. Immediately he stumbled over a terrified Lizaveta Grigorievna who pointed to the far fence with a shaking hand and mumbled:

"The sack… there's a sack, a black one…"

Maksim politely shifted his senile mother-in-law aside and went to the outhouse. There was no sign of Anna. Mystified, he looked around the plot and spotted a bright yellow something in the grass by the raspberry cane. It was a gigantic rubber glove, his wife must have put them on to unclog the pipe. Maksim picked it up squeamishly, and found it strangely heavy. It was twitching…

A bloody hand wearing his wife's favorite ring on its plump index finger tumbled out of the glove. Judging by the shreds of flesh, something had chewed it off just above the wrist.

The villagers got over their dislike of the Usovs as soon as they laid eyes on the hulking Maksim, pale with horror and with tears quivering in his bulging oxlike eyes. They searched every inch of the plot, and the adjacent plots and the streets, but there was no trace of Anna. Lizaveta Grigorievna had given up trying to explain about the black sack and fell silent, trembling as hard as her slight frame could manage.

More and more people arrived on the scene, including the chairwoman and spouse, and also Pashka, as a sort of representative of the active youth sector. They held a quick council and concluded that whatever had attacked and, evidently, eaten Anna had come from the forest. They must make ready to defend themselves from the mysterious foe. Though no one knew how they ought to go about it, exactly.

"We need a barricade! Shore up the fence!" asserted old Volopas.

"Shore it up with what?" Petukhov spread his palms in a gesture of futility.

"The sack, the sack…" stirred Lizaveta Grigorievna.

"You're not getting my cement," Stepanov told them firmly. "I have my foundations to reinforce."

"How can you think about your foundations at a time like this?"

"What, I should let my house fall down? And anyway, we all had to cough up five grand for a new fence just last year, and what did that get us?"

"No, that wasn't for the fence, it was for the water pipes, they were all rusty."

"Are they turning off the water?" someone in the crowd began.

"Have you all fucking lost your minds?" roared Usov. He was at the end of his rope. "Somebody just got eaten!"

The dog breeder Yakov Semyonovich had been making his way through the crowd. With him was his leashed Alsatian Naida, wide and solid as a furry bench. Popping out in the center of the circle, he gave a little cough for attention.

"Naida, if I may, knows how to track," he told them. "I had her trained. The first thing I would suggest, if I may, is that we determine where this creature, if I can put it that way, came from. Alsatians are very smart dogs and if we give her something to, excuse me, sniff... Oh no, no, she doesn't bite."

Naida gave a howly little sneeze and Petukhov came to life: "Well then, go on, go on!"

They led the dog up to the severed hand with its ring. At first, she shrank back, same as the dachniks had. Yakov Semyonovich stood a little aside, holding a very long lead and mumbling how awful it was, how terrible, that they all should live to see something so terrible... His naturally mournful face was truly despondent.

Naida went on to smell the bloodstained grass around the glove, sniffing with obvious distaste, snorting and wheezing like a horse. She circled in place briefly, then headed for the raspberry cane. Petukhov found himself thinking, with a bitter sort of satisfaction, that he'd been right all along about it being an attack from outside: the raspberry cane backed onto the fence, the fence onto the forest, and then... Naida stayed in the bushes and eventually Yakov Semyonovich was forced to get over there and move aside the branches, setting the overripe berries tumbling to the ground.

The raspberry cane masked a corner section, where the perimeter fence guarding the village from the woods met the wooden fence that separated the Usovs' plot from their neighbors'. A part of the corner had been breached. A metal sheet had been pulled away from the bottom of a panel: Naida's head poked out of the triangular hole. On seeing her master, she gave an impatient bark.

Usov's neighbors were horrified to discover that that the mysterious beast had come through their territory, but Claudia Il'yinichna put paid to any hysterics, telling them sternly that the main thing was to figure it out, and they could save the panic for later.

All they could see of Naida was her tail, as she darted among the bushes. Finally, to everyone's astonishment, she pushed at the gate with her nose and loped purposefully down the street, but not toward the woods, the opposite way. If her tracking was true, the trail led right to the heart of the village.

Naida looped around several times and took a few moments of still contemplation before leading them to Lida's gate and nosing it open. She darted to the girasol bushes and whined.

Those that had followed the dog onto someone else's plot in a fever of hunterly excitement now felt awkward. It wasn't right to go barging in, somehow. Someone recalled that the woman who lived here, the one always in that headscarf, looking like a lay nun, was called Lyuda, or perhaps it was Lida... They called her name but no one came out. Yuki and Pashka, noticing the door ajar, poked their heads inside. Dainty little pots and pans, doilies and little icons, and a sickly smell of strawberry jam...

"Excuse me please, are you at home?" Yuki shouted.

All was quiet, excepting the buzzing of the wasps drawn by the sweet berry scent.

Meanwhile, Yakov Semyonovich crouched by the girasol bushes and studied the tiny brown specks that covered the leaves, the fence, and the grass like splashed paint. When Yuki came closer, she actually thought it was paint, at first: maybe they were painting the fence or the fenceposts or something. It took her a minute to understand why the frizzy-haired lady beside her was wailing so bitterly.

"And there I was, wondering all the while, that I hadn't seen hide nor hair of her! I wanted to get some strawberries, for my little Anyuta, but she was never here... I thought she might be under the weather, or else out for a stroll..."

Nikita had started wondering something way back at the Usovs' plot. What kind of creature could carry away or even devour a person entire, leaving only a hand? As though it was too fastidious about the shit-smeared glove to take the hand too. But here everything was gone, except the scatter on the grass. What if it really was paint, or maybe Tamara Yakovlevna's fur babies had had a fight, while this Lida or Lyuda, whichever it was, had just gone out for a walk or something? What if Naida was tracking wrong, and whatever happened at the Usovs' had nothing to do with any beasts?

Nikita turned around, looking for Usov, but instead saw something glimmer in the grass. It was a small red digital camera, lying in a halo of dandelions. Nikita scrolled through the images: flowers, birds, berries, butterflies... and then something dark and indistinct in the final frame. Nikita showed it to Yakov Semyonovich, then Pashka. He enlarged the picture as far as it would go, then shrank it again, peering at it from different angles, close up and squinting, then from a distance... None of it helped. The photo was filled with something blurry-green, its center blurry-black, with a slightly more defined green stick dissecting the shot entirely. "Modern bloody art," Nikita thought crossly.

The woman who had been wailing over Lida and her strawberries looked at the display, then poked her earth-blackened finger in it:

"Girasol."

"What?"

"Look, can you see, that there's the stem. Going across. You can see the little leaf on it. It's girasol. Jerusalem artichoke." She pointed to the bushes where the dog had led them.

"And whose is the camera?"

"That nice red one, that's Lida's for sure."

Nikita squinted at the blurry black thing that blotted out the center of the photo one last time. Then he switched the camera off and put it in his pocket. It was evidence, of a kind.

Having made a survey of the entire plot and taken a rest in the shade, Naida shot off again. Yakov Semyonovich followed hurriedly, with many whistling and verbal cues.

The dachniks were beginning to complain: what was going on, for goodness' sake, and when were they ever going to get to the bottom of it? They had to be thinking about their safety, call an emergency meeting, shore up all the fences, some people had fences barely worth calling that. If something really was gobbling up people, everyone ought to sit tight at home and look after their loved ones, their kids and old people. But here they all were, haring after this self-appointed detective like chicks after a mother hen... Maybe his dog was just wandering around, on its own business. Who even knew if it could track, she was old, wasn't she, this Naida – how many years now had they heard her barking at the mushroom hunters returning home. Maybe she was tracking one of the Usovs. Lyosha was always running wild, out day and night, he would have made lots of tracks. That Maksim probably done his wife in himself, weren't they always shouting at one another, and last year he chased her round the veg patch with a rake, he was that sloshed. Perfect time to do it, you could do whatever you liked just now, and blame it on the poltergeist or on some mystery beast. Who would disbelieve you? Look, you could see that the dog was just wandering around, sticking her nose in randomly. There she went nosing round another gate.

On and on she went, the old lady from Rowan Street, with Yuki nodding along politely. She stopped nodding when she saw it was Katya's gate.

* * *

Nikita forced his way through the crowd flowing onto Katya's plot and called her – once, then again. He pushed at the dacha's peeling white door but it was locked. A jar with orange marigolds stood on the windowsill, those bloody flowers of the dead again. She must have gone fishing, thought Nikita. He didn't see at first that the dachniks were heading further in and looking resolved.

At the back of the property there was a tall fence separating the Beroev villa from Katya's modest demesne, and by the fence, a shed. Ancient and crooked, decked with a mosaic of mosses and lichen, it was the kind traditionally used to store assorted dacha inventory: old bicycles and things that weren't of much use even in dacha life, which is to say all kinds of hopeless old rubbish.

Naida scratched at the door, gave her master a knowing look, and then howled, throwing her heavy head back like a wolf.

There was a rusty padlock hanging from the door. Pashka produced a screwdriver – he always had an assortment of pliers and screwdrivers stashed in the many, many pockets of his cargo trousers – and slid it into the metal loops, prizing them from the rotting wood in a single stroke. He pulled at the door, then realized that it probably opened inward, as the shed was likely to date back to the old days, before anyone worried about thieves kicking the doors in when everyone was away in the winter. Pashka put his shoulder in it, but the door was barely budging, with something propping it up from the other side. Together with a pungent, revolting smell, a noisy spray of flies emanated from the crack.

"Give me a moment," said Tamara Yakovlevna weakly and began to topple to the ground. The other women caught her up and rubbed her hands, patted her cheeks. Zinaida Ivanovna fanned her friend attentively with a lawn handkerchief.

The men suddenly erupted in shouts and movement, shouldering the sensitive and the weak away from the shed. The latter pressed forward all the same; it was interesting in the extreme, and everyone wanted a glimpse of whatever horror lay within. Like on the net, thought Yuki, before... when you'd find a clip of someone getting killed for real and your blood would run cold, but you pressed the play button anyway...

They found it all in the shed. Ruddy-brown spatters and stains over the walls and floor, thin scraps of flesh, bones, a desiccated shell that Gena the former paramedic identified as a skull fragment, some chewed-up tendons and gristle. There were also cloth rags, and when Usov picked one up, identifying it as a piece of Anna's sundress, a small, slim finger fell out of its folds. It was starting to rot already. Nikita heaved over for a closer look, but no, it was not Katya's. Katya had narrow oval fingernails, and this one was square. A none-too-clean, well-worked finger it was, with a callous like a hard yellow pellet below the middle joint.

Nikita had never believed the way that, in movies, people seeing such things would immediately be sick to their stomachs. But now he wanted to puke up everything his eyes had seen, not just from his stomach, from the very depths of him. To shake out, sluice out everything, so it didn't exist, so he had never laid eyes on it at all.

"I said it, didn't I... that she was, you know," said Petukhov pointedly. "You can always tell a psychotic sort of person straight away."

Nikita stared at him. It was coming to him slowly that they were talking about Katya. That according to Petukhov, there were no gnawed-up bones of hers in the shed... that Katya had somehow turned into a cannibalistic monster.

"Why so quick to blame her?" Yuki shouted hotly from the back row. "Maybe she was the first that got... you know, gobbled!" Yuki sniffled. "I came by this morning, but she was gone."

"The shed was locked," parried Petukhov. "From the outside. With the owner's padlock, I might point out, and the owner's key."

"So what?" Yuki persisted. "Anyone could have locked it!"

Someone sniggered. "Sure, the beast must have locked it. With its paws."

Yakov Semyonovich had donned the pair of gardening gloves that still lay on a shelf and was silently picking through scattered rags. He hooked out then smoothed and laid each piece on a box with the stern, important air of a real-life detective.

"When was the last time anyone saw Lida?" asked Petukhov.

Lida's curly-haired neighbor fanned herself feverishly with a burdock leaf: "She told me to come for the berries, didn't she, three days ago. I stopped by a few times since then, and nothing."

"Makes sense," Petukhov nodded importantly.

That was when Nikita lost it. He shouted at them, surprising even himself with the fury and volume he was able to project: that they'd all lost their minds, and of course it was understandable, who wouldn't under the circumstances, but he, Nikita, actually knew Katya, and there was no way that she could, even just physically, overcome the gigantic Anna. And anyway, how could you even suspect one of your own people, your own neighbors, any human being at all, of doing something like this, when it was obviously some strange beast, another of the village curses, a monster from the forest, who had eaten the hardworking Lida, and Anna Usova, and… and Katya too, if she wasn't fishing on the river, though he hoped very much that she had only merely gone fishing…

"Young man," said Yakov Semyonovich ruefully, "do forgive me, but all sorts of impossible things have been happening for some time, and there's no argument against that. They keep on happening!"

"Don't you 'young man' me!"

"Of course, excuse me, Nikita. But just have a look at this," and the dog breeder gestured at the box festooned with bloodied rags, "and tell us if there's anything of your, ahem, so-called friend's, here?"

"How should I know?!"

Yuki elbowed her way inside, snapping back at all the adults that tried to keep her out. The first breath of the rotting meat smell made her gulp, but she pinched her nose shut and crouched down beside the box.

"That's Auntie Lida's headscarf. It had that bandana pattern, I remember... And she had this gray skirt. I don't know whose this one is. This one looks like a piece of a bag...." Yuki lifted her face to Nikita with a despairing, earnest look: "There's nothing of Katya's here."

"So what?" Nikita spread his hands so wide he knocked over a shovel leaning on the wall, the shovel took down a bucket, which in turn caused it to rain down with rusty weeding hooks and gardening shears.

"So you know what that means," sighed Yakov Semyonovich.

Nikita shouldered him aside and went out. He desperately needed to get some air. And to get away from this homespun detective, with his irritating lisp. And he really was sick to his stomach.

"Wait a minute." Claudia Il'yinichna laid a cool hand on his elbow. "You knew her, this Katya. Who was she, where did she come from?"

Nikita gave the chairwoman a dirty look. What was she getting at?

"Does she have any family? How old is she? What's her job, that she can spend all summer out here?"

Something quivered and plummeted inside Nikita's chest cavity, like an apple from a bough. So that's what it meant when they said "his stomach dropped". Abruptly he understood that he knew nothing at all about Katya really, he'd never heard mention of even her family name. His attractive neighbor turned, in that moment, into a person without traits; the frightening unknown briefly made visible through the thin membrane of her familiar shape. She loved fishing, the left corner of her mouth drooped when she smiled, and she said that one time that she couldn't have children; the sum total of what he remembered. He'd wondered, though, and often, at her odd ways, at the things she said... well, didn't say exactly, but seemed ready to say, before catching herself. He had so many questions, and never asked her a single one.

And when she did want to tell him something, he was sloshed, and got spooked – obviously not by the stupid lightning he caught reflected in her eyes, or those orange flowers she'd carted round to his – and he just let her leave. Made her leave. Three days ago...

"Stop scaring people. It's not like she landed from the moon, is it," chided Tamara Yakovlevna behind his back. "You might have just asked me."

With the chairwoman's attention snapping immediately away from him, Nikita took the opportunity to clear off. Tamara Yakovlevna held court for a while, ringed by a clutch of the curious. Of course she knew all about her, that Katya; she used to run about the village as a little girl, when her parents came in the summers, nice, decent people, the mother was called Nina... They used to bring their granny too, she was very old and far into dementia, she used to abscond sometimes, like a little child, and wander the streets, muttering to herself...

The older generation of dachniks were starting to remember too and they grew more lively. Old Volopas related how the granny had once gotten into his shed and made a racket in there, and he didn't know how to get her to leave. Someone recalled that Katya used to sit by the river as a child too, her mother was always looking for one and the other, the child and the granny. There were even smiles, as people rifled through the communal memories of a time without beasts or gnawed bones.

It was comforting to know that it was no strange monster who lived among them for so long in the guise of Katya the angler, but a regular person who had a family, a childhood. That at least was perfectly clear, no dread mystery, at least until the recent turn of events.

"So where is it now, all this family?" said Claudia Il'yinichna.

"You're chairwoman, you'd know best."

"Do you know how many plots we have here? I'm busy enough collecting dues, and all that paperwork, too..."

"Well then, at least we know she paid her dues promptly," shrugged Tamara Yakovlevna. There was a ripple of anxious but approving tittering.

"Until recently, everything around here happened promptly," Claudia Il'yinichna icily retorted. "So when was the last time she came here with family?"

"Oh, seven years ago... maybe more."

"And then she always came alone?"

"I never set up for her nanny, so I wouldn't know." Tamara Yakovlevna was growing irritated. "None of them came for a few years running. Then she started coming by herself."

The chairwoman's husband was shouting. He'd gone behind Katya's dacha, and there was something they all needed to see.

Petukhov carefully opened and shut the gate that led out to the forest, demonstrating that despite his wife's official admonitions it was not properly latched. The lock hung idly on a fencepost. The grass by the gate was flattened; clearly the gate was in use. Petukhov pushed it open once more and they all looked at the narrow path amid the cow-wheat and meadowsweet. Every plot bordering the woods had a path just like it, tamped down over many years' use, and at some gates it was less overgrown than others... and yet... when you put it all together...

Yuki was the first to notice something under the closest birch, by the side of the path. The thing was small, blue and plasticky. Before any of the adults caught on, she sprang forward, on tiptoes.

"Get back!" Pashka yelled, and Naida barked anxiously in answer.

Yuki snatched the strange object and raced back faster than a speeding bullet. Petukhov slammed the gate shut behind her. Just as he'd started berating the foolish kid, he was brought up short by the object she held.

An ordinary plastic bucket, filled almost to the brim with blueberries, blackberries, black rowanberries and others, freshly picked, if a little bruised. They were all the same color, more or less, differing only in hue, which ranged from blue-black to pitch.

"That's crow's eye…" Yuki plucked up a large, shiny berry, with a little floscule still attached. "It's poisonous."

The dachniks whispered worriedly among themselves: she'd gone into the forest, picking berries, poisonous berries at that, and left the bucket by the gate… bait for someone, or else… and anyway, where was all her family, and what exactly was she doing hereabouts each summer, instead of sunning herself by the sea somewhere, or working her plot like everybody else? Why would she spend her days on the river, with those fishing lines of hers – a young woman, not some middle-aged ne'er-do-well with a bottle of vodka in his pocket, looking for any excuse. What was that about? As always, when the villagers were overcome with fear and confusion, the departed Kozhebatkin rose up from oblivion and remembered himself to them. *He* was a strange sort of neighbor too, wasn't he, and then…

"And his body," Petukhov said, suddenly remembering, "did they ever find it?"

The assembly fell to thinking; someone shook their head no.

"When we came, after, he wasn't there anymore," Yuki foolishly volunteered.

"We? Who's we?" spoke several voices at once.

"Me and Katya..." Feeling like the victim of a pop quiz in front of the whole class, she cast a pleading look at Pashka, but he just looked helpless and gave no hint of the correct answer. "No, we weren't together exactly... I mean... I came later, when everyone went home. But Katya, she was just leaving his place, just then. And then we went back, to look for... And Nikita, he came with us too!"

"You're saying she was the last person on Kozhebatkin's plot?" scowled Petukhov.

"Pavlov too, though! Nikita was with her..."

"Did you actually see them leaving together?"

"I don't know... Why don't you ask Nikita, he'll tell you!"

"Sure he will, that one..." said the chairwoman dubiously.

Yuki could always tell that she was blanching by the way the tip of her nose went cold. She'd seen through the gaps in the fence, how Nikita was waiting alone under the streetlamp, for Katya to come back out. And Katya did try to keep Yuki from Kozhebatkin's plot, saying she wasn't old enough for such things.

Yuki put the bucket down and melted into the back row. It was useful sometimes to be small and inconspicuous. She made her way over to Pashka and whispered hotly at him.

"Let's go and find her, ok? Pashka, please, pretty please! She must be on the river, right? Come on, just come with me..."

Her eyes bulged with tears like thick convex lenses. Pashka started on his old refrain of why, what for, they'll figure it out without you. Yuki shook her head violently and lurched away, but Pashka grabbed her by the elbow before she could hare off the devil knows where, and they both quietly walked out onto the street.

At the very first turning they came upon Lyosha-don't, who had been forgotten in the tumult. Other children were all locked up at home, but he was left to amuse himself as best he could. He lobbed a wriggly object at Yuki – this turned out to be a lizard's shed tail – and gave a ringing shout:

"Something's et my mo–om!"

Grabbing a long birch twig off the ground, Pashka gave chase, but Lyosha danced away sprightly across the drainage ditches, giggling and calling Pashka bad words.

"You'll get et too," he cried in their wake. "We'll all get et!"

As always in a heatwave, the river smelled of watermelon. Dragonflies raced up and down along its length like crackling ribbons of orange and blue. From time to time, you could hear a stout lonesome fish bellyflop on the surface. Katya had been telling Yuki all about the different kinds that lived here, while filleting the blood-and-guts-stained fishes on a big chopping board. With pleasure, she showed Yuki the gills – look here, and that's the milt, and here is the float bladder – as she expertly sundered the different parts. Sometimes the gutted fish convulsed briefly; then Yuki, wincing, felt a sickening pity for the cold, senseless creature.

Narrow trails to the best fishing spots wound down from the banked-up roadside. These were not overgrown either, perhaps because just like the woods trail from her back gate, Katya was still using them, going back and forth on her secret business. Katya surely knew something. Yuki had been convinced of that from the time they had gotten rid of the legless girl with her frog mouth. Suddenly Yuki remembered what Katya had called her, the girl: "igosha". Yuki knew her for a witch even then. But now it seemed Katya was something much worse. If, of course, her own gnawed bones were not among the ones back there, in her shed...

"Katya!" Yuki called out.

"Be quiet, you! Gonna wake them all up, them in there..."

"The ones who call?"

"Who else."

"Have you ever seen them?"

"Don't be daft."

An invisible icy finger touched the tip of her nose again. No one in the village really talked openly about those who called from the river. But there was quiet talk of voices heard. Those who had braved the riverbank saw indistinct figures, shadows of some kind, "beckoners" as Tamara Yakovlevna put it. The voices spoke to people by name, saying – so it went – intimate, secret things that only those they called to could know about. That was all that Yuki managed to gather. No need to tempt the devil, said the self-same Tamara Yakovlevna.

Katya, meanwhile, had been spending every day here. She came with her lines and sinkers, and dropped feeder fishing nets. She told Yuki that she always had her music player on, or earplugs in. But one time, she accidentally told Yuki that those who lived in the Sushka now weren't that scary after all. She caught herself, and changed the subject, wouldn't answer any questions. As a grown-up, she could get away with it.

Katya, who had lived in the village for many summers so solitary and inconspicuous, was sure to know everyone by name. And could find out their secrets, if she wanted to. No one paid any attention to her, did they. She moved almost noiselessly – an angler habit, she'd told Yuki, so as not to scare the fish away.

What was it with her, and all that fishing stuff, even the men never spent as much time by the river as she did...

"Katya!"

They were almost by the fence, and beyond it the field, and the now-unreachable residential development across it in the distance. They could see the main gate, where a few weeks ago someone had found a neatly folded pile of clothes belonging to the vanished Valerych. The path split, branching on one side down toward the dark, dank jetty, which once upon a time the village youths used as a springboard into the river.

It was always covered in rubbish – empty bottles, plastic bags, emptied cigarette packets – even a burned-out steel barbecue. But that was before. Pashka thought of how seven months ago, an eternity, he and a bunch of pals had cooked shish kebabs on that barbecue. They chased the meat down with lager and dive-bombed into the warm murky water.

There was no sign of the barbecue, or the rubbish, or any other traces of human fun and games; as though someone had blitzed the whole place clean. All was tidy and green, the sedges rustling.

Yuki started to scramble down but Pashka grabbed her hand. You could see from the top of the path that there was no one on the jetty.

"Katya! Kat–ya–aaa!"

Something heaved forth, splashing hard, just a few feet from the shore: tentacles, or maybe driftwood, but for sure some kind of quivering limbs that gleamed amid the sunspots on the water briefly, then withdrew. Pashka grabbed hold of Yuki, and they retreated at a run, keeping close to the fence and bushes.

"Did you see that?"

"Some pike going mental."

"You… what? A pike?" Yuki stopped dead in her tracks, indignant. "Seriously?!"

"I'm going to leave you here, if you don't stop it! Go and drown yourself, for all I care!"

Yuki knew he wouldn't leave her, and so she looked back over her shoulder and tried one last time: "Katya–a–a!"

Then Pashka was hauling her up over the gravel bank. Below them the river splashed about mildly, smelling of watermelon, buzzing with mosquitoes.

Katya had gone, but not fishing.

* * *

The village did not sleep that night. The darkness was pinpricked everywhere by shivering flashlights and lit up by real, live fires, echoing with overexcited and confused barking from Naida and a couple of chained-up mutts. The villagers were out hunting. Per Petukhov's suggestion, they split the place into quadrants and each hunting party had its own territory to comb.

Yuki dashed about the buzzing streets, avoiding the emptier unlit alleys, variously getting in the hunters' way or bringing intelligence. Volopas, the pensioner, recommended they drive the beast away with ultra-high-frequency sound, and promised to make such a device from this and that, but it would take a few days. Tamara Yakovlevna was refusing to let the hunters onto her plot, saying they would trample her cats, what with the big dogs, while the cats themselves hissed and meowed at the humans, and it was turning into an altercation. Maksim Usov wandered around alone, with a sawn-off shotgun, and looked completely terrifying, and where did he get a sawn-off shotgun anyway? Andrei from dacha number seven, who was a pal of Pashka's and Nikita's, flatly refused to accompany Yuki anywhere, but told her to tell the other lads they ought to join the hunt, as it was vitally important to everyone's survival.

"The survival of the dachnik species," Pashka mused thoughtfully.

He had been holed up with Nikita, drinking, since the previous evening. Or rather, he'd joined Nikita who was already drinking, the previous evening, when he and Yuki looked in on Nikita on their way back from the river. There was nothing for it, except that Pashka should join in.

Nikita seemed determined to finish off his entire stash in one night. As he drank, he talked and talked. First he said that it couldn't be Katya. True enough, all kind of crazy things had happened, and there was no logic or justice to any of it, but how could Katya have turned into a monster literally overnight? It was only three days before that she came to see him, the day before that Lida woman got eaten, and he would have known if something about her was off. He would have known. OK, she was a bit weird, maybe even loopy like Pashka said, but still...

"I never said that, I only said that people said that," Pashka protested, then fell silent, confounded.

Everyone knew that Nikita had a thing for Katya. It was just like in the movies, Yuki thought, in a flash of timid but ardent empathy: she fell in love with him, but he turned out to be a vampire. He fell in love with her, but she was a people-eating changeling. But this wasn't romantic at all, really, and not remotely beautiful.

Meanwhile, through the fume-saturated gloom, Nikita was already expounding a new theory: maybe Katya was keeping the beast close, she'd taken pity on it and sheltered it. Who the hell knew what kind of a monster it was, maybe it looked sweet and harmless like a kitten at first. But then it gobbled up its savior and broke out to run rampant.

"Maybe those berries were for the beast," Pashka offered uncertainly. "Like she was trying to make it go... vegetarian..."

"What berries?" said Nikita.

Yuki told him about the unlatched gate and the bucket with the strange mix of the edible and poisonous berries.

It all made Nikita pine again. "Why did she have to go into the woods in the first place..."

"She knew something," Yuki said with certainty, nodding in agreement with herself.

"Something about what?"

"About everything."

There was only one thing Nikita had not mentioned to anyone, not even here among friends: the way Katya had come to him three nights prior, not just to pay a visit, but with some weird shit about needing a witness, and knowing what was going on. Nikita had spent the last three days watching for her over the fence, plotting how to run into her casually, and apologize or something, or joke it off. But he didn't. Not because he was too proud to, or it was too awkward; because the idea that she really did know scared him. Something came over him that night when she stood on his threshold holding the orange flowers of the dead, something faint and unholy. Though it might have just been the rain-damp draft that made him shiver; that and the silent lightning that rolled across the gray sky and echoed in her eyes.

"She's a witch," said Pashka suddenly. With a start, Yuki realized she'd just been thinking the same thing.

"*You're* a bloody winch... Witch." Nikita got up unsteadily. "If you ladies will excuse me for a moment..."

"She's put on spell on us," Pashka gesticulated passionately at his retreating back. "Come on, you know it's true. Who is she anyway? It's all her doing! I bet you don't even know her last name, do you?"

One of the first rules of being drunk on a summer's night is to avoid looking up at the stars, lest you faceplant the surface of your home planet. There was nowhere else to look, though. Nikita found the old familiar scoop of the Big Dipper and watched it dance a merry jig, which almost caused him to topple over before he caught himself. Flashlight in hand, he began to zip up his flies. The beam waggled haphazardly, plucking forth into light the edge of the dacha roof, then a branch, a rosehip bush...

A shapeless dark form, stirring underneath that bush.

The beast was caught head-on in the flashlight's beam, but it was impossible to tell where its paws were, or its head. The stout, thick body that resembled a black sack, just as the Usov granny said, was covered with scales, or else a rough skin. Nikita froze in horror, which was handy as he was also determined to get a good look at the creature, trying hard to make out anything at all from the featureless mass. Anything familiar at all.

Two crimson eyes flashed like pinpricks from the dark pulsating shape that looked now like a colossal leech – the only thing the creature resembled even remotely. And then a round maw with concentric circles of teeth opened wide, and the beast, executing its ambush, sprang...

Nikita dropped into the grass and hollered hard before he could be eaten. The porch light came on, a door slammed, there was another holler, the clamor of running feet and crunching vegetation, and finally in a hail of mud clots and twigs an indistinct face appeared above Nikita's.

The face spoke with the voice of their mate Andrei who had gone hunting with the others: "That you, Pavlov? You alive?"

Pashka sat on the ground beside him, panting. Wincing with pain, he clutched his leg, his shredded camo pant leg soaked with blood. He had bounded out of the dacha at Nikita's scream and attacked the beast with one of the many screwdrivers he always had on him. Although the creature had had time to chomp on his leg with enough teeth for a pack of dogs, Pashka managed to get a few good stabs into its black leathery side. It took Pashka mere moments to apprise Nikita of all this, since he couldn't stop babbling at high speed. Pashka thrust out his maimed leg, and then his hand, which was splattered with some kind of swamp ooze: it had sprayed, according to Pashka, from the beast's wounds. Yuki paced around them, frenetic, interrupting and clarifying. Andrei kept on asking him something, sounding vehement, and there were other voices filtering in from the darkness. There seemed to be a large assemblage of people on Nikita's plot. Spotting Usov's mountainlike shape in the blinking beams, Nikita twigged these must be the brave hunters, drawn to all the noise.

He got up and wandered away from them. Away from the excited shouting, and the stench of the swamp ooze all over

Pashka and the grass. They shouted after him, calling him back. An old crone in a flowery gypsy shawl, who knew what she was doing among the fraught hunting party, clung to his arm:

"Wait, don't go, you can't possibly…"

"Get off, the leshy take you!"

Nikita shook her off carefully, squeezed through the gate and shut it behind him.

The lights, shouts, and barking now also behind him, Nikita made his way down to the river, slipping and tripping into the fiery embrace of the stinging nettles as he went. And then he was at the little sunken jetty-raft right by the river's edge, someone's fishing spot. Not someone's, hers. Nikita sat down on the dry compacted mud and looked out at the still, black water. It was dawning; wherever the trees were not blocking the sky you could see things clearly. Willows dipped helplessly toward the water, wildly overgrown nettles rose like crenellated black citadels along the banks, and a white fog lay atop the dark funereal ribbon of the river itself.

Then Nikita fell asleep, head hanging on his chest. He dreamed of a long-ago and half-forgotten snowy winter, and his dead grandfather, also half-forgotten. In the dream, Nikita was small, buttoned like a parcel into a stifling rabbit-fur coat, and his grandfather was encouraging him to go down a metal playground slide. It wasn't very big, the slide, and had that inviting, thin coating of ice that made for a gleeful descent. And his grandfather held out his hands, on the ground, remonstrating with Nikita up above: it's so much fun, you've just got to go down, or else you'll grow up a coward, and who will want you then… But Nikita was afraid, he was suffocating from fear inside his sweltering coat.

He woke up just in time; his feet were already in the water. Nikita scrambled back to the tamped-down spot with alacrity. It was morning, and he could see clearly the trees on the opposite side, and the circles made by moving fishes under the river's smooth planes.

The river's edge, just where an arrowhead plant bristled with green blades, roiled and foamed. Nikita saw a dark round object emerge slowly from the murky, viscous water. A head. Then the shoulders appeared, and then the torso, and then a complete female figure, draped in clinging white cloths that looked like a wedding dress or a shroud. Nikita, rigid with shock, saw several small crimson wounds in the woman's side, each of them bleeding a gentle corona.

Pashka and his screwdriver...

The woman stepped up to the bank and bent over Nikita, swiping her hair, streaming and tangled with weeds, away from her face. Her visage was entirely pale, except the sunken circles of her eyes, which stared at Nikita fixedly.

His lips moved almost noiselessly, as he backed up into the bank. "Katya..."

10

WHAT CAME FROM THE WOODS

The dacha cooperative had been built close to the city's exurbs, which meant that land was dear. Year after year, the dachniks defended themselves against rich encroachers, who wanted no less than to seed all the available space with cottages, throw up tall fences, hack down the woods, and leave no trace of the real village, the one that was made of wood and apple-blossom froth, and carved windowsills. Yes, the Beroevs and Usovs and a few more of their ilk had managed to break through, but for the most part the hereditary dachniks fiercely defended their family turf. Anyone contemplating selling their dacha had their entire street of neighbors to dissuade them.

This was perhaps the reason (although it might just have been a simple way of preserving illiquid capital) that there were long-abandoned dachas still standing on expensive plots, their fences and gates slowly caving together with their rusty locks. Nature followed in and conquered, without the kind of wild abandon you got down south, but comprehensively nonetheless. The apples that ripened not for jams or jellies but for their own pleasure, dropped noiselessly into a thick web of elder and lilac branches. Squirrels ran riot along the mossy roofs and fat, skittish wild pigeons roosted under the eaves.

The grown-ups never looked in on the derelict dachas, whether from a sense of propriety regarding the property of others, or for fear of the rampant nettles. The children, on the contrary, worked out endless means of entry, eager to find adventure and berries. The biggest raspberries, the sweetest plums were there on the overgrown plots, and if they ever managed to get inside an abandoned dacha, well, this was a perfect place for a headquarters.

Many years ago, a juvenile Nikita Pavlov had spent time inside just such a dacha – number thirteen, right on the riverbank. This was where he played milk caps with his pals, learned to smoke, and listened to tales of winter burglars who came to ransack snowed-in, emptied dacha villages. Back then number thirteen was a deal less decrepit. The wooden floor had not caved in, pale mushrooms did not festoon the walls, it didn't reek of damp mold. The mice were still wary of people and didn't scamper so shamelessly right under your nose. Most importantly, back then Nikita also didn't spend his time lying flat on the packed earth, nose to the muddy shreds of floorboards, his hands tied behind his back. His legs too, he quickly ascertained, had been tied with some kind of cord, not expertly, but well enough.

The fact that he'd passed out on the riverbank, just swooned like some delicate maiden, was shameful and deserving of censure. No sooner had he castigated himself for the untimely fainting spell than Nikita almost had a second one. At any rate, he experienced most of the mechanics of passing out, once again, when he managed to lever himself into a sitting position and saw, in the doorway, a familiar figure.

She was still wearing that strange dress, bridal or funereal white. It was not quite dry, and the white cloth around the little round wounds was smeared with blood. No chance that Nikita had just imagined it all in an alcoholic stupor, none at all.

He waited a little while and then asked her, in a futile attempt to bring everything back to the normal, ordinary, boring old everyday plane:

"How did you manage to get me all the way here?"

"It's not my first rodeo," Katya shrugged. "I dragged my dad once, all the way from the village gates to our place. I was little, and he was wasted. He had a big rucksack on, so I dragged the rucksack for a while, and then my dad, like that."

She hadn't smiled. To Nikita, her eyes seemed expressionless, two empty black ovals, like back at the river. He was about to ask her where her dad was now, why he didn't come to the village anymore, but Katya took the lead, demanding he tell her what was going on in the village.

Picking his words very carefully, Nikita told her about the beast, and those it had devoured, and the resulting hunt. He shied away from telling her that the dachniks had their suspect, but she prodded him and kept him on track until he finally had to admit everything: the shed on her plot, the gnawed bones. Katya knitted her brows but the look she gave him was impenetrable. Then, with a silent nod at him, she left.

Nikita spent the time she was away trying desperately to escape, but just kept toppling back to the mulchy earthen floor like a broken rocking toy. He banged his nose and scraped his tied hands bloody. His exertions caused his head, already thick with hangover, to ache all the more until, finally, he lay still. What he wanted more than anything in the world was not to save himself from his nightmare neighbor but, simply, to take an aspirin and go to sleep.

When she returned, Nikita saw, with fresh horror, that there were new bloodstains on her white dress. Her hands were bruised and bloody too. She caught him staring, wiped her hands casually on the hem of her dress, and went to the window. Peered out, but instantly drew back and flattened herself against the wall. Then looked out again, gingerly, scanning the overgrown plot. She really did look like an animal poking its finely-tuned nose out of its lair.

"A lair," thought Nikita, "it's obviously a lair." Maybe Katya had a system of tunnels under the village, just like the dead Kozhebatkin. Lairs to sleep in, hidey-holes, tunnels to the hunting grounds, storage pits filled with meat. Maybe even alive meat, so it didn't rot so fast. That pious old maid Lida, hadn't she disappeared without a trace, without a sound? What if Katya dragged her off alive, like her dad and his rucksack that time, not her first rodeo at all, and locked her up in a shed? Lida could be sitting tied-up in the dark right now, on an earthen floor, waiting for the beast to get hungry. When prisoners break out of a camp in the forests of the north, they always take along someone useless but soft. They call it "provisions", living meat. She probably has more than one store of provisions round the village. Going for Anna Usova, a noisy woman with a big family, was a mistake. And so was leaving behind the shit-smeared glove. Disgusted, Katya had tossed the mucky thing aside, and it gave her away. Animals are not so fastidious.

The more solitary dachniks, though, it could be ages before any neighbor noticed, or wondered why they hadn't been seen. Meanwhile the provisions sat quietly in the cool dark. On the earthen floor of dacha number thirteen, safely tied-up.

His belly roiled, stale gastric acid surged up his gullet, and he threw up. And felt much better, if you didn't count the sour reek in his nostrils, because the feverish, raving jumble of his thoughts subsided too.

Katya didn't voice her displeasure, but her face was like that of someone watching a cat foul its place. He could see her thinking the usual "Pavlov, you're wasted again". Oops, said Nikita to himself, this bit of meat is all mucky too. It made him laugh out loud, hacking like a teenage punk.

"You can't run," he told her when the manic giggles passed. "The whole village is looking for you. With dogs."

Katya reached down below the windowsill, tugged out a few large burdock leaves that grew straight from the foundations, and threw them atop the revolting puddle. She kneeled beside Nikita and looked into his eyes – just like at the river – and asked him, quietly:

"You too? You think it was me?"

A piercing, almost sickening feeling of alien presence had roused her from sleep the night before. There came a rustle from the orchard beyond her window, quiet but clear, as though someone was walking up and down. This wasn't the first time Katya had heard the rustling, but it had never been loud enough to wake her up. Before, she only floated up to the boundary between waking and dreams, and skated along it, with the dark shapes of shrubs, the contours of her sleeping house, the muted light of the streetlamp, all swam beneath her closed eyelids. The scent of earth and damp greenery tickled her nose. This was probably how the being that now wandered around in the orchard perceived its surroundings.

Half-dreaming, Katya tried hard to convince it that there was nothing of interest inside the house, separated from the swirling night by only a thin wooden door. A thin, framed-glass, insubstantial, in the usual dacha way, door. Whoever you are, Katya pleaded with her mysterious guest, don't look this way, don't come this way. What use could you have for me?

And then the house really did vanish from the sights of whoever rustled and cracked the branches out there, outside, except it was impossible to tell whether it was for real or only in Katya's disordered imagination.

Suddenly something small but hefty jumped on top of

Katya, pressing on her ribcage and forcing all the air from her lungs. Instantly awake, Katya tried to open her eyes and found she couldn't. Her arms and legs didn't work either, though she could feel them perfectly well. It was so weird, so horrible, to quiver in panic inside your own sleep-slack, warm body, unable to see anything but the ruddy spots beneath your eyelids. Whatever sat on her chest like a dense lump carried on pressing down her ribs, not letting her breathe...

Something in her memories stirred faintly, the same thing. Many years ago. Not long before Granny Serafima died. Then too, Katya was taken by surprise, and couldn't remember at first what must be done.

Moving her lips silently, Katya whispered:

"For good or for ill?"

The dense heavy thing was gone. Katya sat up quickly, gasping for air. Blueish lights skittered across her eyes, her ears were ringing. Katya squeezed her eyes shut, trying to catch her breath and quieten the jagged pain in her chest.

Eventually she realized that the ringing was not in her ears. It was her cell phone, which she had plugged in to charge a long time ago and forgotten all about, chirping its little song. The blueish lights were real too: the phone's display was blinking.

After the initial shock passed, Katya hesitantly picked up the buzzing gadget. There was no caller ID, just two little circles, green and red, for accept or decline. It was all impossible, and she felt a kind of holy dread – as though it wasn't a phone screen sparked to life, but the sacrificial flame of an ancient pagan temple.

Finally, she touched the green circle and held the phone up to her ear. The hissing that emanated from the phone was the same as the noise from Vityok's radio, Vityok who had left his human self in the woods. Only this hissing wasn't stable, it seemed more like the crash of the sea, waxing and waning, other sounds breaking through.

The sounds compacted into words. A susurrating, sexless voice repeated, with modulating timbre and volume:

"For ill... They co–me... Ru–un... Hi–ide..."

The hissing ceased abruptly, the handset winked off and seemed to die in her hand. Katya flung it away like a giant dead bug. Then she climbed out from under the covers, felt for the slippers under the bed, and ran – obeying the order – she knew not where, or from whom. She ran, in just her tattered white lacy nightie, the one she used to dress up in as a child, playing princess.

She fell over something as she scrambled down the porch steps. The something was large and rubbery. It was like falling over an old, beaten-up boxing punch bag, only the bag moved, and stank of bog water and rotted meat. Katya leapt back, heavy peonies slapping her on the legs. Even in the dark, she could make out a shapeless mass, which grumbled thickly and seeped back into the bushes with an unexpected lightness and speed. Katya bolted up the path and out of the gate.

She knew where she might hide. The place she had spent years walking and watching, where every bit of driftwood was mapped, every depth plumbed. Where she had one friend, at least. The river.

"You weren't at the river. Yuki and Pashka looked for you."

"Someone was hiding me."

Facing the window, Katya looked out furtively, every so often.

"Hiding you? Who?"

"Romochka."

The name seemed familiar, though Nikita couldn't exactly remember. Katya didn't give him much time to figure it out, she tossed her head and said:

"So they all think it's me, is that it? That I'm a beast?"

"Everybody, yeah. Who was... you know, calling you?"

Katya turned back to him wearily.

"I don't know. And I don't know what was creeping around my porch steps either."

"Well, I think there wasn't anything creeping around, it wouldn't have let you go just like that... What about these?" Nikita tilted his head at the crimson rips in her nightgown.

Katya touched one of the swollen round wounds gently and turned away again.

"Romochka's payment. They like fresh blood, and so he does too now."

Ice-cold sweat ran down Nikita's spine, like a sticky thread of pure horror.

"Who... who's they?"

"Those who call from the river."

"I know what's happening," he remembered her saying. And the pale flame in her eyes, whose color he still wasn't sure of. His neighbor opposite, the eccentric angler, that nice young Katya...

He felt like laughing again. He hadn't lived long, and he hadn't learned much, but he was definitely going to die a fool...

"Are they still looking for me?"

"How should I know? I left."

"Did you tell anyone–"

"Nope," he interrupted crossly. "I didn't tell anyone anything. Nothing to worry about, go on and feed. Try not make too much of a mess."

Katya froze, but only for a second, then dropped down and crawled toward Nikita. This did not seem to him in the least amusing, or sexy, despite the normal range of feelings one might expect faced with a woman wearing only her nightie and wriggling one's way. In reality it was terrifying, the way she was almost running, on all fours, deftly and easily. Like a true beast.

Nikita leaned away from her until he felt her unwinding the cord around his legs. She tried to slip off the washing line trussing his wrists but the knot was too tight.

"Use your teeth," he quipped, at which she clamped a cold hand over his mouth and cursed him out, under her breath. She cut the rope with one of the many pieces of broken glass littered around, then pointed to the window. Nikita obediently stood up, but Katya hissed at him and made him crawl on his hands and knees, so that he couldn't be seen from the outside. Both his legs were asleep, so he barely made it to the windowsill.

Dacha number thirteen stood in the center of a small clearing ringed by shaggy raspberry cane and gooseberry bushes. Nikita recognized the dark shape near the edge as the stump of a large tree that, a few years back, they'd had to cut down laboriously. An exotic "Brazil nut" tree, it had gotten so wild and overgrown that the nuts would hail down onto neighboring roofs at the slightest gust of wind. It was agreed that they'd simply lie to the absent owner of the plot, if it came to it, that the tree had toppled on its own, and the neighbors did him a favor, in fact, by clearing the fallen giant away.

Now the wide stump supported a flattened, disemboweled fish: innards artfully draped around the stump, the arrangement also doused with blood. Though the bait didn't look especially appetizing to Nikita himself, to the right of the stump he saw the creature make its approach.

This was the first time he'd seen it clearly, in bright light. Its hefty, hairless bulk looked bizarre and awful among the tall grass and bees buzzing in the clover. The beast really did resemble a leech. The jointed black body heaved along with the help of many tentacle-like legs that extended, absorbed, and carried the torso forward, then retracted again. The thing approached the flattened fish carefully and unhurriedly, as though aware or at any rate suspicious of a trap.

Nikita finally tore his gaze away from the view – mesmerizing in its broad-daylight impossibility – and pulled Katya back down, under the windowsill, then breathed into her ear:

"So there's two of you?"

Katya goggled at him and made the are-you-cuckoo sign by circling her index finger by her temple. Outside, there was a crunching. Katya raised her eyes above the sill and saw the beast devouring the fish, literally sucking it up into its round, toothy maw. Bait disposed of, it stretched into a wide black ribbon and wound itself into the bushes. Katya vaulted over the windowsill in pursuit, and Nikita followed, whether to capture her or to save her from the monster, rather unclear in his own mind.

It vanished without a trace. No matter how Katya beat at the bushes and scrutinized the earth and grass for any kind of track, the whereabouts of the thing remained a mystery. Katya even hopped up and down the packed, fermenting soil in the hopes of unearthing a lair, but succeeded only in frightening a muddy-brown field vole: squeaking its panic, it scurried around her feet and also vanished in the grass.

When Nikita finally found her in the fecund orchard jungle, she looked devastated, like she'd just lost the biggest fish of her life. And it was the childlike, utterly miserable disappointment on her face that convinced Nikita to believe her and doubt no more: she was no beast, she had nothing to do with it – at least this time. He smiled his relief at her and was about to go in for a hug, when she flew at him like a furious tornado, forgetting that she was still being hunted, and about all the rules of being undercover, screaming that he'd distracted her, and made noise, and spooked the creature away, when she'd worked so hard to set up the trap, sacrificing her only catch, because she needed to know, had to know what that thing was, where it came from, and why it had framed her in such a sly, clever, human way. Nikita flipped and started to shout back at her: she had no idea what she was playing at, with her idiotic and dangerous ploys, and it was useless to try and chase the beast down in broad daylight because it would, first, gobble her up before she even left the plot and, second, if she did make it out, she'd be nabbed by the dachniks, or else shot by Usov, who still wandered around like a zombie with his shotgun. He had nothing to do with any of it, Nikita, and wasn't going to get killed just to keep her company. He ought to piss off then, Katya swung back at him, and go tattle to the chairwoman, and to Usov too... no, he should call a village meeting and tell them all where they could find the village cannibal. A fine thanks for the cannibal who dragged him like a fainting schoolgirl from the river, and saved him from the river creatures and from the real beast, and...

Simultaneously they realized that they were shouting loud enough to raise the dead, and fell silent. Katya seemed genuinely offended. What an incredible woman, thought Nikita admiringly, to be able to sulk at a time and place like this.

"Forgive me," he said. "I'm glad it's not you eating people."

"There's plenty of takers without me," she grumbled.

"You mean..."

"I mean everybody. Pavlov, there's things living everywhere round here." Katya spread her arms wide. "In the river, in the woods. In the houses. From the beginning, we were never really alone. That's what I was trying to tell you before..."

"You said, I know what's going on."

"I do," she nodded. After a long moment, she said: "Want to see?"

As a child, Nikita loved going to the woods. Trousers tucked into high rubber boots, forehead protected from ticks (at least that was the idea) by a cap drawn low, he would set off mushroom picking. Of course, the village woods were not exactly a real forest; but the mushrooms didn't care that it was weedy and full of litter. In the best years they proliferated in witches' circles even atop rubbish heaps, hoisting up the crumpled plastic bags and beer cans with their thrusting tops. Nikita had really loved the woods just before autumn set in, when the tree stumps were draped in honey fungus and even living trees wore it like pockmarked fur coats. The mushrooms were springy, meaty: you'd grab a handful in one fist and cut away, the knife squeaking as it sliced through the thick flesh.

It had been many years since he last ventured mushrooming, but he remembered it vividly, the sweetish scent of a just-cut mushroom, the quick hot flush of pleasure on spotting the noble brown boletus in a patch of tangled grass, and the mosaic of chance leaves lining his basket. He had roamed the woods for hours, when he was little, feeling calm and at peace. The woods were friendly and generous then.

They'd been scarcely ten minutes inside the woods and already his throat was tight with fear. The worst kind of fear, in fact, the kind that makes you shiver and your palms go sweaty, without really knowing what it was you were afraid of yet.

He'd known it back then, didn't he, during the hunting of the beast – no, even before that he'd had his suspicions – that getting to know his cute neighbor Katya was a sure path to doom. OK, so maybe she wasn't a cannibal – although to be fair there was no conclusive proof to the contrary – but she'd led him into the forest, the one nobody left in the same shape they had gone in. He wondered, as he climbed the perimeter fence, how it was that she convinced him so quickly. He'd jumped down onto the springy green moss and froze in place: there it was, the deadly unexplored zone, which was strictly forbidden, not that anyone in their right mind would want to go there. Katya, on the other hand, scuttled into a small coppice of hazel and rustled along the fence toward her own plot's gate.

When they reached the place, Nikita was astonished at the care and detail everywhere in evidence. Had the dachniks who discovered the unlatched gate looked more closely, they would have seen a system of signs all along the path wending into the forest: branches trailing ribbons, tree trunks marked with chalk and paint, and arrows – laid out with small stones, or else bundles of meadowsweet and willow-herb, tied together and easily spotted from a distance. There were way-signs everywhere, so many that Nikita couldn't help wondering aloud how long she'd been lurking around in secret, setting up her markings. Not that long, Katya told him, she'd only just started researching the forest, and had only marked out three hundred or so meters from the gate. Further than that, you could end up anywhere at all.

Well, that was cheering news. If he hadn't felt obliged to play the strong and decisive male, Nikita would have happily scarpered. Besides, like any heavy drinker, he suffered from excessive anxiety in the best of times; and just then his self-preservation instinct was blaring like a siren.

He was so parched. He put his hand out toward the copious, temptingly ripe, unpicked wild strawberries that dotted the path and was about to pop one in his mouth. He could almost taste the refreshing sour burst on his tongue when Katya leapt at him and whacked it out of his hand:

"Nothing red!"

"Nothing red?" he echoed, looking longingly after the berry rolling away in the grass.

"No picking red berries, only black. No breaking branches or cutting out marks." Katya spoke quickly and without expression, like a lesson she'd long drilled. "And no fire. I checked."

So that explained the berry-filled bucket, edible and poisonous both, but all black. That was her checking. Nikita nodded silently, hoping that if he didn't look especially enlightened, he at least appeared very interested. Obviously, that was how one behaved in a forest, he said, every child knew the rules: no fires, no littering, no chopping down trees… no picking red berries.

"There you go!" Katya pointed an accusing finger at him. "You think it's funny. Again."

"No, I don't, honestly..."

"You said I was a nutcase, that time. I heard you! I'm not a nutcase. Got it?"

"Sure," Nikita said readily.

But Katya, silent and secretive Katya, was finally at the end of her endurance:

"I trusted you! How am I supposed to tell the others? They'll just laugh at me, or else come at me in the night, like Kozhebatkin."

"Katya..."

"But you, I trusted! I can't do it on my own anymore, all by myself. I need a witness who can say he saw them too, you understand?"

"Yeah, I understand."

"Do you? Like shit, you understand."

"All right then, explain it to me!" Nikita felt himself getting hot under the collar.

Yes, he might have behaved better, but she too could have tried harder to make herself clear. So he didn't have to come mooching around the grim woods with a guide who wanted to have it out with him...

Katya suddenly seemed to lose all interest in him, and in their conversation. She scanned from side to side and clicked her tongue:

"Oh, great. Here we go again."

Nikita looked around too. Everything seemed relatively harmless – the path, the pines and birches, to their right a clearing clogged with willow-herb, another one of those ribbons tied to a branch right above their heads. He was about to ask Katya what was wrong, when he saw it for himself.

They had passed through this place already. They'd turned left beyond the tall pine marked with a chalk cross. But here it was again, the pine, looming in front of them. Right here was where Nikita had picked the wild strawberry.

The berry that Katya had knocked from his hand was still here, in the grass. Nikita instinctively reached for it, to see if it was the same one, but remembered himself in time. It really was the same one though, with a slightly dented side, nibbled by some small forest fry.

"It's your fault. You picked that berry, and now he's turning us round and round," said Katya uncharitably.

They walked up to the tall pine again and made a left again. Long ago, a tractor or truck had been down this way, leaving a deep rut covered over with patchy wet grass. Nikita breathed a sigh of relief when he finally stepped into the long track: you couldn't get lost following that, for sure. He took a few wary steps forward, half-expecting the earth to fall away under his feet...

And then there was the meadow, to their right. Bumblebees rumbling above the willow-herb. Young firs. The tall pine just up ahead. He walked a dirt path again, and not a boggy tire track. Nikita stopped still. Something completely impossible was nevertheless happening.

"Don't come off the path," Katya ordered. "He'll spin us round for a while, then let go."

Nikita started to panic again. What if she wasn't going to explain, or show him anything at all? What if it wasn't a witness she needed bringing, but a sacrifice, a gift for whoever it was she seemed so unwilling to name?

They took a right by the chalk-marked pine seven times. Each time there came a moment when everything was changed, instantly and invisibly, so that you couldn't tell when it happened. There wasn't a single join to it, or a dimple, or anything your eyes could hang on to. Nikita started to think that it wasn't a looping reality at all, just him going crazy, wondering if Katya and the pine and the willow-herb were all in on some secret plot.

The eighth time took them down the tire track. He kept craning his neck for sight of the clearing and the ribbon, but the mysterious looping round seemed to be finished. Not the ribbons and colored markings in the tree bark, though. Katya kept a close eye on these, peering around and cocking her ears, making commando hand gestures to direct him to go forward or hang back, and would have passed for a seasoned tracker if not for her dirty, torn nightie.

A twig cracked to the left of the path, beyond a thick clump of hazel. Katya raised a hand in warning and Nikita halted. The hazel rustled again, gave a heavy, throaty sigh. Katya hopped across the track, walked across a dense cushion of moss to the hazel clump and lifted up a branch... It made him nervous – hadn't she said no stepping off the path – but then she turned and beckoned him to come close.

Behind the hazel there was a planted copse of pines, neat rows of them. Once upon a time they'd been put here to replace burned-out or coppiced patches of wood, and the trees had grown wild, interlacing their prickly branches and blotting out the sun. As a consequence, there was barely any grass or forest undergrowth, and so the large copse was easily observable on all sides.

A little old lady in a rustling nylon raincoat weaved in and out of the mossy trunks. She wore a flowery headscarf and carried a rustic basket. Every so often she would bend down laboriously, pluck a mushroom and toss it into the basket without once lifting her eyes from the forest floor. The basket was full, overfull even, and each new mushroom rolled down the mound back to the ground. The little old lady, paying not the slightest attention, was already on to the new one. It was a profusion of mushrooms, in great variety. She didn't differentiate: boletus and fly agaric, russulas and toadstools all went in.

Nikita knew her by her clothes; ancient Granny Nadya from Cherry Street, who wore the raincoat and gypsy-flowered headscarf summer and winter long. He vaguely recalled her from the night before, baba Nadya, whom he hadn't recognized then, as she hung on his arm and slowed his getaway. Instantly, his heart went to her. He had shoved her away, hadn't he, and even cursed her out... All her relations were back in town and she always went on about the same thing at the village meetings, droning on and on pleadingly, when would they open the main gate already, when could she leave, it was hard for an old person on their own, with no help from anyone... Kids and oldies, Nikita's mother used to say, so easily hurt. You might not even notice you'd done it. What if it was the final straw, knowing even that loser Nikita Pavlov could push her around, that drove poor old Granny Nadya into the forest, to look for the way out? And here she was now, lost in the woods not a hundred meters beyond her own section of fence.

He stepped forward: a plastic bottle concealed by the carpet of pine needles loudly crunched underfoot.

Granny Nadya instantly turned to the sound and twisted her neck in quick jerking movements, very oddly, as though scenting for the source of the noise. Then she glowered at Katya and Nikita, who were still concealed in the hazel thicket – Nikita could feel her tenacious, grasping look like a physical thing across his skin – and moved toward them.

"Freeze," Katya breathed into his ear. "Freeze, don't move."

Granny Nadya was now very close. Nikita could see her face. It was stony-set and dirty, the corners of her mouth turned down. A fat mosquito sat on one blue-tinged cheek but she appeared to feel nothing. Before, Nikita would have said she was a cozy-looking, velvety-wrinkled sort of granny, but now she seemed not alive somehow, and stiff, and though she was fast, she dragged her body about clumsily, planting her feet on the ground at random and turning out her ankles in an unnatural way. Her eyes too, they darted to and fro, blank and round like a bird's.

She stopped, looking straight at them, and smiled, or rather bared her teeth at them, wide and predatory. Then opened her mouth wider and emitted a tentative, quiet sound somewhere between "ooh" and "aah." The hair on the back of Nikita's neck stood on end, and not figuratively; an icy shiver fluttered like a flock of birds down his whole body. Suddenly Granny Nadya burst into tears, and this was something she did with natural realism, blinking her myopic, watery eyes pitifully, gray eyebrows rising to form a sad little roof over her face. Nikita lurched toward the poor old lady, who had been wronged by him, to go and console her. But then she stuck out a long pink tongue and began to lick away the tears running down her cheeks. Abruptly, he stopped feeling sorry for her.

After treating them to several more extremely disquieting grimaces, the old lady turned sharply and walked off, still wobbling as she stuck her feet down pell-mell. When she was well away, Katya dropped her head and exhaled loudly, with a long shudder.

"What is with her?" whispered Nikita. He was shaking too.

Without a word, Katya started back through the hazel, the way they came, and he hurried after her.

"If that thing tries to come back to the village, you tell the others not to let it in," she told him, once they were in the thickest part of the hazel again.

"Thing...? She's gone mental, right? Like Vityok?"

Katya made no answer.

"Vityok, you remember. That guy that came back from the woods..."

Katya stopped for a moment to throw him a look over her shoulder.

"Vityok never came back. And that was not Baba Nadya either."

"Wha–a... what d'you mean?"

"It's a changeling. A copy, a fake… Did you see how it made those faces? It's learning. To look like a person. They take whoever ends up in the forest and try to make a copy… Stop staring at me like that, I can feel it with the back of my head."

"*Who* takes them?"

"So you believe me now?"

"Yes, I believe you! I believe you!" He was close to screaming. "Who takes them? Are we gonna get taken too?"

At college, his nickname had been "thirty-three misfortunes". Only he could have managed to get himself into a scrape like this: out devil-knows-where with a witch, or else a lunatic, and a lunatic who seemed to be right about everything, besides.

"Quiet," Katya shushed him. "I told you that I would show you."

"Actually, don't show me!" pleaded Nikita. "Just tell me."

"You won't believe me."

"I will! Katya, I give you my word, I'll believe anything you tell me – aliens, apocalypse, parallel worlds…"

"That goes without saying," she shrugged. "But this, if I told you in words, you wouldn't believe me."

The bushes finally parted and they emerged… into the same pine copse as before. Nikita looked back, hoping to find any kind of trail in the hazel, which had clearly looped them right round again.

Neat, even rows of pine marched away into the forest at his back. There was no hazel at all. Nor any marks on the trees.

They had been walking for an hour or more, straight ahead without swerving, watching the progress of the sun through the treetops. They walked in silence, only swatting constantly at the relentless mosquitoes.

The pine grove seemed to go on forever, as far as the eye could see. Multi-hued lichens hung like rags from the dead lower branches. A thick carpet of pine needles, springy beneath their feet, muffled all sound. The sparse, exurban woods had become very different indeed – a dark, ominous forest, brimming with strange noises. Something enveloping creaked and moaned, hooted derisively in the manner of an owl. Nikita would not have been surprised to come upon Baba Yaga's fairy-tale hut on chicken legs.

But they came upon something else.

First, there was only a shadow that flitted briefly across a mossy piece of deadwood up ahead. Nikita squinted at it but couldn't see anything out of the ordinary. A bird, or a squirrel, he thought, but almost immediately caught a new movement, to the right this time, and closer. Again, nothing there, except for pines and sickly raspberry cane. Nikita sometimes had this after a very heavy bout of drinking: subtle motion on the periphery of his vision, vague shapes, skittish shadows just out of view. The first signs he was about to be away with the devils.

But Katya too seemed to notice something. She stopped and crouched low like a hunter spotting its prey, signaling Nikita to stay silent. A moment later the same shapeless shadow flickered and disappeared. And again. Each time it seemed to come closer, yet was impossible to really see. Show yourself, Nikita raged inwardly, anyone can scare people like that, but why don't you show yourself, so we know if you're scary or not.

A tall narrow mound shot up from under the earth exactly on the spot where Nikita had been looking. Like a mushroom on sped-up film. It grew instantly to the height of a man, and then just as swiftly plunged back down, dislodging the dry pine needles.

In a state of shock, it took Nikita a moment to look at Katya. She was hurriedly pulling off her nightie. He even spotted a triangular birthmark on her left buttock.

The mound appeared again, no more than sixty feet from them, and this time it was taller and stayed longer. Long enough to see what it was made of: earth webbed round with roots, twigs and dead leaves caught up in the webbing, and something sickeningly like muscle spasms rippling up and down the earthen mass. The mound swayed its upper part unhurriedly, snakelike.

Something hit Nikita in the face.

"Inside out!" It was Katya, shaking and slapping him hard. "Pavlov! Turn your clothes inside out!"

She was wearing the nightie again, but with the seams facing out. Nikita had a way of sometimes spacing out, in extremis, to think of really random things, and now he regretted, vaguely, not having seen the entire undressing and dressing act.

"Turn it inside out!" Katya was screaming at him. As he stayed still and stupefied, she had to tear the t-shirt off over his head and tug it back on again. When it came to his trousers, though, he clutched them like an Eastern maiden with her veils and wouldn't let go.

The earthen pillar materialized right in front of them and towered to the pine tops. Needles and twigs hailed down on them like barbs. Nikita tried desperately to spot something, anything, remotely humanlike or even animal-like in the colossus, but there was nothing at all to cling to. Just a gigantic rippling pillar of earth, roots, and leaves, an incarnation of faceless horror. When it reached quite unimaginable proportions, the pillar began to fold, as though... yes, it was bending toward them.

"No ill, but good, master of the wood," Katya sang out brightly, as though reciting the Pioneers' oath of their childhood. "Who here holds sway, from us sinners turn away..."

Nikita couldn't tear his gaze away from the earthen giant who, bent double, seemed to be examining them. No matter how he tried to glean a face in the root-bound dark mass, it didn't work. Even a hint of features – the most monstrous of all that could exist – would have been a relief, because the scrutiny of those missing eyes was agonizing. But now here

was something, starting to coalesce from the packed earth...
something like the crack of a mouth and the hollows of empty
eye sockets...

Then it stepped over them, showering down heaps of
rubbish. It carried itself, like a giant caterpillar to the place
Nikita had almost seen its head... and buckled to the ground
in a heap of dry dust, sinking back into the forest floor.

Katya drove hard into his spine: "Run! Don't look back!"

They ran for it, coughing and stumbling, their eyes and
nostrils filled with dust. They couldn't see whither they ran,
through the ruddy-green haze that filled the world.

Although she managed by some miracle to avoid most of the
tussocks and big pieces of deadwood, Katya finally tripped
over something and crashed to the ground. She skinned her
palms and knees, pain blooming like fire. Sitting up, she
coughed and spluttered and squinted, and then saw through
the teary blurring of her eyes a strip of plastic, cut from
a supermarket bag and tied to a branch overhead, waving
triumphant as a flag. It wasn't long since she'd started
marking trails with plastic, and only because she'd run out
of old rags.

They were, once again, on the track that led to the perimeter
fence.

Katya lay on her back and shut her eyes. Nikita collapsed
beside her wheezily, chest heaving.

"You saw?" she asked, when she had recovered her breath.

"Yeah... what was that?"

"The leshy."

She said it so calmly and coolly that he knew at once she
wasn't joking.

He dredged his memories of kids' books and movies: sly
but on the whole benign oldsters with mossy beards and
mushroom caps. Old man of the forest, even a walking tree

with eyes, OK, or a sort of unfinished Pinocchio – anything at all, but not a sky-high root-bound pillar of earth, no way.

And then a swathe of absurd gypsy-bright flowers bloomed atop his rememberings and drooped, like a funeral garland over an ancient nylon raincoat. Granny Nadya. He hadn't just cursed her out that time, by the gate. He had told her to go to the devil... No. To the leshy...

It was exceedingly strange, feeling instantly guilty without quite yet believing it could be true. Nikita jerked upward. Immediately Katya's fingers locked on his elbow.

"Where are you going?"

"Granny Nadya... It was me... I told the leshy to take her..."

"Good job," Katya grimaced. "It's not Baba Nadya anymore, though."

"But we have to help! What if she's still in there, inside? The real one!"

"You can't help her. And you won't find her."

Nikita wrenched his elbow from her grip:

"How do you know that?"

"I just do."

Katya had a bad crick in her neck. She made to get up, but he loomed over her, keeping her on the ground.:

"Tell me everything."

"Later. When we're out of the woods."

Again she was trying to change the subject, to sidestep without really explaining. Slippery she was, like a fish – probably why she liked them so much. Looking at Nikita fixedly, and even a little warily, she tried to get up but he pressed her shoulders to the ground.

"Are you kidding me? This isn't the place, we need to get out of here!"

Then he put his hand across her throat, carefully but with intent. He even squeezed gently, feeling the cartilage of her esophagus and the frightened beat of her heart under his palm. Her skin was dry and unusually hot.

"Explain."

"What's the point? You won't believe me."

He pressed harder on her hot, fragile windpipe. Then she finally gave in and told him, in a brisk and haphazard way, about her theory. A few minutes of hoarse, hurried explanation was all it took: she told him that since the village shut in on itself, others had come to live there, others she called "neighbors". They were now living all around the humans, and it was likely them that ensorcelled the dacha cooperative, using the well-known fairy-tale formula for the place "whereto no road leads". Naturally there was no road leading *out from* such a place either. The dachniks were turning into other things, not all of them, just some. Maybe these were the ones somehow kin with the "neighbors", or just random subjects of experimentation, like with the changelings. Zinaida Ivanovna and Tamara Yakovlevna, for instance, were witches – the one an herbal witch and the other an animal witch. And stop looking at me like that, it's just what it's called. Kozhebatkin was probably a changeling – an auf – too, only very inexperienced, he'd only swapped bodies instead of transforming. Those who lived in the village now, they were also clumsy at the beginning. But they were learning. That's why they took people, to study them. And they sent changelings for the same purpose, to listen and learn. There was almost sure to be two or three of them in the village now, the ones best at it, that seemed the most like people. The "neighbors" always did it that way, they were curious creatures, and humans were just as unfathomable and alien to them as the other way around. They were just on the other side.

Look at Vityok, when he came back from the woods, he wasn't himself, but a copy. That's why he behaved so strangely, and couldn't stop eating. That was how you knew an auf, it's always hungry. The auf-Vityok didn't like it among people – who could blame it, being trussed up under his loving wife's watchful eye – and wanted to go back to the forest, but she wouldn't let him. So he howled, like a mournful dog. Or maybe he was signaling to the ones in the woods. The deathly doldrums it put the villagers into was probably just a side effect. He listened to the radio because that was how the "neighbors" could sometimes manage to communicate, via the dead and useless radios and TVs. They were getting better at that too. They didn't seem to be able to speak to humans in a direct way, but they called Katya on her cell. They kept her from harm, with that phone call, if you thought about it. You could learn to live with them, Katya reckoned, they weren't that dangerous if you strictly observed the rules. Many of the rules were there in old folktales, you just had to figure out which worked, and the only way to do that was by trial and error. That's what she had been doing in secret all that time, experimenting, studying the new villagers the way they studied the humans.

"Wait," interrupted Nikita. "Can you tell me at least who or what they are? These new neighbors, do they have a species name or something?"

"Sure. Leshy the forest master, domovoy the house spirit. Vodyanoy the water spirit. Mermaids, sirens, kikimoras, vengeful igoshas, devilish mummers…"

"Baba Yaga, Koschei the Deathless, right?"

"No, that's a different story altogether. See? I knew you wouldn't believe me."

Nikita looked at her with genuine compassion.

"How in the world did you come up with all that?"

"I studied folklore at uni," she said quickly. "Believe me, I didn't conceive of anything like this to begin with. But then it was one strange coincidence after another… They're not really like what we get in fairy tales. But they behave the same. And the whole thing with the charms and spells, it works, you've seen it work! We turned our clothes inside out and he left us alone, the leshy, he didn't harm us! That was him looping us around, off the path. Just like in folk tales. You saw it with your own eyes!"

"Actually, I feel like you're trying to shunt something else into this whole scheme, something extremely... strange. That thing did not look like a leshy. Sorry, but it didn't!"

"Oh, so you've seen lots of leshys before? And just so you know, if we don't get out of here, that thing is going to come back for us."

In the time it took them to get back to the fence the sun had hidden away, and evening settled in, shrouded in an uncharacteristic creeping mist. Nikita walked muttering to himself irritably that an invasion of genetically mutated leshys and mermaids was really the least plausible explanation for what was happening to the village. Katya, keeping a beady eye on her ribbons and arrows among the mist, objected that they were not mutated at all, they'd always been that way. When people passed the stories orally down generations, of course anything unusual would eventually end up as the classic "beast of three heads, with fiery tail aloft" or some such hackneyed thing. He couldn't argue with Katya's theory as a whole – he had, after all, seen what he had seen – but he was sure she'd drawn the wrong conclusions. The domovoys who suffocated the unwary by night, in rural tall tales, did not call anyone on their cell, and besides, the suffocation described had long been unmasked as classic sleep paralysis. Mermaids and vodyanoys did not shelter people underwater in exchange for a drink of blood. That went against both traditional folklore and common sense. They were better off harking back to traditional extraterrestrials, evil scientists from underground research labs, or just plain simple monsters from the dark...

It was suddenly dark. They walked straight into it, that dark: a moment ago it had been day, never mind how gloomy and misty, but now it was as though someone flipped a switch, the mist vanished and the light went off entirely. They were walking through a clear, windless summer night. Ahead of them was the contour of the perimeter fence, lit up by the streetlamps on the other side. The air cooled as instantly, with a frosty swell from above.

Nikita turned to look behind him. The forest was pitch-black, nocturnal.

"So he wandered in the woods, that peasant, round and round, hither and back, and when he found his way home at last, then they all told him: "Three full years you've been gone, man, your mother is dead, your wife to another wed...""

Katya's unctuous, sing-song delivery was making the back of his neck spasm again.

"Haven't you read any fairy tales at all?"

"How long were we in the woods, then?" Nikita said, alarmed and picturing a silver-bearded Pashka.

"We're about to find out."

They had ended up exactly where they'd started, on the other side of Katya's back gate. This time it was locked, but Katya quickly found a couple of planks hanging by a single nail and moved them aside. She crawled through, then bent over something by the foot of the fence.

"Light, please."

He shone the flashlight on a thick, meaty stem with rough-skinned leaves.

"My control sunflower," Katya explained. "Every time I get back, I can check how much it's grown. We're OK, we only got spun for a couple of days."

"What if you get spun for a couple of years, though? How would you tell from the sunflower?"

"You wouldn't have a sunflower then. Or you'd have a field of them. Anyway, I've made some markings in the apple trees too."

Despite his strenuous objections, Katya was determined to visit her plot – to change her clothes, first and foremost, and also to see what was in the shed. She hadn't looked inside it for weeks, she said. Nikita tried to lead her away, back to the derelict dacha, and threatened her with Usov who was still prowling around, off his rocker. But she was completely uninterested in his objections, and in him generally, it seemed. She tiptoed inside her dacha and returned properly dressed and smelling of iodine; she'd treated and taped up her wounds. Nikita was dreading her jangling the house keys, or turning the lights on unthinkingly, but she didn't.

The shed still smelled like an abattoir. The human remains were gone, but there were bloody smears on the walls and floor, and bits of bloodstained cloth. Katya swung her flashlight around, then paused the beam at a pile of old planks heaped in one corner, a tarpaulin underneath.

"This wasn't here before," she whispered.

They dragged the planks to another corner, where according to Katya they had originally been stacked, pulled up the tarpaulin and... saw a great big hole in the earthen floor. The way it exhaled cold and damp at them, this was clearly not just a hole, but a proper tunnel.

"That's how it got in!" Katya cried triumphantly, diving into the opening. She got most of the way in, only her feet kicking above the ground, but then came her muffled voice from the bowels of the earth:

"I'm stuck."

Nikita pulled her out by the legs. After spitting out and shaking off a deal of earth, Katya said she knew where the tunnel led, and Nikita snarked that he didn't need to mole underground to know where it led. The location itself, by the wall nearest to the fence, left no doubt that the tunnel could only lead to the Beroevs' plot.

"That's why it stayed locked from the other side. Those bastards tunneled in here with all the bones and stuff." Katya spat on the floor. "I told you, it was just so human, to frame somebody..."

"So the beast... you think it's one of them?"

She shrugged:

"When was the last time you saw any of them?"

Nikita had to think about that. It was a while, actually, since anyone had seen them about, not even Sveta promenading her boys according to the route inscribed in stone. But they had always kept to themselves, that family, they had no particular friends, so nobody noticed.

"You see. I tried to go and see them a couple of times. Just to check on them. Maybe they got spooked and, so… you know."

"I don't know anything of the kind," he snapped. "First it's leshys and kikimoras with you, and now it's some kind of conspiracy."

"Did I ever say there was a simple explanation? Are you coming or not?"

"Where are we going?"

"To visit the neighbors."

There was a tall old pear tree on the edge of Katya's plot, that had long passed its fruitful phase and only occasionally brought forth hard green fruitlets that barely resembled pears at all. It was never cut down though, for sentimental reasons: it had been here for ever so long, it still gave shade, it was a living thing after all. Now there was the additional benefit of thick branches overhanging the high fence that girdled the Beroevs' holdings. That was how Katya had attempted to breach their borders, or at least to get a look of what was happening beyond the fence. Each time, however, Sveta Beroeva appeared out of nowhere, forcing Katya to climb hurriedly down, to avoid an unpleasant exchange.

With much breaking of brittle old branches and skinning of palms, the two of them gained the top of the fence and clumped down to the overgrown grass on the other side. They were both scratched-up and sweaty. The Beroevs had dotted every smooth, tiled white path with solar-powered lanterns, chains of softly glowing orbs that garlanded the plot like

Christmas lights. In the eye of the serene lightshow, the huge house watched them blackly from its opaque windows. A real citadel, thought Nikita, looking at the house, you couldn't find a better lair. It's probably eaten the lot of them, just to make a base at that house. And Sveta... well, she was probably the beast, wasn't she. Just the part for the model wife and mother who'd hacked an old man to death with a garden hoe...

Slowly, avoiding the well-lit spots, they circled around the house, but there seemed nothing amiss. The windows were barred, and the front door locked, as Katya discovered when she risked tiptoeing onto the porch to tug at the handle. Nikita was getting more and more excited. This had turned into a proper quest, the "get inside the haunted mansion" kind, and he wanted to get through it, no matter the real and imagined dangers. Being a thirty year-old loser, he had lots of game quest experience, and so he knew that each level was sure to have some kind of hidden entry point...

There it was, the cellar door. The Beroevs clearly had good underground storage, and in a house this size they weren't pushed for space – instead of the usual hatch in the floor, not terribly convenient for going down with provisions in hand, they could also afford a sloping entry from the outside, with a wide-opening pair of doors that were currently twined shut with wire.

Whoever knotted that wire had meant business, but working together, four-handed, they managed to unravel it. Carefully, so as not to plummet straight in, they opened the cellar doors. Katya stumbled back from the familiar coagulated stench of the abattoir, so it was Nikita who, still moved by his questing ardor, went first into the darkness.

The flashlight's beam picked out shelves laden with oddments and tools, jars of picklings, sacks of potatoes; no matter that Sveta made so much of her English lawn and her European-style villa, the cellar was extremely commonplace, like you'd find underneath any old dacha.

They caught a glimpse of the stairs leading up to the floor hatch. And then something fumbled in the pitch black and emitted an excruciating groan, somehow both hoarse and clammy. The shaky beam jolted toward the sound and Katya shrieked, and hid behind Nikita.

A half-eaten, emaciated creature – not much more than a skeleton – was crawling toward them. Its bones clicked on the floor. Ruddy, ragged strips of flesh hung from some of the bones. In places there were larger patches of flesh with skin still on, that shook with the motion. This nearly devoured thing, that was by some insane chance still able to move, moaned and sputtered, staring at them with its single lidless eye.

Much of the skin and muscle of its face had been flayed, but Nikita recognized him by the coarse black hair at the top of his head, and his square jaw. It was Beroev. The former successful businessman and reputed crime boss came nearer and nearer, upsetting the jars from the shelves and clicking his evermore bared teeth.

"It's captive, right?" Katya gasped, looking at Nikita hopefully, as though he was about to give her a clue. "A captive corpse?"

"How should I know?" And Nikita snatched a shovel from where it had been set to lean on the wall. "Move aside, will you?"

"Wait, you'll make it worse! What are you supposed to do with captive corpses? I can't remember anything about them..."

"Move aside, I told you already!"

Katya crouched down, gathered a heap of rubbish from the floor – pebbles, sand, dry leaves – and flung them away violently:

"Gather all the seed sown wide, if you wish to come inside!"

Beroev responded to this ridiculous maneuver by turning around and crawling away. He dragged his bones along the floor hither and yon, obediently gathering the leaves and stones, before Nikita's disbelieving eyes.

* * *

Katya shot up the stairs and pushed hard at the hatch door – once, and again – until something fell away from it loudly and the lid could be lifted up. They clambered out into some sort of large, darkened room, slammed shut the hatch and stood on top of it, just in case. The flashlight skittered from the curved legs of a wooden side table to a little rug, then the legendary Beroev grandfather clock, whose chiming could be heard by all their neighbors. The clock was still, its face dusty.

"The door," Katya whispered hotly. "Find the door."

"What about some tea, then?" said a pleasant female voice, and bright lights came on so suddenly that Katya and Nikita were briefly blinded.

Sveta Beroeva stood in the door. She wore a velour tracksuit and bunny slippers. The slender rims of her spectacles glimmered just as intelligently and severely as ever. By her feet were the gigantic leathery coils of some beast. Two beasts.

"You must excuse my house clothes," she said conversationally. "You weren't exactly invited."

"You're... they're... what the..." Nikita was choking on the words and pointing.

"What can a mother do but love her little ones. Such as they might be." Sveta gave the saccharine smile of a new mother, dopey with breast milk and joy, from those baby formula adverts. "I do apologize, really, but the children are very hungry just now..."

Undulating like leeches, the beasts lunged for them. When she saw the spreading maws, round and ringed endlessly with teeth, Katya screamed so loud the glass in the windowpanes jangled.

Then something wholly unexpected happened. A white-hot, blinding flash of light lit up the room. Instantly the air was scorching, there was the smell of burning hair. The beasts went into convulsions, growling pitifully like wounded bear cubs.

Their thick hides bubbled and ulcerated. Sveta began to shriek. The suddenly furnace-like air seared Nikita's eyes and throat, he couldn't breathe. He was past thinking, but then someone grabbed him by the t-shirt and dragged him away...

He only came to his senses once they were at the next crossing, in the rain gutter under the streetlamp where Katya had collapsed with him, after running down the length of the street, exhausted. It was raining now, pouring with rain. Nikita raised his singed face to the falling water and worked his desiccated lips open:

"What was that?"

"Those weren't her children, they were aufs," Katya told him through chattering teeth. "Remember when Narghiz took them to the river and they all vanished? The river ones took the children and sent out those changeling things instead. They couldn't make it work with Narghiz, I guess, maybe she was too different from them or something... I mean, who knows. And the aufs, they're getting back to how they really are. And they're hungry. They need to go back to the river, but you'll never get them away from Sveta. They might not even want to go back, now they've tasted human flesh..."

"Enough," Nikita groaned. "I didn't mean that, I meant the fire..."

"Aufs are always scared of fire... He told me that I'm burning..." Katya put her hands up to her face. "But I don't understand. I don't know, I don't know..."

"Katya, listen..." His eyelids were swollen but he struggled to open his eyes again. "Will you just explain already? Enough is enough... You know everything, don't you? Where they live, what the rules are. How do you know all that? Just don't give me that bullshit about folklore at university again, all right? I will believe you. I'm ready to believe whatever you say."

Katya fell silent, watching a large housefly in the last throes of drowning in the little stream beneath the streetlamp. Then she smiled faintly:

"Do you know the old rhyme about the river and the driftwood? My granny used to tell it, but in her own way, like this."

And Katya recited:

River carries driftwood cargo
From the village in the meadow
Let it float, let it glide
Maybe someone lives inside.

11

THE WOMAN AFLAME

By the time Katya was of an age to be more or less self-aware, there wasn't much left of her paternal grandmother, Granny Serafima. What remained of her spent day after day sitting in front of the television in her bedroom or quietly fussing about the kitchen, polishing jars. Granny loved little Katya, and Katya loved her – and if not her exactly, then the tales she told, stories of times when Katya didn't exist yet, but the world, curiously, already did. She could never get used to Granny's odd, sweet-and-moldering scent though. Katya understood early on that this was the scent of dying. Mom said that it was just old age, old people had a specific smell to them, yet Katya's childish black-and-white world view could not accept this: what difference did it make, when old age and death were the same thing?

But in the photographs from the monochrome past, the sun was blinding white and Granny Serafima was a fairy. A fair maiden of radiance, unmatched by any on-screen beauty. Katya couldn't resist this Serafima, of course: she adored her with every fiber of her unformed, preschool soul, unquestioningly. This adoration extended to the magical village of Stoyanovo, whence came her grandmother and all her tales.

It was perfectly clear, when you saw the photos, what drew her grandfather Yuri, a promising young specialist from town, to a poor girl from a backwater village, one touched in the head besides. Granny's peculiarities were an open family secret, though they rarely showed themselves, and were treated with a kind of respect. Little Katya thought this very natural: after all, a fairy had to be a little not of this world, didn't she?

Her grandfather's parents, on the contrary, had not been best pleased, and not just because of their daughter-in-law's strange ways. The ill fame of Stoyanovo village had reached the town by then: there were rumors that people vanished there, visitors and locals alike, that people died of mysterious causes there, and reported strange things – not just the village drunks, but respectable people like agronomists and schoolteachers of long standing. In that decade of crystalline clarity about how everything in the world worked, when they'd just sent a man into space, these rumors were especially disturbing. The rumors never seemed to die down, only proliferate, some of them scandalous in the extreme. They said that a local sculptor, tasked with a memorial statue of Lenin to be erected in front of the village hall for the anniversary of the Revolution, would get drunk and tell people of Lenin coming to him in his dreams, three times – to beg the sculptor not to take him to Stoyanovo, and hand him over to the locals. Not long after, the statue duly went to Stoyanovo and the sculptor to a psychiatric ward. No wonder, that when they considered their peculiar daughter-in-law, Katya's great-grandparents feared a cauldron of madness in the heart of her village, a madness contagious by some method unknown to science.

They were modern, educated people, of course, and were not scared of any old mumbo-jumbo. The pin Serafima's mother-in-law fastened to the door jamb on the day she arrived was not to ward off witchery, but just because.

Back then, when Granddad Yuri first brought his beloved Serafima from Stoyanovo to town, many people still remembered the story of how the Germans went to take the village but never got there.

This was in winter. A small German troop – a scouting party perhaps, or just some soldiers that had become separated from their division – went searching, for some strange foreign reason, after a village huddled behind its woods and of no conceivable use or interest to anyone. During a blizzard, the soldiers spotted a hunter's refuge in a snow-buried wildness and went to ground there. They found some stores inside, and even warm blankets – as though someone had made ready for welcome guests.

It was an old hunter who found them a few days later, his scent hound looping again and again toward the refuge, to fuss and scratch at the door. Like everyone in Stoyanovo, the old man knew not to go in there – a kikimora had taken it for its lair, or else the bear king – for any reason. He went back to the village and gathered some brave and curious farmwives and young lads. Only then did they try the door, with all due caution.

The Germans were all inside, flung helter-skelter around the floor and on top of the long bench. Their faces were blue, eyes bulging from sockets, and mouths contorted in a deathly rictus so wide it tore the corners. The brave villagers were dumbstruck at this: incredible, that their first encounter with the enemy should make them pity that enemy in their hideous demise. Only one of the Germans survived, a young lad, fair-haired and with a pug nose like a small potato. He crawled out from underneath the bodies and set to bawling. The village women began to wail too, from the sheer sight of him. They all had sons at the front, or husbands, and no matter that the Fascist fiend had come to kill them, they pitied the boy fiercely, they couldn't help it. So instead of giving him up, they hid the nameless Fritz and tried to make him well with herbal medicines. He died a few days later, though. He couldn't sleep at all, just sat up all night pointing into the dark corners and screaming the walls down in his own language.

Later, they put it out that the heroic partisans annihilated the German troop as it tried to gain the village, though everyone knew there were never any partisans in the Stoyanovo woods.

Serafima, the future fairy, was born right at the end of the war. And although her father was one of those who had made it back from the front, she never knew him. He was missing a leg, and one of his cheeks, permanently soot-stained, was all crumpled like someone had chewed it up, but he had come back. Even so, the other wives' envy was unfounded: he was broken, inside. He drank and roared, and went for his little daughter Tanya, and his newly pregnant wife. He would whisper, staring down at his missing leg, that when they operated on him back at the field hospital they'd sewn on the leg of a dead Fritz, and no matter where he went, the Fritz followed him, baring his teeth, his lips and face all scorched, only the eyes and teeth left in his skull, and the eyes were pale as water and insolent.

Every night, the legless man punched the air with his fists and threw whatever happened to be at hand into the warm, close darkness of the wooden house:

"The devil take you, white-eye!"

Only Granddad Dmitry had a way of settling his disorderly son. He would tell him that the Fritz was not too bad, he was harmless, just a kid, and how was he to carry on endlessly following after a soldier of the Red Army. Soon enough he would give up and go away...

But it was Serafima's father who gave up first. He limped to the woodshed one day and chopped off his stump with an axe, the one that dead Fritz had been sewed on to. He severed an artery and bled to death, but he died happy, with a smile on his face of victory and the end of his suffering. Before he died, he told them again and again that he'd gone, the white-eye was gone for good.

The day after he died, Serafima came into the world prematurely. Her mother, feeling the first pains, had gone quietly to the banya, away from the corpse and all the things to be done about it. There she gave birth, alone, without anyone beside her to watch out for the banya spirit swapping the baby for a changeling.

This didn't sit well with the women. The village crones came to see the baby girl and worry – no telling what might have hitched a ride on the father's gushing blood, with no one there to keep watch. The war was over, but Stoyanovo was half-empty, and half-starved, and largely defenseless against those others who lived in the woods and the river and meadow. The crones spoke of the others, and explained that you couldn't really understand them, only live side by side like good neighbors, provided rules were followed, and these were not rules set by humans. Those they came to call "neighbors" in Stoyanovo village were neither good nor evil, because they had not hearts nor souls. You never knew what they might do.

So they peered in the child's eyes, looking for the bit of flesh that ought to sit in the corners, and pricked her tiny finger with a pin. Granddad Dmitry swung an axe at her, violently – the changelings were scared of this most of all and would immediately turn back into a log or a broom at the sight of it. The baby shrilled thinly, just as she was supposed to, the mother wept and begged to be allowed to feed her, and even the usually taciturn Tanya joined in with the crying. When they couldn't find any alarming signs, they christened the child Serafima, so that the angels heard their name in hers and came when called, and everyone calmed down.

At that time there was a large meadow between the village and the river. They sowed it with wheat, which helped Stoyanovo to survive the hungriest years. In drought and in wartime – when there were only the women and kids to plow and reap – and in unlucky leap years, and through seasons of hail and freeze, still the meadow gave a harvest. It was said there was a special reason for this, and it was better for regular people not to know the reason. There was a decree to do with the meadow, too: no one was to be there at the stroke of noon. Whether you managed to finish your work or no, come midday you had to leave without a backward glance, come again when the sun left zenith. Children were forbidden to go in the meadow at all, warned off with the ancient but potent tale of little Makar and little Nazar who went to play in the meadow at midday and vanished without a trace. Neither hair nor hide of them ever found, just a small heap of ashes, dispersed on the wind.

Only Serafima, aged ten and scared of nothing, did not believe in fairy tales. She made a secret nest for herself in the wheatfield, where she went to hide from her mother and sister, from her many chores and from Granddad, who was dying for two years already behind his dividing curtain, and cursed and smelled bad. Here was where Serafima kept her treasures stashed under a rock: ribbons, sweet wrappers, an adder stone, and her most precious possession, a broken compact mirror – her older sister's – in a pretty frame. Tanya had dropped it accidentally, and their mother told Serafima to take it away and bury it. The girl took it away, but kept it for her own instead; what a shame it would have been to bury such a pretty thing underground. You could see yourself it in, never mind that it was cracked, or make light bunnies, or tell fortunes during the feast day of Epiphany, like the grown-ups did.

Serafima's hide was all the way across the meadow, near the river where it was cooler. The river was where she went at noon, when the sun began to really scorch your head. She was too scared to break the rule that everyone knew about, but curiosity burned inside her like the sun, too. What in the world was going on in the midday meadow, when even her stern sister who did not believe in God or the devil, when the village headman himself, didn't dare show their faces there?

And then, one day Serafima found herself still in the meadow at the forbidden hour. Maybe her curiosity was to blame, or she just forgot the time, playing. A gust of strange, hot wind blew in from nowhere, skimming abruptly over the wheat and bending it low – and she knew at once that it was too late to run. There was not a stir anywhere else, even the sensitive willows by the river stood immobile on the bank.

Serafima shot to her feet, thinking to hide in a willow copse, but then she saw something that made her drop immediately down again and creep back into her nest, low as the bending wheat. She had seen a tall figure floating high above the meadow in a white-hot, dazzlingly bright dress that billowed over the wheat like a great bell. Where a person would have arms and legs, instead there flared out blinding rays of light. The brightest of these poured from where the face ought to have been. The figure floated above the swaying wheat and swiveled its head from side to side, like a search beam. Serafima had seen a movie about the war once, where they had searchlights just like this, sweeping the sky for Fascist bombers.

The figure radiated a sere, dry heat so intense the girl could feel its scorching breath from afar. She was scared of course, very scared – but also horribly curious. This was happening in broad daylight, after all. Had she met with such a blazing scarecrow by night, Serafima would have run as fast as her legs could carry, but now her curiosity burned her up from inside, and spurred her to have a closer look at the flying thing first, then run. So she crouched low and, shivering with fright, aimed her cracked mirror at the mysterious effigy.

She saw, in the mirror, a thing aflame with bleached fire. Tall as a tree, it floated in the air, turning her head this way and that, sweeping its arms above the meadow and setting a ripple of searing wind across the wheat with the slightest movement. Even reflected in the mirror, the light was so bright and blistering that Serafima had to shut her eyes, her nasal passage thick with tears. And then...

The white-hot beam that glared from beneath the blazing figure's cowl struck Serafima's mirror and shot back into its face. Finally, Serafima saw that face clearly in her little mirror: noseless, white-eyed, with a long crack going ear-to-ear – if you could imagine ears beneath the cowl – for a mouth. It was a woman's face, like that of a corpse left too long in the scorching sun. The woman seemed momentarily blinded by her own reflected light, and scalded; she gave a piercing scream and pressed her hand over her face. A suffocating blast of heat poured into the meadow. Serafima threw herself face down onto the ground. The air was sizzling, things were beginning to crackle and burn. The long, affronted cry that was more like a bird's call than a human scream carried on tolling in the girl's ears. Serafima smelled burning hair and wondered, in horror, whether she was burning up... Time passed. She felt easier, and the air seemed to cool again. She finally dared raise her head and inhale deeply. There was no one in the meadow, nor in the sky either, just the wheat roiling and swaying still.

She came home covered in burn blisters, with hair singed to curly frizz. Granddad Dimitry almost fell off the bed, seeing her. She wept, and when the salty tears ran down her blistered face, stinging it, she howled. She told them how there was a woman aflame flying up and down over the meadow, who had nearly burned her alive. But instead of comforting her, Granddad shouted down the house, threw a glass at her and cussed her out in such language that the little girl hid in the furthest corner and cried her eyes out from pain and sorrow.

Finally her mother came home, but before Serafima could run to her for comfort, her grandfather snarled:

"Your little fool offended Poludnitsa! Run, make amends!"

Her mother froze at the threshold, stupefied. All her life she had lived, like everyone in Stoyanovo, both believing and not believing in their strange neighbors. More than anything in the world, she feared one day having to cross that boundary of belief, in either direction. But Granddad raged on and on, and Serafima – who was covered in real, inarguable blisters – confirmed everything, so her mother made haste to gather up the items Granddad told her were needful into a cloth bundle: a heel of bread, some eggs, a pile of salt...

Just as her mother rushed off to the meadow with gifts, her older sister arrived. After Tanya heard the whole story, it was her turn to scream at Granddad: didn't he have anything better to do than rag everyone with his superstitions, and hadn't he heard that superstition was forbidden by everyone nowadays, from the Party to the Church. She calmed Serafima down, sluicing her with icy water and smearing her burns with egg yolk. The blisters weren't too bad, but her eyebrows were completely singed. It was only the village lads, those devils, teasing a little girl, mumming around in sheets, flicking sun bunnies in her eyes, even tossing burning kindling at her for good measure, Tanya soothed. And Serafima, though the memory was still vivid, felt better for Tanya's words. Didn't the village louts almost drive their neighbor round the bend just the previous year? They'd rigged a whole system of ropes and pulleys to the scarecrow behind her house and put on a show of the scarecrow coming alive by night. They even flickered lights back there, so the old lady almost had a heart attack from fright. Later, she chased them up and down the village with an iron oven fork. Granddad started up again, behind his curtain: damn right she chased them round, the fools, putting up scarecrows and idols, for all manner of things that have no flesh of their own to come and take up. They could have done far worse than just scare the old lady with their pulleys, she was lucky to get off that lightly. Do not make idols, they were told, and wasn't that just what they made. Look at the Lenin they put up in front of the village soviet, the powers that be, no matter how many times they were warned not to do it, lest someone come to live inside that statue. White and swollen-headed it was, the Lenin, like something drowned. And since then, it's been no kind of a life in Stoyanovo, because how could people live like this? He wandered around nights, the Lenin, all white and horrible. Granddad Dmitry couldn't sleep most nights, and so he'd seen the idol from the window a few times, and heard him stomping about, thump, thump, thump.

They gave him some strong drink and he quietened. Serafima they laid out on the long house bench, on her stomach, as her back was covered in blisters. She listened to her wise, grown-up sister talk and began to suppose that no, there was no woman aflame at all, just the usual village layabouts, standing on each other's shoulders in a white sheet, and pelting her with burning twigs. Everything else she just made up, from fright.

In the morning they checked on the offering their mother had left in the wheat, but it was untouched save for a few mousey bite marks on the wrapping cloth. Either she wasn't real, Poludnitsa – known too as Lady Midday, the Noonday Witch, the keeper of the grain – or she disdained their gifts. Granddad ordered Serafima and the others to keep silent and never tell anyone what had happened, or everyone would know at once how the harvest was spoiled and by whom. He had no doubt at all that the harvest would fail that year: he had always been convinced that the reason the meadow prospered was because it was her haunt, Poludnitsa's, and so she kept an eye on the weather and the wheat. Serafima was forbidden to set a foot near the meadow, not that anything in the world could have made her go there now. She would stay indoors at home forever if she could, blistered and browless, a scarecrow. The burns healed quickly though.

"Quick to heal, like a dog," Granddad would say, looking at his former favorite like he wanted to hit her.

Life carried on, and they lived day by day, like everyone else. Except Serafima had bad, terrifying dreams: the woman aflame came to her and bent over her, blowing dry heat. She could see the woman's eyes, white and scorched, run with molten tears that congealed over her cheeks like candle wax. She had wronged her, Serafima, wronged the creature named Poludnitsa... blinded her with her own blaze, and the creature's grievance was oppressive like noonday heatstroke. Serafima tossed and turned, screamed in her sleep and woke sodden with sweat. And then Tanya would croon to her, half-asleep, and comfort her, and make it seem somehow that it was Serafima wronged, and frightened, and only let Tanya find out who these jokers were, she would make them sorry they were born, and report them to the police for good measure.

Later still, the banya hut burned to the ground. More than burned: they came out one morning to find only a heap of embers and ash in its place. There had been no fire, no smoke, no smell. The neighbors had seen nothing, either, so at first suspicion fell on them, as they were in the middle of a years-long quarrel about possession of the very patch on which the banya had stood. It must have been the neighbors, or else a chance bolt of lightning from the storm they heard brewing in the night, though it never broke. Granddad started in on Serafima again, so Tanya led her away, without a word, into the woods, blueberry picking. Raspberries and other red berries were forbidden to the villagers, pledged to the master of the Stoyanovo woods. For especially curious outsiders, it went that raspberries and strawberries pulled up poison from the soil through their roots.

Then something worse than the banya. Their mother burst in early one morning, in tears, and cried: "Night's a-charred all away!"

They thought she'd lost it, at first. But then she pulled them by their hands from the house, still keening, and led them to the barn.

Where their milk cow Nighty would have lain atop the hay, there was a heap of ashes. A heap that had kept the bovine shape in all its particulars, from the barrel-like body with its bony rump and the head, turned sideways, to the tail – it looked to be carved from gray ash as though it were marble. Tanya, who knew everything, who solved puzzles like it was nothing, kneeled down by the cow, stupefied, and poked it in the flank with one finger. A big piece of ash sheared away and crumbled into fine, weightless particles. She hadn't burned, Nighty – indeed how could she have, when the shed stood intact around her, and even the hay beneath her was untouched – she had smoldered like a wet log in the fire stack, the kind that keeps its shape even as it's scorched from the inside.

Their mother wept on. Serafima wasn't thinking about the loss of the milk or their gentle Nighty. Lady Midday had come and seared the cow to ashes with her fiery breath. Even Tanya couldn't explain it away. It was her, Poludnitsa, who had burned the banya too. She was circling, getting closer, looking for revenge. There was no hiding from her white blaze, and nowhere to run.

"Go to the meadow and beg forgiveness," Granddad Dmitry told her. "Go, before your foolishness is the end of us all."

Serafima kept seeing the meadow in her nightmares. Now she remembered it awake, saw in her mind's eye the wheat roiling in the burning air and the tree-sized, white figure overhead. She was hysterical; they had to throw water over her in the end.

A few more days passed. The house was as still and gloomy as though someone had died. Serafima spooked at everything: Granddad, noises outside, the white birches that each looked to her like the blazing-white woman, the pillars of dust the wind whipped up on the dirt road. As luck would have it, the weather stayed scorching, thick like smelted iron, sleep-inducing, but Serafima wouldn't sleep, not while the inhuman face that cried molten tears awaited her there. Every now and then, exhausted, she'd sink into an hour or two of dreamless sleep; either she had nothing left to dream with, or she just didn't remember what she saw anymore.

She tried it a few times: went past the gate and down the path to the wheaten meadow, and made herself walk it, eyes to the ground, against every instinct. Fear would overcome, close up her throat, steal her breath – and she'd turn on her heel and run, run back to the village.

Granddad was telling the truth about her foolishness being the death of them all. A week passed like this, in silent horror, then Tanya fell ill. She woke up one morning in a sweat, complaining first of a headache and assorted pains, but as the day went on, she could barely speak. The cold compresses over her face had to be changed every few minutes, warming up so rapidly it was as though they were being dipped in boiling water. She lay panting hoarsely, her eyes sunken and lips parched and chapped. Serafima knew it even without Granddad's accusing growling from behind his curtain: Tanya was burning up from the inside, with the searing fire, paying for her little sister's folly. She wanted to run to the meadow again, to beg forgiveness, but each time Tanya caught her by the hand and held her back. Tanya's fingers were dry and hot. She muttered, barely moving her eyelashes: "Don't you dare... Granddad's old fairy tales... not I'm in the Communist Youth! Don't you dare..."

"You think your Lenin is going to save you?" Granddad raged from his nest of raggedy blankets. "He's too busy wandering the streets, all white, with holes for eyes!"

Serafima put her fingers in her ears, to escape the delirious torrent from both sides. They were sick, the pair of them, and they smelled sick and all wrong. But where could she go, what could she do to help them? Serafima didn't know. Her mother went to get Granny Lyuba, the village whispering-woman, known in Stoyanovo as a healer and doer of all sorts – they actually called it "all sorts" without ever going into particulars. The village never had anything like a doctor, and Tanya herself, whenever she came to, insisted that it was only a chill from drinking icy water, that she was getting better and no need for that old charlatan or any of her ilk, they'll just cost money and be useless.

Time went on, their mother did not return, and Granddad's cantankerous snores boomed crossly from his corner behind the curtain. Sitting by her sister's bedside, a lonely fly buzzing by the window, the younger girl began to doze. Suddenly, Tanya's fingers tightened around Serafima's wrist. Serafima jolted awake and looked at her sister. Tanya looked back at her. Her eyes blazed white; a pale fire smoldered beneath her skin and capillaries, glimmering like smokeless heat over coals. Tanya's fingers around her wrist began to burn through the skin, but her sister held Serafima tight, and wouldn't let her unclench the searing clamp.

Tanya opened her mouth slightly and produced the sound of grinding metal from somewhere deep in her chest.

"Granddad!" shrieked Serafima.

The grinding was forming into words. It was not Tanya's voice, or a voice that any human being might have, or ought to have.

"The thumb alone... will be mine..." said the thing that was lodged in Tanya's breast. "You will give... it... to me... The thumb alone... will be... mine."

Screaming like it was her suffocating from white flame and not her sister, Serafima broke Tanya's grip and hurtled outside. Then she raced, tripping, skinning hands and knees, to the meadow.

After the long heatwave, a storm was finally creeping over Stoyanovo village. Gloomy clouds hung swollen in the sky, flickering – like Lady Midday's eyes – with silent, unspent lightning. Wind ruffled the willows by the riverbank. Serafima, barely able to see for the hair whipping about her face, scrambled into the wheat and dropped onto her bloody knees. She covered her face with her hands and pleaded, choking back her tears:

"Poludnitsa, I beg your pardon, if you really are real, it was an accident, my word as a pioneer, honestly, just leave Tanya alone. Lady Midday, Noonday Witch, special creature, forgive me, you can have whatever you want, only don't be angry and pardon me..."

A white-hot spear, like a bolt of lightning, struck very near, with a crashing roar so loud it rattled every bone in Serafima's body. Her head swam and she pitched over into the stormy darkness...

When she opened her eyes again, the rain was in earnest, hammering both her and the wheat into the ground. The voice of Poludnitsa, woman aflame, still thundered in her throbbing head:

"The thumb alone will be mine!"

She wondered, as she plodded home under the rain, which thumb Poludnitsa had meant, the left or the right. By the time she walked into the yard she decided on the left. The right would be harder to manage, and anyway, all evil, sinister things took the left, didn't they? You spat over your left shoulder to quell the devil sitting there. That terrible creature would surely find the left more to her liking.

No one saw Serafima return from the meadow in the pouring rain, or walk into the woodshed where her dad had bled his life out ten years before. She placed her left hand on the chopping block, thumb carefully splayed, shut her eyes and brought down the axe, the same one Dad had used to get rid of the dead Fritz. She was plucky, that Serafima, no one could say otherwise...

And in the house, the big woman with the handsome gypsy face – Granny Lyuba, the whisperer – busied herself about her patient. She tried to pour an herbal brew inside Tanya, but the girl resisted and spat it out. She was pale and blotched crimson, one eye swollen as good as shut, but she was alive. Tanya was alive. Their mother wept and kissed her, but stern-faced Tanya turned her nose up at the brew all the more. Find Serafima, she told them imperiously, did the earth swallow up that kid or something, and mind how it was getting dark.

Just then the door creaked open and they saw Serafima on the threshold – sodden, shivering, and silent.

"Simushka, thank God!" Her mother rushed to her, unaware, for the moment, of the way she cradled her hand to her chest, or the blood. "Granny Lyuba's made our Tanya better!"

"Don't know that I did." The old lady shook her head. She moved quickly to Serafima and just managed to catch the child; bony and light as a bird, as she fainted dead away.

That was when Serafima first became "touched in the head" and strange. She might seem normal and speak sensibly, or she might sit and stare into space, not hearing anyone. She could disappear from the house for a whole day and night, without a word of warning, and no telling where the villagers might find her. She saw things, and paced about the house nights, and talked to herself. She told her mother and sister about the little person who was wooly and kind-natured, and lived in their cellar, while the cowshed where Nighty had perished was now the lair of a many-legged beast, who hung from the roof rafters by its claws, waiting in ambush. If it got hold of someone, it would give them bad dreams and drink all their joy away, down to the last drop... One night their mother awoke from a loud whispering, like two voices talking, and the second of these low and hoarse, like a hard smoker's. She struck a light and saw Serafima sitting in bed, arguing with someone unseen. She waved her mother away: "It's just Granddad. He keeps saying snow tomorrow, he's gone all loopy in his old age."

The next day it did snow, which was strange for the middle of June. Granddad Dmitry had been in his grave nigh on half a year by then.

Tanya, mindful of Serafima's desperate, horrible sacrifice, looked after her more tenderly even than their mother. She argued with the little fool that her visions were nothing but nerves and superstition. Granddad was to blame: he'd filled her head with nonsense, ruined her life... This was usually where Tanya started to cry. But never mind, science was so advanced nowadays, they could cure any sickness of the heart or mind. When Tanya got into medical school, she would find the best doctors available, for Serafima. And the missing thumb didn't matter at all, not for a beauty like her sister. Tanya gave her a pretty ring with a blue stone set in it and told her to wear it on her left hand so that people saw the beauty and not the flaw, and so they knew that Serafima wasn't embarrassed about it, not in the slightest.

These were the things she said, but then she fell in love and married young, moving to town to be with her husband, producing a baby boy exactly nine months after the wedding, and forgetting all about Serafima. Not really forgetting – she did visit, bearing treats and clothes, and wept with their mother, over a bit of vodka, at Serafima's evil fate. But then she left again. Of course, she did not go to medical school or anything of the sort.

They had all become resigned to Serafima's remaining an old maid, her mother's burden forever, when a young man was sent over from town, and immediately fell hard for the fey village fool. Tanya had been right about one thing at least – Serafima was an unmatched beauty. He was lost, the city boy, the moment he laid eyes on Serafima in the meadow, crowned with a wreath of flowers. And that was how Serafima followed her sister away from the village.

She too started quickly: first a daughter and then a son who, at eighteen months, burned up with scarlet fever. It was strange, but the father seemed to grieve harder than Serafima herself: the relatives whispered among themselves that it was her peasant upbringing, not to mind too much, the Lord giveth and taketh away and all that... Only a few months later she was with child again, her third. Katya's future father.

Soon after that, her husband who was, after all, a promising young specialist, was given the wonderful, almost magical opportunity of a job posting to the big city, not the capital, but close. His parents worried and tried to talk him out of it: how would he manage there all on his own, so young and already weighed down with two young children, not to mention that holy fool, his wife. The thumbless fairy Serafima, on the other hand, straight away set to packing. She packed so quickly they had to spend the last few days in an emptied room among boxes and suitcases.

The ancient rural axiom "nothing like babies for settling her right down" worked on Serafima. Living a comfortable life in a newly built apartment building with her husband and children consoled her and cleared her mind. Occasionally she still muttered oddly and instituted some strange family rituals like salt over the threshold and gifts for the domovoy, but she didn't seem softheaded anymore and didn't wake up screaming from dreams about the woman aflame. In her old age she was not plagued at all, and the stories of Stoyanovo she passed on to her granddaughter Katya, she told in the manner of fairy tales: about One-Eyed Calamity that danced on the hill not for good but for ill, about the pallid creatures that called from the river, and the mean spirit that lived in the banya hut. She even told her about the vengeful Poludnitsa – Lady Midday, the Noonday Witch. Katya listened to Granny Serafima in a kind of holy dread, still and silent, as though she were not sitting over a plate of canteen dinner in their own kitchen, but high up atop the big house stove of a wooden izba, in the traditional way.

No wonder that Katya was drawn to folklore studies at university; and quickly she was so conversant with the lives of esoteric creatures that her instructor sponsored her for a further degree in the subject. She decided to do one better and focus on new folklore, freshly gathered in the field – at Stoyanovo itself – for her first dissertation. She'd never been to her grandmother's native village, but she knew so much about it from the stories that she was sure she could find any of the places with her eyes closed; the house where they raised a changeling instead of a child, the house of the last village wise-woman. Young and silly she was, so sure that she'd befriend the locals in no time, since she knew of them and they of her already. She would flatter them and listen to them, and they would fill her Dictaphone with more material than she'd know what to do with...

It turned out though, that even her own granny she didn't know very well at all. On hearing that Katya was gearing up to travel to Stoyanovo, frail old Granny Serafima dropped the glass jar she was holding and rushed at Katya, heedlessly crunching the shards underfoot, to grab her by the shoulders:

"Don't you dare!"

Katya was so stunned she could only stand there, blinking. She had never seen her quiet, delicate grandmother in such a state. Granny Serafima was staring at her keenly, and with alarm, as though truly seeing her too for the first time. Her fine-featured face – like an icon, they used to say in the family – had blanched and set to stone. Then her pupils went wide, and stilled, as though she had been looking for something in her granddaughter's face and, at last, found it.

"Woman aflame!" she cried, slapping Katya on the face with her thumbless left hand. The ring she still wore, her dead sister's gift, broke Katya's lip open.

"Woman aflame!"

By the time her father ran into the room, Serafima had smashed up half the kitchen. She threw plates against the floor and geranium pots at her granddaughter, who wept and cowered in the corner, Serafima shrieking in a voice not her own, like someone possessed:

"The thumb will be mine! You promised! You lied to me! Woman aflame!"

Katya had to take herself to the emergency room, where they sewed up the torn left corner of her mouth quite neatly. So neatly, in fact, that in time there was no scar or any sign of stitching. Still, Granny's massive ring must have damaged something in there, because whenever Katya tried to smile, the corner crumpled and pointed down.

After her crazy kitchen performance, Serafima lost it for good and was soon diagnosed by the family doctor as suffering from old-age dementia. Again she began to hold conversations with an invisible partner, to spook at nothing. She kept asking them to draw the curtains, because "she" was "looking in." She seemed to hate Katya utterly, and became hysterical should Katya so much as set foot in her room. But eventually she quietened down, she stopped recognizing anyone and lay staring up at the ceiling with blank, watery eyes, sinking further and further into dementia, it seemed.

Naturally, after that, Katya did not pursue her graduate degree or her planned visit to Stoyanovo. She went quiet too, and grew solitary and morose, spending all her time at home. No one noticed it at first, blaming the change on her just being embarrassed to be seen with the scar on her face. She scoured the internet for articles on psychiatry, and these all confirmed her fears: yes, madness could be hereditary, and more often than not it skipped a generation, falling not on the children, but the grandchildren of the afflicted. What were you thinking, Katya castigated her dead grandfather, agreeing to go to that damned village, marrying that schizophrenic...

She had seen it, of that she was sure, when Granny Serafima stared at her so and seemed to find what she was looking for: Katya had seen her grandmother's eyes suddenly blaze with a blinding white flame.

Katya and Nikita sat on the floor of derelict dacha number thirteen. Nikita was pensively nibbling on the tail of a fried fish, as he waited for the conclusion of Katya's strange story, that seemed so much like one of those horrible ancient tales, only dressed up in modern clothes.

"And?" he finally said.

"And that's it."

"But you said that you know..."

"Yes, I know!" She struck the earthen floor with her fist for emphasis. "Now they've come here. The ones my grandmother told me about. I can see them, all of them... All the creatures and things, from Stoyanovo."

"Why did they come? What for? And why now, all of a sudden?"

Katya said nothing. Nikita felt a flush of pity for her – so much to carry on her own, all this knowing to keep secret, and balancing on the edge of believing and not. The edge that was the curse of Stoyanovo. Obviously, if it even existed, Stoyanovo village, and it wasn't just that Katya being a hereditary schizophrenic...

Now that she had told him everything, it was even harder to believe her. Her connection with the other world, where their taciturn "neighbors" grew and multiplied, was too undeniable now. You couldn't just wave the feeling aside, blame it on a moment's fright.

But Nikita hugged her shoulder anyway, awkwardly, in an attempt to make her feel better and less alone. It was just too horrible, the whole story, even if it was all made up. To his surprise, Katya pressed herself against him and dropped her hot, heavy head on his chest.

"I don't know why. I don't know anything anymore and I don't want to know. Why don't we just hide out here? Wait it out. It's got to end sometime..."

12

CLOSE ENCOUNTERS AT DACHA NUMBER THIRTEEN

The scarecrow was ridiculous and faintly amusing, looking for all the world like a moth-eaten career soldier of times gone by, but the sight of it still startled Katya. It wasn't even a proper scarecrow, just an old brown coat on a couple of poles, headless and not very tall. Some old tin cans hung from the bottoms of the poles, the opened lids resembling toothy, serrated, wide-open mouths. The mice and moths had been at it, too, and its skinny, stained torso had rips in it like ulcers.

"What's that for?" Katya was puzzled.

"For a chat," Nikita told her. He shook the scarecrow up and down and looked purposeful.

For ten days now they had been hiding out at derelict dacha number thirteen. Or rather it was Katya, who couldn't go back to the village, who hid there, while Nikita made secret visits. He had brought the scarecrow – an ancient thing from his granddad's time, it had once guarded the strawberry patch – on one of these visits.

Nikita had earnestly tried to convince the dachniks that Katya had nothing to do with the mysterious cannibal-beast, and that the bones in her shed had been planted there. Sure, she was strange, a bit touched in the head even, no one was arguing with that. No, he had no idea where she was, she probably ran off to the forest, didn't she, through that open gate of hers, and vanished there like the others. But anyway, he wasn't talking about her, he wanted to talk about the beasts. There were two of them, not one, and they were the Beroev kids. Except that they weren't those kids at all, but shapeless leathery things, you couldn't make out anything but the huge toothy mouths on them. He saw them himself, barely made it out of there alive. Sveta Beroeva knew it, maybe she was the one feeding them human flesh, since they were always hungry. No, they weren't the real Beroev boys, they were aufs, changelings, swapped... How was he supposed to know who swapped them, and what they did with the real kids?

Nikita roamed about the dacha village with his story like one of those bothersome door-to-door salesmen of junk with a special limited-time offer ending today: he went to visit the chairwoman and looked in on Andrei and Pashka, and the former paramedic Gena too. He was fixing to go and see the widowed Usov – the man was still stalking around with his shotgun and could well come upon dacha number thirteen – but Gena held him back as he was clearly off his nut and might have shot Nikita on sight. His shotgun was loaded – with pellets – as they all discovered when Naima Hassanovna's other goat came around a corner inopportunely. In real dismay, the old ladies sent for Gena to resuscitate the goat but of course nothing came of it and the village was left without milk.

The intensity of Nikita's activity led to another irregular meeting. Not everyone came – many people were still holed up inside for fear of the beast, although there had been no more attacks since Nikita and Katya had paid a visit to the Beroevs. Claudia Il'yinichna opened proceedings by explaining that comrade, meaning, citizen... oh for crying out loud, Nikita Pavlov over there, wished to convey to them some information he deemed important. The chairwoman said the last part in a markedly disapproving tone, as if to make it quite clear she did not share his view on the matter.

Nikita propounded his version of what happened, looking fixedly away from the not so much suspicious as confused faces of the assembled dachniks. He was nervous and kept getting the details wrong: the details didn't matter at all, but seemed important to Nikita, because they surely grounded the whole crazy story and brought it closer in line with reality. Just as he hit his stride, and dared to hope someone believed him, a shriek of fury cut through:

"You absolute shitbag!"

It was Sveta Beroeva. Pale with rage, fists clenched, she strode toward him through the crowd, and seemed to be drawing herself up as though about to leap at him. Startled, the dachniks shot up from their folding chairs and cleared a path for her, making it look as though she was flinging them aside with the wave of her hand. There was nothing, nothing comical at all in the little spectacles flickering with rage, nor in the battle-ready grasshopper body of hers: gripped by the primeval ferocity of a female defending her young, Sveta was genuinely terrifying.

Nikita caught a whiff of some expensive face cream before Sveta punched him in the nose, awkwardly but hard. Things unfroze, shouting resumed, and Sveta clawed at Nikita's face, cackling: "Bastard, bastard, bastard!"

They pulled her away. As he gingerly essayed his throbbing nose, Nikita spotted, with satisfaction, the burn marks on Sveta's pale skin. The burns were healing already: pink and slick, they had been treated with something shiny. Burn cream, that's what she smelled of. So everything that happened at the Beroevs' villa, including the mysterious fire-blaze, was real, and not a figment of his imagination. He'd started to wonder, briefly, so genuine was Sveta's outrage, whether it had maybe been a spell of some kind, like the ones Katya said were sent to fool you.

Held back gently by the former paramedic Gena, Sveta continued to scream at them. She had heard the whole thing, the horrible rumors people were spreading about her and her children, and it was despicable, beyond belief, and she didn't know, didn't want to know how this could even be happening, she had never in her life learned to understand people's perfidy and envy. Why not just say it outright, after all, it was envy pure and simple, although what was there to be envious of, when things were that awful. Her husband missing for two weeks already, he went to look for a way out, and vanished...

"Two weeks?" Nikita reared up indignantly. "Two months more like! Because he was the first one they ate!"

Sveta wrung her hands helplessly and fell to weeping. Someone brought her a drink, while Nikita got hissed. She gulped down some water then went on. Her husband had gone to find a way out because their boys were sick... at that point Nikita shouted that he'd seen just how sick they were with his own eyes... Sveta raised her voice and carried on, in a manner half-choked with grief and desperation: they were gravely ill, and no herbs or medicines seemed to be of any use. So here she was, all alone with her small children to take care of, and her neighbors all against her, so that instead of helping kindness, all she got was a vile slander...

"Why didn't you tell anyone the little ones were sick," chided the tender-hearted Zinaida Ivanovna. "We would have helped, all together..."

"I couldn't leave them for a minute, I haven't had a moment's peace..." Sveta removed her glasses and suddenly looked very young and defenseless. "Not one person stopped by..."

Then the villagers really did feel terribly guilty: they had, of course, always excluded Sveta from the neighborly circle, hadn't made friends with her, never came over or invited her round... not in the old life and not in the strange new reality either. It was like there was a fence around Sveta just the same as around her villa. They had all thought it was her own doing, but now it seemed not so. It was the village that had not accepted Sveta, taking her for a spoiled princess. No one had seen the businessman Beroev, nor Sveta and the children, for a long time – and no one raised the alarm, not one person went to check on them.

Nikita realized, to his horror, that he was vanquished. All his carefully worded arguments, his proofs, all were swept away by Sveta's tears. So he took a chance, the only one he could see.

"Well, why don't we go and check on them now!"

In the pause that followed, even Sveta stopped crying and was still. The chairwoman, who had been watching Nikita with disapproval and Sveta with compassion furrowed her brow and quite unexpectedly asked Sveta if she minded them heading over there right now, to dispel all doubts, so to say...

"Fine, that's fine," said Sveta meekly and nodded her head. "Certainly."

Shamed and reproved, Nikita tailed the delegation dejectedly. It was like being walked to the principal's office, after breaking the staff room window or something even worse. He marveled to himself that he couldn't get anyone to pay attention, but Sveta just showed up, cried some tears and had them all in the palm of her hand. Even Andrei, his mate since they were kids, was giving him morose and unfriendly looks.

"Doesn't anybody remember how she offed Kozhebatkin?" Nikita whispered to him, hoping to secure at least one ally before it was too late.

"I don't remember, I wasn't there."

Nikita stopped in his tracks: he had been sure that Andrei had been by his side when they'd all gone to storm the crazy pensioner's lair. He had seen Andrei there, he really had. Nikita was dredging up memories like pictures, with Andrei on the periphery. Or was that Pashka? Did Andrei really not remember? Had he sublimated his memory of what happened, like the other dachniks, who never mentioned Kozhebatkin at all, as though he'd simply vanished? God, it was hard, dealing with people. And bloody impossible dealing with people and the new neighbors combined.

They could see the brick villa up ahead, and that was when Nikita realized this had not been a good thing to suggest to the others. He pictured the door flung open, two black monsters issuing forth to tear the whole lot of them to pieces, the overgrown lawn running with blood. They would devour Nikita last of all, in thanks for bringing so much delicious meat to their doorstep. Or worse – they could be greeted by the two Beroev children, pale and coughing weakly, all innocence. Katya was right, there was a glamor – a witching glamor it had to be – over the village. You didn't know what to believe anymore. Maybe Sveta was telling the truth, after all, and Katya was the monster, while Nikita was going off his rocker just like the departed Kozhebatkin. He had seen Andrei there, for sure, and yet Andrei had not been there...

The crowd, with a racket, penetrated the Beroev home, broke into the cool silence within and then stopped awkwardly. Inside, the dim hallway rang and echoed with their whispers, not at all like a normal wooden dacha where sound was absorbed into the warm and dense timber walls. Nikita ticked off every last detail: look at the dust, no one's cleaned in ages, the clock still dead, the wallpaper ripped to shreds, though what kind of housecat could reach so high... And the stained walls, looked like someone had tried to wash off the stains... There was no sign of a recent fire or high heat, nor of the cellar door. It was probably covered up.

The dachniks ascended the stairs, stumbling and getting in one another's way.

"Just don't make too much noise, please," Sveta whispered, pushing open a door.

The stale smell of sick, damaged flesh rushed out at them from within the room. The thick curtains were drawn. Squinting in the gloom, the dachniks began to make out the shapes of a wardrobe, a table, two beds. Something on the beds – alive, stirring weakly.

"Curtains!" Nikita felt almost a surge of triumph. "Tell her to open the curtains!"

The movement from the beds became more pronounced, and there came a quiet sniveling. Sveta, biting her lip, gestured mournfully toward Nikita, as if to say: "Just look at what I have to put up with." Andrei shouldered Nikita aside and suggested, quietly, that he should take a walk outside.

"Let her show them to everyone," insisted Nikita, looking hunted, and failing to meet a single friendly eye.

"Young man, where's your conscience?" that ubiquitous dog breeder Yakov Semyonovich said from somewhere.

His "young man" was really the final straw. Enraged, Nikita pushed inside the room and, almost choking on the coagulated stench, rushed at the window. He tore the curtain aside so hard it came halfway off the curtain rod. A narrow strip of sunlight cut through the gloom, and this was enough.

Two little boys lay in their beds. They were long-haired and covered head-to-foot in some kind of crusty substance, but they were reasonably human looking. Squirming away from the sun, the children started to cry. Their mother was instantly at Nikita, beating at him with her little balled-up fists:

"They can't take the light, it hurts them!"

The children cowered with their heads beneath their blankets and bawled. Two pairs of hands were already securing the curtain back in place.

Nikita was shoved out the front door, while being called every conceivable name, given a few thumps and told to get his head examined. Then everyone let themselves out, mortified and guilty. Only Gena, who volunteered to take a look at the sick boys, stayed back.

"Did you see Gena afterward?" Katya asked, when a completely defeated-looking Nikita came back to her hideout.

"No."

"That's a shame." She went back to unraveling her old-fashioned fishing line. Most evenings, she'd furtively step out to the riverbank – fortunately dacha number thirteen was right by the water – and set her hooks, lines, and sinkers, which were invisible in the grass. She fried up the little bream on an extemporized grill, made from bricks and a piece of chain-link fence. The whole dacha stank of fried fish. Nikita worried the ineradicable smell would give them away, but Katya would counter that they had to eat something. Nikita's own food supply was growing scarce, so he would mutter awhile, then have a good feed.

"So they're aufs?"

Pricking herself on a hook, Katya let out a squeak and a sigh.

"How do I know? Maybe they still remember how to look like people. Or maybe you all just saw what you wanted to see."

"I didn't!"

"Everybody was hoping to see kids and not beasts. Even you. And since there were so many of you in the same place, wanting the same thing… You helped them, you yourselves."

"To cast a glamor?"

"Yup."

The line was untangling, hard, tight knots unravelling into translucent loops. Katya tugged at the next loop with her fingernail and carefully pulled it free.

It was after this failed attempt to come to an understanding with people that Nikita brought over the scarecrow. To try the not-people – if not to work things out, exactly, then at least to communicate.

It wasn't the scarecrow itself that scared Katya, not when its most terrifying feature was an absurd Soviet-era coat, pitilessly tailored to be unfashionable. It was the idea itself. Nikita had cottoned on to a single detail from her tale of the other-infested village called Stoyanovo, the way that her great-granddad forbade the putting up of idols, lest those who haven't flesh of their own take up residence inside. The sculptor who had the furthest plot hadn't disappeared on his own; his angelic pioneers vanished too, as though they'd followed him away.

To Nikita this all meant that something was definitely going on with the village "idols", and if something was going on, they'd better try and make contact with the new neighbors and find out, finally, what it was they wanted.

Katya did not share this desire to communicate. She told him that the others would not be interested, and if they became interested that would not be a good thing. Because, as her granny used to say, not everyone survived the others' curiosity. Katya had tried to speak with the leshy, but he'd paid her no notice. She had tried to converse with those who called from the river, but discovered that they never really answered, just sent back variations of her own thoughts and memories. Maybe the others didn't have that kind of intelligence, in the human sense of the word...

"But they hid you, that time," interrupted Nikita.

"Not them. Romochka."

"Who?" Then he remembered. "That addle-brain? The one who disappeared?"

"He didn't disappear. He went to them, in the river." Katya fell silent and dropped her gaze. Then she raised her face to Nikita's and looked him in the eye:

"I let them have him."

"But... why?"

"He wanted to go. Really wanted to. It's better for him there, with them... than with us. He's not... addlebrained, there."

Again Katya had that distinct aura of something alien and subtle, but clearly related to the mysterious creatures that set themselves up for their new neighbors, and not to the real, normal village peopled with real, normal human beings. Pissed off, frightened, slow to understand things, but normal. Nikita didn't feel like thinking about this too deeply. He would have preferred to put such things out of his mind, and to yank Katya from the strange and hostile dimension she seemed to have one foot in, like a grave, back to the human plane. He wanted to pull everyone back out, but especially Katya.

And he had stopped drinking, for good. Already it was two weeks. A wild energy and readiness coursed through him, and most of all, strength: to move mountains, to save the princess from the dragon, to chase away the fell enchantment hanging over the village, to turn the world upside down...

"We need to ask them why they came. What they want us to do."

"What if they don't want us to do anything?" Katya spread her hands wide, a dense flat sinker spinning heavily from her fingers. "What if they've come for our souls?"

"I guess we'll find out," he said glumly, and went to set up the scarecrow. He was disappointed that Katya, of all people, didn't get him. He had thought of the example of the bait and hook especially for her, the fishing fanatic, but she hadn't appreciated the simile... All his life he suffered from the way that he seemed to be tuned into a different frequency from other people, a wrong frequency, and his being in tune with those around him, even those closest to him, was sporadic at best. Just when he thought he was on the same wavelength as Katya, sensing something familiar, and easy to read, and askew like he was askew... but no, it was the same as always.

At least she didn't object any more. When Nikita reflected some more and offered to put up the scarecrow on his own plot and fly solo, since she was so spooked, she groused that they better do it together.

Nikita came back with flashlights and candles. Remembering the returned Vityok's devotion to the radio, and the mysterious phone call advising Katya to flee, he also brought every communication device he could find: his current cell phone and an ancient, heavy and indestructible Nokia, plus a tablet and a little transistor radio. When he asked Katya what else they needed, in her opinion, she tersely told him to bring an axe.

He really did like her a lot. They put up the scarecrow just outside the window, so it had no chance of evading their eyes, or lying low among the shadows as all the fey creatures are traditionally wont to do. They spread the inventory for their ridiculous séance across the floor: the cell phones, charged to the hilt and glowing softly like cozy nightlights, the quietly hissing radio, the axe, the besom broom of rue, the besom broom of birch, candles in old glass jars, several stout sticks, and a few sugar cubes. Katya had added the sugar for some reason Nikita couldn't fathom and didn't want to ask about. Then they sat down on the floor to wait.

Though both were on edge, there was a solemnity to the waiting, too. They ran their flashlights across the scarecrow and checked the cell phones from time to time, just like in the good old days when the ghostly buzzing in your pocket made you thumb the display button, take a look. The gray night ran with the radio hissing, which also seemed somehow gray.

Neither was in the least bit sleepy. Nikita's pulse raced and thundered like Hindu temple drums, and his stomach gurgled, probably owing to the same dread excitement. At any rate, it was very audible. Mortified, Nikita attempted to stifle the rude noises by pressing an elbow into his belly. Then he heard Katya's stomach gurgle too. They'd been so distracted by their preparations to meet the unknown that they'd forgotten to eat any dinner. Katya must have been thinking the same thing; she smiled at him and turned the radio volume up. Nikita was glad that her stomach was protesting too, because it made Katya back into an ordinary, flesh-and-blood being, weakening her link with the sticky, slippery otherworld that seemed to have some hold on her. Nikita didn't really understand what that link was, but he was entirely aware of it, the way one is with something in one's eye. Around dawn, finally sinking into a heavy sleep, he half-dreamed the link as an unspooling thread, shaded an irritating sort of red. He managed to surface once or twice, trying to remember where he'd put the scissors…

Nothing happened with the scarecrow. The crucified coat hung peaceably from the wooden frame, and the tin cans jangled softly and pleasantly in the morning breeze.

The next night they fell to talking. Nikita, mindful of the way he'd been accused of defending a woman he knew so little that even her last name was a mystery to him, was gently probing Katya for answers. Her last name was so ordinary he promptly forgot it. She worked as a freelance editor, in her past life on the outside, and that's how come she was able to spend the whole summer long at the dacha – she simply brought her work with her. Her family had stopped coming on account of Katya's mother being a committed opponent of digging up and fixing up, and generally keeping things up in that endless dacha way that required unending toil. Once upon a time, they had brought little Katya and Granny Serafima every summer, for the fresh air, as was expected; when Katya grew up and Serafima died, they stopped. Katya herself had no one to bring for the fresh air: perfectly healthy otherwise, she could not have children. There was a husband for a time, and they divorced amicably, deciding that since there were no children there was no family, really, and each should be free to go their own way. Maybe it was for the best. Katya felt easier, more in control somehow, when she was alone. As a child she had never asked for a brother or sister. That was Granny, constantly pressuring her parents, really haranguing them sometimes – one child alone, whoever heard such a thing, that was no way to live, children were meant to come a-handful… But Katya was probably better off alone, after all, living as she pleased with no one to say anything.

"And you can spend all day fishing, if that's what you want," blurted out Nikita. Until now he'd been nodding along quietly, but he couldn't resist. The appeal of solitude was exactly the same for him.

"Why are you all so obsessed with the fishing? Enough already!" Katya cried. "I enjoy it, ok? That's all there is to it!"

"Only because it's seen as a manly hobby," Nikita said placatingly. "Not that I ever got what's so interesting about it, myself."

"You're not exactly manly. It's about the thrill of the hunt, it's exciting. And it's zen too…" Katya fell silent for a moment. "And it's a good place to hide."

"Hide?"

"What do you think people come here for? To hide from everybody else. You've got two lines of defense here, the fence and the dacha walls. You can live however you like. It's not a vacation, people go to the seaside for that. A dacha is not a vacation thing. Dachniks are a special breed now. You, for example, why did you use to come?"

"To, um, drink…" came Nikita's honest reply.

"See. You hide from everybody and drink to your heart's content. This is your lair, your safe space. It's a place to be, for those who aren't quick enough for life. The fast times we live in, when you owe something to everybody, you have to be successful, you have to be happy, you have to conform. Not everyone likes that. Not me."

"Not me."

Although Nikita had never thought about the philosophy of dacha life, he felt, for the first time in many years, that he was inhabiting the same wavelength as another human being.

"That's how you became a dachnik," Katya nodded sagely. "Here you are a discrete person, your own man, no one getting to you or at you. Even the internet… remember how it was always patchy here? And the way everybody brings all their old stuff here, from town, all the worn-out rubbish. The dachas are worn out too, right? The brand-new ones just seem wrong. It's like we're all trying to stop time here, because we're too slow to run along with it…"

Sparrows, woodpeckers, buntings – all that flighty small fry that flocked, chattering, to devour precious cherries and strawberries. They were raiders, the scarecrow's natural enemies. The scarecrow had made himself a collar of them, or a necklace.

Keeping her eyes on the brown-coated figure bedecked with dead bird heads lest it vanish in a flutter of chancy shadows, Katya ran into the house for the axe. She hacked at its single leg – the supporting branch – before she could think about whether the scarecrow now qualified as something alive. It toppled into the grass with a sweep of its sleeves, and Katya took another swing.

By the time Nikita, after much fruitless searching, returned to dacha number thirteen, the dismembered scarecrow lay interred in three separate holes on opposite ends of the plot. Katya, exhausted by the work of burying it, lay asleep inside, in a corner. She looked so cozy, curled up on an old mattress, that Nikita couldn't resist stroking her cheek, like you would with a cat. Then he stroked her shoulder, and then her hip, which just seemed to happen to be there. Then he felt her eyes on him.

"Let me sleep," she muttered crossly, only half-awake.

"I didn't find him."

"Oh, he came back, your scarecrow. Very handsome, all dressed up... I broke it up and buried it. No more trying to contact anything, you hear me?"

"Sure thing." Nikita stroked her again.

"Pavlov..." Katya furrowed her brow at him. "Do you just have to spoil our friendship?"

But Nikita was thinking suddenly that this was the way to cut that twisty red thread, to destroy Katya's elusive connection with the terrifying world of the woman aflame and the headless leshy, and the cannibal aufs... To make her back into an ordinary woman, the kind desired by an ordinary man, that is to say, him. Yes, said Nikita to himself, this is what needs to happen, definitely. Perhaps Katya was feeling that too, because as she carried on grumbling, she put her hands in his and pressed close. She was sleep-warm, even hot, and very skinny. Her skin was dry and smooth like paper, and he worried about scratching her accidentally, or tearing her skin with his ragged fingernails.

Katya woke when it was getting dark again and immediately felt a dislike, seasoned liberally by shame, for Nikita who was snoozing beside her. It was so awkward; now she recalled that he was no looker and not exactly a genius either, and his arms were too long. The main thing was, he drank. Katya's dad liked to drink, not all the time, but hard when he did – like that time she had to drag him, a little girl, all the way to their dacha. When he drank, he became like a disgusting stranger, and that was her own dad, mind you. Pavlov here was known to all the village as a drunkard and wastrel. Her affection for Nikita was evaporating so swiftly that even the smell of him seemed unpleasant now. Hadn't she told him that it would spoil everything? He wasn't the first guy she'd said it to, and it was always the same – men just never understood things like that. It was always more complicated to be on the receiving end.

Katya quietly flicked on the flashlight, pointed it at the window, and crawled up to the sill to gaze at the single remaining pane of glass. Just as she'd thought, she looked bedraggled and crumpled, one cheek was swollen, and there seemed to be new wrinkles on her face. She had no intention of letting that loser Pavlov, who'd spoiled everything, wake up and see her like this. She rubbed her cheek roughly and started to plait her hair, elastic held between her teeth. She would go back to sleep and wake up looking more presentable.

The night moths fluttered like white stains in the weak beam of her light, knocking into the windowpane and unable to think their way around it. Katya watched, yawning. A large butterfly looped closer to the glass until it suddenly covered it whole. Now Katya could see her reflection on white, instead of on black. The white background, she suddenly saw, was marked with black stains. It took her another startled second to recognize they were facial features: blurred dark eyes – one higher than the other – and a very wide mouth with a pair of fangs drawn on, and some kind of rusty spike in place of a nose.

The resurrected and transmogrified scarecrow stared at Katya from the other side of the glass with smudged, coal-black eyes. The face writ upon the old pillowcase was truly ferocious. Katya thought of how she'd emptied that pillowcase of sawdust and mossy mud with her own two hands. Now clumps of wet grass stuck out from the scarecrow's torn forehead and cheek.

Still clenching the flashlight, she rose to her feet. The scarecrow straightened itself too, blocking the entire window. It had remade itself, leaving very little of the human in the process. Its head sat on its torso, its limbs had multiplied, its long crooked back receded far into the darkness...

The scarecrow had also come back armed. It bristled with a collection of nails, sharpened bicycle spokes, and ground locking pins. Even the metal bottlecaps that littered the ground all around the dacha were hammered hard into the scarecrow's wooden body, so that only the jagged edges, flattened and honed, stuck out. Katya pictured tender human flesh sliced open by those edges, just like that... The spikes and blades were everywhere: like dragon claws, they glimmered from its many arms or maybe legs, rose hackle-like down its seemingly endless spine and arced around its fresh new visage like a halo. The spikes comprising the halo were topped by the torn-off birds' heads from before.

Never taking its painted eyes off Katya, the scarecrow moved forward, jangling the remains of the glass, but then recoiled. Numb with icy terror, she held out her hand:

"Wait. Forgive me. I won't hurt..."

The scarecrow froze in place, twitching its head and curving its monstrous millipede spine. It too seemed to be afraid. Katya remembered how she'd gone at it with the axe, how she tore apart the bobtailed old coat.

"A word?" She couldn't dredge up any of Granny's special sayings, and anyway, Katya had never learned the correct form of address for "those with no flesh of their own."

"A word with you? What do you creatures want? Why did you come, who are you?"

The dacha shook with a tinny MIDI rendition of Beethoven's Fur Elise – the ancient Nokia was vibrating, crawling toward Katya across the floor.

It woke up Nikita, who fairly leapt up with a frightened groan. Katya waved her hands without turning to look at him; she was signaling him to be quiet while also drawing attention to the cell phone. When Nikita spotted the scarecrow, his eyes went crazy wide, but he mastered himself, grabbed the cell phone and held it to his ear. A voice that was choked and devoid of breath hissed so loudly from the receiver that Katya too heard it:

"Neigh–bors–sss..."

Then it chattered, in varying tones and timbres, a single phrase:

"Killed me, killed me, killed meeee!"

The scarecrow vanished back into the dark, with a crashing and crackling of twigs. The receiver crackled too and then howled drearily. This had the effect of getting Nikita fully awake and scared to death. He threw the cell phone as far as he could.

"Grab it!" Katya screamed and, snatching up a stick, rushed out the door. Nikita, armed with the axe, followed. His ears were still filled with the furious, inescapably aggrieved hiss:

"Killed me, killed meeee..."

* * *

The scarecrow, unbelievably long and resembling a walking kinetic sculpture, hared around the dark street, trampling bushes and crashing into fences. When Katya managed to catch up with it, she clutched one of its wooden legs and felt it move, almost pulsate, revoltingly, beneath her fingers. The scarecrow easily threw her off, flattened her onto the asphalt and loomed above. The crook-mouthed cloth face still smelled of mice and dust. Katya closed her eyes, not so much from fear even, more that she wouldn't have to see the ferocious pain in the charcoal lines of that face, and the torn wounds on its cheek and brow. A muffled thud of the axe and the scarecrow released its grip. This was Nikita hacking into its back, cleaving off a third of the multi-pawed torso with a single stroke. The separated part rolled into the gutter, convulsing like a vast half-squished spider. The scarecrow flew at Nikita but, faced with the axe again, shrank away. Someone's fence was at their backs. Katya shouted that they needed to take off its head – not that she was really sure that would be enough to stop the thing – but it was too late. The silent monster reared up to its full height, braced itself on the fence and vaulted its coiling body over to the other side.

Katya and Nikita were momentarily frozen with the stupefaction of knowing the monster they had created was heading toward people. Nikita followed it over the fence, but Katya hadn't the necessary strength or height to follow, so she ran to find the gate, which was locked. As she tried desperately to force the lock, there came a shattering of glass and the lights came on inside the dacha, and human-shaped shadows flitted across the windows. Nikita yelled: "Don't touch him!"

Everything was noise and screaming, so heartrending and helpless, that Katya beat impotently at the gate, and screamed back, shredding her vocal cords. "Don't, please, enough," she screamed, and other nonsense, until she sank to the ground and went still, hands tight over her ears.

That was where the villagers, awakened by all the screaming, found her. Luckily Usov was not among them. No one knew what was going on, half-awake as they all came, and they were fearful of Katya too. Unwilling to draw too close, they peered at her from afar, and tried to get a glimpse of her fangs or claws, or maybe even horns. Finally, the bravest of the lot, Andrei and the dog breeder Yakov Semyonovich, came up and lifted her to her feet. There were no fangs or claws in evidence, just a relatively human face, dirty and tearstained. She didn't struggle, just whispered something ceaselessly to herself.

It turned out that the scarecrow had breached Claudia Il'yinichna's plot. All the supernatural creatures seemed to be drawn to that dacha, as though even they knew just who was in charge here. The Petukhovs had not gone to bed yet, and so an old chandelier cascading with plastic teardrops – the kind every respectable household aspired to once upon a time – still glimmered from one of their illuminated windows. That was what attracted the scarecrow's attention. Either it simply made for the light, like a great big moth, or the glittering, sharp-edged teardrops themselves caught its fancy. It would not have been the first to be tempted: the chandelier, pockmarked from the efforts of the Petukhovs' nephews, had been retired to the dacha because it no longer looked respectable.

Drawn by the sound of broken glass and the crash of the chandelier, Petukhov rushed into the room to find to his astonishment, a spiky, tentacled monster who had already stuck a dozen teardrops into its pillowcase head in the manner of a crown and was attempting to claw the chandelier from the ceiling entirely. Petukhov stood thunderstruck for a moment, then grabbed a cast-iron oven fork and went to the defense of his chandelier, and his home, and his Claudia, from the hellish beast. That was when Nikita, who saw it all from the street, screamed "Don't touch him!" though he didn't know whether he meant it for Petukhov or the scarecrow.

It was all over by the time the rest of the dachniks arrived. Glass shards, blood spray, and pieces of the unlucky chandelier lay scattered everywhere. Beneath the window, in a bed of chrysanthemums, lay the dead and broken Petukhov. Claudia Il'yinichna sat on her front stoop, holding on to her left side and looking around with an insensate, primeval stupefaction. When she saw other people, she leaned forward as though she wanted to say something, but just stayed there, sitting, mouth half-open.

Amid the carnage, Nikita, spattered with blood, just carried on hacking. He'd hacked the remains of the scarecrow into kindling, but the little pieces could not be still, they trembled and twitched like spiders. The villagers had not noticed them to begin with, and everyone formed a picture in their minds of Nikita Pavlov, in a fit of alcoholic delirium tremens, who had hacked the unfortunate Petukhov to death with that very axe.

Suddenly Katya broke free from Andrei and Yakov Semyonovich, and flew at Nikita, shrieking:

"You wanted to chat with them, right? Are you happy now?"

"The main thing is to remain calm," said Claudia Il'yinichna. As she broke free of her trance she had straightened and cleared her throat. "The main thing... not to panic... we must all keep..."

She burst into tears, keening and moaning like a peasant.

"Pavlov, why don't you give me that axe," Andrei said in the calm and friendly voice people use with the insane.

Nikita examined the remains of the scarecrow closely, then dropped the axe on the grass.

"Fucking have it."

Pashka had been creeping up on him from behind, limping on his bitten leg and gesticulating to the others how to best overpower and disarm him. Nikita saw him, but he didn't give a shit just then. The scarecrow pieces rustled through the grass in their final agonies, Claudia Il'yinichna sniffled, and Katya mumbled like a mantra, soundlessly:

"Killed me, killed me, killed me…"

13

GINGERBREAD HOUSE

Acquainted since nursery school, the two of them knew one another down to the last little wrinkle and seam; they synchronized even in the way they mangled their names, in a simultaneous fit of teenage rebellion, from Dennis and Anastasia to Denny and Stacy. And neither was sure – not that they ever spoke about this out loud – whether their comfortable, convenient companionship was still friendship, or could be considered a "relationship." They slept together more as a nod to their different genders, than because of anything else. For Stacy, the "relationship" lacked the emotional depth and passion she'd read and heard so much about; for his part, Denny felt that she lacked that knockout dazzle and flair that made a fellow boast "that's my woman." But all in all, being together was so cozy and easy and mutually beneficial that Stacy was even willing to marry Denny one day, if she hadn't met the actual love of her life by then.

It all started when Denny found an old tent, from the outdoorsy Soviet times, in his grandma's attic, and immediately wanted to try it out. The summer nights were still sweltering and the tent would be cramped with two, so it was obvious that Stacy, of all people, should go with him, as long as she didn't whine about mosquitoes and grass snakes, or say she was creeped out. Stacy felt strongly that she was unique among other girls in this respect; nothing creeped her out, she was a strong swimmer and moreover, had a lot of life skills. She argued her case so passionately, that in a trice she found herself sitting on a suburban bus with Denny, the tent, two backpacks, and a bundle of rods. Denny was telling her all about a river called Sushka, which he'd canoed with his parents when he was young, and promising her outstanding natural beauty.

The bus spat them out by an ancient bus shelter, graffitied to within an inch of its life. A huge warning in jagged letters told them to GO HOME from the depths of the shelter. Stacy thought it sweet, the way it was so polite, and even vaguely concerned for the visitors.

Beyond the bus shelter, the road embankment gave them a view of a velvety meadow, dotted with patches of wood, and framed by a little river in the shade of domed willows and overgrown cow parsnip.

"That's what I'm talking about," Denny declared, and went down, hopping awkwardly to slow his steep descent.

Nikita's grandfather, whom Nikita had loved very much, used to say that most pharmaceuticals did more harm than good, and you couldn't beat natural remedies like broadleaf plantain and piss, especially on the march. Nikita didn't have any pharmaceuticals to hand and was dubious about the piss. Perched on a log beside the fence, he was tearing off plantain leaves and gluing them to his many cuts and scratches with spit. The scarecrow had done a number on him: some places needed whole mosaics of the healing leaf stuck on, like pages from a school botany project. Last night he'd felt no pain, swinging his axe like a demented woodcutter, but now everything hurt and stung, his brain felt curdled and his eyes wouldn't stay open.

The chairwoman buried her husband with her own two hands. Or would have done, if the dachniks had let her. For a while they watched her grimly chipping thin layers of clay-seamed earth with her spade as though parsing an expensive cheese. Then the bearded Stepanov came and took the rough, inexpertly planed handle from her hands, which trembled and bled from work to which they were unaccustomed, and began to dig the grave properly. Claudia Il'yinichna stayed by his side: wrapping the shawl more tightly around herself, she gazed at the long bag containing the body of Petukhov, her husband – just a bag for storing winter potatoes – and at the deepening hole. They had chosen a good place, above the river. Though it was just by the banked road, it had a lovely view of the riverbend, and the bowed weeping willows that the beavers had clearly had a go at.

While everyone was busy hunting for a suitable bag or burning the remains of the scarecrow, the chairwoman had sat on her front stoop and glowered at Katya, who was still being restrained by Andrei and the dog breeder. The chairwoman's eyes were swollen and dull with hatred.

"You..." she muttered, just like the drunken Vityok would go looking for the cause of his worldly troubles and alight on Auntie Zhenya. "You..."

Katya said nothing. The others tried to explain to Claudia Il'yinichna that it was no beast that had attacked her home, but some kind of wooden scarecrow. They showed her the twitching kindling strewn all over the grass: every piece they found they threw into the fire. She paid them no heed at all, just shook her head and carried on as before:

"You..."

Finally, they led Katya away, though no one really knew what should be done with her. She didn't protest, just looked at her feet and stayed mum, which made them all even more scared of her. They locked her in the empty corrugated-iron garage where Petukhov had once worked lovingly on his "Volga" and which still housed the ineradicable aromas of auto repair. Katya paused at the threshold: she seemed not to be fully aware of what was happening, and what they wanted from her. No one dared push her in. But then she stepped inside, without a word, and Andrei quickly leaned on the door so they could join the metal bolt holes and affix a lock. They'd all forgotten about Nikita, and now he decided to seize his chance: he leaped at Andrei, pushing him aside, and flung the door open again:

"Run!"

Nothing stirred inside the garage. The door was briskly locked and barred while Nikita, after a brief struggle with Andrei, was pushed out into the street.

Then everyone besides the dog breeder Yakov Semyonovich and Andrei, who volunteered to guard the garage, went to bury Petukhov. Nikita, startled by own willingness to continue a futile protest, remained by the Petukhovs' fence, which he cruised up and down, shouting more of the same, that Katya had nothing to do with it, that the beasts were actually the Beroev kids, and it was them that needed catching and locking up before they ate anyone else. Yeah, OK, it was shitty what happened with the scarecrow, and he was to blame, so they could throw him to Sveta's monsters if they wanted to, he deserved that, but they just had to go and catch the things, and they had to let Katya go... He was sick to his stomach and heartsick, too, with all that had happened, and he desperately needed a drink. He probably would have ended up skulking back to his dacha, to finish off the remains of his stash, and put the hellish scarecrow and the Beroev kids and Katya, whom he couldn't help anyway, out of his mind. But then Yuki, late to the fray, arrived in haste to ascertain what was going on this time.

She tailed Nikita up and down the fence, nodding in agreement with him. Her eyes were inexpertly ringed in makeup – probably the reason she was so late – and very round:

"Right, so that's exactly what I thought..."

It was impossible to know exactly what she'd thought, but it was nice to have moral support.

By the time the villagers returned from Petukhov's burial,

Nikita had organized himself a lookout a bit further down the street. No one looked about to kick him out, and he could see the chairwoman's plot quite well. With a rotting wooden block to perch on, Nikita sat down in the shade of the fence and made himself comfortable. He reprimanded himself for not being able to just go over to the chairwoman's and rescue his crook-lipped princess, devil take her, all by himself like a lone hero. Nevertheless, he remained at his post. Yuki provided not just moral support, but also intelligence; every ten minutes she ran back to report that nothing was happening at Claudia Il'yinichna's. Nikita began to calm down.

He was dozing, and slow to open his eyes at Yuki's approach. It took him a moment to make out what she was shouting as she ran up to him, but it sure woke him up:

"Usov!" Yuki was wailing, "Usov! Coming to kill you!"

Denny was being a brat. First he didn't like it in the shade, then the sun was too hot, or the ground too uneven. He seemed to require ideal conditions for the setting up of the tent. They had left the riverbank because he couldn't deal with the litter. "Regard the remains of an ancient camp of the Homo Shish-kebabus," he'd said, sending them both into fits of laughter as they worked the joke over in different ways.

Now they were in the woods. These were sparse and mossy, shot through with little paths. Stacy had spotted a clutch of noble brown boletus in the grass at the woods' edge and had by now almost a bagful. As they walked, she periodically lowered her face to the bag and inhaled. The mushrooms smelled so delicious it was hard not to eat them straight away. And actually, she was very hungry.

"This is it," Denny announced eventually.

They had come to a clearing, and it perfectly matched

Denny's criteria for the right place: flat and soft with moss and lush grass, the clearing was fringed with thick raspberry cane and shaded from the insistent sun by rangy birches.

The tent was not so easy to put up. Denny wanted to have another look at the instructions he'd googled before they set off but there was no connection to the net. On their fourth try they managed to transform the initial strange assemblage of tarpaulins into a thing that looked very much like a tent, except it had a drooping top and one extra rope that didn't seem to go anywhere.

They crawled inside. Denny popped open some warm beers, and they lunched on their crumpled and soggy but incredibly tasty sandwiches. Eating made them both languorous and dead sleepy. It turned out there was only the one thin blanket, and for a while they tugged it this way and that, laughing, in the cramped tent that still smelled of dust. Then things got more serious as they turned their attention to one another's bodies, damp with cool sweat. And then they snoozed. Stacy always wanted to fall asleep in a romantic embrace after, but Denny managed – just as they both fell asleep – to face the wall, like a normal person.

Nikita burst through the chairwoman's front gate just in time to see the huge, barrel-like Usov smashing the padlock with the butt of his rifle. Stepanov and Andrei hung from his back like hounds on top of a bear, while the rest of the dachniks watched them from a safe distance – which varied from person to person, with some choosing the veranda and others the fence – quivering with both terror and curiosity. The noise was unholy: Usov roared that he would shoot them all to hell if they didn't let him alone.

Nikita leapt into the triple knot of the brawlers. As he pushed someone aside, he felt the cold weight of a gun in his hand and tugged with all his might. The screams became deafening, a bolt of pain sliced through his lower belly and groin. His brain, which seemed somehow abstracted from his body, registered surprise that there had been no sound of the gunshot. Nikita toppled into a rosehip bush still clutching the gun. As the searing pain receded, he caught his breath and was overjoyed to find there was no blood anywhere on him. Usov had not shot him, just kneed him in the family jewels. Kneed him bloody hard, but at least now Nikita had the gun, which was a kind of victory.

The broken padlock dropped onto the stone paving with a clang. Usov flung open the garage doors and stepped inside.

Nikita tossed the gun away and tried to claw his way up from the rosehips. At that moment the dachniks surged forward again, nearly running him over. They clumped in the doorway, pushing and shoving, and no one could actually get inside. A broken scream rang out from the depths of the garage, and Nikita reared up violently among the broken branches, freeing himself. It was Katya screaming.

A blinding white light sparked soundlessly inside of the garage and detonated outward in a scorching wave that bent the grass low to the ground. Everyone scattered, covering their faces from the unbearable heat.

Then all was silent once more.

Stacy woke because she really needed to pee. That was why she didn't actually like beer. She climbed out of the tent and squatted by a nearby bush. She was still half-asleep really.

It was strangely quiet. No rustling leaves or birds whistling to one another, or that dry crackling that seems to come from nowhere in the woods... strange not to hear those noises, especially on a summer's day.

Stacy suddenly found herself fully awake. It was dark. She had thought they'd only dozed for half an hour or so, but they seemed to have conked out until nighttime. She looked up at the dim, starless sky. A very strange sky, and there must have been light somewhere, since she could still make out the shapes of the trees and the tent... She looked closer and discovered that these shapes had their own phosphorescence, as though everything around was swathed in tiny fireflies.

A bright, branching bolt of lightning split the sky. Inky black clouds, vast as mountains, billowed across it, and swirled over the clearing like a winding funnel. The lightning zagged again, starting up a deep booming that grew and grew.

"Denny!" she shrieked, terrified, and ran for the tent.

The echoing, ear-popping silence lasted for a minute or two, just enough for people to recover a little from that blast of suffocating heat. Those closest to the garage had singed eyelashes and eyebrows; hands and faces grew tight and hot, as burned skin began to blister. Nikita finally made it to the door, but the furnace-like heat still blowing from the inside kept him from entering.

"Was that some kind of explosion?" A tremulous voice behind him.

Immediately, with impossible speed, the clear summer sky clouded blackly over, and a maelstrom opened above the village. The branches around them creaked and crunched; a roof slate tore from the Petukhovs' dacha and flew away into the rumbling gloom. Rain and hail crashed down from the heavens all at once, like a heavy, plummeting curtain, making the red-hot metal garage instantly hiss into a cloud of steam. Nikita tugged his wet t-shirt over his nose and dove inside again, but no sooner did he step over the threshold than the garage... it simply vanished. The wretched rosehip bushes were all there, and the grass, but the garage was gone without a trace.

The other dachniks were staggering about the plot, terrified. Nikita ran up to Andrei and shook him furiously, demanding to know where the garage was. Andrei gawped and pointed vaguely off to the side, where the garage stood perfectly still, in its place. But Nikita had moved on to staring glassily past Andrei's shoulder. The Persian lilacs that were the chairwoman's pride and joy were fading, drying out and rotting at hyperspeed, like a sped-up tape. The black, smoldering rot spread, devouring the other trees and bushes. They seemed to be charring before Nikita's eyes, and behind them, a misty, completely different landscape gleamed through: birches and pines, and pine needles on the ground. There was a forest coalescing through the fabric of the chairwoman's plot.

The double vision – it went beyond his eyes, it was seared into his brain, his consciousness – gave Nikita an unholy headache. The pain from the detonation now seemed trivial in comparison, no more than a tickle. He squatted down with a groan. There was moss under his feet, in place of the cement tile path. But also the path. And the moss again. They existed simultaneously, in the same dimension. He felt an icy grip around his shoulders, and a flat, rustling voice by his ear:

"Ssss... Sssave..."

As he startled and turned, the pain in his skull rolled around like a bowling ball. A jagged figure flashed in his peripheral vision, opaque as though stitched together from the stormy rain and gloom. He did catch its inhuman eyes, though, yellow alien eyes with vertical pupils...

The normal, human slamming of the gate brought Nikita back to his senses. This was the former paramedic Gena who demanded to know, at volume and with much cursing, what was going on.

Nikita staggered to his feet and silently pulled Gena over to the garage, then shoved him inside. The heat now seemed bearable, and Nikita even felt better, strangely: inside the garage his insane headache was receding and better still, so was the queasy horror of trying to balance atop a dissipating reality.

Inside it smelled of burned meat.

"Fuck me," was all that Gena could muster.

The tent barely held together under the twin assault of water and wind. Rain seeped through the tatty tarpaulin and dripped onto Stacy and Denny's heads as they huddled together. The earth trembled with the force of the crashing and thundering outside. Instinctively taking on the role of protector, defender, and manly man, Denny was mumbling how there was nothing to be afraid of, it was just a storm. They picked a fine day, didn't they? Those people who did the weather forecast should be shot without a trial, because he'd looked it up at two different websites, and they both said sunny, bright, no precipitation... Stacy was quiet, thinking about how the woods suddenly went dark, and the iron-gray funnel in the sky, and the phosphorescing trees. All while her cell phone was showing three pm.

"Can the tent blow away?" she quavered.

"Shh! What was that? What now?"

Stacy listened. At once she knew what he meant, a new sort of sound emerging through the noise outside. A loud humming, perfectly audible between the thunderclaps, and somehow familiar. Stacy furrowed her brow, thinking, and then it came to her: the sound reminded her of school, when she was about nine. She and her classmates had trolled a nervous young teacher by humming at her, monotonously, the whole class taking turns. Since it was done without anyone's opening their mouth, it was impossible to catch them at it; as the teacher leapt toward one offender, he or she would fall silent, while someone else picked it up. The humming outside was just like that.

Something heavy dropped on top of the tarpaulin, and trapped Stacy underneath. She squealed; Denny cursed and grabbed the flashlight. Now the tarp was puckering and shifting by the tent's opening. Something was blindly poking its way inside.

"Piss off!" Denny shouted in a terrible voice. Thinking some animal was trying to force its way in, he clapped his hands loudly and shouted again: "Get away! Get back!"

The flashlight laced to his wrist oscillated wildly and Stacy felt her stomach heave, from the terror or the swinging, or both. She tugged the flashlight down and pointed it at the opening.

A man was trying to crawl inside. He was wearing a dark beanie. His face, swarthy and high-boned, looked more like a badly executed mask: the nose seriously askew and a blind cavity for a right eye. His left eye tracked rapidly from side to side. His mouth was frozen in a wide, dazzling grin. The monotonous humming was coming from behind those very even, very white teeth.

Denny screamed and gave the man – if the thing was a man at all – a kick. It landed right in the crumpled face, and the creature gave a long plaintive howl. Somebody had Stacy under the arms and was hauling her out. She shrieked, trying to grab on to something, then abruptly found herself out of the tent and under the downpour.

"Stop screaming, get up, we have to run!" Denny had not let go of her. Dazed and terrified, unable to think straight, she shot to her feet obediently but then froze in place, swaying a little. Denny gave her a shove in the back and then they were running, stubbing their bare toes on tree roots.

Behind them, in the darkness, the howling lingered on, and the sound of it made you want to lie down on the ground and curl into a ball and wait for the crumple-faced man to come. But on they ran, hands over their ears, headlong into the forest.

It took Nikita a little while to recognize the heap on the garage floor, with its revolting stench of burned flesh, as the remains of Maksim Usov. Skin and cloth, all was charred to shreds. His head, singed clean of hair, was ruddy-brown. It took another little while for Nikita's hollow stomach to start spasming again.

Katya lay on the ground not far from Usov, unburned but for a few blisters and burn marks. Judging by the copious bruises and the bloody hair at her temple, she looked to have suffered more from her encounter with Usov than from the blast.

Normally, Gena always had his paramedic's first aid kit – just a holdall bag, stuffed with all the medications and instruments in his possession – at the ready. Over the past few months, he'd become the village ambulance, on call for every medical emergency from the grannies' rising blood pressures, to runny-nosed children, and even to the side of Naima Hassanovna's unlucky goat.

This time, he'd rushed out of doors in such a hurry that he forgot the kit. One look at Usov and he shrugged, then attended to Katya. Gena took her pulse, palpated the bleeding bump on her head and told Nikita to bring the Petukhov's first aid kit. They kept it on the veranda, in a cardboard box that their electric kettle had come in. Gena had seen it when he came to take the chairwoman's blood pressure a few times.

As Nikita stepped outside, his vision constricted and the pain chomped down on his forehead and neck again. Hastily he took a step back and shouted into the roaring gloom beyond the garage at the top of his lungs:

"Hey, somebody! The first aid kit! It's on the veranda!"

In mere seconds the requested box, wet from the rain and smelling of a dispensary, was thrust forth. Nikita brushed against the hand that held it: he could have sworn it was thickly and roughly furred. The door immediately slammed shut again.

He didn't mention this to Gena, just placed the box on the floor next to the former paramedic, who got busy rustling the wrappers and clinking the vials.

"Well, how is she?"

"She'll live."

Nikita held a pause, then said snidely:

"And here I'd thought those kiddies gobbled you up..."

Gena didn't rise to this, just handed Nikita a small bottle with a faded label.

"Got a knife? The lid is stuck."

Their city-kid feet, unused to running, ached. Their sodden clothes dragged them down. They'd left absolutely everything behind in the tent: warm clothes, shoes, their precious cell phones. The forest, meanwhile, had transformed into a hostile labyrinth, where sharp stones kept rocking up underfoot and branches did their best to smack you in the face.

The earth suddenly crumbled under Denny's feet and he plunged down with a splash. It was shallow though, the water just higher than his ankles. Another bolt of lightning rent the sky, illuminating the bulrushes, and the dappled water and the willows on the riverbank. Denny was gobsmacked, because it was the Sushka. The River Sushka, which they'd left behind hours ago.

Stacy plopped down beside him and whispered breathlessly:

"Is he chasing us?"

"Will you be quiet? I don't know!"

Again, the lightning sparked through the swollen clouds and Stacy made out in the distance a thing that had not been there before: a dacha. A regular-looking dacha, with an orchard and a fence. It seemed to have popped up from under the ground.

"Denny! Denny!"

"Quiet!"

The water roiled right in front of them, something large and heavy surfacing. Something akin to fingers seized Denny's ankle, tightly and with force. He kicked furiously; for a moment the grip came loose and he leapt out of the water like a scalded cat. Stacy raced after him, slipping in the wet clay:

"Look, a house! It's a village!"

Denny craned his neck but couldn't see a thing in the

dark. The next lightning bolt helped him out, but there was no house where Stacy had been pointing. There was no river either. They were back in the forest.

Gena finished his ministrations and told Nikita he was not to crowd her in but give her a chance to come round. Then he glanced at the remains of Usov again. Nikita could tell how Gena's thoughts were running: if they'd both been in the garage, standing next to one another, how come Katya only had a few blisters while Usov had been incinerated? Nikita had already explained to him about the blast, adding helpfully that there had been just such a blast back at the Beroevs.

"Sveta's boys have burns too, very like these," Gena said unexpectedly. "His are worse, obviously..."

"So that's what her critters are sick with."

Gena seemed not to notice the dig. He was deep in his own thoughts.

"They smelled strange... They stank, actually... And the other thing was, she'd tied them to the beds."

Nikita's eyes went wide at that.

"Tied them to the bed frames by their legs, with towels. They were having fits, she said. So they didn't fall out of bed... I didn't really manage to get a look at them, in the end."

"Shooed you away, did she?"

After a moment Gena nodded.

"I'm not surprised, not when everyone knew you'd stayed behind. Would have been awkward, explaining how they gobbled you up."

Katya stirred and gave a deep, ragged sigh. Nikita and Gena froze in anticipation but she stayed unconscious.

"See here, Pavlov. Let's say..." Gena put his hand out to prevent him from speaking, "Let's say I believe you. About the beasts. But then you have to believe me too. I'm not taking the piss, and I haven't gone crazy, and I'm not... dammit, where is it?"

Finally, he managed to extricate his cell phone from his pocket. Thumbing it on, he scrolled across the screen and showed it to Nikita.

It was a photo, and although it was a very bad photo, grainy and indistinct, it was obvious that it was the Petukhovs' plot. You could make out their dacha, numbered like all the others, and the garage roof. The shot seemed to have been taken from sideways and above, as though the photographer had climbed a tree outside in the street to do it. At the bottom of the photo there was a single word, printed in white:

"DOOR"

"I was sitting around at home, the storm came down, and then... this arrives."

"Um... arrives?"

"Arrives. On my phone." Gena was speaking slowly and with emphasis. "Someone sent it, you get what I'm saying? So then I bolted over here..."

Nikita took the phone from him and scrolled frantically through the menu.

"You won't find a sender. It's all blank. There's no connection, either, just like there wasn't any before. That thing... it came from... nowhere."

Katya sighed again, then scrunched up her face and worked to open her eyes. Turning a dull gaze on her surroundings just once, she closed them again. Nikita hurriedly handed the phone back to Gena and bent over her.

"How are you feeling?"

"Fucking great..." she whispered.

Nikita let out a sigh of relief and smiled. He really did like her a lot.

* * *

Stacy couldn't run anymore. She never managed cross-country at school very well, never mind hurtling through the dark, barefoot, in the forest and in a storm, her heart thudding right out of her chest with fright. And her headache was getting worse too, rolling inside her skull like a lead ball.

"I can't..." She collapsed, moaning, onto the wet forest floor.

Denny hoisted her up and half-dragged half-carried her. He groaned and swore. She sobbed that they ought to go back, they had to find the tent again, this forest had no end to it and they were just circling endlessly, they were definitely just going in circles. Denny grumbled that they were too far from the tent now, they'd never find it, they had to get to the forest edge, and then they'd see a road or a village. This wasn't the Siberian taiga after all, just the exurbs, you couldn't get lost here, the main thing was to find people...

In front of them, a blaze of electric lights. Blinking hard, they saw that the light was coming from the lanterns adorning a large house which had appeared out of nowhere. Washed clean with rain, ringed by a tall fence and brightly, even festively, lit, the house looked very beautiful. You could say magical.

Stacy sank to the ground. A quick look behind them gave her more cause for alarm.

"Denny!"

The forest was gone. It vanished like the River Sushka had vanished – noiselessly and instantly, like someone had changed the channel. The two of them were in the middle of a village street. The air was rife with flowers and compost, soaked orchards rustled beneath the receding gusts of rain. A dog was barking somewhere far away.

The red-brick house, shiny with electric lights, looked like iced gingerbread. Who knew why Denny suddenly thought that – he was probably very hungry. But the house really, genuinely did resemble the giant, traditional gingerbread slabs that his granddad used to bring Denny from Tula, where they were a traditional specialty, gingerbread that always looked hard as stone but was actually soft and pillowy under a layer of thick icing. He thought he could almost smell it...

Whatever was beyond the scratched-up and moss-gummed door Nikita was edging open certainly did not smell of gingerbread. He opened a crack one more time, then shut it. No, the mysterious communication most certainly did not mean the door of the chairwoman's outhouse. He and Gena had already tried the gate, and the doors to the shed, the annex and the house itself, to the puzzlement of the dachniks who had sheltered there from the strange storm. Now it came out that it was not just Pavlov who'd experienced the double, parallel vision that made a person's brain pans creak like a watermelon being tapped at market, and he had not been the only one assailed by whispering voices. Andrei, for starters, had also daydreamed a little person, knee-high, who ran about the house like a frightened cat. Old Volopas was convinced he'd heard someone mumbling "close it, close it, close it" incessantly behind his back, but couldn't catch sight of the mutterer no matter how he twisted and turned.

The storm had petered out into an ordinary cold and gray drizzle. As the dachniks began to emerge warily from undercover, Gena and Nikita went briskly round the plot – not that either had a specific idea of what they were looking for and why. The hopeful word "door" had entranced them; it seemed to point to an exit, and changes, and being set free. Perhaps the message was a clue, and somewhere on the chairwoman's plot there was a secret way out, a bloody portal leading out to the real world...

Then Nikita snapped back to reality. Why in the world would they send the dachniks clues, when they had never helped anyone with anything before.

Except for a single person. They did send a warning to Katya, that one time...

"Nikitaaaaaa!" Yuki screamed desperately from the far end of the plot. A metal clang, so painfully familiar, tolled almost simultaneously with that scream.

The gingerbread house had a small panel with a row of buttons stuck onto the gate. Denny stroked a button indecisively with his fingertip. It was cool and smooth. This house was too expensive to just walk up and ask for help. They'd have to explain that they were not local, and got caught in the storm, lost in the woods, and all kinds of crazy going on back there... They'd get sent packing. But then, that sweet smell of cinnamon, and something else delicious. Maybe they were baking pies in there, with a real chef sweating by the stove, in a mansion like that. Stacy was freaking out behind him as usual, with her endless "Denny, Denny," and he suddenly just wanted to show her that he knew what he was doing, and was not afraid of anything, not like her, all senseless and helpless.

He exhaled and jabbed the button.

"She's unwell! And anyway... where do you get off, locking a person in with a corpse?" Nikita raged, trying to get through the improvised human chain, consisting of Andrei, Pashka, and Yakov Semyonovich, ranged around the garage.

Claudia Il'yinichna stood by the door. She had replaced the broken padlock with a shiny new one. Unhurriedly, she was turning the key.

"Just as well that she's unwell," the chairwoman said tranquilly. "And if she gets hungry, there's something for her to eat, right there."

Pashka, who was not exactly sure how he ended up among the guardians of the garage, snorted wildly with laughter.

"Are you... are you out of your mind?" Just the thought of the burned-flesh smell made Nikita's stomach knot.

"Out of my mind? Me?" Claudia Il'yinichna dropped the key into the pocket of her cardigan. Without warning, she lurched toward him with a terrible grimace. "*I'm* out of *my* mind?! Am I the one who's protecting a cannibal here?"

The human chain looked entirely perplexed, but they held her back too, as she tried to surge forth, channeling the ancient ancestral rage that had made her foremothers thrash their children half to death and chase down husband-snatchers with a pitchfork. It was not from malice that they had raged, but from grief – the kind of grief that is seared into every fiber of one's being.

Nikita saw this not with his rational mind, but with his soul. And he would have withdrawn before such grief, had it not been for Yuki, underfoot as always, who just then burst into tears:

"You're the ones that are cannibals! You should be ashamed of yourselves!"

"Maybe we are ashamed," said Claudia Il'yinichna. Her contorted face cracked. "It's just that people around her keep dropping like flies, my girl! And I stand for the people! You hear me? I'm responsible for everybody here! So if it comes to it, I'll bludgeon her to death myself!"

Yuki dropped to a scared little whisper. "Don't... please, please don't, Claudia Il'yinichna..."

Nikita made another try for the door, but someone behind him pulled him back to the periphery.

It was Gena. "You're fighting with old ladies now? Go on, get out of here, we'll manage without you..." Gena let go. He rubbed his balding head tiredly. "Pavlov, honestly, don't make it worse, OK?"

Nikita couldn't breathe for outrage:

"You... I'll show you... you're all... you'll see... you assholes!" To everyone's surprise, he raced away in the opposite direction, to the gate, where he snatched up a sturdy aspen stick that the chairwoman, in the previous long-ago life, always took on mushrooming forays, shook it at the assembled villagers, and shot out to the street.

The chairwoman held a still silence for half a minute, lips pursed and nostrils flaring, and then collapsed with her hands to her face, transfigured in an instant from a middle-aged but still imposing woman to a bowed and doleful old lady. Gena caught her by the arm professionally, and would have led her back to the house, but she pulled away from him, backing up to the garage door.

"I won't let you..." she muttered. "I won't. I'm the one responsible for everybody here. I'm in charge..."

In the absence of any sound behind the fence, Denny had just about decided to try their luck at the next house over, when the bowels of the lock squeaked and the gate opened a crack. A woman, veiled and rustling in a transparent raincoat cocoon, stuck her head out. She gawped at her uninvited visitors through the lenses of her spectacles, thin and light as dragonfly wings.

"Who might you be?"

Denny took on a lungful of air and rattled off the speech he'd prepared, though it all came out in a jumble: so basically they got lost and could they use the phone, because all their things were in the tent and there was something weird going on, the storm and everything, like the Bermuda triangle, and some psycho had attacked them, maybe somebody should call the police, but they didn't need anything much, just to ask, because they went off the path, which way was it to the road...

The woman interrupted him mid-flow.

"You're soaked right through. Why are you wandering about all alone? Don't you know how dangerous it is around here? Get inside, right now."

Denny and Stacy traded doubtful looks. And then they heard someone running toward them.

There was a man coming at them from the other end of the street. He was wearing rags, which sharp-eyed Stacy saw were covered in red-brown stains, and he looked insane. In his long, monkey-like arms, he carried a ginormous stick. Getting closer, he suddenly stopped, gave a cry of astonishment and then waved his stick at them. He shouted hoarsely, "Stop, don't move!" and raced toward them faster than before.

"Quickly, quickly!" The woman seemed genuinely frightened of him. She pulled Denny and Stacy inside and locked the gate.

They found themselves in a large, slightly unkempt garden. Lush, expensive roses and lilies raised their heavy heads above the overgrown grass. The clipped hedges alongside the path had lost their stark shapes, but the shiny foliage still looked noble and refined. Globe lanterns inclined toward the house like strings of pearls. Little trees, frothy with blossom, swayed in the breeze. It was all very beautiful.

"Wonderful, isn't it? The scent?" The lady of the house inhaled deeply. "These are Chinese apple trees, very luxe, my husband, he..." she seemed to choke momentarily, probably taking in too much of the scent, then went on. "My husband brought them all the way from Beijing. You like it here?"

The gate shook and clanged as someone tried to smash their way inside. The hammering was interspersed with a terrible roar:

"Open up! Sveta, open that gate! Open it right now!"

Stacy struggled to make her lips move, they were trembling that hard.

"Who is that?"

"I told you didn't I, it isn't safe round here. There's more than one psycho roaming around... Go on, get inside the house. We can talk in there."

* * *

From the outside the dacha made a big, not to say monumental, impression; on the inside it seemed, if anything, even more vast. The dark, glossy parquet floor was slippery under their wet, bare feet. The lady handed Denny and Stacy, who were both shivering, a large towel and told them to rub themselves down properly, then sat them down at a little side table in a spacious room on the ground floor – this must have been the living room. In a flash, there were sandwiches and tea. Stacy was so overwrought she couldn't take a bite, but Denny went at the sandwiches with a vengeance, in between guzzling the hot sweet tea. The bread was delicious and obviously homemade; the dusky slices of semi-translucent meat on top looked mouthwatering. Some kind of pork? Or maybe beef, or even game... anyway, some sort of fancy delicacy that would leave a faint salty tang as it melted in the mouth.

"Don't be shy," their hostess pressed them affectionately. "Help yourselves."

Nikita tried one more time to take a running leap over the Beroevs' impregnable fence, but only managed to clamp on to the top with the tips of his fingers for a moment, before he went down again. Then he started beating the gate with his stick, in the manner of a giant gong:

"Open up! Sveta! Open up!"

Stacy knew the hoarse tones of the blood-spattered psycho from the street straight away; she shot to her feet. Sveta too stiffened, the look of sweet serenity evaporating at once from her birdlike face. She tugged the teenagers by the hands:

"Get upstairs!"

Denny extricated himself for a second to come back for another sandwich, then carried on escaping with his mouth full. Sveta pulled him out to the hallway in mid-chew and drove the pair of them up the stairs.

* * *

Nikita was on Katya's plot by then. He finally remembered about the pear tree that had gotten them into the neighboring garden once already. Now the tree was missing most of its branches and sported the kind of gashes on its trunk that made it clear someone tried inexpertly to saw it down but only succeeded in scarring the bark. Blunted her handsaw real nice, that fool, Nikita gloated. He climbed up with difficulty, heaved himself over the fence and dropped down... onto broken glass. The lawn from before was thickly carpeted with glass shards.

"You're dead," he hissed. Plucking a bunch of glass splinters from various soft places, he limped on toward the house.

There was a heap of gardening tools over at a windowless wall – a watering can, a rake, a spade, some poles and string for propping up flowers. Just as he went for the spade, as the heaviest of the implements and most suitable for bringing along on a social visit, Nikita spotted a little rust-speckled hand axe hiding coyly behind the watering can. Nikita gave an irritated cluck: of course, the axe again, where would he be without an axe. But he put the spade back.

She left them in a small room beneath the eaves whose sloping ceiling was covered in stars and airplanes. A windchime glimmered by the window. From outside, there came an insistent clanging. Stacy, hardly daring to breathe, peeked out and saw a dark human form on the porch, hacking. She couldn't see any more because Sveta dropped the blind shut.

"Who... is that?"

"Neighbors. That's the kind of neighbors we've got these days..." Sveta's eyes darted to the window. "Don't you know anything at all?"

"How could we... you weren't even here before! I mean, not the dachas, not anything... It was just the woods! And then everything... And you weren't here at all!"

Stacy was shouting, wringing her hands.

"And where are we, anyway? I want to go home!"

Sveta was suddenly beside her, hugging her. Stacy wept into the woman's blouse. Sveta stroked her hair:

"Hush now, hush. You sit here a minute and calm yourself. I'll be back in just a tick. All right?"

"Don't go, don't leave, he's out there..."

"That's a solid door, imported. He won't break it."

The lock clicked. She's shut us in, Stacy thought dully. She sat on a bed, head down and hugging her knees. It was better not to think, not to try and figure out what was happening, when you could go mental, trying... More than anything in the world she wanted to be back home, in her own bedroom, with Grandma's TV program bleating indistinctly from next door, while Stacy lay in bed and cruised the net on the silvery raft of her cell phone. She was online most of the time, scrolling through social media feeds, texting – mostly with Denny...

She remembered him suddenly, realizing that he hadn't said a word in all this time, and didn't seem to be reacting to anything. Right now, he was happily digging through a brightly colored box full of small pieces of a kids' building set.

"Denny..." she whined at him quietly. "Den, what are we going to do?"

Denny looked baffled, but after a moment's thought, offered her a little green piece of Lego.

At last, Nikita managed to hack a rectangular slit in the smooth wooden door, which was so hard the axe recoiled from it as though from stone. He thrust his hand inside and felt for

the lock. His fingers alighted on something round, metallic –
a handle of some kind, or a deadbolt. Ignoring the splinters
biting into his hand, Nikita tugged and worried at the object,
but it was no use. Sveta had sealed her lair pretty tight. Nikita
looked longingly at the windows, inaccessible behind filigree
ironwork, and went back to hacking at the door.

Their hostess returned with a tray, laden with two cups of
quivering tea and a neat arrangement of the same sandwiches.
The same welcoming smile, the same slim, glimmering
spectacles. The same hammering and crunching from
downstairs. Stacy had a sudden, stunning insight – it stung
her like a burn – that she was being made to participate in
someone else's bout of pervasive insanity, and the temperature
was rising by the second.

Denny snatched two sandwiches and a teacup then went
back to his box. Stacy shook her head no:

"Thank you, I'm not hungry…" She was trying to evade
looking Sveta in the eye.

"Just some tea then. It's nice and hot. You need to warm
up."

Stacy fixed her eyes on the floor. A jolly little rug depicting
colorful intertwining snakes. One, two, three… six snakes.
Two green, two yellow, one black and one red.

"Drink some tea." Sveta's voice was icy. Her thin lips pressed
together into a pink stripe, the pinkish-red of the sandwich
meat.

Although Stacy considered herself a grown woman, wise in
the ways of the world, she still found it hard when grown-ups
were angry with her. She gathered enough courage to choose
the cup with a little less brown liquid in it than the others.

"It's very good tea," said their hostess, softening. "I had
some left, from way back when…"

"When what?"

"When we still had good black tea."

With a terrible feeling of doom, Stacy shut her eyes and took a sip. The tea really was good, strong and well-sweetened. At once she felt warmer. Blood rushed to her temples.

"That's a good girl," Sveta smiled. Her mousy face was suddenly kind and appealing. Stacy shyly smiled back. The wonderful brew had an aftertaste of bergamot; it trickled right through Stacy and settled in her stomach, tickly and soft, like a kitten bedding down in there. It was over, all the horrors of the day, the awful mayhem in space-time. All the monsters had skulked back into the stormy dark, whimpering with remorse. How wonderful that the kind Sveta, who even looked a little like Stacy's mother, had taken pity on them and sheltered them. She had a kind of soft light about her, which made sense, for someone whose name literally means light…

She had not noticed Sveta slipping from the room. She snuggled in the armchair, drinking her tea in small sips and smiling peacefully at the monotonous thudding from below, dozing…

The door swung open and two creatures slunk laboriously inside. She took them for children at first, children playing horsies or doggies, but then she saw the way their contours ebbed and flowed, their limbs unfurling like tentacles, their torsos inflating to shapeless bags then deflating again into fragile, childish bodies. Their skin seemed to pulsate; they were entirely covered with weeping scabs. Their advance seemed tentative, as though moving was difficult for them. Stacy felt sorry for them; she put her hand out toward one, to show it everything was ok, there was nothing to be afraid of.

A spurt of blood, and the little pad of flesh beneath her thumb was gone, sliced clean off. She saw the face clearly now, raised toward her: a scabby forehead and little dark eyes, a child's eyes. And a gigantic round maw, like a sucking leech's, with concentric circles of sharp yellow teeth.

As she screamed in pain and horror, Sveta's soothing, enveloping brew lost its hold. Stacy saw two indescribable creatures thrashing and snarling on the floor. They had sloughed off their human shapes entirely: only the huge, leathery, sack-like bodies were left, remarkably supple for all their awkward physiology, and those hungry, gaping funnel mouths.

"They're very weak, the children, they could do with something fresh..." Sveta said from the doorway, where she stood gazing at them tenderly.

Both creatures leapt on Stacy, but she toppled backward and kicked them off. Squealing plaintively, they made for Denny, who just grinned at them stupidly from the bed. Now Sveta went for Stacy, and when she grabbed the girl by the throat, Stacy saw the ferocious look in her eyes up close. It was the glare of an animal defending her young. This was the scariest thing so far. Terror struck her like a scalding wave, but instead of making her stupefied and helpless, it had the opposite effect. It made her furious. She felt for an object, anything at all, and clamped her fingers around a toy truck, then smashed it into their hostess's head almost with pleasure. The woman plonked down on the floor with a scream. Stacy carried on thrashing everything in sight with the unbroken truck flatbed that had come off in her hand, hard walls and soft flesh and furnishings, until she suddenly sensed a clear space in front of her and dove for it. She fell through the doorway, scrambled over the beautifully polished parquet, and tumbled, head over heels, down the stairs.

Before she could hit the last step, someone grabbed and held her tight. A large dirty hand clamped over her nose and mouth and the someone hissed:

"Quiet!"

She was halfway to asphyxiating when the hand finally let go and she made out, in the gloom of the hallway, the psycho in the blood-spattered rags. She knew for sure now that it was blood. Digging his fingers into her forearm painfully, he turned her around to face him and muttered:

"That's better..."

And swung the axe high.

Curled in the fetal position, hands shielding her head, Stacy lay on the floor hiccupping and sobbing. Nikita had wrapped her bleeding hand with a strip from his t-shirt. He was running his hands over her, gingerly as though in fear of getting burned, picking at her fingers and tilting her chin, turning her face this way and that. All the while he was mumbling, that it wasn't anything weird, he wasn't some serial killer, just checking if she was a changeling, because changelings, they turned back if you scared them with an axe or a broom, and he didn't have a broom, so...

"Did you come from the outside?"

Stacy kept mum.

"You're not... you're not from the village, right?"

Stacy gulped back tears and shook her head no.

"How did you get in here?"

"I don't know!"

"Shush, stop that bawling. Tell me... but only the truth, OK? How is it... on the outside. Is it like it was before? The world, I mean, and everything... is it still there? Nothing's happening?"

"No... nothing..."

"Everything is normal, right? What time is it now? I mean what year is it, or what month even..."

"Um... it's June?"

"What do you mean, June? We've had months of... So time stopped on the outside too?"

"I don't know anything..." Stacy shook her head again and bawled.

"All right, keep it down," Nikita told her anxiously. "If you don't know, you don't know. What's your name, anyway?"

"Anastasia..." She was only ever Stacy to Denny, who was... Who had been...

Then she heard his voice from above, hysterical:

"Stace! Stace, where are you? Staceeee!"

The cries mingled with growling and groaning. Stacy imagined the chomping noises, too, and the squelchy tearing of living flesh. She put her hands over her ears and spun around like a top, just as she had done years ago in nursery school, from pain and mortification, when the new boy Denny – he was still just plain Dennis back then – had tugged as hard as he could on her thin yellow plait...

She knocked into something and it crashed to the floor. Nikita frowned thoughtfully at the curved cabriole legs of the toppled side table, then pushed at the edge of the rug with his toe. The cellar door. At first he was glad to have a place to stash the kid, and even tugged at the handle ring, then recalled the flayed Beroev still crawling about in the dark down there. The simplest and easiest thing would be to just let her out in the street, but she was sure to run away, the little dope, and disappear without telling him anything useful. It's what he would have done. As he turned toward the girl in his confusion, Nikita spotted an understairs cupboard right behind her.

Still muttering something vaguely comforting at her, he stuffed the crying girl into the cupboard – the way you stuff a sick cat into a pet carrier – and snicked the door handle. Then he ran upstairs.

Stubbing his toe over a rug, he pitched headfirst into a little, slope-ceilinged room. The first thing he noticed were the stars on the ceiling, those fluorescent stickers that store up energy during the day and light up with a ghostly glow when it's dark. Only after did he see the shapeless leathery bulks writhing on the floor. A crimson puddle was spreading out beneath them, there was blood on the walls, and even the ceiling was spattered bright red. An arm, gnawed to the bone but with a couple of thick, stubby fingers remaining, beckoned Nikita from underneath the slurping, spluttering beasts. The hand was still twitching. There was a raw, pink hangnail on the index finger.

Nikita screamed and swung his axe – then Sveta Beroeva landed on his back from behind. He never imagined there might be so much strength in her long, slim frame. She twined herself around him like a bindweed round a tree trunk and started to drag him down. By some miracle he got an arm free, the one with the axe, but he could not bring himself to hit her – a woman, and a neighbor, with whom he'd stood in a slow-moving queue by the village store chatting about the weather... Sveta squealed and bit him on the cheek. He tried in vain to throw her off; they tumbled out of the room entirely. She never let up kneeing him sharply in the belly and she shrieked, so hard that froth flecked the corners of her narrow red lips. He just kept on telling her:

"They're not your kids, not your kids..."

Eventually he managed to press her into the floor, but she slithered over the top stair, pulling him with her, and down they went, bumping all the way, step by step.

Everything went foggy and indistinct for a moment, losing urgency. Nikita felt so sleepy... He opened his eyes to the sight of Sveta raising an axe above him triumphantly. The blade crunched down into the parquet and biting pain shot through Nikita's arm, fingertip to shoulder. He looked over at it in horror, expecting to see a bloody stump, but everything seemed in its place. The axe, on the other hand, was stuck in the expensive hardwood flooring. Sveta was working desperately to pull it free.

Nikita leapt up, swerved, and grabbed her by the neck from behind. She was very light, Sveta, like a dried-out grasshopper. He lifted her easily from her feet: she kicked wildly and wouldn't let go of the axe handle. Nikita felt a stab of something like joy: it was almost over, he was going to strangle Sveta, and everything would come out, and the village would be rid of one magic glamor at least...

The axe came free with a hard crunch. Sveta writhed, and at the whistling of the blade Nikita let go. As he backed away, he stumbled over something again. The cellar door. He had only lifted it a crack before, but now his stepping on the lever opened the hatch fully. There was a cold, rotting whiff from the square opening. Nikita looked at Sveta. Slight and disheveled, her golden spectacles quivering on the end of her nose, she somehow seemed to exist independently of the blindly swinging axe. The first time Nikita had seen her, many years before, he'd even fancied her a little. It was at the communal barbeque they had for the dacha village and cooperative's thirtieth anniversary – she was lying when she said that no one made friends with her or invited her anywhere. She knew how to get them all to feel sorry for her, didn't she: a young mother with little children, so much to do... At the barbeque he'd tried to proposition her, but was sloshed as usual and couldn't get the words out properly. She hadn't slapped him, as tended to be the way with other women he fancied, just laughed at him, then vanished into the half-light that streamed with the orange glow of the bonfire.

Strangling with that crisp, cold dread that had once come into the village on an icy cosmic draught, Nikita grasped that there could only be two outcomes: either Sveta would kill him, or he would kill her. Except he couldn't do it, he couldn't live with a dead Sveta inside his head. Having to remember her birdlike face, her long legs and fragile spectacles...

Sveta rushed him, axe high above her head, which was all the more frightening for being so awkwardly done. A bloody gash opened in Nikita's trouser leg. He lurched sideways, and suddenly she was at the edge of the hole in the floor. Right on the edge, her heels over an empty space.

Her gaze cleared. Her eyes still held that same rage and willingness to kill, tear apart, feed the children – but also a reasoning, human horror.

"Sveta, listen, they're not your..." Nikita reached out his hand.

Of course she knew they were not her children. But they were all she had, her sole, crowning achievement in life. The children were her anchor to the wealthy Beroev, who finally had the heirs he needed, and to the good life. There was no Beroev now and no good life, but she couldn't bear to be left behind with nothing and so she clung to what was given her in exchange. By a schizophrenic feat of will alone, her brain had swapped these new children for the old ones. She had cared for them through sleepless nights, fed them and reared them, and now this outsider who had broken into her house was demanding the impossible...

Though he barely managed to pull his arm back in time, the falling blade still razed a slice off Nikita's forearm. Sveta lost her balance and swayed, gawping – clinging onto the axe like a tightrope walker's pole. And Nikita gave her a push. Just a tiny one, with the tips of his fingers. Maybe this was unnecessary, and everything that happened next would have happened anyway. Nikita really wanted to believe that.

Directly, Sveta dropped through the hatch, and Nikita slammed down the cover. There was a thud below. Then all went quiet, if you didn't count Stacy's frantic hammering on the cupboard door. Then a rustling from the cellar, as if something heavy was being dragged across the floor. And then crashing, the shattering of glass jars, and bestial screaming.

Those were not Sveta's real children up above, but her real husband sure was down below.

Stacy heaved at the door, something cracked, and then she could finally take in a lungful of the dusty air that seemed so fresh after the stuffy cupboard. She fell out of the cupboard together with a mop. The man who had locked her inside was sitting motionless on the floor, a little past the bottom of the stairs. There were more bloodstains on his shredded clothing, and his hands were dripping with blood. Stacy let out a strangled moan. The man raised his face, his eyes went wide, and he growled:

"Run!"

She turned to see the black creatures on the stairs; two amorphous sacks juddering down step by step. One of them raised whatever passed for its head: its many eyes flashed red and its round maw opened wide. The monster compressed its unwieldy bulk into a tight coil and sprang three full meters across to Stacy, latching its toothy sucker-mouth on her thigh. Stacy went down in a spray of blood, her own mouth open in a silent, agonized scream. Nikita hurled the changeling aside with the mop, but then the second one sprang onto his chest. Its round maw constricted hungrily over Nikita's face, teeth grinding together, creaking... Nikita poked it in one flickering eye with the broom handle. There was a plaintive, almost childlike sob and the thing dropped off him. He found Stacy's hand and dragged her toward the door, but the girl's legs refused to work. And then another thick, leathery body thudded into Nikita's knees...

Far away, at the Petukhovs', Katya thrashed on the still-warm garage floor and mumbled, though her eyes were shut tight, "Fire, fire... Woman aflame... fire..."

"Fire, fire..." rang out inside Nikita's head. Katya once told him that changelings were afraid of fire. He didn't even have a box of matches on him. He was battering the creatures with the mop handle as he dragged the wailing Stacy toward the door, willing her to come on, crawl, we're almost there – for all that he knew that they were done for. The Beroev changelings had recovered enough to make a pile of blood and bones out of the two of them, same as they'd done with the others. It might just take a little longer.

Then it came again, a faint surge of pale flame. The mop blazed briefly white and then orange, like a normal fire. The changelings recoiled, squealing.

"Aaaaaaaarrrgghhhh!" howled Nikita with primal glee. He walloped the things with the burning mop, its raggedy, dirty head flaming like a torch. The fire spread to the handle, sparks flew, the black hides blistered and hissed... The changelings cowered together, and tried to wriggle away, howling... and retreating.

The dachniks who came to investigate the noise saw an extraordinary sight emerge from the smoke: Nikita Pavlov, with indistinct battle cries of some kind, was beating two monstrous things that looked like vastly enlarged leeches down the street with a flaming staff. The monsters hissed and snarled, working their round, toothy maws, yet slunk obediently down the street as he drove them to the Sushka. There was also a girl sitting under the Beroevs' fence, a round-cheeked, blonde teenager that no one had seen before. She was trying to stem the blood seeping copiously from her thigh and staring at them. Her eyes were swollen from crying.

"Help her!" shouted Nikita. "Don't let her go, she's from the outside!"

All the young people – meaning Pashka, Yuki, and even Andrei, who was still trying to look unconvinced – followed Nikita Pavlov, for a better look at the strange beings. He drove them expertly, keeping to the middle of the road, cutting short any veering off course with a flaming smack of the broom:

"I told you, didn't I... Here they are, your beasts, Sveta's little fuckers... She fed them up big and strong, with live people. Go on, have a good look at them..."

Yuki was looking, and with great alarm, but not at the monsters. She had never seen Nikita so vengeful, and raging and cruel. He looked like a hunter dragging a wolf, still in its death throes, through the snow. Yuki vividly pictured the scene from some book or movie. Nikita looked shredded into strips, ragged and bleeding, and there was one more thing: the tip of the fourth finger on his right hand was sliced clean off. He didn't seem to feel any pain or notice that he was covered head to toe in blood.

They came to the river and stopped at the high muddy bank. Nikita spotted a strip of wood – one of Katya's bottom-fishing rigs – in the grass. The beasts tumbled down the damp muddy bank like beavers or seals. They didn't need any steering now, they writhed toward the water.

"River's out of bounds," Andrei ventured uncertainly.

Nikita waved him aside, forgetting he still held the flaming mop handle, and Andrei leapt back. Then he went down after the creatures.

One after the other, the changelings dove into the brackish water, punching a hole through the green weeds and scum. There were no bubbles, no concentric circles, nothing. They vanished as though they had never been.

"Is that it?" Yuki whispered. Secretly, she had expected the real Beroev children to walk out of the river now, unharmed, and there would be a happy end. Relatively happy.

"Well, they're not going to eat anybody else." Nikita exhaled heavily and lobbed his guttering torch into the water.

Strangers ringed Stacy round: they were all talking at her, trying to touch her, but she couldn't understand them and their words split apart into meaningless syllables that also tried to get at her, surrounding her like a cloud of midges. Time turned slow and viscous as sucking candy, the strangers' mouths slowly opened and closed, opened and closed; she began to

panic again. Then she perceived that these people were much
more frightening than the black beasts and their insane keeper.
Beasts were beastly, they didn't reason, they just wanted to
eat. But she was surrounded by people. Their trembling hands,
spent and swollen faces, gloomy and grasping looks. And the
smell. They all reeked of something sour and sick – a scary
smell. How the homeless in the underground metro stations
sometimes smelled, the ones that tried to guilt the taciturn
passersby with their stumps and boils. The beasts were beasts,
but these people had once been normal, reasonable. Something
happened to them. Maybe they all died, but didn't know it yet,
and carried on getting up in the morning, and getting dressed,
and wandering the earth without any purpose...

"You're dead!" she shrieked. "Dead!"

The dachniks recoiled. This was a possibility they had
considered and discussed, and it was one that frightened them
especially. Grinding her teeth against the pain, Stacy sprang up
and ran from them, limping. They chased after her, she heard
them calling out:

"Stop! Don't be scared! Wait!"

She fled without a backward glance, thinking only of not
fainting, not falling, not letting them get her. When she came to
a chain-link fence, she clawed at it and climbed up, falling over
the top and into darkness. She felt herself sliding backward
and downward, and into a stomach-churning merry-go-round
kaleidoscope of shapes... she was at the fairground, four years
old, and Mom wouldn't buy her the cotton candy...

A few hours passed before the bravest of the lot breached the
Beroev mansion. The cellar was an unholy jumble of broken jars
and building supplies, and among these they found a multitude
of human bones, ranging from small, unidentifiable fragments
picked clean to whole skeletons with rags of flesh still attached.
One of them had enough of its face left that it was unanimously

identified as Beroev. They also found Sveta Beroeva down there. Something had torn her head almost clean off. Her face and neck bore the bruise-purple imprints of fingers.

Nikita didn't return to the Beroevs' dacha; he went to the Petukhovs' instead. The chairwoman was at her lonely post by the garage still – someone had helpfully brought out a chair for her, and she was dozing, wrapped up in a shawl. When she heard the approach, she raised her head and squinted. Unchanging she was, Claudia Il'yinichna, but also a little nearsighted it seemed. When she saw who it was, and moreover the state of him, she shrank back.

"The key," Nikita ordered, thrusting his hand, brown with blood and missing a fingertip, in her face.

The bright green moss was springy under her feet, and the grass was dotted with tight, glossy bunches of brambleberries. Stacy staggered through the woods, swaying like a drunk and whispering some lines from a song in an old kids' animated film, the one about the tiger cub and the monkey and the road and the clouds, that was stuck in her head:

It's so nice to wander back, to wander back beneath the clouds,
When we get to wandering home beneath the clouds...

Her wound was barely bleeding anymore and she was even glad of the cold sweat that pleasantly cooled her forehead. She felt hollow and light. But where was Denny, who dragged her on this blasted camping trip in the first place? She couldn't catch sight of him, though she knew it was him hiding behind the trees, rustling and chirping among the leaves. It was him throwing morel mushrooms – they looked like pieces of white bone – under her feet instead of crumbs, so she could find the way.

The way beneath the clouds…

An earthen pillar, bound up with tree roots, reared up in front of her. Huge, taller than the dark pines along the trail, it rained down pine needles and black forest ants.

It was him, of course. Her Denny. Here he was, all found.

Stacy smiled and stepped forward to meet him.

14

THE RETURN

After everything that happened over the last few days, the village was deflated and dazed. There was no wandering the streets or digging in kitchen gardens, or chopping by the woodsheds. Pashka lay in bed with a high fever – his bitten leg, which he had ignored in big-guy fashion for so long, went swollen and inflamed. Gena made him compresses, swearing at him and threatening gangrene. The former paramedic had enough on his hands without Pashka: he was endlessly changing the bandages on Nikita Pavlov, who'd been scraped clean with an axe and was miraculously missing only the tip of his finger and half of a fingernail. He kept having to shepherd that incorrigible Katya, who was probably concussed, back into bed. Then there was the chairwoman to dose with her dwindling supplies of an over-the-counter sedative; she was not doing well at all, alternating between looking alive and busy, and going on about organizing another village meeting, and hiding in a corner, in floods of silent tears. Everyone had been stunned by how quickly and irreversibly her sudden widowhood had broken her. Claudia Il'yinichna was transformed from a dignified, self-possessed bossy-boots that basically kept the whole thing going, to a pitiful old woman. They had all thought of Petukhov – perhaps justifiably – as useless and henpecked. But it turned out that she needed him, like a solid-looking fence needs a scraggy, blighted little rowan tree to prop it up. Chop down the tree, and the fence, lacking its feeble support, falls down flat.

It wasn't just Petukhov, though. Every night Claudia Il'yinichna had the same dream, in which she chased that girl from outside, the one that everyone kept talking about, down Cherry Street, but could never catch her. The girl kept vanishing, sinking through the ground, falling apart into raindrops. Claudia Il'yinichna wept to have let her get away, this messenger from the regular world, living proof that the village was not abandoned, alone in a universe gone mad... If only she'd been there, she would have stopped her for sure, would have talked her into staying. She could talk anyone into anything, couldn't she, after years of chairing meetings about raised rates. But she'd missed the whole thing, guarding that useless witch Katya.

No one let their children out of doors, so the bold and parentless Yuki was left to bicycle around the village on her own. Lyosha-don't, who had been taken in by the kindhearted herb witch Zinaida Ivanovna, occasionally got away and kept Yuki company by swearing extravagantly at her from street corners or throwing mud at her. It was his way of showing her he cared.

Nikita and Katya had been at the river since dawn, but nothing was biting. Each time he threw in his line, Nikita crooked his bandaged finger out of the way and thought about how strange the shortened digit – disabled in the blink of an eye – would look to him forevermore, after it healed. Stranger still was the thought of Sveta Beroeva being dead. Gena told him that her head had been almost torn off, quite literally, marveling at the brute strength of whoever did it. Nikita tried to explain that it was Sveta's own husband who killed her, but Gena wouldn't believe him. He'd seen Beroev's flayed skeleton among the other bones in that cellar. Katya said that a captive corpse always subsided once it'd had its revenge, and turned back into a normal corpse that rotted in peace... I just pushed her, Nikita told himself, as he stared at the bobbing float, just pushed her, that's all. She might have fallen in all by herself, anyway.

He had to get used to living with dead Sveta inside his head.

Katya sat a little apart. She wore a shapeless old t-shirt and cargo pants caked with river mud. A kerchief was knotted around her neck, and her face was still bruised purple. She had a black eye, swollen shut, like a juvenile delinquent.

Nikita struggled for something to say. After the garage, after the white flame and Usov, after everything that happened. He checked if her head was hurting a couple of times, wondered what was biting round these parts, and borrowed a bit of bait – some kind of gray homemade sludge – only to plop the stiff clump straight into the shallows, accidentally.

"That's why I always go fishing alone, you know," Katya remarked. She still sounded hoarse.

Small fry roiled in the shallows, demolishing the bait with the savagery of piranhas. Beyond the commotion, there were wisps of soft mist floating over the dark water.

"Does that mean heat or rain?" asked Nikita.

"Round here everything means heat. Poludnitsa likes heat..."

"And that's why it's summer?"

"That's why it's summer."

Nikita fell to thinking how he woke to a melancholy tune from his cell phone that morning, falling off the bed and almost passing out from the pain, crawling to the table... only then remembering that he had set an alarm the night before. The devil knew why he'd asked Katya to take him along fishing. Then again, it was her that said that fishing was calming for the nerves. The cell showed five-thirty am, October 31. This is ridiculous, thought Nikita, as he looked out the window at the cherry blossoms blooming for the third time in a row.

Katya gently drew her float toward a clump of fleshy-leafed waterlilies.

"I suppose it was the pale ones cooling the water down," she confided suddenly. "The ones who live down there. That's how come the mist. They're early risers, they like it better when it's cool."

Nikita swiveled his head around:

"They're not going to come for us, are they?"

"I doubt it, they've had enough of me." Katya's derisive little cough made her grimace with pain and put her hand up to her throat. "If they do come, just ignore them. They're going to start rifling through your head straightaway, so you need to think about something else, distract yourself. Did you hear about the Beroevs' fridge?"

What a topic to bring up, distraction notwithstanding. But Nikita kept this thought unspoken, just nodded. The Beroevs' fridge, a freakishly tall contraption sporting fashionable reflective doors, was found to be stuffed with all manner of comestibles not seen in the village for ages. It was quite clear what – or rather who – went into the making of those goodies. There was frozen and smoked and ground meat, and pelmeni dumplings, even something like homemade sausage. A good little homemaker, Sveta had ingeniously planned it all out, for the long-term, so that the children needn't leave the house in search of food, though in the end they did escape to chase after fresh meat. It seemed that Sveta went out hunting herself, to begin with – searching through dachas, or maybe luring people to hers. She had picked out the lonely and the weak, they were easier to manage. Judging by the sheer number of the bones in the cellar, at least half of the missing dachniks stayed in the village forever, rather than vanishing in the woods.

* * *

Katya tugged sharply on her line, and a young bream floated lazily up to the surface like a wide pale stain on the water. Katya reeled him in carefully, right to the silty shallows, then hopped in on one bare foot, to grab the fat-lipped fish by the gills.

"Here comes lunch."

Bream safely stowed in a little holding pond, Katya cast her line again and wiped her foot on the grass.

Nikita had caught himself thinking that any moment now the water would bubble up around her ankle, and steam... Katya somehow caught him thinking it too.

"I didn't incinerate Usov," she scowled. "Or the changelings that time. I don't even know what that was... I couldn't have. It can't have been me, Pavlov, I'm scared of fire. Maybe because of my granny, those stories of hers... I'm scared of burning to death. That's my worst fear, to die like that. I used to dream about it as a kid, the same dream every time: this great big meadow, blazing with white fire end to end. It's all burning, and I'm burning with it... I was screaming so loud at night, the neighbors complained. They took me to doctors, gave me pills. I still kept dreaming. Then Granny said she'd whisper it away, the old way... and it stopped. But I'm still terrified of fire."

As she spoke, Katya could almost smell the lavender: Granny had put little bags of it in the bedlinen drawer. All the pillowcases and sheets were steeped in that cool, somber scent.

The bright light is hurting her eyes. Mother is hovering in the doorway; Granny forbade her to enter. Little Katya sits on the edge of the bed wailing, hands over her face. She's still seeing, in her mind's eye, the wall of pale flame whipped by the wind across the meadow. The fire is devouring the grass and the flowers, and little furball mice burst into flame even as they scatter, instantly smoldering to wispy ash.

"The meadow's burning!" Katya wails. "It's burning!"

Her grandmother bends close:

"Was there a white lady there, in the meadow?" Granny doesn't stroke her head like her parents do or say that it was just a dream. The way she's paying Katya close attention somehow makes it even scarier. Now Katya starts to think that yes, there was a lady, huge and tall, that looked like a pillar of fire herself.

"White lady!" Katya dives under the covers. She only peeks out from her dark, close hidey-hole to watch Granny lash her pillow crosswise with a birch crop. As it falls, whistling, Granny says:

"You come no more! Come no more!"

The steady snap of the birch crop against her faded pillowcase grew louder and bigger, sand shot through with muffled metallic clanging. Nikita heard it too: he got to his feet and looked out, alarmed. They'd picked a very secluded fishing spot, just by the bit of perimeter fence that bordered on the meadow. They could just make out the green top of the fence wobbling above the bushes.

Some long, loud seconds later, they realized that someone was knocking on the iron gates from the other side.

Slowly and gingerly they came up to the main gate: bearded Stepanov, the Dronov brothers, Yuki on her bike, the serial escapee Lyosha-don't with a peevish Zinaida Ivanovna in pursuit, and Yakov Semyonovich the dog breeder, and ancient Volopas, who shouted, struggling to be heard above the racket:

"Who's there?"

There was no answer, but the knocking continued. The fence was high and solid, without any gaps, so there was no way at all to see who was on the other side.

The knocking was reminiscent of the itinerant peddlers who had once upon a time called "Manure, get your manure here!" and "Any scrap metal? Bring out your scrap!" over the fence. As a rule, such riffraff did not gain admittance to the village proper, and the dachniks all politely ignored both the metallic clang and the cries, exotically accented and pitched to beguile. You didn't expect anything good to come from beyond the gate even back when things were normal.

Perhaps they ought to have ignored the knocking as usual, and gone home – the fence was sturdy, so let them knock themselves out – but in an agony of doubt and curiosity, the dachniks simply milled about and looked at one another, hoping that someone would make a decision. The kind of maybe wrong but definitive decision that was normally the prerogative of the chairwoman.

Finally, Zinaida Ivanovna shuffled forward in her felted booties and housecoat:

"Let me get a look in the crack, at least..."

The ancient Volopas was up in arms: no, no, what if they barged through, or pulled her out, what if there was... But Zinaida Ivanovna pointed regally to a knotted iron chain that sealed the two wings of the gate together. After Valerych went and vanished, they'd tied the gate up, so the next hotheaded seeker could reflect, as he sweated over the chain, on the decision to leave.

"Maybe we shouldn't?"

Already they were quietly pulling the bolt free, though the chain sensibly remained in place. Zinaida Ivanovna turned back to Katya and gave her a dubious look:

"Maybe you better keep quiet."

Either the Stoyanovo tales of the evil eye were true, or Gena was right about concussion, but either way, Katya's head abruptly ached. It felt heavy, the way it does at the beginning of a cold, when you can still breathe easy and your throat isn't yet raw and red, but already your eyes are not right, and everything is a bit too much, too bright, too loud, too jittery...

The Dronov brothers tugged the left side of the gate, the chain went taut across the two, and Zinaida Ivanovna cautiously looked into the gap.

"Well, I'll be..."

A bony, narrow hand slid into the gap and grabbed Zinaida Ivanovna by the shoulder.

"Shut it! Shut it!" That was the panicking Volopas. The Dronov brothers started to push at the heavy gate but Zinaida Ivanovna shoved them aside – well, it was more that the docile brothers stepped aside for her, perplexed – and clanged the chain hard, as she hurried to undo the giant knot.

The widening gap revealed Natalya Aksenova – who had driven away on the day the turning disappeared and, with the rest of her family, vanished. Now, that day seemed impossibly distant, belonging to some other reality, and so did Natalya. All that was left of that brassy, vigorous woman was her t-shirt, which depicted a smiling cartoon dog, and which many of the dachniks remembered just for how inappropriately flighty it'd seemed on the day.

The woman before the gate was incredibly thin and bronzed, as though desiccated in the sun. The faded t-shirt hung from her skeletal frame. Natalya's bright blue eyes, once so vivid, were also bleached and faded. Most extraordinary of all, her hair had gone entirely white. That hair – white as milk, white as a new lab coat – coupled with her deeply tanned face, made her look like a negative film of herself, and this was beautiful, really beautiful, in that devastating way that should never touch fragile mortal flesh.

The dachniks stared at Natalya, stupefied. She looked up at them with those parched eyes, and then she smiled, gently and kindly, as though she suddenly felt sorry for this pitiful bunch – in all their bewilderment, petulance and fright.

Everything tilted and went dark, the inside of her skull throbbed, and she felt leaden and feverish, like a full-on flu. Katya started forward anyway, holding onto people and trees for purchase:

"Shut it... shut the gate... shut the gate..." She was mumbling.

Everything spun and shimmered before her eyes and heat washed over her like a wave. She couldn't distinguish anything in the hubbub of voices. Then a brief clear snapshot: little old Volopas launches himself like a ball of fury at the motionless Natalya, but before he can get close, she touches her palm to his forehead. It leaves a red brand on his liver-spotted skin, five fingers clearly visible. Volopas is instantly sedated and still, his pinched face clears, as though he's growing younger. And now the world is drowning again, in the polychrome heat haze.

"Shut the gate..."

Someone caught Katya up, and kept her from toppling. She knew it was Nikita, and she was so glad. Though she could barely get the words out, she panted at him not to let the woman in, they had to get her away, they had to shut the...

Then she saw the crimson handprint, narrow and distinct, blazing across his forearm. And the way he was looking at Katya, with a tender, almost indulgent, smile on his face.

The gates were not shut. On the contrary, they were left wide open. Natalya set off for the heart of the village, down River Street, with the subdued and beatific villagers trailing in her wake.

Claudia Il'yinichna was sitting inside her covered veranda, in a rocking chair that hadn't rocked in a decade: he hadn't managed to fix it in all that time, that useless booby Petukhov, who couldn't even screw a lightbulb in properly, what with his two left hands. She knew it at first sight – a friend of her mother's had brought her bachelor son along on a visit, with obvious intention – here was a booby. Those ridiculous square glasses of his. That diffident, nearsighted gaze, and that droopy fringe, so earnestly patted into place. He was a straight-A student and played the piano, though the only thing he could still remember how to play so long after the many years of after-school lessons was – but of course – Tchaikovsky's *Children's Album*. What did she want with him, the brash and forceful young Claudia, when she made nice to him? What did she mean by asking him probing questions about his frankly uninteresting life, by loading up his tiny beveled jam dish with cherry preserves? Maybe it still burned her, the memory of her first, the man she could not resist, and now she wanted to hide away in something soft and dopey. To wrap herself in someone the way she wrapped her cold feet in a blanket. She was always cold now, Claudia Il'yinichna. She always wondered how those old ladies like Tamara Yakovlevna accrued layer after layer, cardigan on top of blouse, jacket on cardigan, shawl on top of jacket... and off they rolled, like cabbages. One had to comport oneself with dignity. Present oneself appropriately to one's age, sure, but you could still dress well, you were still a woman. These days, cardigans and oversize sweaters and assorted shawls seemed to swell one atop the other almost without her involvement, like soft mold on an old loaf of bread.

She didn't hear the approaching footsteps, and only raised her eyes at the opening of the door. A barefoot woman stepped inside the dusty veranda: she was deathly thin and her hair was bleached white. Her face was extraordinary, tender and impassive all at once. Others followed behind, but these were not strangers – Zinaida Ivanovna, Volopas, a few of the young people. They too seemed different and wonderful... they looked... enlightened. When she found the right word for it, she startled:

"What's happened? What... why are you... who authorized this?"

The white-haired woman stepped toward her and dropped smoothly to one knee. Claudia Il'yinichna couldn't feel the woman's breath or any scent at all, as though her visitor was not of flesh and blood. What she did feel in that moment, and distinctly, was her own feebleness. Claudia Il'yinichna squirmed;

"I've a mind to... Who are you?!"

The woman reached for her. Claudia Il'yinichna shrank back, but still the hand found a place just where her flowery blouse was visible through a spot where the thick cardigan was missing a button.

It seared her, that touch, through the thin cloth, like a piece of coal. The chairwoman made to stand up and push the burning hand away, then saw standing before her, in place of the fleshless woman, her own husband, the departed Petukhov. Never in life had those timid, nearsighted eyes looked on her with such empathy and compassion. Petukhov had forgiven his belligerent, prickly Claudia, who had been so "unrespectful", as her mother-in-law put it. He forgave her for the life they'd had together and for his death, and for not being her first. Hot young blood coursed through Claudia Il'yinichna's veins, commingling with the joy of forgiveness and remorse and absolution. The ache in her back and the pangs in her knees and all her feebleness melted away, her grief flowing from her in copious sweet tears. At last, she was light and empty and free. Claudia Il'yinichna smiled.

And forgot everything.

Nikita Pavlov had felt that same lightness and joy when Natalya, whom he had been attempting to push back out of the gate, suddenly reached out and touched him with the searing palm of her hand. The smarting wounds from his battle with Sveta Beroeva seemed instantaneously salved, and healed – gone without a trace, without a scar. His mutilated finger was whole again. Nikita felt the raggedy bandage catching on his restored fingertip.

The dead Sveta inside his head, meanwhile, laughed good-naturedly – just as she had that time at the thirtieth anniversary barbeque. She didn't hold a grudge, wasn't mad at him anymore. She knew that he hadn't killed her, not really, just given her a little push, he didn't have a choice did he, and she wasn't exactly innocent, going after a person with an axe. They'd both been hotheaded and foolish, and anyway, she would have fallen in all by herself, she was slipping over the edge. So he wasn't to blame for anything, and there was no need for him to feel bad.

Nikita gave a sigh of relief and smiled back at dead Sveta. And he too forgot everything.

This was a very uncomfortable bed, hard and full of sand that needed shaking out. And her cheeks were smarting, as though Granny Serafima had opened the windows again, to freshen the room with wintry air. She hated the dry radiator heat, always saying that it was better to be cold than hot.

Eventually Katya grasped that she was lying not in a bed but in the middle of River Street, someone's little palms hesitantly slapping her cheeks. She caught one, without opening her eyes, just to check... it was a normal, human hand. Warm.

"The woman aflame..."

"What woman!" came a weepy girlish cry. "It's me, just me! Katya let go, you're hurting me! Katya! Don't you recognize me?"

Yuki's frightened, dirt-streaked face hove into view. Her hair hung down like dull black icicles dipped in ash. As she lifted her head, Katya felt the fever rise again, her mouth thick and parched. Yuki babbled at her frantically: it's all gone crazy, you have no idea, everything's gone crazy... This Natalya, she was a witch for sure. When she put her hand on somebody, straight away they weren't themselves. She made them into zombies, but quiet zombies, happy and smiling. She was here in the village, walking up and down the streets, and Yuki just saw her from the bushes, going into the Yegorovs', you know, the ones always canoeing, from Flower Street. Yuki had scarpered as soon as she saw the woman's tricks, hopped on her bike and pedaled so hard the chain almost came off again. Then she was watching from around the corner, and saw something else strange...

Yuki fell silent, realizing that she didn't actually know how things stood: Natalya was a witch, and Katya was a witch too, for sure, but which one was good and which one evil? Maybe she got it all wrong, trusting the evil witch, while it was the serene, smiling Natalya who had come to save the village?

Katya worked hard to focus on the baffled teenager's face, then clapped her hot palms to Yuki's still-pudgy baby cheeks:

"What did you see?"

"She didn't touch you!" Yuki cried out. "She put her hand on everybody, whether they wanted it or not... The dog breeder, he was screaming his head off, and climbing up on the fence, but she grabbed him by the sleeve. But she didn't even touch you, you were lying here in the street and she just went past you... Why did she do that?"

"Woman aflame," Katya grated painfully, and started to get up. It was a slow business as she kept losing her balance.

"What woman? You mean Natalya? Why is she aflame?"

"Poludnitsa... it's all her doing."

"Katya, listen, you have a fever. Gena said you were concussed, maybe that's... or it's your burns. Katya, what if it's the flu? Katya, where are you going...?"

The thoughts roiling in Katya's overheated brain pan, about what was happening this time to the village and likewise to her personally, finally came to the boil and congealed into a thick hot mess. She pushed Yuki aside without a word – so hard, the girl fell backward onto her bicycle – and went to look for the source of both her granny's schizophrenia and the old-timey tales of Stoyanovo village. Its newly found physical manifestation, that was.

Yakov Semyonovich darted inside his gate and slammed it shut. He had been driven home by the single thought of hiding in the house, locking and barring, barricading himself inside, and though the imperative still pulsated in his brain from sheer inertia, he now stopped and paused.

He had been frantic to escape, when Natalya grabbed him by the sleeve, and as he felt the heat coming through the thick cloth, his brain fogged a little, as though he'd just downed a shot of vodka. It was a good jacket, hard-wearing, definitely worth the long queue all those years ago. Even Naida's playful mouthing found no purchase in the durable cloth. Nor had the handprint penetrated, beyond imprinting on the sleeve. He'd checked; there was no mark on his arm, which was sparsely covered in rough hairs. Back there by the village gate, he'd only pretended to go quiet and placid like the others. He'd peeled away from the crowd at the first corner and ran, through the kitchen gardens, to his own plot.

What brought him up short was the sight of his wife sitting on the wooden porch, with Naida lying at her feet. His wife was scratching the dog behind the ear.

Yakov Semyonovich's great secret, one he had not trusted to anyone, was that his wife had left him. A long time before, more than a month past.

She changed when they returned from the forest, having failed to find a way back to the ordinary world. Entirely silent, she wouldn't let him touch her, and began to sleep on a little couch in the hallway, still in her clothes. She never changed them, so the congealing stench got worse and worse. Naida, their beautifully trained Naida, had to be chained up outside because she didn't seem to know her mistress anymore, and kept going for her without a bark or growl of warning – as though determined to rip her to shreds, without any ceremony.

And another thing: his wife ate. God, how she ate. She emptied the fridge and consumed all the dried pasta and rye bran in the house, uncooked. Yakov Semyonovich watched her tear muddy beets and carrots from their beds and devour those too. Having seen the state of Vityok, he guessed the same was happening to his wife but could not bring himself to tell anyone. It was unacceptable, unseemly, unreasonable; it could not be happening to his own wife, so intelligent and refined. He lived in fear of her starting to howl, but she kept silent. Whenever he left the dacha, he locked her in, and she stayed inside quietly, eating. He was even more afraid of having to lie to the neighbors, but there was no need – no one noticed that she hadn't been seen in a while. They had always lived in a secluded way, sometimes didn't emerge from their plot for weeks, busy with orchard and kitchen garden. They only needed one another and Naida, for company.

His altered wife lived with Yakov Semyonovich for a long time, considering. He had squirreled away some tinned goods on the top shelf of the little cupboard they had on the veranda, and lived on those, leaving the rest of the food to her.

One night he awoke to a metallic scraping. His wife was on the veranda: she had found the cupboard and broken in. She was using a kitchen knife to rupture the tops of the tins, then guzzling the contents, cutting her mouth on the ragged holes. The emptied, crumpled tins she threw to the floor. She was almost through the entire supply which she'd long ago dubbed, with great amusement, "the nuclear war stash."

A wooden plank creaked underfoot: his wife turned, still clutching the knife in one hand and a tin of gobies in tomato sauce in the other. She punched through the top with a stiff, forceful motion, and turned the knife to widen the hole, her hand running with red. Yakov Semyonovich knew in that instant, with fearsome clarity, that very soon, mere minutes, that same knife could be punching through his own quivering and terrified guts.

Quietly, he closed the veranda door, returned to his bedroom, and remained there until dawn, motionless and awake, with the covers pulled over his head. When he finally dared to emerge, his wife was nowhere to be seen. The disemboweled tins were scattered across the floor, smelling delicious. Naida was thrilled to see him, leaping around on her chain. His wife had gone.

It was after that, really, that Yakov Semyonovich developed a need to be with other people – from loneliness and horror, together with a ferocious determination to get to the bottom of what was going on and calling those responsible to account. Also because he had barely any food left at home.

And there she was, his wife, sitting on the porch steps. She still wore her old torn and dirty clothes, but she looked restored somehow, refreshed. Like she'd just been on vacation. Her tranquil gaze seemed to be saying "Well, there you are."

Without taking his eyes off her, Yakov Semyonovich backed up through the swinging gate. In a moment, though, something soft barred his way. He turned and saw Stepanov. And the chairwoman. And Nikita Pavlov too. And the white-haired, white-eyed Natalya. He backed away from them, but his wife was coming up the garden path to meet him, and Naida was trotting beside her, rubbing herself against her mistress's legs.

She was smiling so hard you could see all forty-two doggy teeth.

"Oh, God," moaned Yakov Semyonovich. He squatted down and covered his head with his hands, as though waiting to be beaten, smacked right on his balding, kindly and cultured pate.

His wife kneeled on the ground beside him. He squirmed and shut his eyes, but she looked him in the face, then over at Natalya, like a question. Natalya gave a gentle nod.

His wife's little hand settled on his cheek like a burning-hot iron. He let out a feeble scream and opened his eyes. His wife was looking at him with loving concern, like he was a sick child.

"Sonya," he whispered, and wept.

He hadn't spoken her name in ever so long – only "listen" and "d'you know" and "would you mind" and occasionally "my dear," when they were with other people. It was decades since she had been labelled "wife" in his mind, and tidied away into the appropriate pocket of his consciousness as an essential device, well-constructed and convenient in use... Still, he'd missed her terribly, patting the covers beside him, half-asleep, hoping to find the steadily breathing body there that was not his, but so familiar as to be the nearest thing. He'd caught himself straining to catch her footsteps, the awful scent of her chicory coffee, old-people's coffee, every morning. He'd gone out to the fence, shivering with cold and fright, to peer into the gloomy woods. Waiting for her.

"Sonya, darling," he smiled through his tears. And forgot everything.

Someone was lying in wait for the stately procession on the corner of Forest and Rowan streets:

"Get thee gone!"

A heavy wood-splitting axe tore toward Natalya's snow-white head. She caught the axe head in mid-air, snatched it from the wielder's shaking hand, and tossed it easily into the gutter; of the rough wooden handle only a smoldering stump remained.

Katya trailed the axe with a blank gaze. Suddenly she reached for Natalya:

"Good, I don't have to go looking for you. Come on, then..."

A steady white fire blazed for a moment in Natalya's eyes – and Katya's own bloodshot eyes flared in reply. It was like having pepper rubbed in; Katya cried out and winced, her hands flying up to her face. Natalya walked past without touching her.

The unruffled dachniks followed, parting and sidling neatly to avoid touching Katya too, as though she were a leper, undeserving of Natalya's red-hot brand that made everyone peaceful and glad.

"Assholes!" Katya shouted in their wake.

It was as though a swell of desiccating heat burst forth from her chest together with the shout. Again, the world congealed into a fiery mess of colors and shapes. Flowers and trees, fences, houses, all were melting, running viscously to the ground. Her feet were stuck to the liquefying asphalt, and it was cracking, something fiery-red beneath, burning. Katya looked down at her hands and saw translucent flame shimmering from her splayed fingers. What Romochka saw, when he'd told her she was on fire.

Home. Hot and unwieldy, the thought was battering against her skull. She had to get home. There was a water tower, right outside her gate. Cold water, smelling of iron and mold... Her dear old dacha, where you could wait it out, as always, hide away until it was over. Or maybe there wasn't anything to be over. Maybe it was just Katya losing her mind, her inheritance from mad Granny Serafima. Or she was hallucinating because she was still concussed, just like Gena said.

Toward noon, the rest of the villagers began to file back. The ones that were thought to be lost without a trace in the woods and meadow and river.

Vityok and Auntie Zhenya were the first to arrive. They were bright-eyed and hale, though they returned mother-naked, just as they'd left. Vityok, supporting his wife's elbow, held the gate open for her. The rusty hinge squeaked: without a word, Vityok disappeared inside the house and came back out dressed properly and carrying an oil can. While Auntie Zhenya was inside, getting changed, he oiled the hinges. Soon their plot was a hive of activity. Vityok and Auntie Zhenya were setting their holdings to rights, working in tandem beautifully, a whirl of rakes and brooms.

The Beroev boys came back: they emerged from the river down where the village beach used to be, shaking off river weeds and wringing out their sodden clothes. The river also returned the moon-faced Narghiz. She checked her wards were properly buttoned, tidied their wet hair, plucked a leech out of the older boy's ear, then looked them over once again with loving pride and led them home.

Romochka's mom Tatyana came back from the forest. There was no trace of her former grim aloofness, or the way she always looked fundamentally frayed inside, except perhaps the way her hair still refused to lie flat underneath her lopsided headscarf. Romochka did not come back, but Tatyana didn't seem to mind in the slightest. She rolled up the sleeves of her striped "good" top and set to mowing the grass and heaping up the deadfall apples. She beat all the floor mats and hung them on the porch railings to air out.

Valerych came in from the meadow. He was naked like Vityok and his wife, and soaking wet just like Narghiz with her charges. When he got home, he nodded a greeting over the fence at his busy neighbors then got the lawnmower out of the shed.

Three laborers went over the village fence, helping one another. They wore the shy smiles of strangers that no one is glad to see, but everyone must make do with. They made themselves busy sweeping the streets and filling potholes with gravel.

Granny Nadya, whom Nikita had sent to the leshy, returned with a basket full of outstanding boletus mushrooms.

The Aksenovs, father and son, walked in from the meadow, bowed low to Natalya – from the waist, in that old-time way – then proceeded toward their plot.

The solitary old fisherman who sometimes traded tips with Katya came back too, though both his disappearance and reappearance went unnoticed.

More than half of the vanished dachniks came back. Sveta's voracious changelings must have eaten the rest.

* * *

There was no well water to be found, just the tap water for washing hands, stowed in a lightly mossy plastic bucket. Katya drank almost all of it and poured what was left over her head. The water dried before it could stream down. When she put down the bucket, it looked crumpled, like a plastic cup someone tried to fill with boiling liquid. Katya suddenly remembered how she'd ruined half her mother's vinyl records, back when she was a little girl. It was some program on the radio, about easily repurposing unwanted records for stylish and original plant pots. You had to hang the record over a gas ring, holding it high over a weak flame, and the edges would melt downward, making a half-opened black flower with a colorful label for its heart…

The door handle hissed beneath her hand, and it smelled of burned paint. Katya staggered into the room and collapsed on her bed. She squirmed until bedclothes and mattress were on the floor and she lay on the springy coiled-wire frame. She closed her eyes. Lying down was the thing for high fever. She had to stay lying down.

A fat, industrious bumblebee flew in through the window, filling the room with noisy buzzing, and Katya came to. Away with you, she thought. Get thee gone, you wearisome thing. She pictured a clot of heat wrapping around the fuzzy little body, the tiny antennae withering. The too-small, transparent wings shriveled into quivering burned stubs.

No, it wasn't a bumblebee at all. Her cell phone buzzed insistently on top of a chair, slowly vibrating toward the edge.

She took a long deep breath. She pinched the phone between index and thumb, like some repulsive insect. That was how they all picked up the phone these days.

The display was lit up and vacant as usual, no name or number. Just the two bright circles for accept or decline. Katya pressed the red circle.

The phone went on buzzing. Katya tapped the red circle a few more times, with force: decline. A web of tiny cracks dispersed across the screen. The phone buzzed.

Katya held it away from her, as far as possible, and pressed the green.

"The thumb alone will be mine..." rustled the speaker clearly.

Katya threw the phone on the floor and spent a good while stamping on it. Eventually, its fragile components, so elegant and almost beautiful in their microscopic complexity, turned to a heap of electronic dust. She laid the mangled screen on top of the little heap.

She'd dreamed of doing just this even before, when things were normal.

There was something stirring on the veranda. The noise was familiar, though Katya really didn't want to know what it was. She wasn't going out there, but the scraping noise went on and on, twisting itself into her ears and ringing painfully inside her head. Katya picked her pillow up from the floor and clutched it to her chest, in a subconscious attempt to defend herself, or hide behind the comfy shield. Then she went out.

The front door was wide open. On the front stoop there was... a radio. The analog radio that Katya had tossed out the window, when it came on all by itself, on that first night after the turning disappeared. Every summer Granny Serafima listened to the news and her beloved classical music on that radio. Katya always thought that her grandmother had traded the folk songs more pertinent to her background and personality for whining violins and rolling piano arpeggios not through some yearning of the soul but just because it was the city way.

The tuner knob spun wildly and the red needle oscillated left to right. The radio hissed, noisy static interspersed with birdlike whistles and even whispers, hurried whispering that Katya couldn't make out.

The knob abruptly stilled. Something crackled like a stove full of coals. The radio emitted a torturous mechanical squeal and creaked:

"The thumb alone will be mine..."

A blinding white flash sent a surge of heat across the veranda, scorching the net curtains into black smoldering lace. The pillow Katya had been clutching detonated in her hands, the charred feathers swirling like an ashy blizzard. The lightbulb above the door shattered into glass spray. Still the melted tuner knob kept on turning, the red needle moved from side to side like an alert vertical eye, and the hurried whispering grew louder and louder...

Katya booted the radio into the bushes. She heaved the kitchen table upside down with a crash and pulled every drawer from the kitchen cupboard. It had to be somewhere, the spare little transistor radio, it was just hiding away, waiting for the right time. She tossed a chair out the window and tugged a disintegrating lace doily – Granny's work – from the top of the fridge. She wasn't strong enough, it turned out, to upend the fridge. Then she saw that one of the drawers was full of forks and spoons, and useless round-tipped butter knives, all of it old and dull, Serafima's things. She heaved the whole drawer through the broken window, old-fashioned cupronickel cutlery raining down on the singed rosehip bushes.

Wreaking destruction made her feel happy and fierce. She wanted to crush, burn, and kill anything connected to Serafima, that thumbless schizophrenic, who was to blame for it all. Her goddamned doilies and ancient forks, all that flowery china that was so out of style they dumped it all at the dacha. All the quilts and fringed cushions and page-a-day calendars that she'd collected, yellowing bricks with useful advice on every page: "June 21, summer solstice... Easy knitting: crochet yourself a top... continues on reverse."

Katya carried the blankets and everything else out to the yard, breathless from exhaustion and the heat. She heaped them by the porch, started for the house to get matches, but couldn't think of where they might be among the disarray inside. Turned her head suddenly and stared at the embroidered cushion that crowned the heap.

Licks of white flame bloomed atop the cushion like primeval flowers. They skittered across the dusty cloth, filled out and reached up. Katya touched her fingers to the flame – she felt nothing, no pain. An answering flare beat inside her breast, on the left where her heart was supposed to be. She could see the meadow beneath her feet, roiling beneath the burning gusts of wind; it was almost as though she was the white inferno, the great pillar of solar fire...

The vision lasted only for a moment, and then she felt the searing pain again beneath her ribcage and in her head. She ran out into the street, groped for the water column and pumped the handle... There was no water. She was more than feverish, she could feel herself burning, the fire had spread from Granny's condemned possessions to her.

Staggering and falling, skinning elbows and knees – just as Serafima had once run to Poludnitsa's terrifying meadow – Katya ran for the river.

It wasn't only her plot billowing with smoke: everywhere there was a frenzy of cleaning.

People dragged the decrepit and broken things that had collected in every dacha and shed for decades and set them alight with the glee of children burning dry autumn leaves. Cockeyed garden gnomes and plastic ducks, and other ornaments acquired in a sale or just in a momentary lapse of judgement, saggy armchairs and broken folding beds, rotten lumber, holey plastic buckets, granddad's old skis and grandma's rag collection, all went into the fire. Those not employed as inquisitors busied themselves scrubbing windows and floors, laundering curtains, sprinkling clean gravel over the paths, and checking for dead branches left unpruned. There was a ferocious urgency in all this, as though the villagers meant to be rid of all traces of their messy dacha lives once and for all.

The little gangway – damp and mossy even through the worst of the heat – creaked under her feet; her quivering reflection looked at her from the water. It was wreathed in translucent but distinctly visible petals of pale flame. Katya backed up a bit then took a running leap into the river. She hadn't even paused for breath.

Maybe that was why she was always drawn to water, to cool silvery fish. Water was a refuge from fire.

Something hefty and cold shoved her hard, in the side. Katya nearly swallowed water from surprise. She opened her eyes but couldn't see a thing. The cold bulk positioned itself under her stomach, and Katya realized she was being pushed up to the surface, like a dolphin rescue. She decided not to struggle; a moment more, and she was gulping for air, coughing and spluttering.

A bevy of bubbles broke through the opaque water beside her, and a massive wet head appeared. Two golden eyes gave a slow, lazy blink, receding under nictitating lids, and popping out again.

"Romochka," Katya sighed with relief.

She had seen him in his new guise before. The first time, she'd touched the bottom of the river, which was hard and sandy not soft and silty, and let the water fill her mouth and lungs. But she didn't suffocate. She didn't spasm and struggle like the drowning do. The murky pall before her eyes cleared and she saw lacy riverweed, the silhouettes of fish, ribbons of light shimmering as they reached into the water. At the same time, she felt slim pulsating tubes pierce her side, just under the ribs. She saw Romochka – he was standing beside her, mouth wide open, and sharp little proboscises extended from inside his mouth. He was looking at her affectionately with those golden eyes, their pupils vertical like a frog's.

Romochka's top lip crept up, as though he was smiling at Katya, and the little tubes slithered briskly toward her.

"Please don't," she pleaded.

Romochka tipped his head and she knew that he really was smiling at her with his huge gash of a mouth.

That's why you didn't come back, she thought, twitching as the avid tubes painfully perforated her skin. They kept their promise, your girls: you're like them now, how could you go back to people looking like this? And anyway, why should you? There was never any place for you up there, but here they took you in.

Gradually the fever was draining from her body. The pulsating tubes sucked it away, she could see the pale fire glimmer beneath the translucent flesh. When he saw that she understood now, Romochka caught her eye and smiled at her. He raised the limb that wasn't a hand any more from the water and motioned – come down, to us…

Once more they stood side by side on the sandy river bottom among the lacy weeds, breathing water and observing the fish. There were brightly colored perch with stiff prickly top fins, shoals of ablets milling above, right at the surface, and something log-like stirred in a deep rut, a burbot or catfish perhaps, or one of the river-dwelling "neighbors"… A bream swam by, gleaming like a giant golden tray. Must be a five-pounder, Katya thought, a real trophy. I'd love to get my hands on that…

Then she noticed that Romochka had crumpled and dropped his head. His healing tubes looked blackened and singed, his eyes shrouded with an ashy veil. The heat he'd sucked from her was hurting him, so tender and watery. Katya tugged at the tubes still suctioned onto her flesh, but the damaged skin tore off in shreds while the tubes dug all the harder into her side. Romochka waved the things that were no longer hands at her, telling her to stop. He was teetering. He exhaled a little clump of see-through gunk.

"Wormwood and rue," Katya tried to say, but only bubbles came out. She pushed off from the bottom, hoping that up above she'd be able to shake off foolish, self-sacrificing Romochka. A moment later there was a quick flurry of barely perceptible shadows, a multitude of jointed tentacle-fingers wrapped around Romochka, unhooked the burned tubes from Katya's side with surgical precision and pushed her back up where she belonged. So forcefully that she shot out of the water like a cork.

"Romochka! Romochka!" Katya tried to dive back in but the water wouldn't budge. It was viscous like seawater, stiffly salted.

In the end she exhausted herself, not that she had a lot of strength left in her. Her muscles ached with a liquid numbness, and it was almost pleasant. Her body seemed light, almost porous – maybe that's why she'd popped out of the water like that. Katya slowly climbed up on the jetty and lay prone. She felt completely drained, unable to lift a finger.

A splash right by the jetty. The great dark head stuck out from the water and blinked at her with those golden eyes, a little duller now. A quivering little pickerel, bitten through the belly, plonked down beside her on the damp wooden planks.

"A present for Katya, why of course there is…" The striking of the clock, the clinking of champagne flutes… now her father was walking back in from the balcony with the brand-new sledge, bringing with him a bit of the delicious minty-fresh frost, if only she could get there, the winter, the snow…

"Romochka," she sighed with relief. Then she fell asleep, so quickly that the smile stayed on her face; her peculiar smile with the drooping left corner.

At last, the high standard of presentation to which the departed Sveta Beroeva had always aspired could be seen applied across all the dacha plots. Sparkling clean windows were left open to admit a warm breeze, and it ruffled the bright froth of the net curtains approvingly.

And the villagers began to make ready to go.

Claudia Il'yinichna got out her wheeled suitcase and packed her clothes and undergarments inside. Also a little mirror. A photo of the young Petukhov. A stack of plates. Her medicine bottles. An emptied juice carton cut in half and filled with earth and tomato seedlings. A nice vase of yellow flowers that looked like miniature daisies, except they weren't daisies, and no one could ever remember what they were called. The water mixed with the earth, mud running down over Petukhov's anxious smile. With a sigh, Claudia Il'yinichna attempted to jam a small food processor, bought especially for the dacha, on top of everything else in the case. She had to lean on it heavily to get it closed, making the plastic bowl of the food processor creak.

Andrei stuffed his several backpacks with a laptop, a tablet, his smartphone and his headphones, all three pairs. He folded up and tightly lashed a small inflatable boat, packing it in its case. The oars didn't fit in the case, for some reason. Andrei broke each one over his knee, then neatly chopped the halves lengthwise. He stacked them carefully and managed to get them in the case after all, humming with satisfaction as he zipped it shut.

* * *

"Granny, I'm sca–aaared!" Six year-old Anyuta howled from her front stoop in a deep, hacking bass. She had been hiding in the shed from the roar of the terrifying lawnmower, and had only now ventured out.

Anyuta's grandmother was racing about the house, tearing down anything that came to hand: clothes, dishes, books, photos and icons, the last of which she kept well away from Anyuta and dusted carefully every day but was now ripping off the walls like pesky fly-posted adverts. Slap-slap-slap went her galoshes. She tossed everything inside the open maw of a vast old holdall. Anyuta's toys, the wall clock and the electric cooker ring were all at the bottom of the holdall already.

"Granny, don't!" Anyuta cried plaintively.

Granny dropped the mushroom drying rack she'd been clutching and went straight for Anyuta, holding out a stiff, splayed hand. Granny's bespectacled eyes shone clear and bright, unmoving.

Anyuta squealed, tumbled off the stoop, her little feet clattering like shrapnel, and fled.

Katya watched Nikita packing through an open window. His shapeless rucksack – the old-fashioned kind known as "hiker's folly" – was stuffed to the gills, but Nikita carried on gathering up objects and jamming them on top, gathering up what fell on the floor and jamming it back again, gathering them from the floor and… There was a clinking sound from the empties which he had also seemingly decided to bring along.

"Where are you off to, so late?" Katya eventually enquired.

Nikita stopped for a moment, distracted, and smiled at her. She did look amusing, with her collection of bruises, sleep-swollen face, and the riverweed tangled in her damp hair. She was standing on tiptoe and holding on to the windowsill, observing Nikita with a kind of scientific interest.

"It's nighttime, Pavlov. I overslept. But look…" She pointed up, which made her unsteady, then grabbed onto the high windowsill again.

It was bright as day. The sky was swathed in an unbroken white veil emanating a soft glow.

"Pavlov. What a dope you are, Pavlov. She got you almost first of all."

Finally, he let go of the backpack and went to the window. His face was like the veil over the sky, shining and soft. He smiled again and Katya leaned toward him.

"Come on." She glanced briefly at the ruddy brand on his forearm. "Maybe I could use some soothing too…"

Nikita slammed the shutters, barely missing her fingers.

Katya stumbled back into neatly trimmed stinging nettles.

"Why won't any of you touch me?" It came out almost as a growl.

Again that rising, flowing heat in her veins. Not from the nettles, a faint but familiar echo of the fire from before. Katya dropped her eyes to the ground, took a deep breath, and thought of the coolness and the watermelon smell of the river, and how she'd awakened on the jetty with a clear head and a questionable lightness in her limbs. The heat receded.

Everyone else though, the dachniks were enthusiastically working to soothe. Whoever was done packing went outside and roamed the streets in gangs, finding those who had not yet been touched by the all-forgiving, all-explaining hand. The fleshless and noiseless Natalya wandered about with them, appearing here and there, rising from the ground suddenly like a pillar of white.

It was the intemperate young people who particularly resisted joining in with the communal tranquility. They prized Lenka Stepanova out of an electrical exchange booth – she might have been killed, the little fool. The layabout Pashka, despite his wounded leg, managed to climb out his window, crawl under the fence, and melt away into the forest, though he knew as well as anyone else the dangers that lurked in there. They got two other lads down from a mile-high pine. They were covered in pitch and screaming bloody murder. Lyosha-don't, who had scarpered as soon as his temporary guardian let Natalya inside the village, went to ground in Tamara Yakovlevna's cat kingdom, and was seen looking out from her dacha window, and making faces at the crowd that came for him...

The cats. They barred the way like a hissing striped wall, hanging from the gate and the trees, launching themselves from the burdocks. They scratched Zinaida Ivanovna's hand to shreds and Volopas nearly lost an eye.

By this point, Tamara Yakovlevna returned from her storeroom with a hammer and headed for the living room, where the resurrected television set chattered without cease. Unplugging it, before Lyosha-don't, shrieking with laughter, bent the antenna out of shape, hadn't helped. A white-eyed, noseless face stared at them from the screen which no longer glowed but burned, flamed... The face was muttering and muttering and muttering, crooking its slit of a mouth. Barely distinguishable words broke through the hissing static:

"O–pen... let ussss... in..."

A sweltering breeze rocked the branches and the dachniks deferentially stepped aside for Natalya. She walked up to the gate, bare narrow feet barely touching the ground... and stopped. Sitting in the center of the path was that witless striped cat, the one that was always falling out of places or getting stuck in trees, or fatally misjudging its own potency and starting fights with other cats. The cat stared piercingly at Natalya and yowled, ears tucked close to her skull.

Tamara Yakovlevna took a swing and smashed the hammer into the TV screen, right between the blind burning eyes. There was a bang and a spray of sparks. The dacha television set, her pride and joy, was no more.

Natalya's serene and beatified face rippled briefly. She turned without haste, and walked away, drawing the dachniks with her. The stripy guardian carried on sitting there like an ancient mummy and yowling at their retreating backs. Perhaps she could not quite believe in her victory.

Katya went back to her plot. She was surprised to discover a crowd of dachniks milling by her porch, until she heard someone walking on the corrugated roof.

Yuki had climbed onto the veranda roof and was pacing up there like a kitten pursued by dogs, backing up skittishly each time someone tried to climb toward her. The roof extended neatly over the porch, but someone had tried the gutter already – a length of it lay mangled in the rosehip bushes. Yuki had found herself a good place to hide, although it was unclear how she got up there. She alternated between shrieking curse words at the people below and beseeching them:

"Please, please, please... just leave me alone... I'm begging you..." Then at an entirely different pitch: "You frigging zombies!"

Katya made her way through the yielding crowd. Everyone still moved gently aside to avoid contact with her as she went past. Hands on hips – brushing her seeping tube-mouth marks made her wince – she looked back at them from the bottom step.

There was a large fishing hook in her pocket, among bits of rubbish. She pulled it out and stuck it above the front door. She had to stand on tiptoes to do it. A needle or pin would have been better, just like Granny had taught, but sometimes you had to make do...

"No unwanted guest, nor evil pest..." Yuki heard Katya whisper.

Those nearest the dacha all took a step back. Katya breathed a sigh of relief, until she saw Natalya. White-haired and very tall – she seemed to have grown taller since she returned –

the woman was just a few feet from the porch, watching her. Natalya's eyes were leached of all color now, a white flame flickering inside the pupils.

Loud, cheery music broke apart the silence; merry electronic confetti set to a dance beat. Yuki frantically searched through her pockets and eventually found her cell phone, which she flung away. It slid down the veranda roof and fell to Katya's feet. Natalya pointed to the phone and nodded slowly.

Katya picked up the slim buzzing lozenge. She didn't bother pressing anything, knowing that the callers couldn't care less whether you wished to speak to them or not.

The rustling that came forth was quiet and gentle, like murmuring grass in the noonday breeze. Katya knew that you had to greet the "neighbors" properly if you wanted to avoid trouble, but she'd clean forgotten the proper form of address for Lady Midday. Granny had told her about many special creatures, but she only rarely mentioned the woman aflame. You could tell Granny was terrified of her.

At last, something swam up into her mind from the furthest recesses of her memory. Her lips moved quietly:

"Where the good lady goes, the golden wheat grows."

"Ssso... it... issssss..." came rustling from the phone. Desiccated – that was the only way to describe that voice. A desiccated voice.

Natalya had not moved her lips at all: she still wore her gentle smile. But Katya had seen something quiver in her throat, beneath the paper-thin, suntanned skin.

She had spent so much time in guessing, on endless strings of guesses that tangled and tore. She had imagined screaming questions into that blazing face. But here she was, Poludnitsa, standing before her in the guise of her kindly, noisy, long-ago neighbor Natalya in her faded t-shirt with the stupid cartoon dog – and Katya's head was empty of any thoughts at all...

"What do you want? Why did you come?"

"The thumb alone is mine."

"I know that! You've had it, a long time ago. Serafima..."

Natalya gave an almost imperceptible shake of her head.

"She guessed wrong. The thumb alone. You."

Natalya spoke slowly and oddly, drawing out each syllable and taking long pauses between words. Her lips stayed closed, while something labored inside her throat.

Katya squeezed the phone hard in a grip gone slick with sweat.

"Sister to no brother. Wife to no husband. Mother to no babes. Apart in the handful, the thumb alone."

"You're lying!" Katya screamed. "I was married!"

"Not in church, you weren't. No true husband, that one..." the smile seemed to widen. "Only a... sss... swain."

The puzzle clicked together at last into a picture without gaps or unused pieces, and every fragment of it was made to fit together from the beginning. Including Katya's birthday which had gone intentionally unnoticed just before the solstice in June, because she'd reached the age where you didn't feel like celebrating every chime of the clock anymore. Even her birthday, which she had grown used to spending at the dacha, hiding from visitors and congratulations, even that was a piece of the great mosaic.

The pale flame she exuded went red hot again, or maybe Katya was just that pissed off at the creature, Poludnitsa. She had done all this to collect a petty debt. The white lady, Katya's lifelong warder, that's who was to blame for her always being alone... Katya went down to her, to the lowest step:

"So now you've come for me? I've only just hit my sell-by date, is that it? Turned thirty and gone off?"

"Wrong again. Only just ripened."

"So go ahead and take me!"

"What for? I haven't come for the debt. You're ours anyway. You'll stay and live with us."

"Live where?"

"Why, here. It was you, brought us to this place."

"I've brought you?!" Katya shook her head so hard she almost toppled from the steps. "You're lying! Liar! I never brought any of you! Not me!"

"You," the desiccated voice insisted. "You're our door."

Katya went stiff and glassy like seared sand. Then something exploded inside, blasting away the last shreds of the certainty she'd clung to until the end: that it was not her who was to blame for all the village anomalies and misfortunes, nothing to do with her, except possibly, maybe, because of Serafima's long-ago foolishness...

"What goddamn door?"

"To the new place. A good place."

"But why here?"

"You're always free and easy here. And we will be too."

"This isn't your place! You should be in Stoyanovo!"

"Others came. New ones. There's too many now, cramped. We just about gave up, waiting for the door to open."

"But... this isn't a place for you! There's people living here! It's nothing to do with them, they don't even know about you!" Katya peered into the villagers' serene, faded faces. "What are you creatures trying to do? You're killing them!"

"They did it first. Killing. Bad neighbors. Killing. Killing. Killing..." and Poludnitsa began to whisper in the hurried, panicked voice of the unlucky scarecrow, who had once been just a wooden cross in a bobtailed coat, lying quietly in the attic, not harming anyone. But they breathed life into it, then killed it. She'd killed it, Katya, with her own two hands. And then the scarecrow killed Petukhov. So Nikita killed the scarecrow again, and he killed Sveta Beroeva too. Sveta had killed Kozhebatkin and her own husband, and all those other people who would stay nameless, chewed up and sliced up for meat.

"Bad neighbors," Poludnitsa repeated.

"No, just people. Regular people." Katya spread her hands in despair. "They were just scared... You know that, you've lived alongside people in Stoyanovo all that time!"

"These are different. We knew what the old ones were like. But these we can't make out. We tried. There's no living alongside."

"So what are you..."

"I'll lead them all away. Can't live with this kind. Too frightful."

Katya cackled at that, laughing until she cried, until her scraped throat stung. So that's who was to be frightened of, all this time... She caught herself, stifling her rising hysteria, as she remembered that you were not supposed to let Poludnitsa have the last word. You had to ask her questions, she enjoyed that, or else she'd fall silent and that was the end of things.

"Where will you take them?"

"Out of the gate, beyond the fence. We've no use for them here."

Katya was frightened for the dachniks. The woman aflame was being too vague about what was to happen to them.

"But you've, you know, fixed them... Look how docile and quiet they are. You can live with that kind, right?"

"Not fixed. Asleep. They'll wake and start again, like before. What's the use of sleeping ones? Too dreary, living with those."

So, she hasn't sucked their souls out, Katya rejoiced. It's not forever, they can still wake up. Then she asked, terribly meekly:

"Will you let me go too?"

"No. You're our door. The way we came. So here you'll stay, with us."

"I don't want to."

"Even so. You'll get used to it, settle down. Your place is here. You've never been one of them, you're ours."

"Liar." Katya clenched her teeth. "I won't stay here! I'll hang myself! I'll drown myself in the Sushka!"

Natalya's face contorted and flame rolled rapidly beneath her flushing skin. For just a moment, Katya saw her as she really was: huge and white, arms blazing with rumbling flames and stretched wide over the... over the meadow of her childhood dreams. Heat blasted into Katya's face. She raised her arm defensively, wincing.

"You're staying, will you or no!" Like a great red-hot bell, Poludnitsa's voice thundered not from the receiver but directly in her head.

"What use am I dead?" Katya shouted back at her. "Who's going to hold the door open for you then?"

Then the voice went quiet again and soft, crooning from the phone:

"You can keep your swain too, keep him right here..."

Katya looked up at Poludnitsa in disbelief. Then she turned away, biting her lip – that was always how the bargains were struck, in Granny's tales. They could sense a person's weak spots, and once they found them, they pressed hard.

"You'll live here with him, together. And us, alongside. You'll bear him a son. He won't leave you, not like that other one."

"Liar..."

Now she had the weak spot, Poludnitsa twisted her searing fingers round Katya's heart.

"My word. Safer than locks, surer than keys. A family of your own. What do you need the others for? You've no love for them. And they disdain you, too. We'll just keep your swain, keep him back for you..." Poludnitsa's voice was quietening, caressing... "A home of plenty. No trouble with the neighbors. You'll both get used to it. Then the babes will come..."

Katya could only pant raggedly into the receiver.

"A bargain, then?"

"If you leave Pavlov." Katya said at last, in a strangled voice.

"Well and good."

"Will you?"

"That's a good girl. Go now. Don't get in the way."

Katya stepped down. Yuki had been sitting on the roof and holding her breath, certain until the last that Katya had some clever plan, that in the end she would lull the white-haired witch into a false sense of complacency then whip the ace out from her sleeve and vanquish her. Now she fell to her knees, holding on to the edge of the roof.

"Katya, don't! Please, please don't, Katya, dearest!"

Katya was already walking slowly to the gate. She didn't turn, only dropped her head even lower.

Nikita woke – no, it was more that he suddenly became aware of himself, the way you come around after a very long sleep or fainting spell – on top of his perfectly made bed. He was fully dressed, and had a thumping headache, plus another ache, hot and itching, in his forearm. Though his thick curtains were drawn shut, there was just enough light to see a strangely shaped burn on his skin, that looked like a human palm print. It came flooding back to him: the gate, the mind-blowing reappearance of Natalya Aksenova, and after that, only a weightless emptiness inside, and mindless joy. He actually felt sick remembering that maudlin sense of euphoria, it was like being covered in snot.

Nikita raised his head and wiggled around a little, which gave him to know that an unidentified object was lying on the bed next to him. Quickly, he sidled away to the wall. A moment passed; he cautiously reached out and touched the unidentified object, which was a body. The body was hot and it was breathing.

"We're going to stay here," Katya whispered. She squirmed so close he could feel her bony pelvis sticking in his side. "Pavlov, I've come to spoil our friendship some more..."

* * *

"They won't harm us, they promised. If they're not lying, that is. They're always telling lies. Granny said you never know how they manage to trick you... Just don't go anywhere for now. Let's just wait it out in here. We can't do anything anyway, she's going to lead them away. Pavlov, she's going to lead them away like rats... like the pied piper..."

"Wait, what? Who's being led away?"

"You and me, we'll stay here, though. Here in the village. Forever. Everything is going to be ok, right?" Katya gave a sniffle.

"Um..."

"She needs me. It was me she wanted, all along. I was the debt that she set my granny. Remember that text that Gena got, that was them trying to get him to come and fix the door... fix me. I'm the door. It's all because of me."

"What are you on about..."

"We're both losers, Pavlov, that's why we're always here at the dacha, hiding. So now we can hide from everybody."

"Right."

"You don't get anything I'm telling you, right?"

"Nothing. But I'm used to it, I guess."

"So, Natalya... I mean Poludnitsa, Lady Midday... she's going to take everyone else away from here. She took a dislike to them. But we're going to stay behind. Live with them, the new neighbors. That's the deal."

As Nikita stroked Katya's shuddering back, he figured it might not be so bad, to hide forever from everything that hemmed him in and goaded him on, out there, on the outside. He could stay forever in this endless summer. With Katya. If he couldn't pull her away from the otherworld that billowed around her, why not just dive into it himself, the way he'd launched himself into the Sushka from the jetty? Maybe it was better there. Your life transforming from a short gray moment between two kinds of not-being, with existential horror lying for you midway, to something else, weird and enchanted. And terrifying, true – but you could live with it...

"Deal's a deal," said Nikita, and held her tight. "We're staying then, I guess."

"They won't harm us. Just don't go outside, ok? We have to wait it out. And then, you'll see, we... we'll settle. Live our life."

She didn't seem to be shivering anymore and looked calmer. Nikita went on, though he wasn't sure he meant it or if it was just a joke:

"We'll set up house and home." When there wasn't a sliver left of the world you knew, what else could you do but joke.

"A kikimora and an imp, chained up outside... And a bunch of kids. Pavlov, let's have kids, all right?"

"You women, you're all the same..."

"Only a couple, then. Or even just one. And if I can't have more, then we can adopt a changeling, right? We'll find a cute one. Or we'll adopt our very own vodyanoy, Romochka. He's a sweetie."

"Ok. But you're the one doing the feeding. And cleaning up after him."

"All right."

"And sweeping the bones into the cellar. Who's he going to eat, by the way, if there's no people left? Will we have to lure them in from the outside?"

"Pavlov!" Katya elbowed him, then sighed dreamily: "Maybe this is how our real life starts."

"Maybe. Life's always better at the dacha."

"Depending on the neighbors..."

"We managed with the first lot, didn't we? We'll find a way with these new ones too..."

There came the sound of running feet from outside the house. A crunch of twigs, then a girly squeal.

Katya turned away and pressed her forehead to the wall.

"I feel so bad about Yuki, though... I'm not doing so well as an imp, Pavlov. I feel sorry for everybody."

Nikita had been wondering whether he ought to tell her, finding it hard to say it out loud, but now seemed the perfect time, so he just came out with it:

"After Sveta and that garage, I'm not sorry for any of them."

"You're a competent imp, then."

"Doing my best."

They sat quietly for a little while, listening to the hubbub outside. There was another cry; immediately they heard gravel crunching beneath many pairs of feet, moving steadily and in time. A lost lamb returned to the collective.

"Where will she take them?"

"Oh, some kingdom far, far away, sort of thing. Probably. There must be some place that the damned go, and the captive corpses, where they stash people they swapped for changelings..."

"Or maybe back to the normal world?"

"Maybe..." Katya said dubiously.

"What about you? Do you want to go back? Be honest."

"I don't know..."

Nikita's headache was almost gone and he had that after-banya feeling of torpor and relaxation. His eyelids drooped. His mind was a jumble, serious thoughts ran formless and smudged, while flotsam and jetsam began to assume importance. Katya seemed to be dozing on his shoulder, her replies came slower and quieter each time. As he sank, Nikita tried to picture how life would be in the emptied village, with only the otherworldly neighbors for company.

"We're going to have the whole village to ourselves."

"Let's take over the chairwoman's. She got herself the best dacha."

"The Beroevs have a mansion."

"A haunted mansion," Katya sighed.

"You think it's haunted?"

"If it isn't yet, it's definitely going to be... Pavlov, what if she's lying about not harming us, what if it's just more of her riddles?

She likes to riddle people, like my granny with her thumb...
She's not telling the whole truth about that debt, I'm sure of it."

"About you?"

"They always come to collect what they're due. So why did
she say it wasn't the debt she came for?"

"What does she need you for, though, now she has the
whole village to herself?" Empty streets and hushed dachas
in his mind's eye, Nikita imagined the peculiar, solitary hush
that filled dwellings emptied not for humans but of humans.
There was something so restful about it, just the way a very
early morning feels, when there is not a soul around, and it's
as though there are no people in the world, and never were,
and nevermore will be.

"Pavlov," said the imp named Katya, wriggling at his side.
She was having a different vision unfurl toward her out of the
deepening gloom: the smell of wildflowers and the sight of a
meadow, all clouded in yellow dandelions. "It doesn't seem
right, to name the price but then refuse to collect. That's just
against the rules..."

As they wandered sluggishly across the meadow, the departing
villagers left vivid green footprints in the dewy grass. The
chairwoman's solid back swayed in the lead. On her right was
Yakov Semyonovich struggling to restrain the galloping Naida,
and on her left Vityok and Auntie Zhenya, arm-in-arm. Andrei
was with them, and Zinaida Ivanovna the herb witch, and
Narghiz with her charges, and Valerych, and ancient Volopas,
and many others whom you would see every summer and say
hello to without exactly remembering their names, recognizing
them by their bald spots or the way they smiled or even a
sunflower-print housecoat that once donned seemed to bed in
until the end of the dacha season.

There were a few people missing from the crowd. Katya
couldn't see the animal witch Tamara Yakovlevna, or Lyosha-

don't, or the lazybones Pashka. Nor Yuki, whom she'd given up to Poludnitsa, just like she'd let his "girls" have Romochka. Katya felt a flush of joy at the thought that Yuki might have somehow gotten away. Then she recalled that she was not supposed to be there either. She was staying in the village with Nikita, she'd made a bargain...

Katya pushed forward through the crowd, which was thick as syrup: Katya kept getting stuck and flailing. She wanted to say something, to shout at them to let her through, but couldn't make her lips move. It was like they were glued together with that same syrup.

At last, she was on the other side of the human swarm. A female figure walked at the head of the procession, but it was not Natalya.

It was a young girl in a frayed, tatty dress. A thick, fair braid, of a bright burnished hue that had as much red in it as gold, hung down her back.

Katya stopped from sheer surprise. A dry thunder rolled over the meadow, there was a blinding bolt of lightning in the sky overhead, then another, and another. The dachniks halted, faces raised up as though it was a Victory Day salute. Each burst bleached the sky a little more, soon turning a dull, predawn celestial vault to a blazing noonday dome. A scorching wind whistled down the meadow and there appeared in the heavens a flaming sphere like the very sun. Maybe it was the sun.

Katya ran up to the girl and grabbed her by the shoulder. Without turning, the girl clasped Katya's wrist in a searing hold, like a cuff. Four fingers without a thumb. A blue-stone ring on the index finger, her sister's gift, the one that would split Katya's lip many years hence, turning her smile forever crooked, turned down at the corner like a mean or guilty thing...

"Pay the debt," Serafima's quiet voice seeped through the ringing in her ears. "Close the door. No bargain."

Katya managed to move her lips apart, but instead of a scream it came out as a whisper:

"Why?"

"Because you can't treat human beings this way!"

The sun exploded without a sound, poured down in snaking lightning, fell into the grass like boiling rain. Dew instantly evaporating, the grass caught fire. Pale flames lit up the meadow, turning the sky opaque and ashen. A roaring wall of fire tore toward the dachniks, incinerating all the grass and the Martian parasols of cow parsnip that, rising up before the flame, threw strange gigantic shadows and instantly turned to ash.

Katya made to go back, but Serafima stood rooted to the ground like a stone pillar and wouldn't let her go. Not that there was anywhere to run: another smokeless firewall towered between the crowd and the village. Dry heat arced across the meadow while the ring of fire constricted, and all the while the dachniks just stood there, their ruddy faces astounded and worshipful in the flickering light.

"She holds sway while the debt's unpaid," said Serafima, still staring avidly at the pale fire.

"Granny! Tell me what to do, Granny!" Katya pulled the girl back to face her, so hard the tendons in her hand spasmed. Molten tears ran down from Serafima's blank white eyes, pooling on her cheeks like candlewax. Katya did not cower or turn away from the inferno raging in that face.

"There it is, the sun's own fire," Serafima exhaled, like a furnace. "Her mark. Banked low for so long, then flared up in you. You must give it back, before we all perish through our foolishness."

"She won't take it back!"

Serafima broke into a hasty mumbling:

"Take what's due, and what's owed to you, take it and be gone! There was a woman in our village, her dead husband took to visiting her. Third night after they buried him, he came back to lie with his wife. Gave her such a do each night, she could hardly rise of a morning. Everyone thought she wasn't long for this world. Then the whispering-woman tells her: tonight, dress your children inside-out, and sit by the door..."

The first flame licked at Claudia Il'yinichna, who was standing very near. The chairwoman put out her hands as though to ward it away, and instantly both arms were engulfed, flesh melting in the booming fire. She squealed and waved the guttering stumps about, but in a moment was swallowed up entirely. An unexpectedly fragile skeleton – too elegant for such a stocky frame – flashed briefly, then crumbled into ashes.

"... when your husband comes, he'll ask you what you're about. You must tell him you're going to a wedding at the neighbors, the son is marrying his mother. He will ask you: how can it be that the son should marry his own mother? And you say, how can it be that a dead man comes a-visiting the liv–"

Serafima vanished before she could finish, dissipating in the shimmering heat. All around, the chorus of screams intensified, people were bursting into flame like blundering moths in candle-light, immolated bones and all in that raging fire,

Katya woke up from the sound of her own screaming, just like when she was small:

"The meadow's burning!"

On the brim of waking, kicking at her blankets and the charred rags of her nightmare, she understood at last that the meadow in her nightmares had always been the same. The wide and unkempt field running to bittercress and dandelions beyond the dacha village gate.

Nikita ran after her, but she was already halfway out of the gate. She wore her rumpled t-shirt backward and carried a bright red plastic bottle under her arm.

"She's not leading them away, she's going to burn them!" Katya shot out of her front gate and hurtled down Cherry Street, slippers slapping against the asphalt with each step. Nikita set off in pursuit, although he knew instinctively that he wouldn't get her back, not by persuasion nor by force. Their half-mad fantasy of a house and home with a kikimora or whatever chained outside, had crumbled without ever having a chance. Suddenly he grieved for the strange and solitary village where they would now never make a life together, among the new "neighbors". He grieved for Katya too, terribly.

"I thought we were staying!"

"She's going to burn them alive! Lead them to the meadow and burn them all!" Katya's voice was fading as she disappeared down the street.

Nikita slowed to a walk. His sides were splitting, heart tripping and hammering in his throat. It was hard to run fast when your main sporting activity was quietly getting wasted.

"What do you care?" he shouted after her, in desperation.

"You're an idiot, Pavlov!" came her reply from around the corner.

He braced his hands on his knees and tried to catch his breath. To hell with her, let her hare off where she liked, he was going back home for some shut-eye, with nobody to elbow him or scream in their sleep and get hysterical, finally he'd be left in peace... It dawned on him then, the revelation that he didn't want peace. He didn't want anything at all, if he and Katya were never to argue and squabble again, if he wasn't ever to refuse to believe her nonsense again, and feel, not a moment later, such earnest and serious awe at the mere fact of her existence, so different from his. In his past life, he'd experienced such feelings just once – for the first and last time, he'd figured. The object of these feelings was a giggly bottle blonde whom Nikita nearly married.

She had imperceptibly become threaded into his life, his strange neighbor, and hauled him into her weird and terrifying but terribly exciting other world. He couldn't bear to go back to his old drunken solitude. Basically – Nikita was willing to admit it – he'd grown accustomed to her face.

"Katya!"

She didn't brake fast enough and ended up slamming awkwardly into the closed main gate. The sound racketed above the village like thunder. Katya perceived it as an echo of the earsplitting thunder from her dream, the harbinger of the fiery maelstrom to come. She pushed at the gate, dreading the sight of the empty meadow, which would have meant she was too late, or too early, or that the dream was only a dream, and whoever sent it was mocking her. The strange creatures had a strange sense of humor, too.

They hadn't gotten far from the gate, the caravan of villagers laden with holdalls and backpacks and dragging wheeled suitcases over the tussocks behind them. Katya was nearly lifted off her feet by the kind of wild joy that breaks all barriers and switches off instinct. She raced after them.

"Wait!"

Not one person turned around. Katya caught up to them and elbowed her way through, shoving between unharmed, living flesh. She trembled with that earnest awe and wonder at another person's incomprehensible life which is sometimes termed love. Right now, she loved all of them: all the bungling, quarrelsome, persistent botherers of her quiet dacha existence – every one.

The familiar shape of Natalya Aksenova flashed up ahead. Katya ran up to her and emptied the contents of her red bottle over her back and bleached-white head. This was the lighter fluid Nikita hadn't managed to stuff into his rucksack after all.

Natalya turned slowly. Her indifferent, shining gaze skated over Katya's face. Her hair was dripping.

Katya fumbled through the many pockets of her fishing trousers. The little box of spinners, her penknife... she was horror-struck at the thought of losing it, dropping it along the road, but there it was... the lighter she'd found on her veranda. She thumbed the catch, thrust it toward Natalya's soaked t-shirt and shouted:

"Fire douses flame! Fire douses flame!"

She remembered all the stories Serafima ever told her, not just the one she'd dreamed. She remembered the advice given by whispering-women and village crones: you had to get the trickster neighbor to admit some rule had been broken, and everything was awry. They abided by rules, the others, by vows and bargains, by the once and for all time, and they couldn't keep silent when faced with something that went against custom. You could catch them out, then – words were sacred to them. Perhaps that was why people were given language, so they could broker a way of living alongside the "neighbors".

The faint smile flitted from Natalya's face, her lips twitched. Katya brought the lighter closer still and slowly intoned:

"Fire douses flame."

"How can you..." the creature's voice tolled inside Katya's head, still booming but slow and almost pained, "douse fire... with flame?"

The gate swung open and Nikita, breathless and arms akimbo, ran through.

"Katya! Stop! Wait!"

Katya turned to glance back at him, panicking that she'd miss it because of him, the right moment when her words had power. It made her hurry. She shouted:

"How can you name a price but not collect? Take what's due, and what's owed to you, take it and be gone!"

"A clever one, aren't you?" A volcanic roar bored into her temples and the back of her head.

Natalya's face crumpled, then went soft and melted – and began to re-form. Her eyes leaked out into fiery puddles, her nose collapsed in on itself, her lips split into an ear-to-ear crack. She grew until she towered over the meadow, a vast pillar of blinding light.

White flame coursed through Katya's veins, pouring into each cell the heat of the sun, like kernels of grain ripening in an ear of wheat. The heat filled her, then burst through, freed at last from its prison, within which it had smoldered and twisted for so long. But it wasn't painful or frightening, just the opposite – it was as if the sun blazed inside her, illuminating both worlds, the human one and the other one. Katya knew them now, the special creatures. She understood Poludnitsa. There had never been another way.

She flung her arms wide open, sending a white flare over the meadow. Nikita flinched, and when he was able to open his singed eyelids again, he saw Katya consumed by pale fire. She was leaching color and starting to resemble Natalya-Poludnitsa – her hair ran white, her eyes blazed with a steady heat, like molten metal.

"Katyaaa!" Nikita reached for her though his fingers blistered and the bandage on his index finger charred. Finally, he couldn't stand it anymore; he dropped face-first into the yellowing grass, coughing and struggling for breath.

The vast figure bent low over Katya with a dip of its tall flaming headdress, then gathered her up in the ring of white flame that Katya had seen so often in her dreams.

Sparse clouds crept along a dull, ordinary sky. The Sushka sent forth a cool, watery breeze. Frogs croaked with abandon, blending into a creaking chorus. There was a clutch of sparrows rustling in a broom grove. Naida the Alsatian scratched furiously behind her ear.

The dachniks had awaked from a too-long afternoon nap:

they moaned and groaned and sighed, and showed one another their mysterious blisters. Some sat on the ground, in a profusion of cases and bags, blinking confusedly. Others had to be roused. Zinaida Ivanovna they'd barely managed to lift out of a little rut: she kept toppling backward like a dung beetle, groaning and restlessly querying her rescuers:

"Where's Tamara Yakovlevna? Has anyone seen Tamara Yakovlevna?"

Andrei came up to Nikita and silently offered him an arm. Nikita shook his head no; he didn't feel like getting up just yet. He lay on his back and stared at the thin feathery jet plume of a passenger plane that quietly bisected the sky above. The plane hummed gently, pulling behind it the other noises of the regular world, that seemed now so unfamiliar and strange, the villagers couldn't hear them at first. A car honked somewhere in the distance. Across the meadow, in the new development, a lawnmower started up. Each time it fell silent, you could hear barking dogs.

Claudia Il'yinichna righted her mud-stained blouse and stood up straight, though she had to hold on to her left side. Suddenly she cried:

"Look, there's someone there!"

There really was someone there: a fisherman in a red tracksuit top, sitting on the bank of the Sushka, just where it curved beneath a willow.

"Hey there! Excuse me, comrade... I mean, young man, hey!" The chairwoman waved at him wildly.

The fisherman stirred, threw his line in again with a honed, practiced gesture, and went still again in anticipation of his prey.

The dachniks stumbled toward him on cotton-wool legs. Nikita stayed in the grass, watching the tiny plane vacantly, and thinking how much it looked like a little piece of birch bark, stuck to the sky. There was nothing else to think about, and probably no need, either.

Oblivion, enveloping oblivion – it had streamed in with the long-awaited cool of the river. Softly and inexorably, it erased the dachniks' memories of the white flame and the black beasts, the broken Petukhov and disemboweled Kozhebatkin, those who called from the river and those who came from the forest – and those who were there still. Not one of them turned back to see the village – "Bramblings Dacha Co-operative– dissipate into an insubstantial rainbow haze that for a moment still traced the contours of the roofs and fences, and vanish for all time from the human world.

Bor'ka went along kicking the waterlogged touch-me-not balsam grass and thinking balefully about his granddad. The grass was only just flowering, there wasn't a single inflated pod yet that you could explode by just touching. The woods looked new and bright and clean, too, not a speck of dust on the leaves – what possible mushrooms could there be. But Granddad went on and on: the early boletus were through, and his neighbor said that her daughter said that an acquaintance of hers said they were selling them by the railway station. Bor'ka found a forum of mushroom-crazies on the net and read from it out loud for Granddad's benefit: no mushrooms yet, not in their region. But Granddad didn't believe in the internet, did he, all computers and phones and gadgets were "tablets" to him. He said the word like he was spitting. Granddad put his ancient cap on, and his rubber boots, a basket in one hand and Bor'ka held by the other. He confiscated every "tablet" and dispensed a cracked compass instead, then took Bor'ka mushrooming. Bor'ka knew it was really – as ever – to knock some sense into him. Granddad had no faith in the internet, and no faith in Bor'ka, who spent hours on the net doing important things, either. Useless, Granddad used to grumble, useless and senseless, never had a sniff of real life, if you left him in a forest, he'd never make it out. But would anyone leave a civilized person in the forest? And anyway, how would it help Bor'ka, abandoned in a forest, to know that this grass here was touch-me-not balsam, and that bird there, with the shimmering blue stripes on its wings, was a jay? How much real life could Granddad have seen if he couldn't even Skype his relatives without Bor'ka's help? A mean, unenlightened old-timer, that's what he was, Granddad. A proper old leshy.

That was why Bor'ka wandered away from him quietly, pretending not to hear Granddad calling for him. It was easy enough to find the way back since he'd stayed close to the path, and much nicer without the old man. Nobody droning on beside him, poking his stick here, there, and everywhere: d'you know what that one is, and what sort of tree is this one? He'd get it in the neck later, of course, but later was not now.

There it was, flashing like a flaming match among the crumbling old leaves: an orange-cap boletus. Bor'ka couldn't believe his eyes. He jogged over to the mushroom and sliced through the cool springy stem; instantly the pale flesh began to tinge blue. Definitely an orange-cap, so new its cap wasn't fully formed yet. A little to the side, two more – no, three more, fused at their base like a candelabra – shone through the mesh of the grass.

How wonderful. Not only was Bor'ka about to prove to that old leshy he was just fine in the woods, but he'd bring him a bunch of boletus, the handsomest mushrooms in the world, even if these particular ones were confused about the season. Truth be told, Granddad did manage to hook him on hunting out the little variegated caps, and he had a good eye for it by now. As he packed the candelabra in his basket carefully, Bor'ka spotted another red cap, and another a little further…

The path was far behind him, but the mushrooms held him captive still, racing ahead like a dotted line through dells and pine groves, across ditches and tussocks. They peeped out from under bushes and clumped around the few slim aspens, as if to say that this was the perfect woods for them, and if Bor'ka and Granddad had only ever found one or two in a whole season, well, that was because they hadn't paid enough attention. Bor'ka was out of breath, his nearly full basket dragging on his arm, but he couldn't stop himself. He'd bring back enough for several soups and a fry-up, and even a bunch left over for drying. Granddad was sure to come back empty-handed, and then they'd see who had a sniff of the real life. All the mushrooms were perfect, young and fresh – the white flesh looked like marshmallow until you cut it and broke the cells inside, making it tinge blue. Bor'ka even took a bite but had to spit it out straight away: not because it was yucky, he hadn't had a chance to taste it really, but because a large vertical shadow suddenly flitted just past the corner of his eye.

"Granddad?" Bor'ka called out tentatively but heard nothing in reply. This was odd, to hear nothing at all. The woods had gone very quiet, empty of the usual creaking and whistling that fills a forest from tangling roots to leafy, murmuring crowns. Even these did not rustle, as though someone had turned them off.

Bor'ka took another look around, carefully and as slowly as he could bear to. He was lost in a wildness that had no paths or clearings, only deadwood; dead trunks still clinging to living ones or just balancing on thick broken branches, like something that's dropped to all fours. Lichen hanging from the tree trunks like rags, and the ground densely covered in mare's tail and beefy ferns, it was like Bor'ka had blundered into some prehistoric bubble. There was no easy way of getting through, he'd have to crash about and climb, and get tangled in shrubs, careful to turn his head before some branch whipped back to smack him in the face. He hadn't noticed how far he'd come off the path, he only dipped again and again to pick up the next mushroom, and there was nothing out of the ordinary...

Bor'ka forbade himself to get scared. He thought of looking at the map for the nearest village, then remembered that Granddad had his phone. So he had to dig out the bleeping compass, though he'd really tried with Granddad, explaining how there was a compass app, that would show you the direction on your phone and give you the whole route too. But no, he was stuck with this made-in-China thing that was at least twice as old as Bor'ka and probably broken.

The quivering needle swung one way and then the other, then simply rotated around the dial without stopping. Broken, he knew it. Bor'ka shook the compass furiously. There was a creak. Not from the useless device, but overhead – a deafening wooden creaking, like one of the dead trunks was already falling on top of his head. Bor'ka snatched up his basket and ran, vaulting adroitly over the piles of deadwood. The creaking never ceased, though nothing fell on Bor'ka either, and seemed to be chasing after him, ever louder and nearer, like something huge was crashing through the trees in pursuit.

Then he saw a break in the trees up ahead, and daylight. And through the break, something that he least expected, but fervently wanted to see: a fence, and rooftops, and chimneystacks. A dacha village, a stone's throw away – Bor'ka even made out someone's garden gate. Inspired by the proximity of rescue, he finally dared turn back and get a look at whatever was breaking branches behind him, but only caught a glimpse of the tall, upright shadow from before. It had gone from tall to gigantic, no longer the height of a person but towering as a tree, and it was much closer than before, so close he couldn't understand why he still wasn't able to really look at it.

Up ahead, where the fence beckoned like a life raft, a deadening white light flared out like a projector. It blazed through the trees, throwing tall twisting shadows, formed into a vast shining sphere, and rushed up toward Bor'ka.

Ball lightning! Bor'ka dove headfirst into some raspberry cane. Above his head the forest crunched and roared like a tornado. He curled up and squeezed his eyes shut, until all he could see were the floating spots beneath his own eyelids, red like mushroom caps.

A very ordinary tapping on his shoulder brought him back to his senses. Someone tapped once, then again, and then the someone took him by the shoulder and gave him a shake. It was a lady – just a normal-looking lady in rubber boots, saggy trousers, and a sweatshirt. The hood was pulled forward over her face, like she was a villain or a monk or something, out of a cartoon or videogame, trying to hide their face. Or a ghost. Bor'ka could see her face perfectly well of course. The lady was probably worried about getting a tick in her hair, all the women were scared of that – none of them seemed to know that ticks lived in the grass and didn't fall out of trees.

"And where exactly did you come from?" the lady asked him.

"I'm... the mushrooms... and he was chasing me... this big thing, and then a lightning bolt..." Bor'ka babbled, perfectly aware how pathetic he must look, and flushing ear to ear. It was a shame, because on the inside he was a grown-up and not scared at all anymore.

"Not to worry, we get a bit of that round here. It was just a... boar. There's wild boars, roaming about. Getting a little too bold lately, though, mucking around just as they please." The lady raised her voice. "Behaving too much like pigs."

The upright shadow that was first the size of a man and then the size of a tree hadn't looked like a wild boar, but Bor'ka believed her. He clung to the ridiculous explanation simply because it had to be something, that shadow, didn't it?

"On your feet now and be on your way." As the lady bent toward him, her braid slipped from her hood. It was pretty long and tied with an elastic hairband. The lady stuffed it quickly back inside, but not before Bor'ka saw that her hair was entirely white. Not blond, not silver-gray. White as milk.

Well, his cousin was always dyeing her hair, pink and green and all sorts.

He got up obediently and took a step toward the village. The lady caught him and turned him back to face the forest.

"Go that way. Back where you came from."

"But the wild boars," Bor'ka tried to protest.

"They've all run off by now. Go back, there's no coming into the village. I won't let you."

From the calm way she spoke and her strong grip on his shoulders, Bor'ka understood that she meant it. The woods seemed so dark and forbidding that he almost burst into tears.

"Please! I don't know the way!"

"Look, can you see the mark on that tree?"

He looked up at a little piece of fabric knotted around a branch.

"You go toward that. Then you'll see the next one after, and then straight on from there. Don't swerve and you'll get to somewhere. You can't get lost in little woods like these."

"I'm…"

"Get going," she gave him a shove. "Go quickly and don't look back. Or you'll be sorry."

Affronted and frightened, he took one step and then another and was soon wandering back the way the lady had sent him. The knotted rags were probably leading him straight back into the heart of the woods, where a terrifying beast with a tree-sized shadow lay in wait…

It took him a little while to realize that he was back on the path, the one he'd abandoned running after mushrooms. His basket, brimming with bright boletus, hung heavy from one hand. His other held the compass. The compass needle had stopped spinning and was diligently pointing where it was supposed to.

Although the strange lady had forbidden him to turn around, he couldn't resist. Behind him was a crisp June woodland, with a narrow path that ran into the trees. A jay sat in a swaying hazel copse. How quickly things are lost in the woods, Bor'ka thought to himself. You take a few steps away from some fence or person and they're gone.

Granddad let him have it, obviously. But it wasn't to do with Bor'ka's long absence – Granddad hadn't seemed to notice that at all. He was proud of Bor'ka's haul, though, examining each mushroom delightedly.

Bor'ka got it in the neck for lying, of all things, when he tried to tell Granddad what happened to him. He didn't even mention the ball lightning, just his flight from the beast and the village with the strange white-haired lady.

"Try and make it believable, at least!" Granddad fumed. "I've been coming here for twenty years, there's never been any village."

He went on for ages, arguing, trying to get Bor'ka to wager on it – a grown-up wager, for money or washing dishes – they could even look it up on the map in Bor'ka's "tablet," see where the nearest village was. A regular leshy, Granddad was, Bor'ka said glumly to himself. A mean old leshy, and that was that.